THE DESIGNATED COCONUT

BY JOHN TRAVIS

D1707278

METRO VANCOUVER   DOMINION of CANADA

The Designated Coconut

This Trade Paperback Edition published
April 5th 2013, ISBN 978-1-927609-00-2

First Edition, jacketless, hardback published
October 5th 2012, ISBN: 978-0-9866424-8-7

Electronic Book published October 5th 2012,
ISBN: 978-0-9866424-9-4 (all file types)

Cover design by and copyright © 2012, Sunila Sen-Gupta

Typeset in "Warnock" & "Seabird"

The "Atomic Fez Publishing" logo and the molecular headgear
colophon is designed by, and copyright © 2009, Martin Butterworth of
The Creative Partnership Pty, London, UK (www.CreativePartnership.co.uk).

PUBLISHER'S NOTE:

This is a work of fiction. All characters in this publication are fictitious
and any resemblance to any real places, sororal mystery writing
teams, or persons — living or dead — is purely coincidental.

10   9   8   7   6   5   4   3   2   1

ATOMIC FEZ PUBLISHING
3766 Moscrop Street
Burnaby, British Columbia
V5G 2C8, CANADA
WWW.ATOMICFEZ.COM

**Library and Archives Canada Cataloguing in
Publication entry available upon request**

Table of Contents

Dedication

For Mum, Dad and Sharon, for love,
support and Sunday night Poirot.

THE DESIGNATED COCONUT

‡ ‡ ‡

A Benji Spriteman Mystery

Prologue

‡ ‡ ‡

HARVEY 'THE TEETH' O'KEEFE had a face like a wallpapered armpit and made about as much sense. 'Say it again,' I told him. *'Slowly.'*

'Tell cas a clar larls,' he said, enunciating as best he could under the circumstances, 'are clal nunnun vom lan-lan.'

I screwed up my face. '"England?"'

'Less. Lng-lan.'

'Okay. Carry on.'

'Thez e vor a vuc voor. Lesez san Nalalala le Loot.'

He stopped to see if I understood him. Apart from what sounded like the word "lettuce" I thought I was doing okay. I told him to continue.

'Than vuv verb ter zee zoo.'

'And you're sure it was my name you heard? Not someone else?'

'Less. Zoo.'

Frankly I was stumped. As I stood there trying to think it through with the traffic whizzing past us, I watched Harvey reach inside the bag slung across his shoulder and produce a clear plastic bottle filled almost to the top with sludged-up vegetables. Then, after jamming one end of a plastic straw into the top of the bottle, he jammed the other end into the small gap between the discoloured white bars of enamel that dominated his face. Sucking in a mighty breath, the discoloured mush in the bottle began to judder up the straw into Harvey's mouth. When he gulped his whiskers twitched.

It wasn't an ideal situation, getting your information second, or sometimes even third or fourth hand from a six-foot-four Rabbit with an extreme dental problem on a street corner,

5

but there it was. It made me feel nostalgic for the dim and distant days of the year before last, and a permanently grumpy Tortoise called Arnie. He may not have been the easiest fella in the world to get along with and had more wrinkles than an Elephant stuffed full of walnuts, but at least I didn't have to ask him to repeat anything.

Looking at the oversized Rabbit again, I decided I was being unfair. I was hardly perfect myself, especially not this early in the morning. I'd been wearing the same suit for four days, my coat was a mess, and I was sure I had a furball coming. But at least I had the option to take off the suit.

My fur hasn't been the same since The Terror struck; its thickness and texture changed overnight, along with everything else. Gone forever is the silky coat I once possessed, replaced by something more akin to human hair than anything — and it didn't keep me warm. But it could be worse — Harvey's teeth being a case in point — you make do with what you have. None of us has any choice in the matter. And compared to Harvey I had it easy: at least when I awoke on that fateful night to find myself roughly sixty inches taller *and* vertical, the process had already stopped, like it had for most animals the world over. Just like it had for Harvey too; or at least most of him. Because unfortunately his two front teeth just kept on growing and growing, so that now his lower jaw is fenced in by them; 'malocclusion' the Sappies called it. And they *still* keep growing — sometimes, after long and difficult conversations with him — such as this one — I swear I can see a difference. As you can imagine, this extremely cruel twist of fate made talking and eating troublesome. Sucking all the gunk up through a straw, it had been so long since he'd chewed anything that his face sagged where it should've bulged, leaving him with the kind of cheeks usually only seen on ancient trumpet player's. As a result, he looked a lot older than however old he really was.

Suddenly I felt uncomfortable, like I always did after looking at those teeth for too long. When he'd finally vacuumed up the last of his breakfast, I asked, 'What you've just told me, does it have anything to do with —'

He shook his head. 'Uths sumsum tha sur.' Just something he'd heard. I asked him then what I *had* come to see him about.

'Eth...'

It took a while but, as usual, Harvey had turned up a fair bit of stuff on the case I was working on that I hadn't already known. Harvey had this knack of getting closer to certain animals than I ever could. Because of his predicament, finding work was almost impossible: one look at those oversized choppers and nobody took him seriously. Most creatures assumed because he couldn't talk properly that meant he couldn't listen either. But there was nothing wrong with his ears, and for an informer that's what's important. As a result, he often picked up titbits of information that otherwise I'd never get my mitts on.

Thanking him for the information, I took several bills out of my pocket and handed them over. With lightning speed he shoved a couple into the bag the bottle had come from, while the majority were tucked into his vest. The money that went into the vest I knew was for day-to-day living, and the bills that went into the bag were for the operation. It was usually a fifty-fifty split, but not today.

'You nearly have enough?' I said, nodding towards the bag. Shaking his head sadly, he told me he was thinking of doing it himself. The very idea of it made me wince.

I came over all unprofessional and felt sorry for him — what the hell. Reaching back into my pocket I took out another couple of notes and stuck them in his paw.

'Consider it a bonus,' I said, patting him on the shoulder as I moved away, 'a down payment on a chisel or something. Just make sure your paws don't shake.'

On my way back to the office I thought about the information he'd just given me; what he'd told me first went clean out of my head. At least, the words did. The second I walked away from Harvey I began to feel edgy, like something bad was going to happen. I assumed it must have something to do with what he'd just told me — the case I was working was starting to deepen, and the deeper it got the nastier it became. The thing was I'd only ever felt this distracted, this *antsy*, about a case once before, and it wasn't something I was keen to repeat. But looking at it now, at what Harvey said that day — or rather the stuff he said that I could made out — it wasn't worrying at all; there was nothing to indicate anything out of the ordinary was about to happen, especially not with the first thing he told me.

What he told me was this: two female crime writers from overseas were coming to do a book tour. Somewhere they'd heard about me and wanted to meet up; why, I'd no idea. Among it all, and with seemingly no connection to anything, he'd mumbled the word "lettuce". At the time I just assumed he'd been talking about his breakfast. Whatever it was, none of it really made any sense and certainly didn't seem important. So I forgot about it. Now, I realise this was the reason my nerves were tight as piano wire that day. And any chances that I might remember it were lost when the seasons changed.

When I say the seasons changed, I mean *changed* — from a blowy but pleasantly mild spring, into a summer that saw the hottest recorded temperatures for twenty-five years. Of course, twenty-five years ago — hell, even just over *two* years ago — the world was populated by humans; those largely hairless creatures who, on waking from their dreams or their jobs or their leisure time, suddenly found that cats, dogs, birds, rabbits, reptiles, and virtually every other creature under the sun had either grown beyond what had been their usual dimensions or were in the process of doing so as they watched; many now upright, walking on two legs instead of four, talking in human languages; animals that were at the very least as terrified and angry and confused as the humans all around them. Humans, that contradictory species who, within the space of a few months were virtually wiped out with the possible exception of the odd few here and there hidden away in cool, lightless caves, never seeing the sun from one day to the next, and who, despite their vastly reduced circumstances, at least now never had to worry about sunstroke.

It happened a few days after I'd spoken to Harvey: one day I was worrying about my hat blowing away in the wind, the next the broiling heat was making me sweat so much that large clumps of my fur began knotting together to form a series of ugly little braids all over my body. At least, the fur that didn't fall out did. One day I moulted so heavily that when I removed my hat the inside looked like a bird's nest. My socks were full of fur, my underwear was full of fur, *everything* was full of fur. A day or two later going to the Laundromat, a sign in the window informed me that the machines were so clogged with animal hair they wouldn't work anymore. Still, it had only been a few days, it wouldn't last much longer... and sure enough it didn't; a week later, the weather changed again.

And became even hotter.

It was at this point that some animals began to take drastic measures.

‡ ‡ ‡

In the twenty-four months that had passed since The Terror, the city had gone from being completely lawless and uncivilised, to being slightly less lawless and marginally more civilised. As someone put it in a letter to the local rag, it was still like the Wild West, only now we spat in the trashcans. We had a police force who by and large tried their best, despite being sorely understaffed and short of resources — like most places after The Terror, the Station had been easy prey for looters — but, along with the rest of us, they had to make the best of the situation we'd all been thrown into. By and large, things had settled down: most animals settled into the occupations that their owners had previously had, currency came back into fashion instead of robbery, routines were established. Conventions were observed.

One of those conventions I've mentioned already. As I said earlier, animal fur these days is not what it used to be — its main function now seems to be as a reminder of what we once were, a relic of the past. It looks nice enough, but it doesn't retain heat. So nobody was more pleased than I was — for aesthetic reasons if nothing else — when animals started to wear clothes. Even on reasonably hot days some kind of clothing was needed. It was generally agreed that clothing was a Good Thing — right up until the weather went haywire, then all of a sudden it was okay to strip off again. Only this wasn't enough for some animals; they decided that the fur had to come off too.

Not all of it, of course — I mean, that would be *too* much — but fur began to be shaved from chests, backs, heads and various other places where a supposed benefit might be felt. Of course, it looked dreadful: within days the streets were teeming with what looked like walking patchwork quilts of fur; previously hidden birthmarks and blemishes were visible for all to see, *fleas* could be spotted scurrying across badly shaved patches of blotchy flesh; and when this flesh got sunburnt, sunscreen had to be applied. The problem here is fur, particularly Cat fur, grows back quickly and because of the heat most animals didn't have the patience to shave every day, so the sunscreen wasn't applied properly, with the result that when the cream melts in the sun it looks like sap coming out of a diseased tree. It's grotesque; and also quite funny if you're in the right mood.

At least for a while it was. Soon the joke became as thin as my fur. When a would-be client came by the office one day and remarked that my carpet matched my coat I sent him away with a flea in his ear. But the weather became even hotter still; furless animals had to remain permanently indoors for fear of frying, while anyone who had a dark coat found themselves being bleached in a matter of days. Tempers frayed, fights started over nothing, traffic accidents doubled, the crime rate soared, and among it all the case I was working on was just starting to get interesting.

Then, one day, seemingly out of the blue, my nerves began to sing the way they had before. I put it down to the weather and left it at that. Not for the first time in my life, I soon discovered I was way off the mark.

Part One: Heatwave

‡ ‡ ‡

1. MANUSCRIPTS

IN CASE YOU MISSED it somehow, I'm a private detective. Benji Spriteman, formerly the well-fed pet of Jimmy Spriteman, who ran the Spriteman Detective Agency right up until The Terror turned the world on its head. I used to spend my days sleeping in a basket and looking disdainful; now I sit in a chair doing the same thing but pretend otherwise.

A typical day runs something like this: I wake up, usually after too little sleep, and decide where I am. If I'm at home I'll have breakfast: milk, followed by tuna, then I'll try and overdose on scalding coffee. At some point I'll get washed and dressed then look in the mirror. There I'll see an oversized Tortoiseshell with brown eyes, a small pink nose, long, thick white whiskers and black, white and brown fur that could do with some attention. I'll look at the reflection for as long as it takes me to flatten down my fur, but no longer. Between leaving my apartment and getting to the elevator, the chances are I'll bump into at least one of my neighbours: usually a grumpy Parrot who's stalking the corridors looking for his Old cats. Depending on how I feel I may or may not grunt back at him. After the elevator has dropped me fourteen floors to the ground, I walk the short journey to my office. My secretary will be hard at work, or, if there's nothing to do, making it look like she is. I'm clean. I'm fresh. I'm ready for the day.

Only I don't always wake up at home.

When I don't wake up at home it's because I wake up at the office. A typical day here begins with me slowly raising my head from the desk and cursing the fact that I didn't go home. As there's no food in the office, I have to manage with coffee until I can drag myself out to Moe's Coffee Pot for a late breakfast. After finishing the coffee, I go into the washroom across from my office and tidy myself up a bit. On days like this I can't bear to look in the mirror. Having nobody else to grunt at, I grunt at myself until the feeling passes. After breakfast I go back to the office and drink more coffee until Taki arrives. I'm dirty. I'm rumpled. I'm in a foul mood. Add the tropical weather to the brew and you have the makings of a pretty yucky day.

That's how it was the morning things began to get interesting again. Getting back from Moe's — after navigating my way through the shaved animals, melting sidewalks and blaring car horns — the ripples from the heat haze were still playing across my eyes. Slumping down in my chair, back to the window, I could still see it through closed eyelids, wave upon wave of grey static pulsing like an alien force-field, the kind you went into as a normal being but came out the other side some horrible, mutated creature, dripping and shambling, trying to find someone, *anyone,* who could satisfy your now insatiable craving for blood —

Opening my eyes I laughed long and hard; partly because of the idea that a world full of talking animals would be bothered by mutants, but mostly because of the case I was working on. I'd spent so much time reading those kind of stories that almost immediately on waking my imagination would overheat.

Not that I didn't like that kind of story to begin with. It's one of many things I've inherited from Jimmy, a love of lurid and gaudy fiction. In the early days after The Terror, discovering that I could read, I spent many days reading his old crime paperbacks, wondering how much of what Jimmy read was true and how much was escape. But I didn't stop at the Shamus stories; when the agency got going again, Taki brought in a pile of old magazines for the waiting room; spook stories and science fiction and tales of strange worlds and the even stranger creatures that populated them. I read everything I could get my paws on and the stranger and blood-thirstier they were the more I liked them. When I found myself running out, I'd go searching cheap bookstores and market stalls for Old thrills which were new to me.

Then about nine months ago, my prayers were answered with the world once again in some kind of order and the essentials of life taken care of. Except for certain shortages, matters began to turn to luxuries: art, music, books. Magazines.

To say that *Dismemberment Monthly* and *No Shit Sherlock* were immediate successes would be a gross understatement. Both titles became so popular so quickly that even the publishers seemed taken aback. Wasn't there *enough* unreality in the world already, some wondered? Apparently not. We wanted more, it didn't seem to matter about the quality as long as there was lots of it, and with both magazines being monthly, there was.

Of the two, I prefer *Sherlock,* for obvious reasons. I'd virtually been weaned on crime stories, after all. With *Dismemberment Monthly* I found I had to be in the right mood for it, but ever since the 'Letters' pages got nasty, I haven't had a choice.

The haze finally gone from my eyes, I was just about to pick up the new *Sherlock,* when I heard the outer door open and close, followed by what sounded like a heavy bag being dropped on a desk. A few seconds later the glass part of my office door darkened and the handle turned. A pair of ocean-blue eyes peered around the frame.

'Here again, huh?' Taki said, dumping a large padded envelope on my desk. 'Four mornings in a row. Should I stop bringing my key?'

Without answering I looked down at the brown bulk in front of me. 'I don't like this mail, I know what it is already. Bring me something else.'

17

'That's all there is today. Sorry.'

Looking at the pile of unopened manuscripts, I sighed, wishing that I hadn't suggested it to either of them. I also wished I could get my paws on the animal who sent the letter saying we'd find what we were looking for in an unpublished manuscript.

'Couldn't Linus take a few more?' Taki said sweetly, as she returned to the outer-office.

'He has enough to do with the missing mutt,' I called out to her. 'And I've told you, don't call him that. You know he hates it.'

Sticking the large padded envelope full of smaller envelopes on top of another pile of unopened envelopes, I sighed again and waited for the smell of coffee to bring me back to reality. When it did, I drank it as fast as my throat would let me. Then, taking a deep breath, I opened one of the large envelopes, hoping that the stink inside wouldn't be too bad this morning.

They say that everyone is a critic. This is without doubt true. What is also true, but is never said, is that not everyone is a writer. They only think they are.

I'd been going through the submissions for *Dismemberment Monthly* and *No Shit Sherlock* for what felt like months, but in truth had only been about a week, after Patch Finnegan, the editor of *Dismemberment*, received another of the creepy letters. There'd been a lot of this stuff over the past few weeks — this kind of thing brings out the wackos in their droves — but one particular series of letters stood out, and one letter among them in particular. It read: *A shame about what's happening huh if it was a storey no one wud believe it (should they) keep cheking the mails.* The writing was the same as other letters that had turned up in the past few weeks, each dropping none-too-subtle hints, some of which had been true. And the claw-marks on the envelopes — nearly all of the letters had been delivered by air and either dropped through open windows or wedged into their frames — matched those other letters from the same author. Thinking that I'd got the letters' real drift, I had the bright idea of asking Finnegan to send me any stories with incidents in them that could *possibly* be relevant to the case. I specifically remember saying *possibly*.

Then the stories began to arrive; dozens of them. Exasperated, I phoned Finnegan to ask what he was playing at: I only wanted stories that might relate to the case I told him, not every damn thing he was sent. He told me that these *were* the stories that might relate to the case and were only a fraction of what he received on a weekly basis.

So with a heavy heart I started to wade through stories with titles like 'Crawling Without Legs', 'The Melting Mind of Martha', and my absolute favourite, 'Boots in Puss'. The stories were terrifying, but for all the wrong reasons: it had never occurred to me that some of the trash I'd read in *DM* was actually the best of a very bad bunch. When I finished reading that first batch of stories I felt like I'd been battered around the head for a few hours with a billy club. Several of these stories came from the same author, a Grover S. Nelson. I hadn't seen the name in the mag before.

Two days later I got a call from the editor of *Sherlock*, Rusty Laidlaw, who'd also received an odd letter which he read out to me over the phone. Word-for-word, it was almost the same letter Finnegan had received. Wearily, I told Laidlaw to send along any stories he too thought might be relevant. In the first batch was a story called "The Invisible Feud" written by someone claiming to be called Jake Lake. Laidlaw had ringed and underscored the title in red ink. Reading it through, it was an almost blow-by-blow account of what had been happening at both magazines over the past few months.

2. LETTERS

THE TROUBLE STARTED IN the 'Letters' pages of *Dismemberment Monthly*. In Issue Six, a story called 'Sick Relish' had upset a lot of readers, its content proving too literal for some creatures to stomach. Among the expected I-didn't-buy-the-magazine-for-this-kind-of-filth, and please-cancel-my-subscription-forthwiths that appeared in the next issue, a letter from someone signing themselves Daphne DuMoralize was also printed:

> *I'm sure I'm not alone in thinking the author of this story (among many other authors in this vile publication) will one day meet their just desserts. In fact I can promise them that. If it's terror and revulsion the 'Editor' wants, I can promise both — DDM.*

Finnegan, assuming that the typed letter had come from Mungo Bickeridge, the author of 'Sick Relish' as a publicity stunt (Bickeridge had pulled the same trick before; Finnegan had recognised his writing from previous letters), printed it, also with the hope that the attendant publicity would perhaps increase sales. But a few days later when Bickeridge called the *DM* office about another story he'd sent, he denied having written the letter.

The letters themselves seemed to be divided fairly evenly between supporters of the tale and detractors; for once, the letters pages were more entertaining than the fiction. But not all the letters were amusing: *I think certain authors should take care when going out at night,* someone calling themselves 'Bumper Fodder' warned. *They can only be lucky so many times.* Then, a few days after Issue 8 hit the stands, a rather washed-out looking Jack Russell turned up at the office and I put down the magazine I'd been reading. His clothing was rumpled, his fur was dull and his eyes were blazing. I told him to sit down. Before his seat was warm he'd reeled off half the story, and told me he knew who was responsible.

'Who?' I'd asked, although I knew what he was going to say.

Finnegan looked down at the copy of *No Shit Sherlock* on my desk. 'If you've read that, you'll know.'

It was well-known there was no love lost between the two editors — Laidlaw regularly sneered at *DM's* 'low-brow content' (which was a bit rich, considering the title of *his* publication), while Finnegan was forever accusing *Sherlock* of elitism and snobbery. In fact, a few minutes before Finnegan walked in I'd been reading Laidlaw's latest editorial, commenting on the furore caused by Bickeridge's story: 'It seems as if certain magazines (not to mention names) have fallen foul of their own policy to plumb the depths of bad taste, only to find that the same sick tendencies not only exist in their readership, but far outstrip them.' The fact that both magazines sometimes published the same authors seemed to have been pushed to one side.

'So he doesn't like the mag,' I said. 'It's not a criminal offence.'

'Trying to kill one of my writers is,' Finnegan shot back.

'Which one?'

'Mungo Bickeridge. Someone threw a brick threw his window yesterday.'

'If I'd written a story like that I'd have thrown a brick through my own window,' I muttered. Finnegan glared at me.

'You read the magazine?' he said eventually.

'Yup. Enjoy it too, for the most part. What makes you think someone smashing Bickeridge's window has anything to do with his story? It might have been Kittens or Puppies.'

'Kittens, hell. Laidlaw's trying to discredit us.'

'Discredit? How? I'll bet your sales are going through the roof.' *And right into Laidlaw's office,* I thought to myself. 'Listen, think about it. If Laidlaw wanted to discredit you, giving you free publicity's a pretty dumb way to do it.' Finnegan mumbled to himself.

'Okay. Maybe you're right. But someone's looking for trouble. Look at these and tell me different.'

The small package of letters he passed across the desk weren't pleasant, the ones he had printed were kid's stuff by comparison.

'You tried the police?'

He shook his head. 'I'm sure it's Laidlaw. But I'll look like a fool if I accuse him publicly.' Suddenly he looked anxious. 'This arrived this morning,' he said, handing me a sheet of paper from his pocket: *Next time it won't be a brick and it won't be a writer — DDM.*

'And you think Laidlaw sent this? Where did you find it?'

'Sticking out of my doorframe on the sixth floor. He could have done it while he was walking up to his office. He doesn't take the elevator, I know.'

'It doesn't fit. Why go to all that trouble?' Looking at him across the desk, I think he realised the chances of it being Laidlaw were remote, whether he'd admit it or not. But he was frightened. Getting the rest of the story out of him, I took possession of the notes and told him I'd see what I could do.

The next day, after leaving the magazines' offices having talked to the staff, I arrived back at my office to find a frail-looking grey Whippet in a brown corduroy suit sitting in reception.

'You're Rusty Laidlaw,' I said, recognising the editor's photo from his magazine. He blinked at me in surprise.

'I like to read detective fiction,' I told him. 'One day I might actually learn something. Come on through.'

Sitting where Finnegan had the day before, Laidlaw told me roughly the same story, only he said the trouble had started just a few weeks ago. As he spoke I decided straight away that Laidlaw wasn't responsible for the letters to Finnegan; because if Finnegan was scared, this Dog was petrified.

'These started arriving at the office four, five days ago.' Producing a batch of envelopes from his corduroy jacket, the Whippet laid them carefully on my desk. 'And of course there's the one in the new issue. I thought printing it might shame them into stopping, but we've had three since Monday.'

The letters were the same kind of thing Finnegan had been receiving, but with two main differences: they were all paw-written in crayon and signed with the name 'Giddyfits'. I was still looking at that sinister childish scrawl when Laidlaw said, 'Have you read it?'

Looking up, he had my copy of *Sherlock* in his long, slender paw.

'Only your editorial. You say there's one on the 'Letters' page?'

'We've had several but I decided just to print one.'

Taking the mag back I leafed through to the end: ' *"Have to say I was amazed that you chose to publish a story called 'Punching a Ticket' — an odd thing to punch, I thought... Punching an editor I can understand. Or even better, stringing him up by his tail... best wishes, Giddyfits."* ' I remembered that story, which was pretty inoffensive. But Giddyfits... Giddyfits...

'Someone letting off a bit of steam, that's what I thought at first,' Laidlaw said, his voice rising in pitch.

'You haven't noticed anyone suspicious hanging around your office?' Laidlaw said he hadn't, continuing 'if it's who I think it is, I wouldn't expect him to,' he added.

'You suspect someone?' I said wearily.

23

'Patch Finnegan, the editor of our main... competitor. Somehow, I don't think it's any coincidence this started after I mentioned his problems.' In among the fear, a glint of anger showed.

It'd taken him longer to get to Finnegan than I'd expected. 'Why are you so sure that it's Finnegan?'

Taking a shabby-looking copy of *Dismemberment Monthly* out of his pocket he slapped it down on the desk. 'Page 76,' he said, folding his paws across his chest. Sighing I picked up the magazine and turned to page 76. The first thing I saw was the author's name — M. Schnauzer Sabreman — an improbable one, even for an animal named by an eccentric owner. Then I saw the story's title: "Giddyfits".

I asked Laidlaw the same question I'd asked Finnegan — why go to all that trouble? When he said it was just the kind of level Finnegan would sink to, I didn't believe it any more than Laidlaw appeared to. I asked why he'd come to me and not the police, and he gave me some hooey about it not being serious enough to take to the police (the fact that he'd thought it serious enough to involve a private investigator I let slide).

Again, I told the editor to leave it with me and I'd get back to him.

One thing was clear straight away: unless they were in on it together, neither suspected the other of involving me. Also, I was intrigued by the fact that both editors were strangely reluctant to go to the police. And on top of that, why had they both come to me?

Looking again at the copy of *Dismemberment* that Laidlaw left behind, I phoned up their office and asked for Finnegan.

'Who's M. Schnauzer Sabreman?' I asked.

There was a long pause before Finnegan spoke. 'Oh, it was a pseudonym for an author in Issue —'

'Issue one, yeah. Page 76. What's their real name?'

'Well, I'm not sure that they'd want me to say —'

'Why not? It wasn't a bad story from what I remember.'

'It was...'

'Who?'

'Me.' Finnegan sounded pained as he admitted it.

'*You?*'

'We... we didn't have that many good stories for the first issue,' he said defensively. 'We needed something to put in the back. So I put one of mine in under a pseudonym.'

'Who else knows it's you?'

'Lots of folk. But I didn't tell anyone.'

'So how does the name get used in the "Letters" section of *Dismember* —?'

'I don't know. We got a few letters after the story appeared from readers who said they knew it was me. But I'm sure I told no-one.'

Putting the phone down my head began to spin. I was working a case where both of my clients were blaming the other one for something that I was sure neither of them was responsible for. Plus, or seemingly despite the fact the only thing separating them was a floor, neither appeared to know that not only was I working for *them*, but also for the animal they felt was responsible. Unless of course they *did* both know, and were stringing me along as part of some bizarre publicity stunt; and they had both come to me within a day of each other...

Perhaps the greatest thing about being your own boss is that you can leave whenever you like. Making my way through her office, I told Taki not to bust a gut on my behalf. I'd hardly pressed the button for the elevator when I heard her heels clacking on the floor behind me.

'I'll make it up tomorrow,' she said, following me into the elevator.

‡ ‡ ‡

For the next few days I carried on without really getting anywhere. The only thing I thought I'd figured out was why they'd both chosen me to look into the letters.

A few weeks after both magazines were launched, the business had been going through one of its quiet patches. It happens from time to time and I can never figure out why. During periods like this I get so bored I end up doing things I'd usually never think of doing — watering the plants, clearing out my desk drawers, filing things away... One day I was so stuck for something to do that after reading both magazines I took it upon myself to write to the editors. In their published replies, both wondered if I was the same Benji Spriteman who'd been involved in the Carlin case a while ago? I regretted writing both letters there and then. The last thing I wanted was to be reminded of the Carlin case*.

So I talked to the staff of both magazines, *Dismemberment's* first, asking if they'd had any strange calls lately or if anything unusual had happened; then, heading up the back stairs of the Henderson building to make sure I wasn't seen, I went into the *Sherlock* offices and asked the same things up there. I also asked Laidlaw if he knew anything about M. Schnauzer Sabreman. To my surprise, he said he'd no idea who they were. Then, as far as I could, I looked into the finances of both editors and their magazines; both were in extremely fine shape. As for enemies, both Laidlaw and Finnegan appeared to be well liked, if not by each other.

That seemed to leave writers with grudges. Had either of them had any writers who'd reacted badly to reviews or rejections? Plenty, they both told me. Could I check through the files, see if anything showed up? Certainly. Both friendly and cooperative. Both, I was sure, hiding something.

It took me the best part of a day to get through the mound of letters from disgruntled writers regarding their masterpieces. A few made legitimate points among thinly-disguised anger about their stories. Others, however, were just bizarre:

Sir:

I am writing back to you following the return of a story I sent you, 'The Mystery of the Fifteenth Corkscrew.' Whilst I am glad that you have actually read the story and commend you for praising its "pleasingly old-fashioned turns of phrase" and its "authentic uses of local colour" I cannot accept the rejection letter you sent along with my story.

Your letter (it seems to me) is the work of an editor who, with the best intentions I'm sure, has to turn away so many stories of inferior quality that when he is gifted one of superior merit, he is disbelieving of its obvious genuine quality, and consequently rejects it by mistake. You conclude the letter you sent me with the words "I do not believe that your heart was in this story." I could — and indeed do! — say the same thing for your letter!

Therefore, I am enclosing the story again. I will make no further mention of your error to any of my associates as long as the story is published before the end of the year.

Yours at all times,
Quentin P. Wiedlin

Most though were just impolite — disbelief giving way to disgust followed by terrifying threats 'not to buy the magazine again'. Reading through the pile I noticed that a lot of these letters came not only from animals who couldn't write but also couldn't spell. An idea popped into my head so I contacted Harvey.

It took him a few days to get back to me but, after babbling on about lettuces, he told me something very interesting about a certain newspaper editor. By the time I'd looked into it, the weather had gone haywire.

And so had the case: the letters were becoming more and more frequent and sinister. Then I received a call late one evening from Finnegan to tell me his office had been trashed. I asked if anything had been taken and he said no. He asked when I was coming over. I told him I wasn't. I told him to call the police and that I needed to see him about Fuller in the morning. Before he had a chance to argue I slammed the phone down. Within an hour the phone rang again. This time it was Laidlaw, telling me that *his* office had been turned upside down. I started to tell him the same thing I told Finnegan. When he began to protest I told him I knew about Fuller. Hearing that name, he rang off without saying another word.

‡ ‡ ‡

'*You!* I knew you'd have something to do with it.'

As they stared at each other I called over to Moe and ordered breakfast.

'And what about your friends?' Moe asked.

'No friends of mine,' I told her. She looked at me, at them, then back at me. Laidlaw and Finnegan were still carrying on their staring contest. I was just finishing off a roll when Laidlaw spoke.

'Are you going to tell me why you've dragged me out here?' he asked me, ignoring Finnegan's presence.

I must've chewed that last piece of roll forty times before bothering to reply. 'I haven't dragged you anywhere,' I said. 'If anything, it's you two who've done the dragging.'

'What's that supposed to mean?' Finnegan asked defensively.

'It means several things. It means you didn't tell me Fuller was involved. It means that I know both of you are in cahoots, even if you do hate each other's guts. It also means that now this thing has escalated beyond a silly game, the police can take over and I can walk out of here once I've finished my breakfast. I'll send you my bills.'

My words hung in the air for a few seconds before Laidlaw replied. 'He knows about Fuller, Finnegan. He knows what we're up against.'

Boy, did I.

When The Terror transformed the world, it seemed to be an unwritten rule that whichever creature remained in a property after they changed, that creature took possession of said property. Unfortunately for us, once the humans had fled, the only living creatures of note in the offices of *Fuller News* were the illiterate Rats in the basement. I'd had dealings with Fuller and I didn't like him; I didn't like his arrogance, his drunkenness, or the fact that he and his 'staff' couldn't put a paper together without misspelling every other word. I'd wondered if some of the hoax letters were his doing. But after talking to Harvey I realised Fuller wasn't responsible for the letters.

'He blackmailing you, something like that?'

'Not blackmail as such,' Laidlaw leaned forward, as if Moe cared about what we were discussing. 'He told us he was setting up his own magazine and wanted us to join him. We told him that we were more than happy where we were. He implied that wouldn't be the case for much longer.'

'He said he was going to wipe the floor with us,' added Finnegan.

'Then one afternoon I got a slurred phone call saying we hadn't heard the last of him —'

' "Hadn't heard the last of him"!' the Jack Russell spat.

'— not long after, the letters started arriving.'

'But the letters started because of "Sick Relish," ' I reminded them.

'The hell they did,' Finnegan said, 'I've published sicker than *that*.' Laidlaw sniffed at that. I did, too. 'We just used that as an excuse.'

'We both suspected him straight away. But you know the kind of power he's got around here. If we'd accused him publicly he'd have played the victim and ruined us anyway.' Which was true; even for a soused rodent, he was devious.

'Then Finnegan remembered a letter of yours he'd printed. We thought that if we got you involved and *you* found out it was him, it wouldn't look so bad for us.'

'— and if Fuller blamed us we could say we never considered it would be him,' Finnegan added.

'So I get the flack and *you* end up looking like the victims.' They bowed their heads when I laughed. 'The thing is, it isn't Fuller.'

'*What?*' they said in unison.

'It isn't Fuller. He's gone off the idea, and it seems that without either of you on board he has no-one to run his magazine. Besides, some of the hoax letters are quite literate; I doubt he could even spell some of the words you've read, even if he was sober.'

Both editors sat quiet for a time.

'So who the hell's doing it then?' Finnegan said.

'Who indeed,' I said quietly.

3. DOGS AND DETECTION

IT WAS ABOUT LUNCHTIME when I got through reading that first package of manuscripts, and my eyes felt like they'd been deep-fried. I didn't think there was anything among them that warranted further investigation. There was a story about someone who got a kick out of sending out poison-pen letters, but the manuscript was so shabby it looked like it had been doing the rounds for years, as in 'pre-Terror'. You'd think that the editor of a crime magazine might have noticed that, but he sent it to me anyway.

Standing by the open window I inhaled heavy, stagnant air through the drawn blind. Outside I could hear the faint hum of cars below, the occasional flapping of wings as someone passed the window. I let out the air I'd inhaled, deciding it was probably bad for me. Turning, I looked at the still unopened envelopes on my desk.

Despite the police's involvement after the break-ins, my workload seemed to have increased. The letters showed no signs of abating (although the hoaxer who suggested I keep 'cheking the mails' had fallen silent) and there was seemingly no end of manuscripts to read. But I was getting nowhere; I still had no idea who Daphne DuMoralize, Giddyfits or Bumper Fodder were, and the writers I'd managed to speak to had told me nothing, and the ones I really wanted to talk to — Bickeridge, Nelson and Lake — I couldn't get hold of. On a whim I'd added Quentin P. Wiedlin to the list; he sounded too interesting to pass up.

Deciding Taki was right, I gave the Mouse a few more stories to read. Giving one of the envelopes a quick once-over, I picked out any gory tales for myself. He was still wet behind the ears, and I didn't want Ma Spayley squeaking at me down the end of a phone line for corrupting her offspring. After separating the stories into piles, I stared at the wall and wondered what I should do next.

It was as I sat there in the dull, baking heat of my office that I noticed that same sense of creeping anxiety I'd felt after talking to Harvey. Normally I'd have brushed it aside, but the feeling was too strong, disproportionate to the case. I remembered the last time I'd felt like this; and immediately tried to forget. Just the heat, I told myself. Then the thought vanished as I heard a squeaky voice coming through from reception. *'Don't call me that!'* it piped, *'you know I hate it!'* The floor seemed to vibrate, closer and closer, before my door was pushed inwards.

As usual the Mouse was out of breath. He was always out of breath, even when he wasn't doing anything. Closing the door behind him he came in and sat down. A small note of complaint sounded from the chair.

The Mouse — Linus Spayley, my only other operative, was a different rodent from the sulky cheese-botherer that I'd taken on initially as a driver after The Terror, although I daresay the large red '1' Ma Spayley had drawn on his back to identify him (she'd drawn numbers on all of the backs of his thirteen brothers and sisters) was still there. He'd changed a lot since then; like many of his brothers and sisters: he'd begun to pile on the weight, and even now, as a Cat, I find it a bit unnerving to be dwarfed by a 240 pound Mouse. Also, with each Mouse now looking completely different and Ma Spayley being able to tell them apart, she'd given her offspring names. Linus didn't like being called "Linus". Which is hardly surprising.

'Any luck?' I asked.

'No more,' he said, wiping his face. 'No more letters.'

'Birds?'

'Plenty, but none of them stopped. And I asked Mr. Laidlaw and Mr. Finnegan if they'd seen anything, but they hadn't.'

I'd had the idea that maybe we could catch one of the Birds in the act of delivering the letters. Against Ma Spayley's wishes, I'd had the Mouse keeping an eye on both offices overnight.

'Can I go home now?' he asked.

'Yeah, sure. Get some rest.'

But the Mouse stayed where he was.

'You have something on your mind?'

The Mouse squeaked and puffed for a few seconds. 'It's this missing dog case, Mr. Spriteman.'

'What about it?'

He squeaked and puffed some more before answering. 'Nothing's happening. There's no evidence to suggest he was taken. I don't know what else to do.'

Despite being a different species, I'd started to look at the Mouse almost like a much younger brother. He was loyal, earnest, eager to please, and sometimes I felt, far too innocent to be involved in this line of work. 'I told Miss Foxton that,' I said, 'but she's convinced he was snatched. The dog means a lot to her.'

Alannah Foxton, a well-to-do Singapura, kept dogs; Old dogs. Her devotion to four-legged mutts was quite something. A couple of days ago, Trix, her Dachshund, had gone missing. From the start I thought it had probably just run away and would come back when it was ready. But she said he wouldn't do that, somebody must have taken him. I'd told Miss Foxton that she was wasting her money but she wouldn't listen: she wanted him back.

'Can't I do more on the proper case?' the Mouse pleaded, 'more on the hoax letters?'

I was just about to say that looking for Trix *was* a proper case but I couldn't lie to him like that; we both knew the mutt had walked and that was that.

'Okay. That pile of stories on the edge of the desk. They're yours. See if anything in them relates to the hoax letters. But only after you've looked for Trix. Okay?'

The Mouse, after a slight hesitation, decided this was as good a deal as he was going to get. In fact, as he made his way to the door with the package under his brawny arm, he looked quite pleased.

I'd barely had time to think about what a good employer I was, when that feeling of apprehension began to make itself felt again. It seeped into me for a long time before the phone rang in the outer office, then seconds later rang next to me.

'She says you'll know who she is,' Taki said before putting the call through.

'Yes, hello. Could I speak to Benjamin Spriteman, please?'

The voice sounded mature, like overripe fruit, with a smokiness and briskness to it that suggested breeding. Needless to say, I didn't know anybody like that. And she'd called me "Benjamin"; it wasn't "Linus", but it was bad enough.

'Speaking.'

'Good afternoon to you. This is Angelica de Groot. Spelled A-N-G-E-L-I-C-A, like the plant. Then D-E —'

'So?' I interrupted.

There was a slight pause before she went on. 'I believe you were informed that I was coming. Is that not so?'

Something in my stomach tightened. 'Say that name again.'

'Angelica de Groot. The crime writer.'

Then I remembered: Harvey. 'Yes, I remember now. You want to meet me for some reason.'

'Oh, come now. Not just any old reason: *The Carlin case.*'

'The Carlin case.' At the mere mention of it, my innards seemed to shrivel.

'Yes, of course. Why else? My sister and I read about it months ago and we both decided that when we came to promote our new book we simply *had* to speak to you about it. And Lieutenant Dingus, of course. He played more than his *rôle* in the proceedings, I understand.'

In the Old days they used to say that certain animals — cats, dogs, horses — could sense when a thunderstorm was coming. Since The Terror, I've had moments that have felt similar; usually it's something banal, such as correctly predicting how many items of mail I'd get that morning, or the feeling that a store would be out of a particular item I wanted. These moments have proved so rare that I've never given them much thought. But once, not long after The Terror, the feeling was much stronger. The next thing I knew I was involved in the Carlin case, which ended with the deaths of ten humans and animals, including Jimmy Spriteman, who I'll never stop missing. I had no reason to believe at the time that this 'bigger' feeling was anything other than some dreadful fluke, or that such a thing would ever happen again. I'd spent the past year-and-a-half trying to keep it out of my thoughts, and have generally succeeded.

Now a plummy voice on the other end of a phone line was trying to drag it all back up, and that feeling had returned.

'You say you read about it,' I muttered, mainly for something to say. 'Where?'

'Oh, it was in some crime journal or other. It must've been quite a famous case if we got to hear about it.'

She was right; it had been a famous case — at least for a while. I wondered if Dingus knew our fame had spread overseas.

'Look Miss de Groot, I can't speak for the Lieutenant, but personally I don't like to talk about that case.'

'Whyever not? It was a wonderful piece of detection. Your finest hour, surely. Of course, you may have had other cases since, which —'

'If you've read this article or whatever it is, you'd also know it was my worst hour.'

There was a brief silence on the line. 'If you mean Mr. Spriteman —'

'I do.'

Again, a moment of silence. 'We all lost people because of The Terror. That was "then". We have to think about "now"; move on.' Before I got a chance to reply, she did just that. 'Anyway, let me tell you about the book my sister and I are working on. It doesn't have a title yet, but it does feature a Private Investigator, and despite our *heritage* as it were, we know next to nothing about that kind of thing, so what we'd like to do is —'

'Hang on. Just how many books have you had published?'

She seemed surprised by my question. 'Why, nine. What —'

'You must be very imaginative, you and your sister. And you've written all those books without the help of a Private Eye?'

'I told you, we've never written about one before. There are details which we —'

I felt like I was edging close to saying something I'd regret. 'Look, I'm afraid I'm very busy at the moment. I don't think I could fit in a chat with you and —'

'Lettice —'

'— and I'm sure I wouldn't be —' I stopped, swallowed. *'Your sister's called "Lettice"?'*

The voice that replied sounded a bit wary. 'Yes, Lettice de Groot. I thought you knew —'

Suddenly I felt giddy, I was shaking all over. *'Lettice?'*

'Yes. I don't understand. What's wr —'

That was it for me. That build-up of creeping anxiety I'd been feeling came out in a gust of laughter so strong that I dropped the phone. I'd just started to get myself under control again when I heard a voice shout from the dangling earpiece:

'If you change your mind we'll be at the book launch in a couple of days. We'd love to see you there —'

The line went dead. For some reason the sight of the earpiece swinging in midair set me off again. When Taki came in a few seconds later to see what the joke was, I couldn't tell her. There wasn't any joke to tell.

4. QUENTIN P. WIEDLIN

WHEN I FINALLY CALMED down I looked across at the pile of unread stories and decided that my nerves had been jangled enough for the time being. I was wondering what to do instead, when Taki came in with lunch. Dropping the sandwiches on my desk, she gave me a strange look before going back to reception.

Lunch seemed to involve a lot of chewing but not a lot of swallowing; my throat felt half closed. I was still anxious after the phone call, wondered what it all meant, and where things were heading. I decided that I needed a bit of light relief.

Searching back through the letters I got lucky, finding an address and a telephone number. Dialling the number, I got lucky again. Writing down directions, I hung up and grabbed my hat. In reception Taki glanced up at me from a file but said nothing. 'Going to see someone,' I said sheepishly.

In the street, animals baked in their cars, windows down, sunroofs open. Sometimes I felt like the only animal in the city that couldn't drive. It was strange that I couldn't, because Jimmy had been able to. The Mouse had offered to give me lessons more than once but I always turned him down. I wasn't sure why. Most of the cases I worked were local anyway, and most public transport was pretty good now, and the cabs were fairly regular. It was also said that the buses and trains had started running to timetables a few weeks ago, but I think that was probably just a rumour.

The subway was a different matter — it wasn't being used exclusively as a latrine anymore, but it was hardly efficient. Getting my ticket from the grumpy Hamster behind the grille, I joined the ranks of animals on the down escalator while my eyes tried to adjust to the on-off flickering of the lights.

Wedged between a Bulldog and a Gerbil, I tried to take my mind off the stench of sweat and hay by looking at the posters pasted to the tunnel walls: *Buy Harris's Litter Trays, for all your Old cat needs. Terry's Tuna Tastes Terrific.* "*The Jagged Stiletto of Ursula Prim*" *by A & L de Groot, out now in bookstores.* By the time I'd taken it in, the poster was several feet behind me. Turning to look at it again all I saw were the small pink eyes of the Gerbil glaring down at me. When I turned back, my train was pulling into the platform.

Between leaving the subway and walking the block-and-a-half to Derry Park Flats I saw another three posters for *The Jagged Stiletto of Ursula Prim.* 'A rip-roaring read' apparently, 'a real page-turner from beginning to end'. I wondered how the de Groots could have produced nine books in such a short space of time. I decided they must work in shifts.

From the outside at least, Derry Park Flats bore more than a passing resemblance to my own apartment block — twenty-odd floors of honeycombed brownstone topped with a flat roof — although this place looked older, and unlike Shefton Heights it was liberally spotted with pigeon droppings. Inside, an elderly Siamese sat in the lobby on a lumpy sofa, reading a newspaper and tutting.

By the time the open-cage elevator had made its way to the nineteenth floor, I realised that the Flats were several notches below Shefton; nearly every creature I saw walked with a bent back, used a cane or looked underfed. Between floors when I caught a whiff of some unwashed Mutt or Moggy it was like being back in the subway; not the kind of place I'd expected the author of "The Mystery of the Fifteenth Corkscrew" to be living.

Stepping out of the cage, I was looking down a long corridor an exact duplicate of the eighteen below it: narrow, with faded pea-green walls, the monotony broken only by a score of stained brown walnut doors. The whole building reeked of failure and despair; the open window at the far end of the corridor looked like an invitation to jump. Most of the doors I passed had gouges in the wood, as did several of the off-white numbers stuck haphazardly on them: 1918, 1920, 1922. The door after 1924 had no numbers. The second I knocked on it, it crept open a few inches, its place held with a discoloured silver chain. In the faint light, a pair of black eyes peered at me before their owner spoke.

'*Yes?*' the way he said it, it sounded like the longest word in the dictionary, as though uttering it was painful.

'Benji Spriteman.'

'Ah, right. Well, you'd better come in.'

Shuffling my way through a narrow hallway, I followed the grey-headed figure into his living room. When he got there, the Dog turned with lightning quickness and a stern look on his face. But to all appearances Quentin P. Wiedlin looked like most Schnauzers. It's hard to look anything but stern when your eyebrows are longer than your ears.

He was a good six inches shorter than me, but roughly the same build. Apart from the lighter gushes around his eyes and mouth, his fur was mostly iron grey, short and wiry, somehow uncomfortable-looking. Despite the weather and the heat in his apartment, his shirt collar was buttoned up to the neck.

'Would you like some tea, Mr. Spriteman?'

'Tea would be good.'

'Won't be a minute,' he told me. Before I had a chance to reply, I sneezed so hard it took my hat off.

Looking around, I tried to make out if the apartment was small or just cluttered; three walls were covered with bookcases, all full; any space not large enough to house a book was filled with other ornaments or figurines coated in dust.

Books on the bottom rows of the bookcases were obscured by more books on the floor, haphazard piles that blotted out the carpet. A pair of drawn orange curtains blocked out much of the sunlight but none of the heat. Squashed between the books in the middle of the room two small sofas faced each other, a coffee table inches between them. Coming back in with the tea tray, Wiedlin told me to sit down.

The dry air in the apartment had given me a thirst. As soon as Wiedlin stopped pouring the tea, I started adding sugar, waiting for the inevitable reaction. Dropping the last lump in my cup, my host blew out an exaggerated breath of air, and the thick fur around his mouth shivered. 'Seven sugars,' he said without emotion.

'Sweet tooth,' I told him, taking a sip.

'You mentioned something about a story of mine on the phone,' Wiedlin said in the same disinterested tone.

'You're no doubt aware of the threatening letters Laidlaw and Finnegan have been receiving lately, so I'm checking on any writers who've had run-ins with them.'

'You haven't got that long to live, believe me,' Wiedlin snorted. 'Besides, I wouldn't say I've had any "run-ins" with them. I don't even send stories to that other rag.'

'Why don't I have that long to live?'

'Because they're both idiots.'

'One of those idiots has seen fit to publish you in the past, Mr. Wiedlin.'

'Yes they have,' he said, leaning forward so far that I could see the dust on his fur. 'And what did you think of my effort, Mr. Spriteman?'

'Oh, I liked it,' I said a little too quickly.

'Did you,' he said, taking an eternity to lean back again. 'Did you really.'

'And how many stories has Laidlaw rejected?'

41

'Altogether, or of mine?' he said, waving a paw lazily in the air. 'Just that one. And you want to know why I reacted the way I did, I presume?'

'Seems like a fair question to me.'

As he started to speak he began to tap the claws on both paws together. 'I did it in a fit of pique. I was bored, that's all. In fact I'd forgotten all about it until you called.' As I watched him knitting invisible sweaters with his nails, I wondered if that was true.

'Do you know who Daphne DuMoralize is?'

'No.' He shook his head, still clicking his claws.

'Giddyfits? Bumper Fodder?' Another shake of the head.

'Interesting names though,' he said, leaning forward again. 'I mean, "Bumper Fodder"...? Has anyone been struck by a car at all?'

'Not that I know of. You expecting it?'

Wiedlin laughed. 'Not me, Sir.'

'What do you think about all this: the letters, the threats?'

He took a deep breath, as though I was tiring him out. 'Well, it's quite entertaining, I suppose. Have you spoken to the author of the story that started the ball rolling?'

'Mungo Bickeridge? You know him?'

'Of him. Writes the most *awful* garbage apparently and then gets all precious about it.' I managed to hide my smirk just in time with my cup. 'I have to say though, I find it hard to believe it all began as a result of one story. It's almost as though someone just wanted an excuse to start something.'

It was the first time he'd said anything I agreed with. I asked why anyone would want to do that. Shaking his head noncommittally, he began to gather the tea things on the tray. Apparently my audience was over.

Coming back in from the kitchen he tried to usher me towards the door. He wanted rid of me, which was as good a reason as any to stay. I pulled up suddenly, the way he had when I came in. I said the first thing that popped into my head, mainly to annoy him.

'Sorry, I was trying to remember what breed you are. A Schnauzer, right?'

'Well done. Give that Cat a mackerel.'

'That's interesting. You said you don't submit to *Dismemberment Monthly*. Ever read it?'

'Once or twice. It's not to my taste.'

'It's just that there was a story in the first issue called "Giddyfits". It appeared to have been written under a pseudonym —'

'M. *Schnauzer* Sabreman, yes? Was it me under an assumed name? No. Sorry to disappoint. I think you'll find that story was written by none other than the magazine's editor.'

I tried to pretend I didn't care. 'Really? Who told you that?'

'It's a well-known fact. I can't remember who told me.' Again he tried to move me forward. I shuffled forward a couple of steps before stopping again.

'I expect you must be pretty excited at the moment.'

He sighed, as tired of me as I was of him.

'And why is that?'

'Well, the arrival of the de Groot sisters. I believe they're in town at the moment.'

'I believe so. Signing their latest offering, I heard. Before you ask me what I think of them I'll tell you, shall I? They're rather good; about fifty percent of the time. No doubt Laidlaw will go sniffing around them, trying to crowbar them into his magazine regardless of whether they have anything suitable or not.'

'Sounds like sour grapes to me.'

'I don't really care what it sounds like to you. Now if you don't mind...' Deciding the fun was over, I walked out of the apartment before he had a chance to push me.

In the elevator, I pulled my shirt away from my back and coughed the dust out of my lungs. I decided Wiedlin was guilty of nothing except having an ego the size of a truck and a talent the size of an egg. Maybe deep down he even knew it himself: among all the books and magazines littered around his apartment I never saw a single copy of the *Sherlock* he'd appeared in.

Back in the subway — when I wasn't being shoved around like a rag doll — I spotted more de Groot posters; their arrival in the city was certainly big news. Outside, the sun's rays hurt my eyes. Beneath my fur, my skin felt prickly. By the time I reached the office I was soaked with sweat and exhausted. For the first time I wondered if maybe I should learn to drive after all. Knocking back several cups of water, I stuck the fan on full power and called Laidlaw. Wiedlin had said something that hadn't occurred to me before and I wanted to see if he was right.

'What do you know about the de Groot sisters?' I asked him.

'I know I'll be at their book launch at Sidwells,' he said. 'I'd like to interview them for the magazine.'

'Do you think any *Sherlock* contributors will show?'

'I'll say. Writers and fans alike. Should be a good day. Why?'

'I was just wondering whether perhaps some of those writers and fans might turn out to be not so friendly. Bear the odd grudge or two.'

'You mean the letters?' Laidlaw said eventually. 'I never thought of that.'

'Tell me where and when this launch is.'

As I scribbled down the details, I realised that in a perverse sort of way I was looking forward to meeting the de Groot's. I was just about to ring off when Laidlaw heard me laughing and asked what was so funny.

'I think it's the idea of a lettuce that can write,' I told him.

5. MUNGO BICKERIDGE

THE BOOK LAUNCH AT Sidwells was still two days away. After contacting the police, filling them in and asking if they could get Dingus to give me a call, I was in the middle of having a scratch when the phone rang. Picking it up, a muffled voice said: 'I need to see you. Now.'

'Who is this?'

'I'll tell you when we meet.'

After breathing down the line as aggressively as I could, I said 'You'll tell me now or I don't leave my office. And here's a tip: you might find it easier to talk if you remove the handkerchief you've got pressed over your mouth.'

'Look, I really need to —'

'Nuts. Now listen. I've just come back from dealing with one drama queen and I'm not especially in the mood for another. It's like an oven outside and I'm going to need a damn good reason to get up out of this chair.'

After a short pause a thick voice said, 'It's Mungo Bickeridge. Someone just tried to kill me.'

Sometimes, but not often, the direct approach works.

'Where do you want to meet?'

'You know Palfreyman's? I'll be in a booth by the washrooms.' Before I had a chance to sigh disdainfully down the line, he hung up.

Of the three writers I was still trying to get hold of, Mungo Bickeridge was the one I least wanted to talk to. My

45

gut told me that he had nothing to do with any of this — as Wiedlin pointed out, it seemed unlikely all this had kicked off because someone had taken a dislike to a story they'd read. And after re-reading the back-issues of *Dismemberment Monthly* I was reminded of Finnegan's remark that he'd published sicker writers than Bickeridge. More prolific ones too: "Sick Relish" was only his third story in the magazine. Amazingly, it was also the best of the three.

Palfreyman's was an exclusive-looking place tucked away in a side street full of once-prestigious law firms. When your eyes got used to the poor lighting — the poorer the lighting, the better the clientele, I've noticed — your ears had to get used to the silence. The various animals standing at the bar or sitting at the small, polished wood tables or booths rarely said anything in voices above a whisper, making it feel more like a reading room than the private members club it so obviously wanted to be.

After ordering a tuna oil on the rocks, I looked over at the small black leather booths that made the place look like it had rubber walls. In a booth next to the john a newspaper twitched, the large smudge of darkness behind it trying hard not to be seen. I took my drink over and sat down opposite the newspaper, which quivered slightly. Finally getting my chance to be disdainful, I let out the breath I'd wanted to on the phone, causing the newspaper to quiver some more. I gave him a few seconds to introduce himself while I took a sip of my tuna oil, which wasn't bad at all. Still no movement.

He was either hamming or scared; or dead, I supposed, but that wouldn't explain the twitching. Taking my chance on the first, I flicked out one of my claws and stuck it into the top half of the newspaper, shearing it in two. Through the flapping, separated curtains of newsprint I could see the animal behind it was definitely breathing.

Of all the Dogs I'd ever seen, Mungo Bickeridge was among the ugliest. He had small, black, wide-set, billiard-ball eyes, which probably looked further apart than they were due to the dirty-white growth of fur sprouting above them. At the top of his flat head, a thick salt-and-pepper quiff arced out like a fin before splitting in two and falling in front of his piggy eyes. His mouth was big and sloppy; his dewlaps looked like they were about to drip, and every so often his small discoloured tongue flicked nervously at them. Even in the dim light and with the remnants of the newspaper in the way, my guess was he was probably as tall sitting down as standing up. Trying to tear my eyes away from him, I wondered from which hideous breeds he'd originated. I took a guess at one part Boston Terrier, one part Chinese Crested and two parts Goat.

'You aren't taking my plight seriously,' he hissed, throwing the newspaper on the table.

'How did someone try to kill you, Mr. Bickeridge?'

'I was coming out of a diner a couple of blocks away,' he said, eyes looking fearfully around. 'This car came up on the sidewalk — right up on the sidewalk — and kept coming towards me. I managed to avoid it and get level with a parked car further down the street and hid behind that. Then it drove away.'

'Anybody else see this?'

'No. The street was empty.'

'Get a look at who was driving?'

'The car had a black windshield. I couldn't see a thing.'

I let his tongue flick at his mouth a few times before I spoke. 'Why would anyone want to kill you?'

Straight away he began to overheat. 'Why?' he said, rubbing the quiff of fur roughly. '*Why?* Because of the story in the magazine!'

'It's just a story. Why go to all that trouble?'

'*Because,*' when a few patrons looked over he lowered his voice. 'Because what I write — the things I write — are difficult for some animals to accept. I deal in the truth; and most of us don't like having to face the truth.'

47

'So you're an artist,' I said, trying to keep a straight face.
'You're paying a heavy price for your art.'

'That shouldn't mean I get my windows smashed!' grabbing the fur on his head again, he corkscrewed it between his claws.

'Why didn't you contact me sooner?' I asked.

'Because since my windows were smashed, I've kept moving. I stay a different place every night; I can't stay at home any more. They'll kill me.'

'Any ideas who "they" might be?'

'I've thought about it a lot and nobody springs to mind.'

'Had any threatening letters before for other stories?'

'No. I've never written anything that good before.'

'Any of the letters come direct?'

'No. Always straight to the magazine.'

'So you've no idea who Daphne DuMoralize, Giddyfits or Bumper Fodder are?'

He laughed bitterly. 'Somehow I think I've just met Bumper Fodder. There was a story in the first issue of the magazine called 'Giddyfits' — Finnegan wrote it under a pseudonym. But I doubt it's him. That wouldn't make sense.'

'Ever heard the name Quentin P. Wiedlin?'

'Sure. He had a story in *No Shit Sherlock*.'

'Earlier today I asked him all the questions I'm asking you now. I didn't much care for his answers, but he did say this, and I think it rings true: why would everything that's happening — that's the letters, the death threats and the break-ins — come about because of a short story in which a Cat serves his dinner guests a pickle made from Hamster vomit?'

'Because it's real life. Things like this happen in real life. It's the *truth*. And like I said, most of us don't like dealing with the truth. Which is why they're trying to stop me and the magazine for publishing it.'

'So the whole thing is a conspiracy?' I said, trying to keep calm.

He leaned forward again. 'Exactly! But nobody believes me. Hey! Where are you going?'

'Mungo, I never thought I'd hear myself saying this, but you've got one hell of an imagination. I suggest you call the police.'

'The police? I can't trust them!'

'You can trust them more than you can trust me at the moment. Goodbye.' Without looking back I left him there. It's at times like these I wish Cats weren't allergic to alcohol.

It was after four and I was nearer Shefton Heights than the office. After a quick wash and something to eat, I phoned Taki to see if anything new had come in.

'You only just got me,' she said. 'Lieutenant Dingus returned your call. And someone called Grover S. Nelson phoned. Said you wanted to speak to him.'

'I do. He leave a number?' I jotted it down. More than a little warily, I called him, expecting to get my third fruitcake of the day, but he sounded surprisingly sane. After arranging to meet him in the morning, I called Dingus.

'Had any luck on those break-ins?' I asked.

'I spoke to Officer Toffee, but he says nothing stands out. You?'

Telling him about my interviews with Wiedlin and Bickeridge, I asked if he'd been told about the book launch.

'Sure. We'll work something out.'

'Have you, um, spoken to the authors yet?'

'Wiedlin and Bickeridge and the others? I'll probably leave that to Toffee. There's this other case I'm on and it's —'

'I meant the de Groots.'

'The de Groots?'

'The writers whose book's being launched?'

He sounded puzzled. 'Why would I want to speak to them?'

Explaining the de Groot's interest in the Carlin case, the Lieutenant gave a small moan at the other end of the line. 'I hope they're not going to bring all that into the open again. What time's this book launch?'

'So I'll see you there?' I asked when I'd told him.

'You will,' he said quietly before hanging up.

Looking out the window, the sun was still blazing in a cloudless sky. It wouldn't be dark for hours, but I decided to go to bed anyway. It had been a long and trying day. By and large, I could cope with trying. What I found harder to cope with was the feeling of creeping unease pulsing through me, that and the nagging uncertainty of where it was all heading.

6. GROVER S. NELSON / LETTICE

NEXT MORNING WHEN TAKI walked in to find me sitting at my desk, she could barely contain herself.

'Again! Really, you should go to a doctor: you look terrible. Don't you like your own bed?'

'I was in my own bed last night,' I snapped, 'and slept twelve hours straight through. I should look wonderful.'

'You don't. You look appalling.'

'Why, thank you.'

It'd been a long time since I'd slept that long. I awoke feeling that I'd dreamt lots of horrible things but couldn't remember what they were. I was drenched with sweat and had a headache; that bit was hardly surprising; the air in my bedroom was so thick you could chew it.

Leaving Shefton Heights I felt a bit better. The street was slightly less muggy than my apartment; maybe, just maybe, the weather was finally going to break. Then it occurred to me that it was cooler because I was up so early. By the time Taki rolled in, things were getting sticky again. I still had an hour to fill before Grover Nelson showed up. I phoned Finnegan to see if he'd had any more letters.

'Just the one, from "Bumper Fodder". It says "Won't fail next time". Any idea what they're talking about?'

I told him about my talk with Mungo Bickeridge. 'Somebody tried to mow him down in the street. He's not contacted you?'

'No. Is he okay?'

51

'Physically, yes. He thinks somebody out there hates his work so much they want to kill him and bring you down with him.'

'He's... I wouldn't judge him too harshly.'

'I'll try not to. He also knew you wrote "Giddyfits", as well as another writer I talked to who doesn't even read your magazine. You're sure you don't remember telling anyone it was yours?'

He thought about it. 'No. I'd have no reason *to* tell anybody. Who's the other writer?'

'Quentin P. Wiedlin.'

'Yeah, I've heard of him. Writes for upstairs. How the hell does he know?'

'He says it's common knowledge.' Ringing off, I called Laidlaw, but he had nothing new to report.

I was still mulling things over when I heard a knock at the outer door. Someone said something to Taki in a hushed voice, and she buzzed through to me.

'Grover S. Nelson,' she said as someone coughed in the background. 'And he says to tell you he's sorry he's early.'

I looked at my watch; nearly half an hour early. I told Taki to send him through. My door started to ease open very slowly and quietly, and after a while a large slipper-shaped ear brushed the doorjamb. On the ear alone I took a quick guess at the breed. Corgi.

'Again, I'm sorry I'm so early,' the Corgi said, closing the door quietly behind him, 'but I'm intrigued to know what all this is about, and as we seemed to keep missing each other —'

'That's okay, Mr. Nelson. Take a seat.'

As he did, I looked him over. He was wearing a white cotton shirt nearly identical in colour to the ruff of fur at his neck. The top button was undone but didn't sit right, and I guessed if it hadn't been for the heat he wouldn't normally have been so informal. He perched on the edge of the seat, with his small white paws crossed on the desk and his large innocent eyes blinking at me. He was the last animal on earth I'd suspect of writing horror stories.

'One the phone you said something about the poison-pen letters that keep appearing in the magazines,' he said.

'That's right. But I wanted to talk to you in particular about the stories you've sent Patch Finnegan.'

He blinked at me several times more and squeezed his paws together. 'But none of my stories has ever been published.'

Or are ever likely to be, I thought. 'I know.'

'Have you read them?' he asked hopefully.

'I've read four of them. One of them, "The Hatred of Damien Fitch" is about a writer who gets so sick of having his stories rejected that he makes the editor's life a misery; "The Horror of the Small Press" is about another writer that can't get a publisher and feeds several of his rivals through a mangle; "Fat-Man Becomes Flat-Man", on the other hand, is about a *successful* writer who meets an untimely end when he is knocked down by a steamroller —'

'Yes, about "The Hatred of Damien Fitch" —'

'— and "The Curse of Disembowelment Quarterly" is about some Mutt who kills his favourite author and feeds him to his pet snake. Four stories and all of them roughly about the same thing: a frustrated writer jealous of, and angered by, the success of others.'

'Good heavens, you're right,' he said, 'they're all the same plot. Could I have a drink of water, please?' he said a few seconds later. 'It's awfully hot in here.'

Getting him the water, I couldn't decide what would be worse: if this clown was joking with me or if he was serious. Clown or not, he was polite, thanking me before and after drinking the water.

'Mr. Nelson —'

'Oh, Grover, please. I only use the rest for the stories.'

'Grover, I don't know how to put this, but those stories are quite similar to the events I'm investigating. Writers and editors have been threatened. The offices of *Dismemberment Monthly* and *No Shit Sherlock* have both been broken into. One writer has even had his windows smashed and yesterday someone tried to run him over. Can you give me any explanation why your stories are mirroring what's going on?'

'I'm afraid I can't,' he said earnestly.

'None of them?'

'Well, "The Hatred of Damien Fitch" was written almost a year ago. That covers that one. But the others...' he shook his head. 'They've all been written quite recently. In the past couple of months in fact.'

'And it never occurred to you, with all this going on, that stories like these might make you a suspect?'

'No,' he replied, blinking some more. 'They just seemed like good ideas for stories.'

The thing is, looking at his vacant face, I believed him. He was no more capable of masterminding what was happening than he was of writing a half-decent story. Nevertheless I went through the rigmarole of asking if he knew who Daphne DuMoralize was, or if he knew who wrote "Giddyfits", but he knew nothing. On his way out, I asked him if he was aware that the de Groot sisters were in town; he looked at me like I'd sprouted another head. That was the last I ever saw of him.

As I sat there dumbfounded, I realised that Nelson was right about one thing: it was awfully hot in here. I figured it must be the heat that was stopping me from seeing what was really going on, because I seemed to be as far away from any answers as I had been at the start. I'd spoken to three of the four writers, Wiedlin, Bickeridge and Nelson; one was arrogant, one was nuts and the other pathetic. That left Lake... again I tried the number I had but no answer. After slamming down the phone, I slammed the desk in frustration. Perhaps Harvey had it wrong: maybe Fuller was involved after all; maybe something had changed. I called Harvey's number but he wasn't there. Rather than sit in the office and bake, I decided to pay the Rat a visit myself.

Approaching the anonymous-looking grey-brick building, I thought back to the other times I'd been there. As a rule I tried to stay away from the place, as the experience was always rather dispiriting.

It started the moment the elevator door opened onto the fifth floor. The cleaners wouldn't go up there anymore because of the abuse they got from the paper's staff, so the corridor was littered with old editions of the paper, plus the food cartons and bottles that could no longer be squashed down into the overflowing office garbage can. After wading your way through that, you opened the door with one paw and held your nose with the other. The office itself was full of semi-comatose Rodents covered in food particles, slowly slipping out of their chairs. And if you were really lucky, you'd see a large brown Rat stuffed into a small white chair in a cramped office on the right. He'd have sharp yellow teeth and breath you could chop a tree with.

'Whaddaya want?' he shouted as I walked in unannounced.

'Social call,' I said, taking a seat. 'You know how well we get on.'

'Yeah, I remember. What's it this time?'

'A dickie-bird told me you were thinking of publishing a fiction magazine. I told them you already did. No, a *real* fiction magazine, they said. Pictures and everything. Sounds interesting.'

'Well, that dickie-bird of yours is wrong. I went off the idea. No money in it. Besides, we got two magazines locally already. And look at the trouble they're having.'

'Are they having trouble?' As a treat he gave me his best scowl. 'So who do you think is behind it? If you were to care about such a thing.'

'If I were to care about such a thing I'd be doing your job,' the Rat said, scratching himself noisily under his desk, 'But if

I *did* care... I'd think it was just a prank that got out of hand. Drink?' As I shook my head, he broke the seal on the bottle of scotch on his desk, the cap ending up on the floor. 'No? See, that's your problem, fella. You never lighten up.'

I watched Fuller glug back the whiskey like it was tap water. 'And that's it?'

'That's it,' he said, slamming the bottle back on the desk. 'Nothing more, nothing less. Whoever's behind it, they should lighten up too.' Picking up the bottle again, he glugged some more.

I reeled off the names of the writers I was looking into, in case they were all somehow in it together, but no reaction. When I left his office he was still glugging away. When I stepped out of the building a few minutes later, I wondered if he'd finished the bottle yet.

It had nothing to do with Fuller, I was sure of that now. The problem was, I was equally sure it had nothing to do with anybody else I'd spoken to either. I went back to the office.

'You've had three calls,' Taki told me before I got a chance to ask, 'all from the same animal. Wouldn't give her name.'

'She say what it was about?'

'Nope. She had to speak to you and you only.'

I decided to try Lake again. I was reaching for the phone when it started ringing. I smiled. Whenever you think of someone... picking up the receiver I was just about to ask where the hell he'd been when a dull, accusing voice said:

'Benji Spriteman. I want to talk to Benji Spriteman.'

'That's me,' I said, trying not to sound like I was guilty of something. 'How can I —'

'My name is Lettice de Groot. I believe you spoke to Angelica.'

Her voice was markedly different to her sister's; perhaps they came from separate litters. The smokiness was there, but it didn't suggest breeding, it suggested cigarettes; ashtrays full of them. And while Angelica de Groot's voice was a touch overripe, this one was positively gamey.

'Yes I did. If it's about the book launch —'

'It is about the book launch.' She said, talking over me. 'Have you any idea how far we've both come to see you, Mr. Spriteman? It wasn't an easy journey.'

'Your point being? Besides, I was led to believe you were here to promote a book, not talk to me.'

She ignored that. 'It is *essential* we talk to you. Our next book depends on it.'

'If it's so *essential* why couldn't you have just phoned me from overseas?' a frosty silence blew into my ear.

'Mr. Spriteman,' she said eventually, 'we are both extremely busy. We have deadlines to meet. I can't see why a brief chat should prove so difficult for you. I think if we can make changes to our schedule —'

'Lettice, Lettice. You're busy. *I'm* busy. The heat in this city is unbearable. I'm working a case that's tying me in knots and my fur is falling out. The last thing I need are nuisance calls from two pushy felines wanting to rake up parts of my past that I want to forget. And frankly, talking to me like I'm an imbecile is not helping matters. Kapeesh?'

The pause wasn't so long this time, but the paw I was holding the phone in suddenly felt about twenty degrees colder. 'Tomorrow we shall be launching our latest book at a shop called Sidwells. Do you think you could *somehow* manage to attend?'

'Yes I could. And if you hadn't interrupted me you'd have heard me say that I was going to be there. Whether I now want to be there is another matter entirely. Can I speak to your sister?'

She sounded surprised. 'Whatever do you want to do that for?'

'I don't know. It'd just be nice to hear a friendly voice.'

'She's not here.' With that, Lettice de Groot hung up.

With the echoes of her voice in my head, I made some coffee before doing what I'd intended to do before being so rudely interrupted. Unfortunately, Lake wasn't there.

Finishing my coffee, I put my paws on the desk and my head in my paws. After letting out an almighty yawn I wondered where the sisters were staying, and if either of them ever read *No Shit Sherlock*. They'd certainly never appeared in it.

7. JAKE LAKE / BOOK LAUNCH

THE MORNING OF THE book launch I had a surprising phone call from a female who said I'd been trying to get in touch with her.

'What's the name?'

'Jake Lake,' the soft voice said.

'Jake Lake. *Jake.*'

'It's a long and boring story,' she said, as if she'd told it a thousand times before. 'But you do want to talk to me, right?'

'If you're Jake Lake, I want to talk to you.'

I arranged to meet 'Jake Lake' in the park; at least then there'd be lots of other animals around should things turn ugly. She might be claiming to be female, but the way things were going, I decided I didn't want to take any chances.

The morning streets were busy, everyone wanting to get their business out of the way before the real heat kicked in. The sidewalks were full of animals selling ices and sunhats, large Birds made extra money by standing in offices and flapping their wings for a fee; apparently it was more effective than air conditioning. As I walked, I realised I was getting used to the sight of shaved midriffs. The sooner the rain came, the better.

In the park the grass was the colour of straw. Sunlight reflected off a hundred pairs of sunglasses and hurt my eyes.

I'd arranged to meet Lake by an ice cream stand across from a pond where Old ducks splashed about in the water, the only contented creatures I'd seen in weeks.

'I'm sure if you jumped in nobody would mind,' someone said behind me.

'Maybe,' I said, still looking at the Ducks, 'but my clothes would stink to high heaven afterwards.'

Turning to my right, a vision in pure white fur blotted out the sun, a Turkish Angora with light blue eyes, a small pink nose and a voice you could make pillows out of.

I laughed. *'You're* Jake Lake?'

'Yes.'

'Then why —'

'Ice cream?' I followed her over to the stand.

'My owners thought they had a sense of humour,' she said, handing me a cone, 'I mean it rhymes, right?'

'But you're a Jane, not a Jake.'

'Obviously the joke was more important than the facts.' She pointed to a nearby bench. Nudging in beside a pair of Mallards who refused to move, we sat down. 'Anyway, I find it helps with the writing. I seem to be more successful submitting to magazines as a male.'

'Are all your stories as good as "The Invisible Feud"?'

She smiled behind her ice cream. 'You like it?'

'I did. Trouble in the publishing world... very realistic.'

'Ah.' She laughed. 'Yes. The idea was too good to leave. I'm surprised nobody else has done it.'

'How do you know they haven't?'

She blinked and smiled at the same time. 'Have they?'

I filled her in — the letters, the break-ins, everything. She looked shocked.

'But I didn't write about any break-ins. I knew nothing about them,' she said as she crunched into her cone.

'Perhaps. But everything you had written, up to the point the story ended, was accurate. That's why I've been wanting to talk to you.'

'I've been visiting relatives in the country. I mailed the story the morning I left. I thought the letters were a joke, so I changed the names and used the idea.' She looked out across the water then back at me. 'Has anyone been hurt?'

'Not yet. But it's heading that way. I don't suppose you know who any of these letters' writers are? It would help me tremendously.' She shook her head. I tried her with a few of the writers, even mentioning the de Groot sisters.

'I've heard of Wiedlin; he's been in *Sherlock*. I don't know about the others. But I've heard of the de Groots, of course.'

For a while neither of us spoke; instead we looked out at the water and the sun coming through the trees. Finally she asked, 'Am I a suspect?'

'About as much as everybody else is,' I replied, still looking at the water. 'Okay. Last question. What do you think this is all about? I mean: *really* about?'

She laughed again. 'Aren't you supposed to be the detective?'

'I never said I was any good. Come on, what's it all about?'

She gave me an unreadable look; unreadable but enjoyable. At least, I enjoyed it. 'I've really no idea,' she said. 'Money? That's what most things seem to be about, isn't it? Even these days.'

Standing at the same time, we watched a large Duck as it came into land, skimming above the water gracefully before landing on its surface. 'If you do jump in I won't tell anyone,' she whispered.

'I will if you will.' She didn't answer.

As I was walking away she called me back. 'Don't you want to check my alibi?' she said, smiling. 'Where I was staying in the country?'

My fur covering my blushes, I took my pad out of my pocket and went back to her. The idea had never entered my mind.

‡ ‡ ‡

It was now eleven thirty. The book launch was at one. On my way back to the office I stopped in at Moe's to pick up tuna sandwiches for lunch. By the time I'd got out of the elevator, mine had gone.

'The Mouse was in about half an hour ago,' Taki told me, once she'd recovered from the shock of me buying her a sandwich. 'Said he'll meet you at Sidwells. He also said he had something important to tell you.'

I grunted back. Usually when the Mouse had 'something important to tell me' it wasn't very important at all. 'Anything else?'

'No,' she said, tucking into her sandwich. 'It's just another long, quiet, lazy day.' When I grunted this time it was with feeling.

Before leaving I went into my office and closed the door, listening to the traffic purring below. For some reason I found the noise quite soothing and it helped me to think. I needed it to help me now. But when I left five minutes later, I was none the wiser.

The heat of the day was about to reach its peak, and the streets were almost empty. As I walked, I wondered if the letters' writer would be at the bookstore, and what trouble they might cause if they were.

I arrived at Sidwells with ten minutes to spare and found the place packed solid. The only books I could see through the window were those on the upper shelves, the ones below being obscured by fur, feathers and tails. Pushing my way inside, I almost knocked over a stack of copies of *The Jagged Stiletto of Ursula Prim* piled up on the floor. The elderly moggy on the cover looked at me over her *pince nez* like I had.

The heat inside was even worse than in the street. The odours of various species mingled in the air, words from half a dozen half-heard conversations snaked through my brain. As I looked for Dingus and the Mouse, I kept banging against tables groaning under the weight of the de Groot sister's works. Jammed between two Alsatians in beach shirts, I examined a few; books with bright but tasteful covers sporting titles such as *A Rest Cure for Mr. Jellinek* and *The Poisoned Piston of Peter Pinter*. The books all looked to be short, but again I found myself wondering how they'd managed to produce so many in under two years.

'I wouldn't bother even *attempting* that one,' one of the Alsatians said as I picked up the intriguingly named *Death by Winkle*. 'The title's the best thing about it.'

Putting it down, I grabbed *The Final Gasp of Wallace Miles*. 'What about this one?'

The mutt's eyes sparkled. 'Now you're talking. Didn't see the ending coming at all. Wonderful stuff.'

Despite myself I was interested. 'What about the others?'

'Well, it's a bit of gamble, I'm afraid. *Rosa Worth, Rest Cure, Pinter...* each one an absolute gem. But the others — *Gift-Wrapped, Enemies, Butter...* they're bad beyond belief.'

It was increasingly difficult to hear above the cries for drinks. 'Sorry, I thought you said "Butter".'

'I did — *The Last Words of the Dying Butter*. Absolutely dreadful. It should say "Butler" but whoever did the cover spelt it wrong. The rumour is that it was done deliberately, so you'd keep reading to see how butter could talk at all, never mind what its last words were; the picture on the cover even matches the misprint. You certainly wouldn't keep reading it otherwise.' With that the Alsatian moved away, asking anyone who'd listen where the buffet was.

It took me a while, but I eventually found the Mouse backed into a corner between a shelf, a ladder, and a large animated Rabbit that kept stamping its foot on the floor as if it was making some important point. Considering it my duty to rescue him, I waded through fur and flesh, waving my paw at him. As the Mouse moved towards me, I made a mental note to try and contact Harvey again.

'Trouble?' I asked.

'No,' he said, looking across at the bunny who'd now collared someone else, 'just a chatterbox. He didn't stop to breathe.' He wiped his face with the back of his paw.

'Taki said you had something important to tell me.'

Before he got the chance, the room fell silent.

'Can I have your attention please,' a voice called out, seemingly at the other end of the room. 'As you may have noticed, Sidwells is rather cramped today and the air conditioning isn't working. So today's launch party is being held in the gardens at the back of the store, where refreshments as well as books will be available. So if you'd like to make your way outside —' Nobody waited to hear what was said next; instead, the crowd surged towards the shaft of sunlight that had appeared at the back of the store.

'Talk about a room-clearer,' I said, turning to the Mouse. But he'd gone too.

With most of the animals gone, I made my way through the empty aisles, scenting the air for cigars, only to be surprised when I didn't catch any; I'd imagined Dingus being there before any of us. Unless he was already outside...? Opening the door to the garden, I stepped out into the dazzling sunshine.

It was quite a scene. The garden — which had been concreted over with the exception of an area around a tree at the far end — was now a bustling jumble of animals, books and refreshments. Trestle tables set around the edges of the garden sagged under the weight of large silver tea urns, china cups and saucers glittering sharply in the sunlight. The only things not sparkling were the huge pile of books on the tables underneath the tree.

Making my way over to the refreshment tables, I saw someone I hadn't expected to see.

'Not a word Spriteman,' the Parrot said, flapping away, 'not a word.'

Shove Off — real name Captain — was the grumpy Parrot I sometimes grunted at on a morning, and of all the Birds in the city, I'd have said the least likely to be working as a fan. 'The money'll come in handy,' he snapped as I opened my mouth, 'I have to feed the kitties somehow, you know.'

'They pay well?'

'Well enough. Don't you get enough crime in your life?' he said, nodding towards the books.

'I'm working on a case. What are the sandwiches like?'

'I wouldn't know — I haven't had a chance to try one. The salmon are going quickly. Nobody's touching the other ones.'

'What are they?'

'Cucumber.'

'Where are the crusts?' I asked, picking one up.

'They cut 'em off. Don't ask me why.'

I took a bite, then spat it straight out. 'They cut off the best bit,' I said, picking up a salmon sandwich, which, like the cucumber, was the size of a postage stamp.

'Who died, anyhow?' Captain asked. 'I've spotted at least two cops since I've been here.'

'Which ones?'

'Tober and Toffee, both in plain clothes. Either they're working or they can read. I'm guessing the former.' He looked at me in that way only he could, a mixture of defiance, sly humour and impatience.

'You could be right,' I said, popping another postage stamp into my mouth as I walked away. 'Keep flapping those wings, Cap.'

'Shove off,' he said heartily, sending a breeze up my back as I went.

For maybe half an hour I walked around picking up nibbles and eavesdropping on conversations, on the lookout for anyone who looked like they might cause trouble. Most of the conversations, not surprisingly, revolved around books and the brilliance of such works as *The Final Gasp of Wallace Miles* and *A Rest Cure for Mr. Jellinek* against the abject failures of *The Enemies of Edgar Silliphant* and *The Last*

Words of the Dying Butter. 'It makes you wonder how they get away with it,' a middle-aged Siamese said at one point. 'I doubt they would if they hadn't followed it with *Jellinek*,' an elderly Poodle replied. Exchanging a few brief words with Tober, he told me the Lieutenant would be along later. When I asked where he was, he shrugged. 'You know the Lieutenant. He likes to play his cards close to his chest.' Then, standing on his own in a corner, viewing the events the way a Vulture views a carcass, I spotted Quentin P. Wiedlin.

'Mr. Spriteman, how wonderful to see you again,' he said as I approached. 'Any progress with the case of the threatening letters?'

'I'm surprised to see you here,' I said. 'You seemed rather lukewarm on the de Groots the last time we spoke.'

'I seem to remember saying they were satisfactory fifty per cent of the time. I'm here on the off-chance that the new book is one of the good ones.'

'Quite a few animals seem to agree with you. Why, what's so wrong with, say, *Death by Winkle?*'

He snorted. 'If you have to ask, you obviously haven't read it. Murder by poisoned seafood? Absolutely ludicrous! Perhaps if it'd been well-written they might just have pulled it off, but *really...*' As he was talking, a brown corduroy jacket came into view near the writer's table.

'I see you've spotted our esteemed editor,' Wiedlin said. 'I wonder how much he'll pay them to appear in his magazine? Interesting that he's wearing a jacket that colour, isn't it? When he's finished brown nosing them, it won't show.'

As if he'd heard what Wiedlin had said, Laidlaw looked up. But it was past Wiedlin and back towards the door.

'Well, it looks like they've finally decided to arrive,' Wiedlin sneered.

For some reason, I knew straight away that Angelica de Groot was the one smoking the pipe. It looked old and wizened, and protruded from the side of her mouth like a second tongue.

Once I'd got over the pipe, I started to take in the rest of her. There was a lot to take in, too — the patterned dress she was wearing had either shrunk in the wash or she liked the feel of all those faded roses pressing tightly against her fur. Either way, one swift movement and something was going to give. Not that she looked capable of swift movements; she was roughly the same width as the Mouse, but about six inches shorter. For a Blue-Cream Longhair, her fur was unusually thick and she had large patches of grey around her ears and shoulders, and her whiskers were also long and thick. Her eyes were a deep sherry colour like her purse, the pupils bright and shiny like a kitten's, despite her not being in the first flush of youth.

'Good afternoon, how-do-you-do, good afternoon, how-do-you-do,' she said as she bustled her way through the rapidly retreating bodies. Passing us, I caught no scent besides a natural one. For some reason I'd expected to be overcome by lavender.

'My God,' Wiedlin said when she was safely out of earshot. 'Is this the sister?'

Lettice de Groot looked exactly as I'd expected her to look: mean. She was about the same height as her sister, but there the similarity ended. Despite being slightly younger and maybe a quarter of the width, she didn't look as sprightly as her sister. She was wearing a baggy grey trouser suit and, instead of a pipe, a thin cigarette protruded from the side of the mouth. She looked frail somehow, and her fur, a mixture or black and brown, was greying faster than her sister's, particularly around the neck. As far as breed went, if anything she was a Rex. If she greeted anybody on the way to the table I didn't hear it. While Angelica greeted the Birds in the tree with a cheery wave, good naturedly asking them to 'mind their aim', Lettice slumped down in her chair. After sitting down herself, Angelica de Groot spoke.

'First of all, our apologies for being late. We were rather held up in Rockway by circumstances beyond our control —'

'Let's just get on with it,' Lettice de Groot said.

Her sister didn't react. 'Yes, you're right; we should. Well, thank you for coming to the launch party for *The Jagged Stiletto of Ursula Prim*. It's our ninth novel, and I'd have to say of all our novels this is one of the best.' Beside her, Lettice winced before coughing a few times. 'So, if you'd like to form an orderly line in front of the table we can get the signing under way, and at the same time answer any questions you may have.'

'Thinks she's the queen,' Wiedlin said, looking at his watch. 'I think I've seen enough.'

'Aren't you buying a copy of the book?' I asked.

'I'll wait for the paperback,' he said, barging his way through the tide of animals towards the exit.

Standing next to an empty food table, I watched proceedings from the sidelines. Officer Toffee tried to look inconspicuous behind the tree the sisters were sitting beneath, while Officer Tober chatted to the Mouse at the edge of the queue. Nothing looked out of the ordinary. Apart from Rusty Laidlaw who stood rubbing his paws together expectantly next to the table, I saw nobody that I recognised. Above the chattering of the line, one voice was plain above all others.

'To *whom?* Agnes? Oh, how lovely. I hope she enjoys it,' Angelica de Groot said, passing a signed book back to a terrified looking Greyhound. When they put the book in front of Lettice, she signed it but said nothing.

Twenty minutes later the line was no shorter. Angelica talked enthusiastically to everyone who approached her. Lettice said nothing, only barking out an occasional 'next'. Toffee had retired to a hammock at the back of the garden, his hat titled over his face. Everyone looked worn out with the heat except the sisters, the large tree branches hanging over their desk providing them with shade. Rusty Laidlaw was still standing next to the table, like some unnoticed flunky. Catching his eye, I signalled him to come over. With some reluctance he began to move away from the table. Then he stopped. Lettice de Groot was speaking. In sentences.

'*Uneven*? Well, that's just great,' she snapped at the flustered Chow Chow in front of her. 'I'm sorry if you preferred *The Haggling of Rosa Worth*. Let's just hope this one doesn't disappoint too, shall we? And even if it does, there'll be another one along soon, which makes it okay, doesn't it?' Beside her, Angelica greeted the next fan as cheerily as ever.

'Interesting pair,' I said to Laidlaw when he came over.

'I'd heard she was temperamental,' he said.

'I've heard several animals say the quality of the books isn't exactly consistent.'

'No. Generally it's one good one followed by a bad one. If the pattern holds, *Stiletto* should be a good one.'

Perhaps as a result of Lettice's outburst, the queue began to dwindle. When it was down to three or four animals, Laidlaw joined it. Then, despite the stink of pipe and cigarette smoke emanating from the sisters, I caught another odour behind me: cigars.

Shambling onto the concrete, Lieutenant Dingus looked just the same as he always did: like a balloon someone had been letting the air out of over a long period of time. Despite the weather he was wearing the same shirt, waistcoat and trench-coat that he always wore, and as usual didn't look any hotter for doing so. Waving a paw at me, he waited for Tober to come over and brief him. At the back of the garden Officer Toffee tried to disengage himself from the hammock without being noticed.

Back at the signing table, Laidlaw got his wish and was buttonholing the de Groots, the bookstore owner smiling politely next to them.

Then, as Laidlaw was apparently asking Lettice a question, she pointed at me and seemed to ask the editor one of her own. Hearing his answer, she moved out from under the shade of the tree and made a beeline for me.

69

'Are you Spriteman?' she barked out while she was still about ten feet away. I waited until she was standing next to me before telling her I was.

'So,' Lettice de Groot said, 'now you can tell me what you know about being a private investigator.'

'Don't you want to wait until your sister's here?'

'Why would I want to do that?' she snapped. 'We're not joined at the hip, you know.'

What followed was the verbal equivalent of a mugging. Not used to answering questions, I did my best to bat them away. The whole thing probably only lasted a minute, but when I spotted Laidlaw, the store owner and the other de Groot sister coming towards me, I had to stop myself letting out a cheer.

'Mr. Spriteman? Good of you to come,' Angelica said, holding out her paw for me to shake. 'I see you've already met my sister. I hope she hasn't been giving you *too* hard a time?' Lettice shot her a look but she didn't notice; instead, she looked at me and tutted. 'You haven't got a book,' she said. 'Let's go and get you one' and she marched back to the table. Not wanting to face this alone, I looked around for the Lieutenant but couldn't see him anywhere.

Stepping into the shade of the branches, I tried to ready myself for the interrogation that would surely follow.

'Right then, first things first,' she said, looking up at me with her lively eyes, 'the book.'

No sooner had the words left her mouth than the leaves above us began to quiver. We all looked up. As we did, several small white pellets appeared among the greenery, dropping onto the nearest copy of *Stiletto* in a series of small *pats*, smearing the cover.

'Sorry about that,' an embarrassed voice called from the branches. 'It just sort of... slipped out.'

Looking at the book, the old biddy on the cover looked like she'd been hit with a bucket of whitewash. Unable to help myself, I could feel a laugh coming on, but Angelica de Groot got there before me. She laughed so hard her pipe fell out of her mouth, its contents spraying the table. Beside me, Lettice was stony faced, her paws across her chest.

Wiping her eyes, Angelica picked up the soiled book and put it to one side. Taking the next one from the pile, she opened it at the title page and signed it.

'Never have liked that cover,' she said, handing Lettice the book. Angelica looked like she was going to laugh again. After adding her rough squiggle to the page, Lettice pushed the book at me. Angelica had written: *To Benjamin Spriteman — for assisting us with our enquiries.*

'So, Mr. Spriteman,' she said with a smile, 'tell us about being a private investigator. Without giving *too* much away, of course; I'm sure you have your trade secrets.' Looking at her in a way that I hoped conveyed thanks, I asked what they wanted to know. Before Lettice had a chance to butt in, Angelica began to ask questions.

What followed was no less an interrogation than the one I'd had from Lettice, only this time it was friendly. She asked about my workload, my staff, the kind of cases I took, if certain kinds of animal were more likely to commit certain crimes than others; in short, she asked nothing about the Carlin case. She'd just started to ask me what I knew about poisons when Lettice suddenly announced in a strained voice that she was going to the washroom, pushing past anyone unfortunate enough to be in her way, sucking on her cigarette as she went.

'She's not been feeling well since we left Rockway,' her sister said, trying not to make it sound like an apology.

'Where are you staying?'

'The Plaza. Do you know it?'

'I've never been to Rockway,' I said.

'Really? You'll have to come and visit us,' she said, tapping out her pipe against the side of the tree. 'Maybe in different surroundings you'll feel like discussing the Carlin case.'

The look she gave me was gentle but persistent; her eyes smiled, but not her mouth.

'Perhaps,' I sighed. Before an awkward silence had time to develop, she asked me what I was currently working on. Jumping at the change of subject, I told her as little as possible about the *Sherlock/Dismemberment* investigation as I could get away with.

'Good heavens,' she said when I'd finished. Then, 'That magazine you just mentioned. Isn't that the editor —?' she turned to face Laidlaw but he and the storeowner had gone. 'Just asked us to do an interview?'

'Rusty Laidlaw,' I told her. 'Are you going to?'

'Reluctantly, yes,' she said, pulling a face. 'He asked us for a story too. But I can't say I'm sure I want to appear in a magazine with a name like that, though.'

I laughed. 'Believe it or not, they publish some good stories.'

She looked surprised. 'Do they really? I shall have to buy a copy and see.'

We were still discussing *Sherlock* a few minutes later when I spotted Dingus at the other end of the garden, hovering around a tea urn. Eventually catching his eye, I called him over.

'Who on earth is that?' Angelica de Groot asked as he slouched over, only stopping to pick up cucumber sandwiches.

'Lieutenant Dingus,' I told her. 'Not your conventional police officer.'

'I'll say. Not what I expected at all. Good heavens, no.'

As we were watching the Lieutenant's progress with his tea and plateful of sandwiches, Lettice reappeared and shoved past him. She looked even worse than she had before; she was bent over, clutching her stomach, coughing up cigarette smoke. The look in her eyes said her mood hadn't improved either.

'I don't suppose for one minute you've asked him,' she said to her sister as if I wasn't there.

Angelica looked pained. 'No, Lettice, I haven't. I thought we could —'

'This isn't the time or the place,' I said.

'Why not?' Lettice said, coughing again. 'We're not here forever, you know.'

Dingus finally joined us. 'Have you tried these sandwiches, Benji?' he asked, 'they're really something.'

For several awkward seconds nobody spoke.

'Who are you?' Lettice finally asked.

'Oh, Lieutenant Dingus, ma'am. You must be the de Groot sisters?' he looked first at Angelica, then at Lettice.

'I hope you're more helpful than he is,' Lettice said, wincing before hiking a claw in my general direction.

'I'm sorry ma'am?'

'I was just trying to explain to Miss de Groot here, Dingus, that the Carlin case was a difficult one. *Very* difficult.'

'I think we should discuss it now,' Lettice told her sister. 'Somehow I don't think we'll get another chance with these two.'

'We wouldn't want to know anything that would compromise either of you,' Angelica said, her gaze suggesting she didn't want trouble.

By now the heat was just about unbearable; my fur and flesh felt like it'd fused together with my shirt. I was sick of this case and sick of the heat — all I really wanted to do was go home and sit in a cold bath.

'I'm afraid I wouldn't be able to make it today,' Dingus put in. 'The case I'm on is at a very important —'

'I don't believe this!' Lettice said in a voice somewhere between a cough and a laugh that caused her to stoop even further. 'Is this the way you normally do business? If it is, it's a wonder any crimes over here get solved at all.' It looked like she was going to say more, but her voice turned into a watery cough.

It was Angelica's turn to speak. 'Even if we could conduct an interview now dear, I hardly think you're in a position to participate. You need to see a doctor.'

'Doctor nothing,' she said, clutching her stomach. 'It's just a stomach ache. I'm in better shape than these two amateurs. So they had a tough time on a case, so what?'

My blood was starting to boil now. 'Now you listen to me, *Lettice*. I don't sit behind some desk all day eating dainty biscuits and drinking tea. And I'd hardly think that someone who does and has heard about the Carlin case fifth hand is in a position to lecture anyone about a tough time. You have no idea what you're talking about.'

'Oh, don't I?' she said as she gripped her stomach, 'I know that Jimmy Spriteman got himself shot in the back after chasing some lunatic into an abandoned building. And I also know how —'

That was it. I finally snapped. *'Can it, sister,'* I shouted, the words hissing out of me like boiling steam. Lettice de Groot looked at me like I'd gone insane. Everyone else seemed to hold their breath. All around me I could feel dozens of pairs of eyes staring at me.

'Benji.'

It was Dingus. He was looking down at my paws. After a few seconds I did the same. Thick red dots pooled around my claws. It took me a few seconds to realise I'd clenched my paws so hard that my claws had punctured my pads. As I licked the blood away, what sounded like horrible, throaty wheezing laughter came from Lettice.

Looking into her horrible black eyes, my anger melted. She looked terrified. She was clenching her stomach even harder now, her teeth bared in a rictus grin. Almost doubled over, she grasped for the edge of the table to steady herself but missed, her outstretched paw catching a pile of books, scattering them everywhere. A horrible tortured whine escaped through her clenched teeth. Another spasm hit her like an invisible punch and she jolted backwards, bent double with pain. Her legs collapsed under her and she fell backwards, her head smacking the concrete with a sickening thud, her sightless bulging eyes staring up into the branches above.

Lettice de Groot was dead.

8. CLEANUP

W HEN I FINALLY LOOKED up from the body it was into a sea of furry faces, each with frightened eyes. I wanted to say what I hoped they already knew — that I hadn't killed her, but the words wouldn't come. Time froze. I waited for someone to speak, to break the spell. Then, just when I thought I couldn't take any more, I smelled cigar smoke.

'Okay, I need you all to go back indoors so we can sort things out,' Dingus said, walking past. 'Tober, make sure nobody leaves. Where's the nearest phone?' he asked the bookstore owner, then followed him back inside. On the way they pushed past the large white bulk of the Mouse, who had a pained look on his face. As I looked at him that feeling of anxiety reared up in me again. *You knew this was coming,* the voice in my head told me, *you knew this was coming but there was nothing you could do to prevent it.* The knowledge didn't help, but it burst the bubble I felt I'd been standing in.

Looking back to the scene, Toffee was standing next to the body, trying to keep his gaze away from those sightless eyes. Next to him, Angelica de Groot looked... crestfallen. Making my way over to her, I readied myself for her accusations. Only they didn't come.

'We weren't close,' she said with a sigh, putting her pipe back in her bag, 'but that was no way to go.'

'No,' I agreed, looking down at the body.

'It wasn't your fault, you know,' she said. 'I told you she hadn't been feeling well all day; kept complaining about "stomach cramps." I daresay your coroner will find out the cause.'

'Coroner?'

'That's who Lieutenant Dingus said he was going to call. Some chap called Clancy. Do you know him?'

'Everyone knows Clancy,' I told her. 'He has a habit of making himself known.'

'Sounds interesting,' Angelica said brightly, putting her paws behind her back and looking around her.

As I was trying to decide whether she was heartless, witless or something else, the Mouse finally came over and looked at the corpse. 'Oh,' he said, his eyes big as dinner plates. But it was twice the reaction of the victim's sister.

Nudging him away from the tree and out of Angelica de Groot's earshot I asked 'Seen anything suspicious?'

'No.' he shook his head vigorously, his breathing even heavier than usual. 'Officer Tober thinks maybe it was the heat.'

'That's Tober for you. If it was the heat, half the animals here would be out cold. I hear you're bringing Clancy in on this one,' I said to Dingus when he reappeared. 'I'd heard he was on vacation.'

'He is,' the Lieutenant said, massaging one of his large ears. 'He just very forcefully reminded me of that fact.'

'Why not use Barrows? He's good.'

'True. But he's not as good as Clancy.'

I wondered what Dingus knew that I didn't. Whatever it was it must be serious if he was willing to put up with one of Clancy's moods. But I knew better than to ask. I'd find out eventually.

In the hour it took for Clancy to arrive, I took a back seat and wandered back and forth between the garden and the bookstore, trying to gauge reactions to what'd happened. In the store as the cops took statements, I noticed that some of the shock had gone out of the situation: a few animals had begun muttering among themselves, complaining because they couldn't leave. Then a story got round that Lettice de Groot wasn't dead at all; it was all a publicity stunt.

'Hey, they're here to take her picture!' someone shouted when the police photographer turned up. 'Remember and tell her to smile.'

Following him out back, I watched him photograph the body, almost becoming as absorbed in his work as he was. 'It is fascinating, isn't it,' the remaining de Groot sister said enthusiastically.

'Perhaps you should take notes,' I muttered.

'Hmm.' The way she said it, I wondered if she was considering it. I was just about to say something when a sharp voice said 'Well perhaps you could do that for me, huh?'

His medical bag swinging in his paw, Clancy stomped towards the scene, grumbling to himself. Instead of his usual garb he was wearing a loud pair of beach shorts and a Hawaiian shirt, undone at the neck. His reddish fur was wet and tangled. As he got closer I could smell the chlorine. Trailing in his wake was his assistant Teo, who looked more sheepish than usual.

'You'd better have a good reason for dragging me away from the pool,' he snapped at Dingus. 'Why didn't you call Barrows? *Huh*?!'

When Dingus took him to one side to explain, the coroner calmed down. A few seconds later his eyes grew wide. '*Really*?' he said, looking at Angelica de Groot.

Introducing himself, Clancy was the model of decorum. 'I'm sorry for your sad loss,' he said. 'I understand that your sister complained of feeling unwell?'

'That's correct. Said she had terrible stomach cramps.'

'Perhaps you'd feel better inside?' he suggested. When she waved the idea away, Clancy shrugged. Seeing an unoccupied seat away from the tree, she made her way over to that instead.

With the photographer finished, Clancy went over to the body, Teo close by. A muted conversation went on between the two of them. Eventually, Clancy nodded.

'Okay,' he said, 'we can't really tell anything here. Teo, chalk the body then we'll get her out of here. Well, what are you waiting for?'

'I can't,' Teo said, looking at the ground.

'What do you mean, you can't?'

'We don't have any chalk,' Teo told him, looking more sheepish than ever.

'*We d—*' Clancy burst out. 'What do you mean, "we don't have any chalk"?' he said, lowering his voice a fraction.

'I mean we don't have any chalk. We used the last of it at the Rodman shooting. We're short of all kinds of things since Ashton's introduced the budget cuts. I tried to tell you when you came in, but —'

'*Ashton? Why I'll* —' it looked like Clancy was gearing himself up for one of his specials when he remembered that Angelica was still present. Snapping his claws, he said 'This is a bookstore, right? They must have chalk here. Ask the manager for some.'

'I did, before you came in. They haven't got any.'

'Well what about art shops, places like that? They must have tons of the stuff.'

'That's where we've been getting it from for months,' Teo said. 'But they've finally run out too. I told Ashton about it, but —'

'I don't believe this.' Clancy said, looking at each of us in turn. 'Chalk, that's all I want. One lousy piece of chalk. It's not a lot to ask!'

'It's the shortages,' Dingus explained to Angelica de Groot. 'Since The Terror there's not as much call for some things.'

'We have similar problems at home,' she replied, the body of her sister lying only a few feet away. 'Do you know, I can't get an egg-slicer for love nor money? What are you short of over here then, besides chalk?'

'Oh, lots of things,' Dingus told her. 'I mean, there's —'

Showing remarkable restraint, it wasn't until Dingus had rattled off eight or nine items that Clancy exploded. 'Teo, get me chalk. *Now!* I don't care how you get it, *just get me chalk!*' Scuttling towards the exit, Teo looked relieved to be out of harm's way.

We all stood like statues for a while after that, nobody knowing what to say or do. Mouths opened and closed without anything being said. So when one of the Birds that had flown away on Clancy's arrival flew back into the branches of the tree, we all turned to watch. After settling itself on one of the lower branches and ruffling its feathers, it tucked its beak under its wing. As it was preening itself, a small white globule fell to the floor with a small *splat,* a few feet from the body. Still nobody spoke. At least not straight away.

'Hmm...' Dingus, massaging his dewlaps, walked around the signing table, past the trunk of the tree, and over to the Bird dropping a yard or so from the body. Then, putting one of his scuffed shoes into the offending globule, he dragged the sole along the concrete, leaving a faint but discernible white line in its wake.

Lieutenant Dingus looked across at the coroner.

'Oh no,' Clancy said, shaking his head violently. 'Uh-uh. Not even as a last resort.'

Everything went quiet again.

When Teo came back minutes later he looked pained. 'Sorry, Clance. There's no chalk anywhere.' All eyes turned to Clancy.

'We need to do that outline,' Dingus told him.

'This is just —' Clancy stopped himself, shaking his head. Eventually he said, 'Hey, you in the tree? How many friends can you get here? *Quickly.*'

'Dozens,' a voice said from the tree. 'If you don't start yelling again.'

'I won't,' Clancy replied, sounding defeated. 'I promise.'

The Bird flew off.

When it returned, it was followed by a buzzing of wings hovering just above the trees. Clancy told them what he wanted them to do and where to do it. The Birds settled into the branches of the tree, directly above the body.

'I *really* can't believe this is happening,' Clancy muttered to himself as he walked out of the line of fire. Passing Angelica de Groot he said, 'I'm sorry about this. I'm truly, truly sorry.'

'Oh that's alright,' she said. 'It's not as if anyone will get to hear about it.'

'No,' Clancy said. 'I suppose not.'

'Besides,' Angelica de Groot said, 'who on earth would believe it?'

Shaking his head, Clancy shouted out for the Birds to be careful with their aim.

It took about ten minutes, and like everybody else I was dumbstruck for a while, squinting into the bright sunlight as the grey concrete slabs around Lettice de Groot's corpse turned white while the branches above her shivered beneath the weight of the Birds as they worked.

'It's like huge snowflakes,' I heard the Mouse say close by.

'I was thinking along the lines of a painting,' Angelica said a few seconds later. 'The way her outline's starting to appear. It's quite beautiful in its way really.' As I looked at her in disbelief, she wiped a tear from her eye.

Me, I had nothing but the sun in mine, reflecting off the buttons on Lettice's jacket.

'Okay,' Clancy shouted up at the tree, 'that's enough. Thanks for your time.'

The branches above the tree wobbled as dozens of Birds flew from the garden. Clancy and Teo moved forward, only to be stopped when another of our winged friends flapped towards them.

'Hey!' Clancy shouted. 'I told you, it's done —'

But it didn't appear to hear. Swooping below the branches and straight towards the body, it landed on it for the briefest of seconds before taking off and flying out of the garden.

'Didn't you guys hear me?' Clancy shouted up at the remaining Birds in the garden. 'We've got enough; that one landed in her mouth!'

'Nothing to do with us,' one of them snapped. 'Honestly, you try and help...' With that the remaining Birds left.

'What was all that about?' Clancy asked.

'I think I know,' Dingus said. 'That was a Jackdaw, wasn't it? I kept seeing something glinting off the body. I've just figured out what it was.' Making his way back to the corpse, Clancy and I followed. Around Lettice's neck, a small silver St. Christopher was visible.

'It was trying to get the necklace,' Dingus said.

With just the outline to be sorted before the removal of Lettice's body, Dingus insisted that Angelica went back inside the store. Careful not to touch the body, Clancy and Teo smudged the droppings together with their shoes so they formed one continuous body-shaped line. When it was done, a couple of Dogs came forward with a stretcher.

'Not very dignified, is it,' Clancy said, nodding at the droppings that had splattered her face. 'Tsk. That damned Bird tore her jacket too. Look.' He pointed, then stopped.

'Wait,' he called to the stretcher-bearers. 'Give me a minute, will you?'

'What's wrong?' Dingus asked.

Crouching on his haunches, the coroner reached inside Lettice's jacket and pulled out several long brown strands.

'What the hell is this?' he asked.

'Probably tobacco,' Dingus said, taking a look. 'She was smoking earlier.'

Clancy took a sniff, 'No, it's not tobacco.'

'Let me.' Dingus , who was known to have the best nose on the force, took the strands from Clancy's paw. 'You're right, it's not tobacco,' he said, taking a long sniff.

'So what is it then?'

'Don't know. It reminds me of something though. Something...' he started to drum the side of his face with his blunt claws. Then, with a sudden exclamation he shouted: '*Coconuts!*'

'Pardon me?' Clancy said.

'Coconuts; Those threads are coconut hairs.'

'How the hell do you know that?'

'Because around this time of year a bunch of animals come over from England and have stalls in the midway. There's this game called a "Coconut Shy": you hit a coconut with a ball, you win the coconut. I won one last year for my nephew. It shed everywhere.'

'And those threads are coconut hairs?'

Dingus nodded. 'I'm sure of it.'

'Well, whatever they're doing there, now's not the time to debate it,' Clancy informed us. 'Come on, let's get her loaded up. What is it now?'

The Lieutenant was kneeling before the body. 'There's a pocket on the inside of the jacket,' he called back at us.

'Yeah, where I found the coconut hairs,' Clancy told him.

'No, another one lower down, folded over. There's something inside it.'

'Probably just her money,' I said.

Reaching into it, Dingus pulled something out and whistled. Looking up he said, 'It must be her life savings, then. Look.'

Standing up, he flicked a wad of bills at us so thick you could've beaten a Gorilla to death with it.

'Maybe she was planning on buying a few books,' I said lamely.

‡ ‡ ‡

All in all, it had been a strange day.

Before the Mouse took me home, I had a brief chat with the Lieutenant, who suggested that we needed to talk. Angelica had suggested the same before Dingus arranged for someone to take her back to the Rockway Plaza. For someone who'd just seen her sister die an agonising death, she was in remarkably good spirits.

'I have to say Mr. Spriteman, that was bizarre,' the Mouse said in the car. To my surprise he seemed quite calm.

'Certainly was.'

'You know, Ma reads their books. I was going to ask them for autographs.'

'She likes them too, huh?'

'Yeah, but she says their books are weird. Apparently one book will be really good and —'

'The next one will be really bad. I know.' The Mouse turned to look at me but said nothing.

We drove the rest of the way in silence. Pulling up outside Shefton Heights, I remembered something.

'What was this important thing you had to tell me?' I asked.

The Mouse laughed shyly. 'It doesn't seem so important now, Mr. Spriteman. Not after that.'

'Try me.'

'Well, it's those stories you gave me to read — to see if any of them tied in with the hoax letters?'

'One of them does?' I asked, surprised.

'No, none of them. But one of them seems to fit in with our missing dog case.'

'What?'

'To Trix. The details of his disappearance, his breed; even the names in the story are similar. I suppose it could be a coincidence, but —'

'Yes,' I said, stifling a yawn, 'I suppose it could be. Go home and get some rest.'

That night I couldn't sleep. Random words and names whirled through my head like pieces of wind-blown litter — Daphne DuMoralize, Giddyfits, Bumper Fodder, the de Groot sisters, Trix, Bird droppings, the whole caboodle. Then, just when I was finally starting to feel drowsy, one last image crept into my head, dragging me back from sleep.

'*Coconuts hairs?*' I said into the darkness, 'why coconut hairs?'

Wide awake again, I got out of bed and went for a glass of milk.

Part Two: Rockway

‡ ‡ ‡

9. TRIX GOT LOST / ALIBIS

THE RAT MUST'VE GONE on a real bender, because it took two days for the following article to appear on the front page of *Fuller News:*

GUMSHOO IN DE GROOT BOK SHOCK!
Leading crime riter Angela de Groot is said to bee «distrort» following the dearth of her sister and writing patner, the much-luved Lettice de Gorot. The two where at Sidwells, lunching their latsest novel as part of their book tour when Lettuce collapsed and died during an argument with local privet investugator Benji Spiriteman. «I don't know whatt I'll do without her» a teaful Angelic said at the scene. At the tim of going to press Spritman was unavailale for comment.

As usual, the Rat had done the city proud. Of course it was possible one of Fuller's cronies had been at the book launch, crawling their way between the tea urns and cucumber sandwiches; but if they had, I couldn't help thinking they'd have at least heard about what happened after Clancy arrived, and Fuller would've had a field day with *that.* And as for Angelica's distress at her sister's loss... no, Fuller had done what Fuller always did: heard half a tale, thrown away the bits he hadn't cared for and added some bits that he did. A true pro. On another day I might have gone round there and let him know what I thought of him and his article, but it had been a productive couple of days and I didn't want to spoil my mood. And on the plus side my name had been spelled wrong. Twice.

The morning after the book launch my mood wasn't so hot. I managed to sleep in and didn't get to the office until after eleven. 'The Mouse left something on your desk,' Taki said, giving me one of her looks '— about an hour and a half ago'.

Flopping into my chair I looked at the pile of bulky envelopes in front of me. At the top of the pile at an angle was a single manuscript, its right-hand edge bending towards the desk like a branch to a river. Pulling it towards me, I removed the paperclips and began to read.

"Rex Got Lost" was a fairly well-written pot-boiler about a Dachshund and its wealthy owner. A day after the dog goes missing, Rex's owner receives a ransom note demanding a thousand dollars for the safe return of the pooch. Rex's owner, Helena Hockston, unable to cope without him, leaves the ransom money at the designated place and returns home, safe in the knowledge that Rex will be returned to her soon. Only he isn't; the days pass by with no sign of him. It turns out that Rex escaped his captors after the ransom note was sent and tried to find his own way home, but heads in the wrong direction and is taken in by another family. The story ends with Rex being miserable, the dognappers getting away with the loot and Helena Hockston crying into her lace handkerchief. It cheered me up no end.

Grabbing the phone, I called Rusty Laidlaw.

'Yes, I remember that one,' he said. 'There's a kidnap in it or something. I nearly didn't send it along, but the tone of it worried me.'

'Tone?'

'The ransom. The lady in it was being held to ransom. It kind of feels like that here. After what happened yesterday, it's —'

'Have you had any letters today?'

'Just one. Same writing as the "cheking the mails" note. It says "You can't pin that murder on me it had nothing to do with me not my fault". No punctuation. But the writing's really shaky this time. It's more frightening than the message.'

'How did it arrive?'

'Beak mail. Wedged into the window frame.'

'At least it isn't a threat. Anyway, this story: can you tell me who wrote it? There's no name on it.'

'That was another reason I sent it,' Laidlaw said. 'I mean, who sends a manuscript anonymously to a publisher?'

'You got me.'

'Mr. Spriteman, about what happened yesterday: *was* it murder, do you think? Something to do with... well, with what's been going on?'

The Whippet's voice had taken on a pleading quality. I felt dangerously close to feeling sorry for him.

'We don't know that it was murder,' I told him, 'let alone anything to do with the letters. And now with the police being involved...' I tried to make that sound like a good thing, at least as far as he was concerned. I was going to add that any potential killer would have to get past Finnegan first but changed my mind. Instead I asked if he'd heard from him lately. 'We exchanged words,' he said tersely. 'I still can't help thinking that if that damned story hadn't appeared in his magazine —'

Interrupting him, I told him to drop the latest letter off, then called Finnegan. Even though he hadn't been at the signing, I asked him for his thoughts on what'd happened.

'Well, I don't think it's anything to do with the letters,' he told me. 'I mean, why take it out on Lettice de Groot?'

'I don't know. But it's spooking the hell out of Laidlaw.'

'Don't I know it. I've just had him down here, showing me the letter he got this morning — which I also got — and telling me it could be one of us next. But if that was the case, why haven't they done it already? I told him, if they wanted to waste us they could do it anytime, cops or no cops. But did it calm him down? Ha!'

'Maybe you should keep an eye on him,' I said. 'I don't think he's as thick-skinned as you are.'

'You want I should wet-nurse him?' he snorted down my earpiece.

'Not exactly that. I mean...' I stopped, trying to decide exactly what I did mean. 'I mean that it would be in both of your interests.'

'How?'

'Well, say someone *does* come to your building looking for trouble, whose office will they land at first?'

'Ah.'

'And, between you and me,' I said, lowering my voice, as if that would make the lie more acceptable, 'I think Laidlaw looks up to you in a way.'

'What? He has a funny way of showing it!'

'It's just a feeling I get, that's all. I think maybe he sees something in you,' I told him, screwing my face up against the whopper I was about to utter, 'that he lacks in himself.'

The line went quiet, and I waited for the laugh or the insult but neither came. Instead Finnegan said, 'Okay. I'll see what I can do,' before hanging up.

After lunch the Mouse came back in. We discussed the story for a while and how the search for Trix was going. Then I reached for the phone.

'Who are you calling?' he asked.

'Alannah Foxton. We need to go round there and tell her about the story.' The Mouse's face dropped. 'Unless you've already told her?'

'No, it's not that...' he squirmed, little dots of pink coming to his face.

'What then? Oh, hello, Miss Foxton. Yes, Alannah, of course. Benji Spriteman. I wondered if it's convenient to come 'round?'

When I put the phone down, the Mouse looked relieved. 'You don't need me then?' he said. 'Well I'd like you to be there,' I told him. 'Why, what's wrong?'

We were nearly halfway there before I got it out of him. 'It's just that she's... she's very friendly with me, Mr. Spriteman. I mean *very* friendly. It's... it's like I'm a baby or something.'

'Oh,' I laughed. 'Another one.'

Perhaps it was the combination of size and shyness, but for some reason certain female clients seemed to fall madly in love with Linus; at least in a maternal sense. Last winter one old Chow even went so far as to knit him a pullover so he wouldn't catch cold while looking for prowlers in her back garden.

'It's not funny, Mr. Spriteman!'

'Enjoy it while it lasts,' I told him, trying hard not to laugh, 'you won't be cute forever.' The look he gave said that was fine by him.

Alannah Foxton's house was bang in the middle of a long row of large, detached houses and looked so pristine it seemed a shame to step on the gravel. A procession of surprisingly green topiary dogs tiptoed along the varnished fence surrounding the garden. While the Mouse parked the car, I buzzed the button on the gate. 'Go round to the garden,' a disembodied voice said. With barely a creak, the gate split in two, both sides retreating towards the lawns. No sooner had we walked through when they began to close.

The grass running around the side of the house wasn't as green as the hedge, but it wasn't brown either. I wondered if she did the garden herself or got somebody in to do it for her. Seeing a small mound of earth over towards the fence I decided it was the former; I couldn't imagine Alannah Foxton letting an employee off with something like that, no matter how friendly she was.

I was just beginning to wonder where her dogs were when a Great Dane came bounding around the side of the house, running straight for the Mouse, leaping into his arms before knocking him to the ground. After much licking and slobbering, it ran back the way it came, wagging its tail and barking.

'That's Sooky,' the Mouse said, getting up off the grass. 'The others will be here in a sec.'

'The others?'

Suddenly a jumping, licking, tidal wave of fur, paws and wet noses gushed around the side of the house and engulfed us. 'It's best to just go with it,' the Mouse shouted over to me. A few moments later and seemingly without having walked there, we were standing at the bottom of the garden. Alannah Foxton waved at us. As she did the dogs began to move to different parts of the garden.

'Do they always do that?' I asked the Mouse.

'Every time,' he said, out of breath but laughing.

'I hope the dogs didn't upset you,' Alannah Foxton called out as we made our way over to her. She had large, black-rimmed almond-shaped eyes that never seemed to blink, giving the impression that she was permanently surprised. Her short fur was a lightly bronzed cream, most of it covered by a long patterned dress she wore which glided an inch or two above the grass.

'Would you like some lemonade, Benji?' she asked, rising. 'I don't have to ask *you* now, do I?' she said, smiling at the Mouse. 'Liney here loves my lemonade, don't you Liney?' she walked off towards the house.

'*Liney?*' I said when she was out of earshot.

'She got it out of me,' the Mouse squeaked. 'And anyway, it sounds better than L —'

'Here we are,' she announced, coming back with a tray. 'Home made.' She handed me a glass of cloudy, off-white liquid.

'Tell me about that day again,' I said after taking a sip.

'It was around breakfast and the dogs were feeding,' she recalled. 'It was really hot so I left the back door open for them while I went upstairs to take a bath. When I came back down, the dogs were in the garden, running around. That's when I noticed the fence panel was out of place.'

'You hadn't noticed it before?'

'No. It was fine the day before, I'm sure. But even if it wasn't, I've never had any reason to suspect any of the dogs would run away. You've seen them, they're happy here. It doesn't make sense.'

'When was the last time you saw Trix?'

'He's always one of the first to come out when they hear me rustling the bowls. When I went up to take a bath he was nosing around in the kitchen. That was about nine o'clock. When I came back down twenty minutes later he was gone.'

'And there was nobody else here that day? Just you and the dogs?'

'Yes. But you know this already.' She looked at the Mouse then back at me.

'The reason I'm asking is because of this.' I handed her the story. 'Unless it's a huge coincidence, it looks like somebody else was here that day after all.'

While she read it, I looked around at the garden, at the well-tended plants and neat borders; so neat I doubted the dogs went anywhere near them. Then I saw the fencepost that had been moved, its bottom nail missing, the wood around the top one rough and splintered. It looked like it had been kicked from the street, then pushed aside. The Mouse, unused to sitting still for so long, twitched at my side before wandering off.

When she put the story down, Alannah Foxton looked shocked.

'Somebody's been watching me,' she said. 'Most of this is true. The times, the house — they've even mentioned how they took him. It's —' putting a paw up to her mouth, she took a moment to compose herself. 'Where did you get this?'

'It's part of another case I'm looking into.'

'Another? But the details —'

'At the moment it doesn't make a lot of sense to me either. Did you see anyone new in the area hanging around before Trix was taken?'

'No, besides Betsy I don't see many other animals at all.'

'Betsy?'

'Betsy Oatland. She comes in once a week to clean. I do most of it myself but she helps out with a few things.'

'She wasn't here the day Trix disappeared?'

'It wasn't her day, no. She has other jobs the rest of the week.'

'Do you know who with?'

'No. I hired her through an agency. I can get you the address.'

While she got it, I went looking for the Mouse. I found him surrounded by fussing dogs, each one desperate for his attention.

'This cleaner, Betsy Oatland. Have you spoken to her?' I asked him.

'I haven't been able to get hold of her. She's only here one day a week and wasn't here last week at all. I've tried the phone number Miss Foxton gave me but there's no answer. I was going to try her home address yesterday but the bookstore seemed more important.'

Alannah Foxton came back out with a small card in her paw. 'Here's the agency address. Betsy's home address is on the other side.'

'I believe Miss Oatland wasn't here last week?'

'That's right, she said she had to look after someone in her family who was taken ill. Why?'

'What's she like with the dogs?'

'She's very good, they all trust her. You don't think she's —'

'Probably not,' I said, putting the card in my pocket. 'But we'll have to check. We'll be in touch.'

Coming out with us to the gates, Sooky at her side, Alannah said, 'That story... it's the same apart from the ending. I haven't had a ransom note.'

'That's a good sign,' I told her. 'If someone had taken him you'd have had one by now.'

'Which means he's gone missing.' She didn't sound any more relieved by this. 'And that story, it's so sad.'

'It's still only a story, as far as we know.'

'I know. But I've got this feeling...' Her smile was sad, resigned.

'I get those.'

'Do they ever come true?'

'Not very often,' I lied.

‡ ‡ ‡

'Where to?' the Mouse said, starting the car.

'Miss Betsy Oatland's.' As we drove away, Alannah Foxton stood behind her big gate, waving, surrounded by her beloved Dogs.

'You think she's involved, Mr. Spriteman?'

'I'm not sure.' When Alannah Foxton had asked me the same thing a few minutes earlier, I was in two minds. But seeing her and the Dogs at the gate like that, it was hard to imagine one of them standing by while one of their number was taken against its will. Unless it was by someone they trusted. As Alannah had pointed out, why would any of them run away from a set-up like that? But why take him in the first place?

We pulled up outside Betsy Oatland's place just in time to see a flabby Bullmastiff squashing itself into a small striped canvas chair on a rickety porch surrounded by foot-high weeds. Getting himself comfy, he eyed us carelessly as we approached.

'We're looking for Betsy Oatland,' I told him, stepping gingerly onto the porch.

'Huh,' the Mastiff muttered. 'Betsy Oatland.'

'Is she here?'

'She hasn't been here for two weeks,' he said, sticking a claw between his teeth and poking it around. 'Left in the middle of the night. Neighbour across the road heard her go. Said she had a case with her. Car pulled up, she got in and left. Owes me a month's money.'

'And you've no idea where she might have gone?' He shook his head.

'What does she look like?'

'Ordinary. Wouldn't cause trouble for anybody. Huh. I got her wrong.' Fishing the claw out of the side of his mouth, he flicked it at the porch. Something soft and wet hit a rotted beam in front of him.

'Thanks for your help.'

'Pleasure.'

The Spick 'N' Span Cleaning Agency was on the other side of town. With everyone stopping inside because of the heat, it meant an hour's journey took less than twenty minutes, even with all the cracks in the roads.

'Betsy Oatland you say?' a prim Guinea Pig in a trouser suit asked as she flicked through her index cards. 'Here we are. Betsy Oatland. Cleaner. Works part time. One morning a week at Deventon's Toy Market, for a Miss Foxton at a private address, and does alternate weeks at JLM Holdings and Shimmy Shirts, both of which are in the Henderson Building. Oh,' she stopped.

'The Henderson Building!' the Mouse piped up. 'That's where —'

'Is something wrong?' I asked the Guinea Pig.

'Well, it's just that according to this, she hasn't been to any of these addresses in the past two weeks. And we haven't been able to get in touch with her.'

'The two places in the Henderson building — which floors are they on?'

The Guinea Pig looked at the card. 'Fifth,' she said.

'Just below Finnegan and Laidlaw!' the Mouse squeaked.

'Why, is she in some kind of trouble?' the Guinea Pig asked.

'Thank you for your time,' I said.

Back in the car the Mouse wouldn't stop talking. 'The two things must be connected,' he said again, taking another bend too quickly and wearing another quarter inch off his tyres, 'they have to be. We've got the missing Dog case and the poison-pen letters. Betsy Oatland cleans for Alannah Foxton but *also* works in the same building the letters are going to. Nobody's seen Trix for a week and Betsy Oatland for two weeks. And besides Miss Foxton she's the only one who'd know enough about Trix to write about him.'

'So let me get this straight. You think Betsy Oatland took Trix, wrote a story about it, and then sent it to a magazine?'

'Who else could have written it?' he asked, looking over at me.

It was a dumb idea, but it was more than I had. I couldn't think about it in the car: if I was going to tie myself up in knots properly I needed peace and quiet to do it in.

When the Mouse dropped me off at the office, he told me he was going to go looking for Betsy Oakland. When I asked him where, he said he didn't know. I watched as he zoomed off back up the road, tongue at the corner of his mouth.

After thinking about it for a while and getting nowhere, I called the station and asked to speak to Dingus but he wasn't in, so I passed on my info about Betsy Oatland to the Desk Sergeant. Then I phoned Finnegan and Laidlaw to ask them about their cleaners, only to find they employed the same one — her name was Peaches, she came in every other day and she was very reliable; and the name Betsy Oatland meant nothing to either of them. But it was still possible Betsy Oatland had something to do with it all. When I asked Laidlaw and Finnegan for a description of Peaches they both struggled to come up with one. Nobody notices cleaners, especially in busy offices. Perhaps she *did* write stories? Hell, *maybe* even poison-pen letters; who knows? All I could do was keep working my three main suspects — I was pretty sure I could discount Grover S. Nelson.

First of all I checked Lake's alibi, phoning the number she'd given me. I was informed by an elderly-sounding Cat that *yes, her niece had been to visit her,* and *no she hadn't been away at any time for longer than an hour or two,* which, considering that the old lady's place was at least three hours away, meant she couldn't possibly have broken into the magazines' offices. Still, that story of hers was accurate, and so was the 'Rex' one... I gave her a call.

'Hello?'

'Benji Spriteman. I just checked your alibi.'

'Oh good,' she said, her voice even softer than I remembered. 'Did you like my Aunt Rebecca?'

'She sounds very nice. I was just wondering if you've written any other stories lately. I'd be only too happy to read them.'

She laughed. 'Nothing since "Invisible Feud" I'm afraid. But thanks for the offer.'

'Nothing at all lately? Nothing about missing Dogs, that sort of thing?'

'Missing Dogs? God, no. What would I want to write about missing Dogs for?'

'I've no idea. I don't know what goes on inside a writer's head. But the offer still stands. About reading your work, I mean.'

'I'll keep you in mind. Any luck on your case? I heard about what happened to Miss de Groot in the bookstore. She wasn't a suspect, was she?' I tried to think of something witty to say, but nothing came. I wondered if she could hear my brain liquefying over the wire. When I mumbled something incoherent she laughed, a noise like wind chimes.

'Goodbye, Benji,' she said, the laugh still in her voice.

Annoyed at this weakness, I decided to take my frustration out on Mungo Bickeridge, but as usual he wasn't there. That left Wiedlin. And I was just in the mood for him.

'Hello?' before he even knew who was there he sounded bored.

'Just a quick call, Mr. Wiedlin.'

'Ah, Mr. Spriteman, as I live and breathe. And hopefully for a *little* while longer yet, I trust.'

'You heard what happened.'

'Why, of course. I suppose I should be grateful you haven't popped round. Who knows what might happen?'

'Who told you?'

'Who? It's all over town. I only wish I'd stayed around long enough for the floorshow. I've never had anyone die on me before. Tell me, what did it feel like? You never know, I might get a story out of it.'

In danger of puncturing my pads again, I moved away from the mouthpiece, took a deep breath and came back at him with both barrels. 'I imagine you could get a story out of anything, Mr. Wiedlin. Perhaps I could tell *you* a story; a shaggy Dog story. Interested?'

'Not especially.'

'Okay, here it is. There's this Dog and it goes missing from its wealthy home; Dogknapped. The animal responsible for swiping the Dog decides it would be amusing to write a story about it and send it to a local magazine, along with a bunch of threatening letters. But who would do such a thing? The kind of animal that would reject a rejection letter from a publisher, perhaps. Why did you leave the book signing early, Mr. Wiedlin?'

For a second Wiedlin was stunned into silence. 'Wait. Back up a second. Are you saying that I've *stolen someone's Dog*?'

No, I was just letting off steam. 'I might be.'

'And could you tell me where in the sprawling palace of my apartment I'm supposed to *keep* such a Dog?

I didn't answer. I didn't have to. Somehow or other, I'd touched a nerve.

'And I'm supposed to have done this while directing a campaign of poison-pen letters against a magazine that's refused to print one of my stories?'

Again I said nothing.

'And then, finally, despite the fact that I wasn't even *in* Sidwells at the time of that old bag's death whereas *you* were standing next to her, I somehow managed to kill her?'

'That's about the size of it, Quentin.' I said, enjoying myself now.

'Oh, Mr. Spriteman,' Wiedlin chuckled down the line, in control once more, 'if only I could be so imaginative. Pray tell, why would I kill Lettice de Groot? Because half of her books weren't up to scratch?'

'I don't know yet,' I said, stretching and yawning, 'but I'll have fun finding out.'

'I'm going to hang up now,' Wiedlin said, the sniff firmly back in his voice. 'I suggest you only call again if you have something sensible to say.'

'I hear you, Mr. Wiedlin. Merry Christmas.'

The line went dead.

Putting the earpiece back in its cradle I let out a contented sigh.

It was strange with Wiedlin: verbally as smart as anyone I'd ever met, but apparently unable to translate that smartness into success, living in a pokey shoebox in Derry Park Flats. Was that why he was so twisted? But twisted enough to be a Dogknapper, or a killer? I didn't think so. But something I'd said had rattled him.

It had to be the letters.

10. STRYCHNINE AND SECRECTS

THE NEXT MORNING I was still in my apartment when Dingus called.

'Clancy's just finished the autopsy on Lettice de Groot. Want to come along?'

'I'll be there as soon as I can. Will be Angelica be there?'

'She can't make it. Something came up.' Before I got a chance to reply, the Lieutenant hung up.

I wasn't entirely surprised to get the call from Dingus. After our respective paths crossed during the Carlin case, we both found that we could be useful to each other where certain cases were concerned. And God knows the police needed all the help they could get. So if the Lieutenant wanted me at the autopsy, he'd have a good reason, although it didn't necessarily follow that I'd be privy to that reason straight away. But he'd tell me. Eventually.

Out on the street the sun shone in my eyes like a puppy's flashlight, its unrelenting rays puckering my bald patches. Stopping for a Popsicle at a vendors a couple hundred yards from Shefton Heights, I ended up with a half pint of warm orange juice in a funny-shaped carton.

Chugging back the juice, I made my way across town to the ugly office block that housed the coroner's office. Parked right in front of the double doors and cluttering up the sidewalk was Dingus's ancient grey jalopy, looking for all the world like it had fallen out of the back of a very large garbage truck.

A small sign made from a cereal box was taped to the back window saying NOT TO BE TOWED AWAY THANK YOU. It seemed to work: since he'd stuck it up, the Lieutenant hadn't had to retrieve his car from the junkyard again.

Riding the elevator to the tenth floor, I found Dingus and Clancy in the latter's office, Dingus smoking a cigar, Clancy wafting the smoke away. Without a word he took us through to the morgue and over to a metal table covered with a sheet. Pulling it back, the three of us looked at the lifeless body of Lettice de Groot. As in life, she looked like she was sucking a lemon.

'What killed her, Doc?' Dingus asked.

'Strychnine poisoning. A fairly large dose. She must've died in agony.'

'She'd been feeling unwell that day,' Dingus said. 'But according to her sister she'd eaten nothing since breakfast. I take it that it must've been put in her food?'

'It's the most likely possibility, and it can take a few hours to work. But she could have got it on her fur somehow and she licked at it.'

'Either way, Strychnine's bitter, isn't it? Wouldn't she have noticed it, complained?'

'She had kippers for breakfast,' Clancy said, 'and a ton of butter. I imagine they masked the taste somewhat.'

'I got the impression she did nothing else but complain anyway,' I put in. 'I don't suppose Angelica thought this complaint was any different to the others. Any chance that Angelica administered the poison?' I asked.

'It's possible, but she says her sister had a late breakfast, alone. She was the only one in the dining room at the time. I checked.'

'Anything else?' Dingus asked Clancy. Shaking his head, the coroner covered up the body and we left.

'Oh, by the way,' he said as we walked along the corridor, 'you'll both be pleased to hear I found some chalk.'

'Where?'

'In my jacket pocket,' he said, looking sheepish. 'Well, in the lining anyway. It'd fallen through a hole. You know why she was carrying all that money around with her yet?' he looked at Dingus eagerly.

'Not yet. Perhaps she was just a hoarder. So you mean we went through all that for nothing?' With a cheery wave, Clancy bade us farewell and headed back to his office.

Despite what we'd just seen, I felt hungry. 'Fancy breakfast?' I said.

'Sure.' Dingus led the way to the canteen. As we walked I waited for him to speak, to tell me why he'd wanted me there. But he said nothing.

Picking up a bagel and a coffee, I found an empty table and started without him. I was almost finished when he came over with something brown and steaming on a plate. It looked like the sort of thing Clancy might pull from the inside of a diseased corpse.

'What the hell's that?' I asked.

'Devilled kidneys,' he said, sitting down and shoving a forkful of it under my nose. 'Want to try some?' It smelled better than it looked but I still declined.

'Smells spicy,' I said.

'It is.'

'Spicy enough to disguise something like strychnine?' I chewed off another piece of bagel.

'Maybe. I know what you're trying to say Benji, but I don't think she did it. She doesn't strike me that way.'

'Did she ask you about the Carlin case?'

'Uh-huh. Tell me about Betsy Oatland,' he said, changing the subject.

As he shovelled glistening brown lumps of meat into his mouth, I finished my coffee and told him about the cleaner, Trix, and the shaggy Dog story. In return he gave the impression of polite interest.

'The last I heard they hadn't found her yet,' he said between chewing soggy pieces of toast. 'But you don't think she's behind the letters? You think it's Wiedlin?'

'He's enjoying all this too much. How's Miss de Groot bearing up?'

'Pretty good. She's a tough cookie. Oh, and she asked after you. Says she wants to talk.'

'About what?' He shrugged.

'So what did you talk to her about?' I asked.

'Oh, nothing much. When they'd arrived at the hotel, how they got there, her sister's behaviour; those sorts of things.'

' "Those sorts of things".' It was like pulling teeth. 'What I can't understand is why you went to see her at all.'

He looked momentarily surprised. 'Excuse me?'

'You're obviously working on something big at the moment. I'm surprised you could fit her in. Why didn't you send Toffee down there to talk to her?'

'Because the something big I'm working on is in Rockway.' The final piece of toast disappeared. As he chewed he squinted at me in that way only he could. I was being stonewalled.

'I've never been to Rockway before,' I said, getting up to leave. 'Maybe the change of air will do me good. I'll keep an eye out for you.'

Without looking up, he picked up his coffee cup, took a mouthful and put the cup back on the table.

'I'll see you around, then.' I said. It wasn't until I was a few feet from the door that he spoke.

'When you go to see her, I'd appreciate it if you didn't mention the money we found.'

I turned to face him. 'What about the coconut hairs?' I asked.

'Just look after yourself, Benji,' he said. It seemed a strange thing to say under the circumstances, but his expression was neutral.

When I walked into the outer office the look on Taki's face couldn't have been more different. 'There's a Pigeon in your office,' she told me, as if she couldn't believe it herself.

'Why didn't you shoo it out?'

'Because he wants to talk to you.'

I waited patiently for an explanation.

'I kept hearing this tapping noise, it was driving me crazy. I popped my head around your door and he was sitting on the ledge outside, pecking at the glass. So I let him in.' She gave me a brief but radiant smile before pretending to get on with paperwork.

'Okay,' I sighed. Opening my door, I went inside.

He was sitting on my desk, his small grey feet planted between the bundles of letters and manuscripts. On one of the bundles was a rolled-up note that hadn't been there last night.

'I was told I had to deliver this in person,' the Pidge said, nodding fiercely at the note. 'As it were.'

'Well, here I am and now you have. Thank you.' He ruffled his feathers then blinked at me stupidly. Neither of us spoke for what felt like a very long time.

'I'm sorry, do I tip you now?' I said eventually. 'I'm afraid I don't know the... etiquette for th —'

With a sudden flap of wings, the Pidge turned and flew out of the window, leaving a cool draught of air in his wake. After checking my desk for accidents, I picked up the note:

Mr. Spriteman — I wasn't sure if the good Lieutenant would remember to pass on my message (I rather get the impression he may be prone to absent-mindedness) so to make sure I decided to send my own. I have something I'd like to discuss with you that I think could turn out to be mutually beneficial. Perhaps you could come to the Rockway Plaza at your earliest convenience? I shall certainly be here for at least the next couple of days.

Respectfully yours, A de G.

'Hmm,' I said aloud.

'Hmm?'

It was Taki, standing in front of me with coffee. Leaning across the desk, she looked at the sheet of paper upside down.

'I was just wondering why she's sent this Pigeon post. She knows I've got a phone.'

'I daresay Miss de Groot has her reasons.' Beaming, Taki turned on her heel and back towards the door.

'Good thing this isn't about you. What did you make of our enigmatic visitor?'

'Not a great deal. He just said he wanted to see you. He wasn't very talkative at all.'

'Hmm,' I said again.

Looking at the note once more, my eyes kept falling on the phrase 'mutually beneficial'. Why was everybody being so secretive at the moment? I decided to phone Miss de Groot and find out. But picking up the receiver, I put it straight down again. No. She wasn't the only one who could be secretive. She'd see me all right; but unless she had a crystal ball she wouldn't know when.

‡ ‡ ‡

After lunch I phoned my two favourite magazine editors. Neither had received any letters or stories that they deemed relevant. It was as if things were returning to normal. Well, almost.

'Between you and me, Finnegan's been acting a bit strange,' Laidlaw confided.

'Strange how?'

'He's been up here twice, sniffing round. He never comes up here — on the rare occasions we do speak it's on the phone. When I asked him what he was doing here he told me not to worry about a thing and that everything would be okay. I think this whole thing's getting to him.'

The Mouse breezed in not long after. 'Can't find her,' he said as he flopped into a chair.

It took me a second or two to catch up. 'You've spent all this time looking for Betsy Oatland?'

'Not quite the whole time. But I thought I'd find her.' He looked dejected.

'So where else have you been?'

'I went back to Miss Foxton's to see if she'd had any news, but she hadn't. Then I asked around the neighbourhood to see if anybody remembered anything. But nobody did.' He shook his head, then yawned.

'You look beat,' I told him. 'Go home and get some shuteye. I'll call you bright and early.'

I stuck it out for another couple of hours before the heat beat me. During that time I tried Bickeridge again but with no luck. Then I tried Fuller. On the thirty-fifth ring I hung up; if he wasn't sleeping off a hangover, he was drinking himself towards one. Finally I phoned the police to see if they'd had any word on Betsy Oatland. But they hadn't.

Locking the office behind me, I strolled along the still-hot sidewalks back to my apartment. Despite sweating like a Pig and the case I was working on going nowhere, I felt okay; it wasn't until I reached Shefton that I realised why. I was still beaming about it when I met Shove Off in the corridor.

'I don't know what you've got to smile about,' he said jovially.

'Pardon me?'

'The paper,' he said. 'You're the villain of the piece. You haven't seen it?' he could hardly keep the glee from his voice. 'Wait there, I'll get it for you.' Waddling back into his flat as fast as he could, he re-emerged with the paper in his mouth and several cats around his feet. Removing the paper from his beak the way you'd remove cheese from a mousetrap,

I read the article. ' "Unavailale for comment", huh?' I said, smiling. 'Funny, but I don't remember him contacting me.'

'I wouldn't take it too seriously,' Shove Off said when I'd finished. 'That Rat's an imbecile, everyone knows that. That's the way,' he said, clapping me on the back with his wing when I allowed myself a small smile. 'Anyway, see you around.' Snatching the paper back, he and his cats went back inside his apartment.

Going into mine, I thought about my other Bird-related meeting earlier and found myself idly wondering what kind of Bird had delivered the letters to the magazine offices. Birds were doing big business these days; they delivered things, they even fanned your building. Who knew what else they'd do if you gave them enough grain. Filing the thought away for future reference, I had a cold bath, a quick meal and went to bed early, actually looking forward to waking up for once.

Because in the morning, for the first time in my life, I was going to the seaside.

11. THE HOTEL AND THE DETECTIVE / DELUGE

DESPITE THE FACT HE'D been to Rockway before, the Mouse was more than a little excited when I told him. 'Really?' he squeaked, his voice shrill in my earpiece. 'Oh wow.' This was followed by further squeaks as he told his brothers and sisters, the resulting noise vibrating the hairs in my ear to an alarming degree. 'Ma wants to know why we're going to Rockway,' the Mouse said when he came back on the line.

'Tell her we're going to visit one of her favourite writers,' I said.

As I waited in the lobby, I listened to the comments of various animals as they came in from their early morning walks. Almost all of them were complaining about the heat. 'World's gone mad,' an old Tabby in a pair of shorts muttered to himself on the way to the elevators, 'preferred it in the Old days. Didn't have to buy fans *then*. Just sat on the rug and licked my ass. Good times.'

Hearing the familiar roar of the Mouse's car I stepped outside, ready to shield my eyes against the fierce glare of the sun. Instead, everything looked grey and washed out. They were right about the heat though.

'Ma says it's going to rain today,' the Mouse informed me as I opened the passenger door. I said I hoped she was right.

'What's all this?' I asked, gesturing towards the two shopping bags on the back seat.

'All Ma's books. She's asked me to get them signed.'

Leaning across, I opened the nearest bag. The now familiar face on the cover of *The Jagged Stiletto of Ursula Prim* looked up at me reproachfully, as if she knew I hadn't even opened my copy of the book, let alone read it. 'Has she read this one yet, the new one?'

'She finished that the day she bought it. Said it was the best one so far.'

'Better even than *Death by Winkle?*'

He looked over at me like he hadn't heard correctly. 'Excuse me?'

'Never mind. Let's go to Rockway.'

We left town just as the roads were starting to fill up with rush-hour traffic. Every car window was down, and before we'd even got onto the freeway we spotted two cars that didn't even have windshields; I wondered if they'd been smashed or removed on purpose. God help them if Ma Spayley was right. Quarter of an hour later, we were driving past baked-hard mud fields. With the patches of heat-haze rippling around us, it was like driving through aspic.

'What's it like, Rockway?' I asked.

'Oh, it's great, Mr. S. You've never been before?'

'Never got 'round to it.'

'Maybe if you could drive,' he said, looking at me. 'You know, if you ever want those lessons —'

'Yeah. I'll think about it,' I said, looking out the window.

Rattling along through the hills, one breathtaking drop followed another. Up here the sun was shining, the sky below us a deep blue. The heat-haze looked different too; I was thinking of mentioning it to the Mouse when I saw a small boat sail across it.

Suddenly the road dropped once more into a valley full of brown grass, cows, and thin trees bent over by the wind. At the top of the next hill a small sign read ROCKWAY WELCOMES CAREFUL DRIVERS. A blink of an eye later the town appeared, crouched on the edge of a cliff, its buildings huddled in beside what looked like a weatherworn fairytale castle just above the sea.

'What's that?' I asked.

The Mouse looked at me like I was kidding. 'The Rockway Plaza,' he said.

'It looks like it takes up half the town.'

'I haven't been inside, but it's big. It was quite famous once. You do want me to stay, right?' the Mouse said, afraid I was going to send him back to town.

'Certainly, if you want your books signed.' Puffing out his cheeks in relief, he drove even quicker.

For someone used to skyscrapers, traffic snarl-ups and sidewalks bustling with life and noise, Rockway was a bit of a shock. With the exception of a few hotels, most of the buildings were two, maybe three storeys at most, the roads were home to largely moving vehicles, and the sidewalks were so narrow that one fat animal with a shopping bag was enough to hold everyone else up. But the air smelled good, the streets looked clean, and by and large nobody looked guilty. The constant cawing and wheeling of 'gulls I would have to try and get used to. Apart from a few Kittens and Pups out with their parents, most of the creatures I saw looked elderly. Before I could make any more observations, we were pulling to a halt in the Plaza's large parking lot.

Close up, the Rockway Plaza reminded me of a great big Owl made out of stone, its large, grimy windows looking out to sea. Above them, a pair of grey turrets stuck up like ears, listening as the 'gulls screeched around the cliffs. The brickwork had perhaps once been black or brown, but was now a faded mixture of grey and white streaks, most of which were presumably Bird droppings. Birds nested on the deep ledges of many of the windows, several of which looked as if they hadn't been opened in years. Walking up the right-hand side of the hotel's yellowing marble staircase, it puzzled me why a large black board was placed across the left-hand side. When I opened the door I found out why.

'Move!'

The voice seemed to come from my midriff. In front of me, a wizened creature of indeterminate species was hunched up inside what looked like a wicker basket with a wheel on each side, its dried-up paws hovering above them. 'Well, what are you staring at?' the creature said without appearing to open its mouth. I was about to say I wasn't sure when the Mouse nudged me to one side. Wheeling past us, I expected it to aim for the board, but instead it went for the stairs, crashing down each one in turn, its head shaking about so violently it looked like it might fall off at any second. Before we were assailed by anything else, we stepped into the Lounge and realised that it wasn't called that for nothing.

At first I wondered if maybe they were short of beds. It was a large open-plan affair dominated by a great white staircase leading to the second floor, and was fitted with a faded burgundy floral carpet, several tables, a selection of dying potted-plants, several large black leather sofas and an array of equally leathery-looking creatures dozing, napping or snoring their way through the morning under the protective cover of tartan blankets. I'd just started counting the walking sticks leaning against the sofas, when a phlegmy voice close by gave me a start.

'Morning,' it said. I was just about to ask who for when I realised what they meant.

The Whippet standing beside us could've been an elderly relative of Rusty Laidlaw's. He was garbed in a pair of black trousers, a white shirt, and a small peaked cap. A pair of round, grimy spectacles hung on the end of his long nose.

'Are you here for rooms?' the Whippet asked hopefully.

'No. We're here to visit someone.'

'Well, you'll want to be joining the line.' On the far side of the room, a few animals hovered in a crooked line next to a long counter. 'Good day t'yer.' The Whippet hobbled off towards the door.

We joined the back of the line behind a mangy Tom wearing a checked suit, too much aftershave, and a comb-over that was fooling nobody. The rest of the line reeked of mints, liniment and mothballs, fitting aromas for God's Waiting Room.

'Can I help?' a harassed-looking black Cat asked when it was our turn.

'We're here to see Miss de Groot,' I told her.

'Yes, she said she was expecting visitors today. I'll give her a call.' She'd barely finished dialling the number when a fuzzy voice came through her earpiece. 'Yes, that's right,' the receptionist said, giving me a strange look.

'She says to go straight up. Elevator to the sixth floor, then up the stairs. It's the turret overlooking the sea.'

Eventually we found the elevators, both of which were hidden behind one of the large pillars to the left of the staircase. In front of each, several Cats and Dogs queued, along with a Hamster bent almost double over its walking stick, coughing its guts out. Both cages arrived at the same time, their charges stumbling out while the new ones bustled their way inside.

As is usually the case, we picked the wrong one. Our elevator stopped at every floor, and by the time we'd got as far as the third floor, the Mouse and I were squashed flat against the back wall, listening to an argument between two Persians; a female wearing a grey flannel dress, the male the most ridiculous wig I'd ever seen.

'Well it wasn't *me*.' The female hissed. 'I didn't know where to put my face.'

'I could've told you,' her partner said after he'd stubbed his cigarette on the floor. 'But I don't think you'd have appreciated my answer.'

'Oh? And what would that have been?' she snapped. At which point the doors opened and they left.

I was hoping I'd get to hear Wiggy's answer before the doors closed, but instead my attention was drawn by the elevator's latest occupant. While I was looking at him I heard a shriek of indignation from beyond the door. Then, we started moving.

The new passenger, a Wirehaired Pointer, was a few inches taller than me and had deep yellow eyes and thick, greying black fur. Instead of standing with his back to me, he stared straight at me, his yellow eyes never blinking, the ruffs of fur above his eyes remaining steady. I stared back, not much caring for the yellow and going straight for the pupils. By the time we'd reached the fourth floor he was blowing heavily through his dry, black nostrils. The door opened and another bunch of senior citizens entered, wide-awake and full of good cheer. The Pointer and I continued to stare each other down until the door opened on the fifth floor. His eyes never leaving mine, the Pointer reached back and wedged the door open with his paw. Squeezing past the other animals, he left, eye contact only ending when the elevator doors closed.

'Wow,' the Mouse said as the cage rose. 'Do you know him?'

'I've never seen him before in my life.' I said.

'Then —'

'My guess is that's the Hotel Detective,' I told him as the door opened on the sixth floor. 'I'd also guess that he's as crooked as they come'

After judging — or rather guessing — the turret's position from outside and where we might be now, we turned right, along a corridor with a lengthy run of gleaming red doors. At the end of that corridor was another door, this one painted green. It had a porthole window and a view of maybe a dozen steps leading up to another door which was varnished dark brown. When I knocked on it, the sound seemed to be swallowed by the wood.

A faint voice from behind it shouted 'Enter.' So we did.

From the parking lot the turrets looked quite small, but even with the bedroom and sitting room rolled into one it was surprisingly large and naturally lit by the three porthole windows looking out towards the sea. Below the furthest one and next to a closet, Angelica de Groot was sitting at a small desk, the expensive-looking pen in her paw gliding across a sheet of paper already crammed with words.

'Be with you in a second,' she said, scribbling a word from existence with apparent relish. 'There; that's got it. I'm glad you've responded to my summons promptly, Mr. Spriteman.' Capping her pen, she placed it in the pocket of her blouse. 'And you seem to have brought someone with you,' she said.

Unused to such pleasantries, it took me a few seconds to catch on. 'Forgive my manners. This is the Mouse, my main operative. Besides me, that is.'

'I can *see* he's a Mouse, Mr. Spriteman. We spoke briefly at the launch if you'll remember but we weren't introduced. I'd like to know his name.'

I squirmed a bit, looked round at the Mouse. 'Well, we just call him the Mouse, you know.'

Miss de Groot was having none of it. Turning to him she said, 'What's your name, dear?' He told her as quietly as he could.

'Speak up, dear. I won't bite, you know.'

'Linus!' he said far too loudly.

'Linus? How unusual! Well,' she looked at her watch, 'I think it's time for refreshment. Tea?'

'Why not,' I told her.

Picking up the phone on the desk, she called downstairs and ordered. 'Isn't the view wonderful?' she said, watching the Mouse looking out to sea. 'It's a little light when you're trying to get to sleep of course, but after a day of sea air you tend to drop off easily enough.' Dingus was right — she *was* bearing up well. Too well. It was as though seeing her sister drop dead a few feet from her had skipped her mind.

'I was surprised you weren't at Clancy's offices yesterday.' I said. 'I'd have thought something like that would have been right up your alley.'

She didn't take offence at either the remark or my tone. 'I was busy here,' she replied. 'And anyway, the Lieutenant has kept me up to speed. Poisoned. So sad.' She looked towards the window.

'Doing what?' I asked.

She turned back to me. 'I'm sorry?'

'Busy doing what?'

'I'll get to that later.'

'So, the Lieutenant was here yesterday afternoon?'

'That isn't what I said. But yes, he popped round yesterday afternoon and we had a long chat.'

Another one, I thought. 'Maybe he forgot what he'd asked you before. In that Pigeon Post you sent me you seemed to think he was forgetful.'

'I said I thought he *might* be forgetful. He's a strange creature. Do you know, I've spoken to him twice in the past two days and I've no idea what either conversation was about?'

'You don't say. I gather he's spending a lot of time in Rockway at the moment.'

She either didn't take the bait, or had no idea I was offering any. 'I'm sure I've no idea.'

The tea arrived soon after that, and for some reason, a plate of bread and butter. After eating a few slices and refilling her cup several times, she reached into her handbag and brought out her pipe. 'I'd be interested in your thoughts regarding our latest novel,' she said when the bowl was lit.

'I haven't read it yet. Say, why don't you bring up those books Ma Spayley wanted signing?' I said to the Mouse. Happy to be doing something, he dashed out of the room.

'I managed to get hold of a copy of that crime magazine you mentioned — you know, the one with the title,' she said, picking up a copy of *Sherlock* from the bedside table. 'Some of it was rather good. I've decided I'd let that editor have his interview after all, despite what's happened. It's good to keep oneself busy in these situations.'

'Laidlaw's been in touch with you?'

'Supposedly to see how I was coping. So transparent.' After taking another suck on the pipe she drained yet another cupful of tea. I decided it was time to get to the point.

'Forgive me for saying so, but you don't seem unduly upset by your sister's death.'

Slowly, she placed the pipe down on the coffee table. 'No, it's all rather sad,' she sighed. 'We weren't *real* sisters anyway; different litters, you know. But I don't think it's hit me yet. Or if it ever will.'

'I got the impression that she wasn't easy to like.'

'No, she wasn't,' she said, sighing again. 'I think she resented the fact that I came from a better breed; at least she thought I had. These days it really doesn't matter, does it? But I still don't see why anybody would want to kill her, especially over here.'

'Can you tell me why she was so anxious to speak to me?'

She looked up from the table. 'I didn't know she was.'

'She phoned me the day after you called. Said it was *essential*. Her emphasis.'

She looked genuinely surprised. 'I did mention that you might not be available for the book launch. But I'm amazed she called you.'

'At the launch she made some crack about you and her not being joined at the hip.'

'Well, that much was true. She was always off gallivanting on her own. I can't say I discouraged her too much.'

I recalled something else Lettice had said to me. 'What was your journey over here like?'

'On the boat? Absolutely dreadful. Why?'

'I can't imagine the sea being rough at the moment.'

'Oh, it was nothing to do with the crossing. My sister managed to rub a few animals the wrong way as usual. In fact she was even more disagreeable than normal. In the end she requested her own cabin. I was cock-a-hoop.'

'You strike me as being pretty unflappable,' I told her.

It took her a while to reply. 'Usually, I am.'

Changing the subject, she'd just started asking about the poison-pen letters when there was a knock at the door. Opening it, she was confronted by a stack of her books and a Mouse eager to put them down.

Angelica de Groot's eyes lit up. 'My goodness! Have you got them all? Come in! Now. Who am I signing these for?' she asked, eagerly taking the pen back out of her blouse pocket. 'Your mother? And her name? Imelda? Splendid!'

With seemingly great pleasure, I watched Miss de Groot pick up each book in turn, and sign it. I couldn't weigh her up; was this her way of coping or was she being callous? Or did she have something to hide?

'Incidentally, Mr. Spriteman, I saw that awful newspaper accusing you earlier today; absolute tommyrot,' she said as she was signing the last of the books. 'It's not giving you any trouble, I trust?'

She sounded genuinely concerned. 'Not that I know of,' I said.

Handing the last book back to the Mouse, she returned the pen to her pocket. 'If you'll both excuse me for a minute,' she pointed towards a closed door on the other side of the room, 'nature calls.'

Hearing the bolt fasten I made a quick decision. 'I want you to stay in the hotel,' I whispered to the Mouse.

'For a few hours?'

I thought about it a second. 'The night. There's something going on here but I don't know what. Get a room as far away from this one as possible and dig around, see if you can find anything out.'

The Mouse looked shocked. 'You don't think Miss de Groot killed her sister?'

'I don't feel like I know anything at the moment, that's the point.'

'Then why don't you stay?' he said.

'Because if she sees me she'll know that I'm keeping an eye on her.'

'But what if she sees *me*?' he hissed back.

It was a fair question, and one I didn't have an answer to. Luckily I didn't need one, because at that moment Angelica de Groot came out of the bathroom, all bright and breezy.

'Well, Mr. Spriteman, I think it's time I told you the reason I wanted to see you. Something rather peculiar has occurred in this hotel and I'm at a loss to explain it. The manager asked us to look into it, presumably because we wrote crime novels — not that Lettice was interested of course — but frankly, I'm out of my depth. The hotel has its own detective: a rather intimidating old Dog called Burt, but —'

'A Pointer? I think we just met him. So what's the problem? Has something gone missing?'

'Well, it's the safe. By the sound of things it wasn't full, but it's still a substantial amount of money, I'm told.'

'Forgive me for saying so, but if someone's stolen money from the safe, the manager should go to the Police, not its guests.'

'No, you don't understand; it isn't just the money that's gone. It's the safe itself.'

'*What?*'

'Exactly! A great big heavy thing, and it's completely vanished. No sign of it anywhere. The manager thinks Burt had something to do with it, but hasn't the nerve to confront him about it. Besides, he wants to keep the police out of it because of the publicity it would attract. So I was wondering whether you could... take a look around?'

The Mouse was there before me. 'Mr. Spriteman, I could do that,' he suggested. 'I could stay here overnight and see if anything turns up. It would be good experience for me, wouldn't it?'

'Hmm, that's not a bad idea,' I said, hopefully playing along a little more subtly than the Mouse. 'That is if Miss de Groot is agreeable?'

'It think it's a wonderful idea. First things first, I think we should see about getting you a room.'

While she fussed over the details in reception I found out the times of the buses back to town. It turned out I'd just missed one, so we all trooped back to her suite for more tea and pipe fumes. After the first half hour the Mouse stopped coughing.

'Do you have anything to read for your journey back to town?' Angelica de Groot asked. I told her I hadn't. 'Soon remedy that,' she said, slipping a book into a bag for me.

When I went down to wait for the bus, they both came with me. 'You haven't asked me about the Carlin case,' I said as we sat on a bench outside the hotel.

'No,' she said, with a smile. 'I think I understand your reluctance now, after everything that's happened. Lettice and I might not have been close, but... well. Some other time, perhaps?'

'Perhaps.' Overhead, the skies were darkening. Thunder grumbled in the distance. By the time the bus pulled up, a few spots of rain had started to fall. Taking a seat at the back of the bus, I looked out to find them both still standing there, an ageing Cat and a sprightly young Mouse, looking for all the world like grandma and grandson despite being different species.

We hadn't been going a minute when the heavens finally opened. Despite being stuck inside a humid metal box, a small cheer went up in the bus. On the sidewalks, animals began removing their clothes and dancing in the streets, open mouths tilted up to the skies. Then the rain got heavy, bouncing back up off the pavement: three, four inches. The streets began to clear as half-drowned Cats and Dogs rushed for cover in shop doorways.

As the excitement died down, I noticed that we hadn't travelled very far. Ahead, a bus identical to ours grew impatient; mounting the sidewalk and driving past the obstruction, it gave us a clear view of the hold-up.

Below us there was a van with its back doors wide open, and two Dogs crouching on the floor in the back between two blue benches, with something on the floor between them. It wasn't until they covered whatever was on the floor with a blanket that I realised the van was an ambulance and the something was a some-*body*. A small, uneasy murmur went through the bus. Our driver, following the other driver's example, suddenly mounted the curb and sped past. A few passengers muttered disapproval, but after spending the last few hours in a mausoleum, that was the last thing I wanted to see.

As the traffic thinned once more, I thought again about Angelica de Groot. Had she been listening behind the bathroom door when I suggested the Mouse stay at the hotel, and got there ahead of us? But if she had, why was she so willing for him to stay? Maybe there really was trouble at the hotel after all. Either way, I couldn't let go of the idea that she had something to do with what was going on. She was too casual about it all for my liking, too detached from its consequences.

Or maybe it was just the creative mind at work. Taking the book she'd given me from its bag, I read the blurb, and laughed. With no expectations I turned to the first page, to find out who Peter Pinter was and how a cylindrical disk covered in cyanide could be used to dispose of an elderly relative.

12. READING

'EXCUSE ME. SIR?'
A Cat in a white shirt was standing over me. 'Yes?'
'We're here sir,' it said. 'Far as we go.'

It was now two twenty-five, the streets were dry and I was forty-odd pages into *The Poisoned Piston of Peter Pinter*. I felt like I'd had the same clothes on for a month, and despite spending most of the day sitting down, I found I wanted to do so again. I made my way back to the office as fast as I could without breaking a sweat.

When I opened the door Taki didn't even pretend to be busy.

'Good book?' she asked, filing a claw.

'Yeah.' I went into my office.

I called Patch Finnegan first. 'Anything new?' I asked.

'Not since the day after the murder. No new stories either. Maybe it's the heat.' I called Rusty Laidlaw and asked him the same question.

'I've managed to secure an interview with Angelica de Groot; she's coming back to the city,' he told me, sounding like all his birthdays had come at once. I told him I meant the case he was employing me to work. 'No, nothing. Do you think maybe it's stopped?' I told him I didn't know and hung up, feeling deflated. Even though the two things may not be connected, I had an odd idea that the murder of Lettice de Groot might have opened up some aspect of the case. Maybe my 'feelings' weren't so hot after all. Jabbing at the phone again, I called Alannah Foxton, who asked me if I had anything to report.

'Not yet. I don't suppose Betsy Oatland's contacted you?' but she hadn't. Calling the police, they said they didn't know where she was. When I asked to speak to Dingus they said they didn't know where he was either.

Hanging up the phone, I made a few frustrated noises. I was starting to wish I'd stayed at the hotel. Then I realised that was a lie: the truth of the matter was the hotel depressed the hell out of me; I could imagine myself in a place like that one day, shuffling around with nothing to do. But hey, here I was in my office instead, with the Mouse checking up on Angelica de Groot and Dingus looking into the murder. I had no idea where Trix had gone and the poison-pen letters had dried up.

After racking my brains for a few minutes I tried to get hold of Mungo Bickeridge but — surprise surprise — there was no answer. Out of desperation I even gave Grover S. Nelson a call, but nobody picked up. *The Poisoned Piston of Peter Pinter* was on the desk in front of me. I picked it up and turned to page forty-six.

How long I read I wasn't sure. All I know is that I wanted to find out what happened at the end of chapter fifteen but the room was so dark I couldn't make out the words any more. Flicking up the blinds, the sky above the buildings opposite looked like a rough block of discoloured granite. A rumble of thunder sounded overhead. Snapping on the light switch, I settled back down to my book. I'd barely started chapter sixteen when the rain began to fall.

Below I saw the same kind of response there'd been in Rockway when the clouds opened, but this time it wasn't as interesting. With the thunder grumbling in the distance, I went back to my chair, stuck my paws on the desk and carried on with chapter sixteen, the wonderfully comforting sound of torrential rain washing the sidewalks in the background.

At some point during the next two hours it stopped raining. Finishing the book, I slapped the covers shut, swung my paws off the desk and sighed. All was quiet next door; Taki was long gone. I looked down at my watch, seeing it was just past seven. Grabbing my jacket, I locked up the office and headed for Sidwells.

It was nearly closing time when I got there. The manager was talking to a member of staff next to a cash register. As soon as he saw me, he made a beeline for me, wanting to know if I had any news.

'You'll have to ask the police,' I told him, 'I'm here as a customer. I want to buy one of the de Groot sisters' books.'

'Certainly. Any particular one?'

I thought about it a second. 'How about *The Last Words of the Dying Butter*?'

He looked at me a second, raising what on another Dog would've been eyebrows. '*The Last Words of the Dying Butter*?' he repeated, a little shocked.

'You have still got a copy?'

He looked at me like that was a silly question. 'I'll go get you one.'

As I paid, I asked if the police had been back. 'Once or twice. They've got rid of that outline, thank goodness. Customers were spending more time looking at it than at the books.'

By the time I got home it had started to rain again. After opening the living room window and putting on the percolator for coffee, I dried myself off in the bathroom, listening to the twin rumblings of coffee pot and returning thunder. I felt strangely calm, an emotion I'm not altogether familiar with. Perhaps it was the book I'd just read. Sitting by the open window with my coffee, I opened my copy of *The Last Words of the Dying Butter* and wondered if it would have the same effect; it surely couldn't be as bad as its reputation suggested.

I was right; it wasn't. It was much, much worse.

At least the fifty or so pages I managed to get through were. I did briefly consider persevering with it, in the hope that my copy was a special magic one in which the butter *did* speak, letting slip the identity of the murderer in the process. But after a day spent among the severely aged at the Rockway Plaza Hotel I decided that life was too short. Despite the increasingly loud rumbles of thunder and sharp cracks of lightning seemingly just above the building, I thought an early night was the best option. I stood up and turned off the light, plunging the room into darkness.

Then, a curious thing happened: as I was heading for the bedroom, a jag of lightning threw the room into sharp, eyeball-piercing brightness. Turning instinctively, I found myself looking back across the room, where, on the table, illuminated by the lightning, I saw a detail from *The Last Words of the Dying Butter*'s cover; an embossed skull and crossbones on a silver butter tray being held aloft by a servant.

For some strange reason, I was glad I wasn't having kippers in the morning.

13. SUSPECTS AND SECRETS

THE NEXT MORNING WHEN I got to the office, I found the Pigeon waiting for me on the windowsill.

'Not coming in today?' I asked.

'I like the breeze,' he said, shaking his head. 'Another note for you here.' He nodded at the paper he was standing on. As soon as my paw touched it he shot off into the air. I unfolded the note:

> *Mr. Spriteman — I wonder if you could see your way clear to a return visit to the hotel? Young Linus told me a bit more about your present caseload last night and I think that I may be able to help you; and vice versa. Again, yours, A de G.*

Picking up the phone, I told the operator I wanted the number for the Rockway Plaza Hotel. When I got through to reception, I asked for the Mouse, deciding I'd get more sense talking to him.

'Hello?' he sounded edgy, like he'd never answered a phone before.

'It's me. What the hell is it with her and these notes?'

He didn't answer straight away, and then not my question. 'It's this hotel, Mr. Spriteman. There's something going on here.'

'Is Miss de Groot involved?'

'I don't think so. I've been with her most of the time.'

'Has she mentioned her sister's death at all?'

He thought about it. 'No.'

'What about the hotel dick? Seen much of him?'

'I've spotted him around a few times, and he looks really suspicious.' He stopped, but I got the feeling he wanted to say more.

'Anything else?'

'Well... I'm not sure. I just heard something. But you said you didn't think he was a suspect anymore.'

'Go on.'

'At breakfast a lot of the residents were talking about a hit-and-run here yesterday afternoon. Apparently one of the old ladies in the hotel was there when the ambulance arrived. She says that when the ambulance staff were checking the body for ID they found a letter in the Dog's pocket. She overheard the name of the animal the letter was addressed to: Grover S. Nelson.'

'Nelson?'

Before I got a chance to take it in, the Mouse was talking again. 'Mr. Spriteman, I've got to go now. I think Miss de Groot's at the door and she said she didn't want me using the phone.' He slammed the phone down so hard the resulting crack set my teeth on edge. I, however, put my phone back in its cradle like it was a sleeping baby: slowly and softly. Then I looked at it for a while, as if that would give me answers to the questions zipping around in my head: What the hell was going on at that Hotel? Why was Angelica de Groot so reluctant to use the telephone, and who did she think she was forbidding my operative to use one? And why on earth would anybody want to kill Grover S. Nelson?

Buzzing Taki, I got her to look up the time of the next bus to Rockway. A few minutes later she buzzed back — there was one in half an hour.

Looking again at the note and its offer of help, I bundled up all my letters and papers then stuck them in a bag. I thought

127

about taking the stories, but there were too many of them. Besides, I could imagine her response to a story like "Sick Relish". But God, was I tempted. If she asked, I could always give her a few graphic descriptions.

'If that damned Pigeon comes back, tell it I've gone to the beach,' I said to Taki on my way out.

This time it was a more comfortable journey: the roads were quiet and since the storm had cleared the air, the bus didn't feel so much like a sauna with leather seats. Passing the spot where Nelson was killed, I wondered who was responsible? Had 'Bumper Fodder' succeeded with Nelson where they'd failed with Mungo Bickeridge? The problem with that theory was Nelson had never been published. As far as I knew, the only animal besides myself who'd read his stories was Patch Finnegan.

When the bus stopped outside the Plaza I was the only one to get off, the Mouse and Miss de Groot waiting for me.

'Miss de Groot said you'd be on the next bus,' the Mouse told me, looking pleased. Beside him, Miss de Groot looked pleased too; too pleased for someone who must know she was a suspect in a murder investigation. So I decided to try and wipe the smile off her face.

'So, here we are again, safe and sound. Any other suspicious deaths I should know about?'

'Only Miss Gilchrist,' she told me.

'Miss —'

'Gilchrist. One of the residents. Not suspicious though — poor dear died in her sleep. She's the third one since I've been here. Sometimes it feels more like a hospice than a hotel. Right,' she said, rubbing her paws together, 'you must be thirsty after your journey, Mr. Spriteman. Shall we have some tea?'

'I'll have coffee,' I mumbled, following her inside.

Initially, the three of us sat in the lounge in silence. Every so often Miss de Groot would lob over a piece of small talk, which

I batted back impatiently. After the third or fourth of these sallies she seemed to get the message.

'I see you've brought a bag with you,' she said. 'Are you thinking of staying?'

'I haven't decided.' Turning to the Mouse, I said, 'What's all this about Grover S. Nelson?'

'It's like I said on the phone. He was found dead in the middle of the road with a tire stripe up his back. We just spoke to Miss Sayers before you arrived.'

'Who's Miss Sayers?'

'The Cat who was there when the ambulance arrived.'

'And she didn't see anything el — did you just say "we"?'

The Mouse blinked at me, like the Pigeon had in my office. Miss de Groot answered for him.

'Mr. Spriteman, I've spoken to Miss Sayers a few times since I arrived. I only introduced them, that was all. I didn't say a word after that.'

'I'm surprised you didn't send her a Pigeon. Can you tell me why my operative was forbidden from using the telephone?'

'He wasn't forbidden. I merely —' looking round, she lowered her voice. 'I merely advised him that under the present circumstances it wasn't such a good idea.'

I gave her a good, hard stare. She never even blinked.

'Are you suggesting that the phones in the hotel are being bugged?'

'I'm suggesting, Mr. Spriteman, that whatever's going on here is an inside job. How else could a safe go missing? And whoever is responsible must know where various animals are at certain times. The phone seems a logical way of finding out.'

I blew out a long breath. 'Lady, you read too many detective novels.'

'I hardly think that's fair,' she said, puffing herself up like a peacock.

'Okay. If it's an inside job, who's behind it?'

'The Hotel Detective, Burt.' I asked if she'd any evidence. Shook her head. 'Just a hunch.'

'You get any dirt on him last night?' I asked the Mouse.

'No. He's always watching to see if anyone's following him.' I turned back to Miss de Groot. 'This safe; how big is it?'

'A few feet across, if the indentations it left on the carpet are anything to go by.'

'You said before it was heavy too. So how exactly did such a weedy mutt manage to carry it out of a busy hotel without anyone noticing?'

'I don't know. I'm not ashamed to say that I need help,' she said, sitting up primly. 'And neither should you be.'

'What's that supposed to mean?' I looked across at the Mouse, who just blinked again.

'Linus hasn't told me anything, Mr. Spriteman. He's a good boy.' When she patted him on the head, I found myself blushing on his behalf. 'But we did have a conversation last night — a general one, nothing more — and, reading between the lines, it sounds to me like you need a fresh pair of eyes. And now that one of your suspects has been found dead...' she shrugged, all eyes and shoulders, still good humoured. I was getting nowhere fast, so I tried her with something else.

'Miss de Groot, I find this rather hard to believe. You needing help, I mean. You're nothing if not inventive.' Her shoulders fell slightly but her eyes were still wide. 'It's hard to imagine that the co-author of *The Poisoned Piston of Peter Pinter* would need help from anybody. I was very impressed by it.'

'Why, thank you.'

'So impressed that I decided to try another of your books: *The Last Words of the Dying Butter*. And after trying to wade my way through that one, I'd go so far as to say that not only do you read too many detective novels, Miss de Groot, *you also write too many*.'

I could almost see her deflate before my eyes.

'Ah,' she said quietly, 'the world's worst literary secret uncovered at last.'

'So who wrote what?' I asked. Between us, the Mouse looked completely stumped. But he'd catch up.

'I wrote *Piston*. I also wrote *Rest Cure, Rosa Worth, Wallace Miles* and *The Jagged Stiletto of Ursula Prim*. Lettice wrote the others. They were released alternately: one of mine followed by one of hers. It was the only way we could do it and hope to get away with it.'

'But your novels are the ones everyone likes.'

'Lettice wasn't a writer,' she said, fishing her pipe out of her handbag, 'she knew it and I knew it. But when I sent the manuscript of *Wallace Miles* to Alicia's old publishers and they accepted it... well, the pound signs lit up in her eyes. And at that point the publishers didn't know I was Alicia Hartley's cat.'

'Hang on a second,' I interrupted. 'Who's Alicia Hartley?'

'Alicia Hartley, the renowned pre-Terror crime novelist. Surely you've heard of her?'

'My reading habits haven't extended much to your side of the pond. So how come you write under the name de Groot?'

'A concession to my sister; or half-sister as she was so fond of reminding me.' The pipe now fully lit, her voice came to me through a succession of small, pungent clouds.

'Lettice became jealous. Very jealous. She said I must've traded in on our famous owner's name and if I could do it, so could she. So she started to write her own novel. After about a week she'd just about given up when she found a box of Alicia's half-finished stories. From them she managed to stitch various old plots together and fill them out with her own ideas. The result was *The Enemies of Edgar Silliphant*. She let me read it before she sent it off to the publishers. When she asked me what I thought of it, I tried to be kind, but it simply wasn't very good. She said that was just sour grapes and posted it to Alicia's publishers anyway, along with a letter making sure they knew fine well that, like me, she had been one of

Alicia Hartley's pets. I fully expected it to come back with a rejection slip attached. But a couple of weeks later they phoned her to say they'd accepted it.'

'Is it as bad as *The Last Words of the Dying Butter*?' I asked, pulling a face.

'Not quite,' she said. 'And, putting modesty to one side for a second, I'd say — and the publishers agreed — the reason for this was that despite having Alicia's old manuscripts at her disposal, Lettice also borrowed several elements from *The Last Gasp of Wallace Miles*.'

'If that was case, why did they accept it?'

'Money! Why else?' She said, puffing out a huge plume of pipe smoke. 'The world had settled down again and animals started to read books, and do you know what kind of books were selling? Murder mysteries; the kind of books that Alicia Hartley had been writing before The Terror. And then we came along, writing the same kind of stories... the publishers couldn't believe their luck: they had an opportunity to clean up. They wanted as many as we could produce and as quickly as possible. The only problem was my novels were much better than Lettice's.'

'So they got round that by publishing the novels as collaborations.'

'Precisely. The publishers reasoned — and rightly, as it turned out, as the sales for Lettice's books match mine — that the book-buying public would forgive a bad book if it was immediately followed by a good one. The publishers made their money, Lettice and I made ours. In theory, everyone was happy.'

'Everyone except you.'

'I don't think Lettice was either, in truth, even with the money being split fifty-fifty and her getting her own way most of the time. It was because of her we ended up with this silly name, despite her kicking up all that fuss that everyone should know we were Alicia Hartley's cats. Just before *Wallace*

Miles was published, she suggested we use another name Why she picked such an ugly one I can't say. I'm sure there's some twisted reason behind it though. Whatever it was, it seemed to amuse her greatly. I had hoped that going along with it might pacify her a bit. Anyway, when the books came out, it was always mine that got the praise. I offered to help her with hers but she rejected the idea out of hand. It wasn't too bad at first, while she still had Alicia's cast-offs to work from. But after *Gift-Wrapped for Murder* she'd exhausted them all, so books like *Dying Butter* or *Death by Winkle* were entirely her own work. I knew someone would catch on sooner or later. In a way I'm relieved it's out in the open. I'm not proud of the deception I've been involved in, Mr. Spriteman, but I did not kill Lettice because of it.'

Her confession over, she finished her pipe in silence. I realised that I'd misjudged her: she was a different type of animal, that was all, from a different world to mine.

'You said in your note that I might be able to help you.'

'Yes,' she replied, putting her pipe in her bag and snapping the clasp shut with a loud click, 'I rather think you can.'

14. REQUESTS AND DETAILS

ECAUSE I WAS SICK of travelling back and forth, I decided to book a room for the night. After getting my key, I made my way back to the turret. I was hardly in the door when Angelica said:

'I want you to look into my sister's death.'

I'd expected her to ask me to look into the missing safe.

'I don't see what I can do, Miss de Groot, with the police looking into it. If Dingus is involved he'll get to the bottom of it.'

'I'm sure he would, but I get the feeling his mind is on other things at the moment. And it's "Angelica", if you don't mind. I can't abide all that formality.'

' "Benji", then. I don't much care for it myself.'

'But what about Linus? He calls you "Mr. Spriteman".'

'I've told him not to, but he keeps on doing it. Short of docking his wages I don't see what else I can do. When you said you could help me,' I reached into the bag I'd brought with me, 'I presume you meant with these?' I handed her my bundle of papers.

'There's certainly plenty of it.'

'There's also a load of stories back at the office. If you get anywhere with this lot I'll let you have those as well.'

'I think this is more my line of expertise,' she said, flicking through the sheets. 'Plenty to get my teeth stuck into here!'

'You can see why I'm getting nowhere with it.'

'Oh, it wasn't a criticism. And heaven knows I need something to take my mind off... you know. So will you do it? Look into her death, I mean?'

Figuring I had nothing to lose, I nodded. 'Okay. Where do you want to start?'

'The letters sound intriguing. Tell me about them first.'

'Not Lettice? Or the safe?'

'Lettice can wait for a while. As for the safe, I thought young Linus could look into that.' While we'd been talking, the Mouse had been glued to one of the porthole windows, staring out to sea as if hypnotized.

'Huh?' he said, turning round.

'Angelica wants you to find out what Mr. Burt is up to. And Linus —'

'Yes?'

I winked at Angelica. 'From now on, call me "Benji".'

He thought about it for a second. 'Sure, Mr. Spriteman,' he said, heading for the door.

After giving her the background to the case, we went quickly through the letters. She glanced at each one in turn, making no comment until she'd reached Wiedlin's rejection letter.

'Oh dear me,' she tutted. 'Not very professional at *all*. And this character is one of your suspects?'

'If he isn't, he wants me to think he is.'

'What's his work like?'

'The one of his I've read was mediocre.'

'Hmm. What about the others?'

'Well, Nelson's stuff was so bad he made Wiedlin look like a genius. I never really had him as much of a suspect.'

'Until he got himself killed.'

'Until then. Jake Lake wrote a story about the poison-pen letters but at the time of the attempted knock down and break-ins she wasn't in town.'

' *"She"*?'

135

'I'll tell you another time. Which leaves Mungo Bickeridge, the author of "Sick Relish".'

'This "Sick Relish",' she asked tentatively, 'what's it about?' Feeling in a devilish mood I told her.

'Absolutely disgusting,' she said, wrinkling her nose. 'Still, I suppose I'd better read it at some point. So if you had to pick a main suspect, who would it be?'

'That's just it, I can't. Of the four, I'd say Nelson was the least likely.'

'Of course, in a book that would make him favourite. You say there haven't been any letters for a few days?'

'Not since the day after Lettice's murder.'

'And now this Grover S. Nelson has been knocked down and killed?'

I made a few incoherent noises before replying. 'Nah. I still can't see it.'

We sat quietly for a while. 'So where does the Dog story fit in?' she asked eventually. 'Linus mentioned it in passing last night,' she added quickly.

When I told her, it really seemed to catch her attention.

'How interesting... do you think the animal is still alive?'

'Until the "Rex" story turned up, I had him down as a runaway. I thought he'd find his way home sooner or later. Now I'm not so sure.'

'I think he's alive,' she said, rubbing the fur around her neck. 'Yes. I'd definitely say he's still alive.'

'Why?'

'I don't know; just a feeling. It's a pity you didn't bring those stories with you. Still, I can always get them when I go through to the city for my interview.'

Hearing a clock chime in the distance, she looked at her watch. 'I don't know about you, Benji,' she said, picking up her bag, 'but I'm ready for a spot of lunch.'

15. RELATIONS

'Y<small>OU LOOK PLEASANTLY SURPRISED</small>,' she said.
'I am. With the hotel the way it is —'
'You thought the town would be the same.'
I shrugged.

To begin with I wasn't disappointed. The first thing we passed on leaving the hotel was a small antique shop next door. Their definition of the word 'antique' seemed to mean anything that had existed before The Terror.

'Fifty bucks for a pack of playing cards,' I grumbled. 'Who the hell buys these things?'

'Elderly Cats who inherited all their owners' money when things changed,' Angelica informed me, 'and now can't spend it fast enough. A few of them live in the hotel.'

'It seems a strange place to live if you're elderly,' I remarked, grunting my way to the top of the next hill. 'You'd need damn good brakes on your bath-chair.'

She laughed. 'I get the impression most of the hotel's residents venture no further than the balconies overlooking the sea. They certainly wouldn't cope well with Main Street.'

'And where's Main Street?' I asked.

'Right in front of you. Would you like to take my paw?'

Ahead of us, the narrow road cut dramatically away, twisting down towards the beach. Either side of it were dozens of small, cramped-looking shops selling everything from tattoos to

137

candyfloss, their doors barely a yard from the passing traffic. Drop your change here and you could wave goodbye to it.

'I think I'll manage,' I assured her. 'What's down at the bottom besides the beach?'

'Amusements, ice-cream parlours; and just 'round the corner, a very good fish restaurant.'

Strolling along the narrow pavements past half-dressed tourists, with the cawing 'gulls all around us, I decided I liked Rockway. Nearing the bottom of Main Street Angelica pointed at the window of a joke shop and laughed, every inch of its space taken up with leering masks, bald wigs, whoopee cushions and itching powder. Reading the small sign next to it — BANK SAFE GROWS LEGS; "WHERE'S OUR MONEY?" SAYS MANAGER — I wondered at first if it was part of the joke shop display. Grabbing a paper from the stand, I paid the vendor.

On the flat, we took a few seconds to squint into the bright silver glare of the sea across the road, and at the kids playing there. I suddenly wished I was younger, and could go over and join them.

'Where's this restaurant?' I asked.

When we were seated and waiting for the fish to arrive, I unfolded my copy of the *Rockway Herald*. To my surprise the main headline wasn't the safe, but the death of Grover S. Nelson. HIT AND RUN HORROR IN TOWN, the headline screamed. Reading the story, I was impressed: unlike Fuller's rag it was well written, and if there were any spelling mistakes I missed them. The details, however, were vague. At around one o'clock the previous afternoon, a Corgi named Grover S. Nelson had been killed outright by a hit-and-run driver on the outskirts of town whilst in Rockway visiting relatives. As I read it, I couldn't help thinking about the letter-writer calling themselves 'Bumper Fodder' and Mungo Bickeridge's near miss. And then, just as the fish arrived, I remembered something else.

' *"Fatman Becomes Flat-man"!*' I exclaimed. The waitress gave me a funny look.

Angelica stared at me. 'I beg your pardon?'

'Nelson — one of those stories of his was about a writer that was knocked down and killed in the street. But as far as I'm aware nobody else has read his work.'

'Maybe someone had after all,' Angelica suggested, 'and wanted to get him back.'

I had intended to read about the Bank's safe as I ate, but the fish was so good I couldn't drag myself away from it. It was with some regret that I pushed the plate away.

'You look like you enjoyed that,' Angelica said, smiling.

'I did. I could eat it again.' Picking up the paper, I found the article on the safe and read it aloud to Angelica. Its tone was hardly serious: *'We all know about bathtubs and tables having legs,'* the article joked, *'but safes? And as well as having legs, this particular safe appears to have had its own key too, because according to Max Fletcher, the bank's manager, the room which contained the safe was* LOCKED *from the* OUTSIDE*!'*

'Just like the Plaza,' Angelica remarked when I'd finished. 'A locked-room mystery.'

'Hmm. Only the Plaza's manager managed to keep it out of the papers. You still think Burt has something to do with this? I mean, it's possible he had a hand in taking the hotel's safe, but the bank's as well?'

'I'm certain he's involved,' she told me. 'I can feel it in my water.'

I laughed at that; so hard several diners looked round.

'You find that expression amusing?' she asked once I'd settled down.

'Not so much the expression, more the sentiment,' I said, explaining the way I'd been feeling lately, what with my meeting with Harvey followed by the phone calls I'd had from her and her sister, and finally Lettice's death. 'The last time I had a 'feeling in my water' was during the Carlin case. And look what happened there. Jimmy survived all that time and then —' but I didn't want to say any more.

'Ah, Jimmy Spriteman,' Angelica said after a while. 'Do you know how Alicia died? Poison. She saw what was going on around her and poisoned herself, right in front of my eyes. I didn't even realise what she was doing until it was too late.' She tried to force a smile.

'Did Lettice see this?' I asked.

'No. She'd run outside to see what was happening. Afterwards she even resented the fact that I was there when Alicia died and she wasn't.' Taking a small lace handkerchief from the sleeve of her cardigan, she dabbed at her eyes and sniffed.

I asked my next question carefully. 'How many of your books are about poisoning?'

She sniffed again, but didn't seem to take offence. 'Oh, all of them, in some way or other. All Alicia's books were too. That's why she had the poison in the house in the first place. Years before she'd worked in a chemist's — a drugstore to you. And they ask writers where they get their ideas from.' Waving a paw in the air, she signalled the waitress for the check. 'My treat,' she said when I reached for my wallet. Deciding it would be ungentlemanly of me to protest, I kept my mouth shut.

'I hope you enjoyed your meal,' the waitress said, looking at Angelica. 'Is there anything else?'

'Yeah,' I said, having a sudden brainwave. 'You could tell us where Bailey's Crescent is.'

'Back up the hill and turn right at Milner's Lane,' she said. 'It's about half a mile away.'

'Thank you, my dear,' Angelica said, 'and keep the change. Up another hill,' she said as the waitress left us. 'Do you think you're up to another walk like that?'

'I'll have to be,' I said, rising sluggishly, 'If I want to meet Grover S. Nelson's relatives.'

‡ ‡ ‡

'You know, it's quite strange really,' Angelica remarked, stopping at the top of the hill, 'about Nelson having relatives. Most animals would've been separated from their litters before The Terror.'

'You had a relative,' I reminded her, also stopping.

'*Half* relative. But back then most animals were pets, so they had owners. Unless you can remember back before The Terror, you'd have no idea who your relations were.'

'Jake Lake has an Aunt Rebecca in the country. I talked to her on the phone.'

'Didn't that strike you as odd?'

'No. Why should it?'

'Two Cats apparently living so far away from each other knowing they're aunt and niece?'

'It's not impossible,' I reasoned. 'Maybe Lake didn't like the country and moved.'

'No, fair enough. Jake's a damned funny name for a female though. Tomboy, is she?'

'No. Quite the opposite, I'd say.'

'Well, as long as your feelings don't cloud your judgment,' she said, looking straight ahead.

'They're not. We're here. Bailey's Crescent.'

The Crescent was made up of perhaps fifty or so identical bungalows.

'Excuse me,' Angelica shouted across to an old Labrador mowing his lawn on the other side of the street, 'can you tell me where Miss Nelson lives?'

'Number forty-seven,' the Labrador shouted back. 'But if you're a reporter she'll send you away with a flea in your ear.'

'Oh, we're not reporters,' Angelica shouted back. 'Thank you!'

The Corgi who opened the door of number forty-seven looked so much like Grover S. Nelson I had to look twice. If it hadn't been for the dress and the slightly higher voice they could have been twins.

'He mentioned you when I spoke to him, the day before it happened,' Lily Nelson told me when we were seated in her front room. 'I think he found it exciting, being involved in a real-life detective case. Not that I could tell, of course.' She smiled sadly. 'He was the same Dog after The Terror as he was before it. He lived in his own little world most of the time.'

'He told you why I spoke to him?'

She nodded. 'About the threatening letters those editors were receiving. But if you met him, you'll know he wasn't capable of anything like that.'

'I don't think he sent any letters. I was more interested in the stories he wrote about editors and publishers being killed.'

'Those stories,' Lily Nelson replied irritably, shaking her head. 'They were all terrible. But I didn't have the heart to... you know. They gave him an interest, you see. That's why he moved out of here: he got it into his head that he'd sell more if he lived closer to the city.' Angelica and I exchanged a quick look. 'You're not here because you think someone *deliberately* knocked him down, are you? Because of his stories?' as she looked at me with big, frightened eyes something sharp cut through the dullness of grief.

'I don't think so,' I told her, deciding honesty was the best policy, 'but I thought I'd check.' The next question I asked I already knew the answer to. 'Did Grover have any enemies that you know of?'

'Enemies?' Lily Nelson laughed. 'He didn't even have any friends. As far as I know I was the only creature on earth that had anything to do with him.'

'Well, that was useless,' I said to Angelica when we were outside. 'Maybe it was just an accident after all.'

'Maybe,' she said, 'maybe not.' Raising her sleeve, she looked at her watch. 'Goodness me, look at the time. We need to get back to the hotel. Dinner starts at five o'clock.'

I looked at my watch: nearly three thirty. 'Why the rush? Besides, we've only just had lunch!'

'We're not going back there to eat. I want to have a look round Lettice's room.'

'But w —' I started.

'Because meal times are the main event of the day in the Plaza. It's the only time we're not likely to be disturbed. So come on. Chop chop.'

Unable to think of a decent reply, I marched after her.

16. DISCOVERIES

OF COURSE IT WASN'T as simple as just going into Lettice's room. We were almost back at the hotel when Angelica mentioned that not only did she not have the key, she didn't have permission either. I said if I'd known about her plans earlier, I could've brought along the set of skeleton keys I had at the office.

'Really, Benjamin, there's no need for anything as seedy as that,' she told me as we entered the lobby. 'It's just a matter of asking for the key, that's all.'

'If it were that simple my life would be a hell of a lot easier,' I said.

Of course, she was right. Going up to the desk and spinning the most ridiculous sob story I ever heard, the receptionist handed over the key without a moment's thought. 'And I really hope you find it,' she said with a concerned look. 'Me too, my dear,' Angelica said with a small smile. 'Hatpins are so hard to come by these days.'

'Right then,' she said to me, obviously enjoying the look of disbelief on my face, 'let's go and have a root about.'

'Are you're sure this was her room?' I asked when we were both inside and the latch clicked on the door.

'Doesn't have a lot to recommend it, does it?'

'You're not kidding.'

Besides a single bed and a small, chipped wardrobe pushed against the wall to our right, the room was bare of furniture.

The décor was even more miserable: a faded brown carpet curling away from the off-white baseboard and dappled wallpaper which was yellow only because in the past the room had been used by heavy smokers. The window, with its view of the hotel across the street, looked like it had been painted shut. Despite this, the room felt cold.

Yes, this was Lettice's room all right.

'Are any of the other turrets occupied, do you know?'

'As far as I know they're all free except mine. Why?'

'It's just hard to imagine giving one of them up for something like this. What makes you think we'll find something here?'

'It was the Lieutenant. I heard him tell the manager that *under no circumstances* was Lettice's room to be let out because it still contained vital evidence. But later I overheard him tell Burt that the room was to remain closed *despite* the fact it no longer contained anything of any relevance to the case. Why would he do that, do you think?'

'You say you overheard this?'

'I imagine anyone who wasn't asleep in the lounge must've heard it, he was speaking so loudly.' She sniffed. 'Why are you laughing?'

'Good old Dingus,' I chuckled. 'You check the wardrobe, I'll look in the bathroom.'

'There's nothing in here except a few of her suits,' she called through a few minutes later. 'And — oh.'

'Something wrong?'

'One of her cases is packed. Usually the first thing she did in a new room was unpack her things.'

'Really,' I said as lightly as I could, remembering the large amount of money we'd found on her body. 'What about the suits?'

'Nothing. They're all empty.'

'Right.' In the bathroom, I checked the side of the sink, along the window frame, even the top of the cistern, but came up with nothing.

'Can I come in?' Angelica asked.

'Sure. Maybe you'll have better luck than I'm having.'

'No, I mean can I *come in?* Too much tea earlier, I'm afraid.'

Sitting on the bed, I waited for her to finish so we could leave. It seemed I'd overestimated the great Lieutenant for once.

Seconds later, a sharp exclamation from the bathroom made me jump.

'What's the matter?' I asked.

'Nothing,' she said. 'Give me a second to rinse my paws and I'll show you.'

When she came out she was waving a single sheet of white toilet paper covered in writing. 'A message.'

'What does it say?'

'It says '*We need to talk — D*'. And below that there's a number.' She passed me the sheet of paper. 'Is it the Lieutenant's writing?'

I nodded. 'I'd know it anywhere.'

'Do you recognise the number?'

'No. I've never seen it before.'

'Well then,' she said, snatching the sheet of paper back, 'the sooner we get back to my room, the sooner we can dial it.'

No sooner had she said this when we both heard the metallic click as a key rattled in the lock. Turning together, we saw the doorknob slowly turning, first right, then left, its creaking painful in the still air of the closed room When the door wouldn't budge, the knob began to twist violently, first from side to side and then roughly back and forth, the effort shaking the frame. Then, as suddenly as it started, it stopped.

After ten seconds or so, it seemed safe to breathe out again, so we did. Angelica opened her mouth to speak just as something heavy thudded against the bottom of the door.

Holding our breaths, we waited to see if the door would be struck again. Then after a few moment's more, Angelica spoke.

'Listen,' she said.

At first I couldn't hear anything. Then, out in the corridor I could hear voices, laughter.

'Whoever it was they must've gone. They must've been distracted by some animals coming out of the lift.'

Nevertheless, we decided to leave it a little while longer before opening the door. Waiting until the chatter rose to a peak and then began to recede again, I popped the catch on the door and took a look into the corridor.

Apart from something grey shuffling along at the far end, it was empty. Letting Angelica out of the room, I eased the door shut as quietly as possible.

'They certainly left their mark,' she said, pointing to the large muddy boot-print eighteen inches up the door.

'Hmm. Let's go and check that phone number.'

17. DANCING AND DEAD-ENDS

'You still haven't explained what's going on,' Angelica said as I hung up the phone, the number on the toilet paper eliciting no response. 'Why would the Lieutenant go to such trouble?'

'He'll have a reason, believe me; just like he had for telling you one story about Lettice's room and giving Burt a different one while you were in earshot. He knew it'd get back to me.'

'But why would he want it to get back to you?'

'I don't know. But I intend to ask him.' Picking up the phone again, I dialled police headquarters and asked to speak to Dingus, but he wasn't there.

'So what now?' Angelica said.

I wasn't altogether sure.

'Let's go find the Mouse,' I said eventually.

We found him in the dining room, sitting at the huge window overlooking the ocean, watching the tide inch its way towards land as he finished his meal.

'So who was it, do you think,' she asked as we made our way over, 'on the other side of that door? My money's on Burt.'

I agreed. 'I doubt there's anyone else in the hotel capable of raising a leg that high, let alone kicking a door like that. Present company excepted, of course.'

Angelica smiled. 'Presumably he wanted to check the truth of what the Lieutenant told him.'

'But why wait so long? Dingus told you about the room, what, two days ago? I imagine he'd have been in there as soon as he saw Dingus's car shudder out of the parking lot.'

'Maybe something cropped up that stopped him going in, or he was just waiting for the fuss to die down. Or maybe he *had* been in there before but hadn't found what he was looking for and was going back for another look.'

She had a point. But if he had been in before he'd missed the message on the toilet paper too. 'But why would it matter to him what was in her room?'

'Maybe he isn't just implicated in the removal of the safe,' she said.

Sitting down beside the Mouse, I asked him if he'd seen much of Burt.

'Some,' he said, sucking up the pulp at the bottom of his orange juice. 'But he's not the easiest of animals to tail.'

'Somehow I don't think we'll see him again tonight.' I told him about our little escapade. 'I think it's perhaps time to speak to the manager.'

'I had that idea myself. But he's not back until late.'

'Supposing Burt did have something to do with Lettice's death; what could he gain from it?'

'Money?' the Mouse said. 'Th —' I gave him a look to remind him that Angelica didn't know about that yet. His mouth snapped shut.

'Well, perhaps,' Angelica replied. 'She was very secretive. But if money were the reason, surely I'd have been the obvious target? I mean, I was the one staying in the turret. She'd barely set foot in hers before she decided she wanted a room on the ground floor. And you saw the room Lettice picked out for herself; nothing about it suggests she had any money. Unless Burt knew who she was already, he'd have no reason to think she was wealthy.'

'Maybe they *did* already know each other,' I said.

She sighed. 'Well, that's possible — I've no idea who she associated with. Besides using the same by-line and sharing the same house, we had very little to do with one another. But even if they did know each other, it comes back to the same thing: why go to the extent of killing her?'

'If only we could get hold of Dingus,' the Mouse said gloomily.

'Well, we can't.' Grabbing her bag, Angelica stood up. 'And as far as I can see there's nothing else we can do for the time being, so I suggest we get ready for the dancing.'

'*What?*' The Mouse and I said in unison.

'Tonight's dance night. Didn't I say? You're both coming, surely?'

'Angelica, I'm beat. Really. Perhaps if I just —'

'Nonsense. I'll see you in there in half an hour.' With that, she marched off towards the elevator.

The Mouse and I sat in silence for a while.

'Tuna oil, Mr. Spriteman?' he asked.

'Very civilised of you, Linus,' I said. 'Thank you.'

When he came back with my drink, it took longer than I expected for him to finally say his piece.

'You know boss,' he said, faking a yawn, 'I've had a long day too, so if you don't need me, I'll —'

'Uh-uh. You'll be there —'

'Oh, Mr. S!' he squeaked.

' "Mr. S" nothing. If I have to suffer this, then so do you.'

Each under our own thunder cloud, we left the bar in silence.

‡ ‡ ‡

When I stepped into the ballroom I couldn't see Angelica or the Mouse anywhere. It was a vast cavern of a room, its only concession to light at that moment the glittery curtains covering the stage. The dance floor was empty. Around its edges were dozens of small tables occupied by mostly female animals sipping drinks.

'You couldn't wait to get here, I see.' Turning, I saw Angelica, wearing yet another floral dress, this one loose fitting.

'There's no dancing,' I said, trying to sound disappointed.

'That's because the band haven't arrived yet. I've heard they're very good.' She was pointing to a small poster on the door that I'd missed: TONITE, BACK BY POPULAR DEMAND; THE CLAUDE STUBBLEFIELD QUINTET!

'I've never heard of him,' I said.

'He's probably never heard of you either,' she told me. 'Ah, Linus!'

Looking round, I caught the Mouse slowly edging into the room.

'Neither of you have changed,' Angelica noticed. 'Ah well, never mind.'

Following the eyes of those around me to the stage, I saw a small, wiry-looking mutt in a tuxedo standing on the raised platform in front of the glitter curtain. When he leaned forward to speak, a small squeal of feedback came from his microphone.

'Welcome friends,' the Dog said, its croaky voice filling every corner of the room, 'to tonight's special treat. It's been a while since they were last here but we finally managed to get 'em back. So please raise the roof for... *THE CLAUDE STUBBLEFIELD QUINTET!*'

Nothing. Nobody clapped, nobody moved. Nobody said a word.

'Right. Well, here they are anyway,' the Dog said, taking the mike with him huffily.

The curtains opened to reveal a Bulldog on drums, a very tall, thin Cat playing double bass, another Cat on guitar and an ancient-looking mutt holding a saxophone. To the right of them a gigantic Pug plonked away at the keys of a baby grand.

'It's nice to be back in Rockway, folks,' he shouted out in a voice as thick as molasses. 'This one's called "T'aint Nobody's Business if I Do!"'

151

Suddenly the dance floor was full and the seats around me were empty. I realised just in time what was coming: Angelica, her paw reaching for me across the table. Managing to swerve to one side, she grabbed the Mouse instead, leading him onto the dance floor, where they were soon swallowed up in the swirling procession of furry limbs; it seemed my crack about no-one being able to raise a leg around here was wrong. Safe in my seat, I could enjoy the music.

The band were good, especially Stubblefield. A split second before "The Sheik of Araby" started up, I saw the Mouse trying to escape; but Angelica grabbed him and he was lost to the music once more. I didn't see him again until the middle of "Abercrombie Had a Zombie", by which point he looked exhausted; also like he was enjoying himself, as was Angelica and all the other residents.

'I think it's time we had a short break up here,' Stubblefield announced after "Your Feet's Too Big". 'It's thirsty work, you know.' Grabbing a bottle of beer off a nearby table, he knocked it back in one go, at the same time signalling to the mutt in the tuxedo for two more.

'I hope you're going to give me the pleasure of the next dance, Benjamin,' Angelica said as she sat back down, dropping the Mouse into his seat like a wet rag.

'Drinks?' I asked. Both Angelica and the Mouse nodded. In the end I timed it just right; by the time I got the drinks, Stubblefield was back on stage. As Angelica led the Mouse back onto the dance floor, I tried to show my disappointment in a world-weary shrug.

'I hope you're all havin' a good time,' Stubblefield called out, draining his third bottle of beer. 'Ain't Misbehavin', nothin' like that.'

The song started slowly. With nothing much to see, I eventually looked away. As I did, two things happened at once; one, the drummer woke up and began pounding the tom-toms like he meant to burst them, and two, I spotted something flit past towards the exit. For the briefest of moments Burt's eyes locked with mine; then, realising who I was, he ran.

With the drumbeat still echoing in my ears, I shot after him towards the lounge.

By the time I reached it there was no sign of him; the lounge was empty. The only evidence that anyone had passed through was the scrunched-up rug someone had tripped over near the elevators. As I got there, the doors of the second elevator were closing; the light on the first one said it was heading for the sixth. I decided it was too obvious, and he'd probably pressed both buttons as he was picking himself up off the floor. I headed for the two doors in front of me. One lead to bedrooms; the other looked private, so I chose that. Easing it open slowly, I held my breath.

To my left was another elevator at the end of a long corridor. Ahead of me was a green fire-door, a large metal band across its middle. Pushing it open, it looked out over the back of the hotel onto a large piece of open cliff-side, with a stable over to the left. Next to it, a Horse grazed away without a care in the world.

'Has anyone just run past here?' I asked it. The Horse kept chewing. It was difficult to tell with them sometimes: of all the creatures that changed after The Terror, Horses were one of those that appeared largely *unchanged*, staying roughly the same height and remaining on four legs. The big difference was that some of them could talk. Repeating the question, I got the same response.

Looking along the cliffside I saw nothing except a few 'gulls sweeping overhead in the breeze. Maybe Burt had gone into the elevator after all. Annoyed, I went back inside and was just in time to see the door of the elevator at the end of the corridor opening. Only nobody got out. The door remained open, revealing a space inside twice the size of the hotel's other elevators. When I walked towards it and the smell of detergent stung my nostrils I realised why. This elevator wasn't for elderly patrons: it was for laundry. Inside it, there was only one button to press. When I did, the doors eased shut.

It seemed to take a long time before they reopened. I wondered if maybe this was one of those elevators that went up and down of its own accord for something to do but I doubted it: somebody had pressed that button, and pressed it from below. When the cage wobbled to a stop I pressed myself against the left-hand wall, hoping that if someone was there, they wouldn't see me straight away. With painful slowness, the doors began to open.

I stood for a few seconds listening, but there was nothing to hear. I stepped out of the cage gingerly, the smell of washing becoming even stronger.

It reminded me of a parking lot. The wall and floors were bare grey concrete but, instead of cars, large white box-shaped machines sat against the walls, along with dozens of cage-like metal baskets fitted with wheels. Keeping to the centre of the room now, I checked the ranks of machines and baskets, looking for any sudden movements. The smell of soap powder and detergent blocked out other scents, but I was still sure there was someone else there.

In a small alcove on the right I saw a lone clothes basket, its top covered with a sheet, and I knew I had to check it out.

I walked over to it on tiptoe, trying to breathe softly through my nose. Getting closer I noticed that the sheet was stretched across the top of the basket. Before I could talk myself out of it, I grabbed the sheet and yanked it back, hard.

It was the oldest trick in the book: you're looking at the thing in front of you when the thing you're really after comes at you from behind. So, as I pulled the sheet away I spun round at the same time, hoping to catch whoever was behind me off guard. But that was too clever. As I turned round, the sheet still drifting in front of my face, someone sprang up from inside the laundry basket and whacked me on the back of the head, turning the world as grey as the walls that surrounded me.

18. A SAFE EXPLANATION

'WELL,' ANGELICA SAID AS I opened my eyes, 'it looks like you got out of that dance after all.'

I was lying in bed, presumably in the room I'd booked earlier, but I wasn't sure because all I could see were the four furry faces standing at the foot of the bed, studying me. The one I didn't recognise stepped forward, one apology after another tripping off his tongue.

'Mr. Spriteman, if there's anything we can do for you, name it. Please.' Instead of answering, I looked across at the three faces I knew, and the only one I was surprised to see there.

'This is Mr. Sanders, Benji,' Dingus said, 'the manager of the Hotel.'

I should have guessed. Sanders was a fragile-looking, underweight English Setter with a spotted face. If Burt was on the make he'd have no problems with someone like Sanders.

'How do you do,' I said.

'What happened, Benji?' Dingus asked.

I explained about seeing Burt near the ballroom and racing after him, and the wallop I got on the back of the head for my trouble.

'A member of the laundry staff found you in a basket covered with a sheet,' Sanders put in. 'Gave them quite a turn.'

'I'm sorry if I upset them. What time was this?'

'It was after midnight. They came and told me straight away.'

'What time did you go chasing after Burt?' the Lieutenant asked.

I looked across at Angelica who looked across at the Mouse. 'Between eight thirty and nine?' she asked him. The Mouse nodded.

'Wait a minute,' I said, suddenly aware of the bright light streaming into the room. 'What time is it now?'

'Coming up for eleven,' Dingus said.

'You mean I've been out cold for fourteen hours?'

'Well, not out cold. You were delirious for a time, though. Luckily, there's a doctor staying in the hotel. He thought it best for you to stay here so he could keep an eye on you.'

'But fourteen hours? Anyway, what are *you* doing here?'

'I'm here about Burt, same as you. When I heard what'd happened, I got over here as soon as I could.'

'Did you find him?'

Dingus shook his head. 'We've looked everywhere. He seems to have vanished off the face of the earth.'

'And none of the hotel staff saw anything?'

Again, Sanders looked apologetic. 'I'm afraid not. The ballroom gets quite rowdy around that time and most of the staff are on hand if help is required.'

'Rowdy?'

'A couple of weeks ago the bar ran out of ginger ale,' the manager said, shuddering. 'The shortages, I'm afraid. But you are alright, Mr. Spriteman? I'd hate to think...' he looked like he couldn't wait to get out of the room. I wondered why.

'I'll be a lot better when I've had a couple of pills for my headache.' To the Lieutenant I said, 'So, this safe. What do you think happened to it?'

The Lieutenant looked at me stupidly. 'Pardon me?'

'The Hotel's safe. Seems to me it must be the same creatures who took the one in town.' Dingus's expression hadn't altered. But Sanders' had. 'You haven't told him,' I said.

Sanders rubbed his paws together and looked at the floor. 'Well, I thought that maybe the Lieutenant had more important things on his mind —'

'You mean you didn't want the publicity,' I interrupted.

'Well, there is that,' he admitted in a voice barely above a whisper. 'We had an outbreak of food poisoning here a while ago which was bad enough. Quite frankly, we can do without rumours of a thief spreading among the residents, most of whom are elderly. I'd rather not upset them unnecessarily.'

'If what I saw in the ballroom last night was anything to go by, most of the residents are only elderly when it suits them,' I told him. 'And as for rumours, I bet most of them can't get enough.'

'Well, Mr. Sanders?' Dingus said. 'Do you want me to take a look?'

The look on his face said no. 'Only if it's not too much trouble,' he said meekly.

Leaving me to have a bath and sort myself out, I arranged to meet them in fifteen minutes.

‡ ‡ ‡

Sanders' office was on the ground floor at the back of the hotel. As I opened the door, I heard Dingus as close to anger as I've ever heard him.

'And you "didn't think this was important enough" to report to the police, Mr. Sanders?'

'Well, it's just so ridiculous,' Sanders replied as I walked in. 'I mean you'd only have my word for it that there was a safe in the first place. You might have thought I was trying to scam the insurance company or something.'

'But if you didn't have a safe, what caused those marks on the rug?'

The rug was next to the wall, its tassels thick with dust. But with the exception of the indented square crimping its edges, it looked as good as new.

'Try to look at it from my point of view, Lieutenant,' Sanders said. 'A safe — not an ashtray or a few towels, but an entire *safe* — vanishes from my office — which I always keep locked, by the way — and you want me to go to the police? They'd laugh in my face. And now you're saying that the House Detective is involved —'

'He said nothing of the sort,' Angelica said, puffing herself up. 'It was you who asked me to check-up on him.'

'Okay! So, maybe Burt *is* involved,' Sanders admitted at last. 'But I still don't see how he could have got that safe out of here on his own even in the dead of night.'

'So he had an accomplice. Who does Burt associate with at the hotel?'

'He isn't paid to associate with anyone, Lieutenant,' Sanders snapped. 'Besides, he keeps everyone — myself included — at arm's length. Which suits me fine.'

'You're intimidated by him,' I said. Sanders didn't reply.

Pacing the room, Dingus unwrapped a cigar and lit it.

'Something about this room is wrong,' he said.

'There isn't a safe in it anymore?' Sanders suggested under his breath.

'What's out there?' Dingus said, pointing to the far wall.

'The edge of the cliff,' Sanders replied.

Dingus left the office. We all trailed after him.

Outside, we weren't far from the spot where I'd been looking for Burt. As before, the Horse stood grazing near his stable. But the Lieutenant seemed more interested by a mound of earth near the cliff's edge.

'What's this?' he asked, crouching beside it.

'A Molehill,' Sanders said angrily, kicking at it. 'Can't get rid of the damn things. I've tried everything to get rid of them, including poison, which is probably illegal. Not that they'll touch it. If it was up to me I'd kill the lot of them, or at least try to ban them and stop them from coming here. I don't know how you'd go about something like that, but I'd be damned willing to try.'

'That wouldn't help,' the Mouse put in. 'Ma says if you try and ban things they just go underground.'

Angelica threw back her head and laughed. It didn't take much for me to join her. 'What's so funny about that?' the Mouse asked, making us laugh even harder.

'*Moles!*' Dingus shouted out. '*Of course!*'

We all turned to look at him. One of his paws was pressed against his wrinkled face, the cigar jammed between his claws now little more than a cold stick of ash.

'Moles!' he said again. 'Don't you see?'

I didn't, but it did remind me of the small mound of earth on Alannah Foxton's lawn.

'So it's a Molehill,' I said. 'So what?'

'Benji, I've been so stupid. Boy, have I been —'

'*Poison?*' Angelica blurted out, as if the word itself was toxic. 'What *kind* of poison, Mr. Sanders?'

The hotel manager flinched. 'Well, strychnine's supposed to do the trick, so I used that. But I've never found a dead Mole yet.'

'You see, Benji? They're *clever* too.' Dingus waved the remains of his cigar at me. 'How on Earth could I have m —' he hurried back inside.

'*Strychnine?*' Angelica shrieked behind me, just as the door slammed shut.

Back in Sanders' office, Dingus was looking at the rug again.

'Tassels,' he said to himself, 'something as simple as tassels. And the earth of course.'

'What about the tassels?' I asked.

At that moment, Angelica, Sanders, and the Mouse came back into the office. The Mouse and Angelica were talking among themselves.

'It *must* be the same poison that killed Lettice,' she was saying.

'But what would your sister be doing at a Molehill, Miss de Groot?'

'I don't know. Who knows what she got up to? And it's *Angelica*, please, Linus. I've told you before.'

Suddenly all eyes were on the Basset Hound in the shabby coat. He could barely contain himself.

'You have the floor, Lieutenant.' I told him. 'Take it away.'

'Interesting choice of words, Benji,' he told me. 'I may have to, at that.

'Those tassels — the ones against the wall — what do you notice about them?'

'Well, they're flush against the wall,' Angelica remarked.

'Not quite. *Most* of them are flush against the wall. But some of them are tucked under.' He was right: a dozen or so strands were folded beneath the fabric. 'And then there's the smell of the earth.'

'What earth?'

'The earth under this floor,' he looked at us in turn. 'None of you can smell it?'

We all started sniffing the air.

'I can't smell anything except cigar smoke,' Angelica said, *sotto voce*. 'What on earth is he talking about?'

'The Lieutenant's known for having the best nose on the force,' I told her.

'But it still doesn't make any sense.'

'It will,' I assured her.

Crouching next to the rug, he said 'The reason I can smell earth in this room is because of those tassels. And if I've got this right, they're not tucked under the rug; they're trapped under the floorboards.'

Grabbing an edge, he pulled at the rug. I had a sudden flashback of the sheet in the laundry room and flinched. But instead of the rug leaping up, it stayed where it was. He pulled at it again, harder, but it still held fast, the tassels straining against his force.

'So how come they're trapped under the floorboards?' the Mouse asked.

'Because when the Moles broke in and took the safe, they didn't check the floorboards were level before covering their tracks. That's how I can smell the earth.' Giving the rug a much sharper tug, it suddenly came away from the floor, raising one of the boards a fraction. Suddenly I could smell earth, too.

'I smelled the same thing at the bank when its safe went missing,' Dingus continued. 'Only when they did the job there they must've put everything back the way it was, but the smell lingered for a while. Such a small thing,' he marvelled, 'and that's how I find out how they're doing it.'

'But exactly *how*, Lieutenant?' Angelica asked.

'The same way Moles have always done things. They might live underground, have a poor sense of smell and taste, and be almost blind, but boy, can they dig. And what they dig are burrows; tons of them. They even dig 'false' burrows to confuse predators and are extremely aggressive creatures. Also, they're clever: when they do break the surface and tunnel back into the earth, they cover their tracks by throwing the earth back so nothing can follow them. And that's *Old* moles. Imagine how big a *new* Mole could be; maybe six times the size they were before; perhaps even bigger. Think about the power they'd have; and how much bigger their burrows would have to be to accommodate them. Their tunnels are probably big enough for us to comfortably crawl around in, at least. Both the Rockway Plaza and the bank are on the cliffs, and there's maybe only a mile between the two. And it certainly wouldn't be difficult for them to tunnel up through the floor of this office. Once they're in, they dig a hole big enough for the safe to go down, then lower the safe into the hole, and move it along the tunnel to another burrow. In the meantime, other Moles would be covering their tracks. Before they replace the earth in the hole, *these* Moles could put the floorboards back in their original positions along with the rug, and *then* pack the earth back below the boards, so nobody knows they've been there. It's almost perfect.'

'Only this time' Angelica added, 'they made a fatal mistake: when they were putting the rug and floorboards back, part of the rug got caught at the side of the board, which meant it wasn't a perfect fit. And because of that, you were able to smell the freshly-turned earth through the gap.'

'But they'd still need help,' I said. 'Someone above ground telling them exactly where to dig, if their senses aren't that hot. Someone who'd know when the office was empty and for how long. An insider.'

'*Burt!*' we all said together. Sanders looked ill.

'I think I need some fresh air,' he said.

'I'll come too. I want to look at the Molehill again,' the Mouse said.

So we all trooped out, a slight breeze playing around us as we stood around the little mound of earth.

'So you think this whole cliff could be full of them?' the Mouse asked Dingus.

'Could be. Old ones and new ones, side-by-side, living separate lives. And unless we catch the new ones at it there isn't a damn thing we can do. We can't poison them, we can't smoke them out, and putting explosives down there would only de-stabilise the cliffside.'

'Is there a stream round here somewhere?' Angelica asked then. 'I'm sure I can hear running water.'

'I think you'll find it's our friend in the corner,' I told her, pointing towards the Horse as wisps of steam played around the joints in his legs.

'Oh my goodness,' Angelica said, looking over. 'He *is* desperate, isn't he? Doing it "like as racehorse", as they say.'

'What?'

'Oh, nothing. Just an expression I heard once.'

In such situations it's hard to know what to say. A minute later, the Horse's flow showed no sign of easing. Angelica was starting to look uncomfortable.

'So,' I said to her above the roar, 'what does it feel like to be in a real murder mystery for a change? Death, poisonings, mysterious disappearances — you shouldn't be short of material for a while.'

'I doubt I would be in this hotel anyway,' she snorted, squinting against the sun, 'the way the residents keep dropping like flies. It really *is* like a hospice in this place!' Remembering that Sanders was still there, she said 'I think I'll go over and have a word with him.'

'Mr. S,' the Mouse said, lowering his voice slightly, 'I was meaning to ask you before. What exactly *is* a hospice?'

'Well,' I said, looking at the Horse and the ever-widening puddle, 'if he's anything to go by, I should say it's about half a gallon.'

'Huh?' the Mouse said.

Behind me, I could hear a certain female crime writer tutting her disapproval.

19. HIDEAWAYS

'*SMUGGLING?*'

'Smuggling. It's been going on for months. We never knew how they were doing it. Until now.'

We were all in Angelica's suite, except Sanders who was in his office nursing a cup of hot sweet tea, the shock of it all proving too much for him.

'So this is the big case you've been working on?' I asked Dingus, who nodded.

'The whole area's being swamped with counterfeit goods coming in from abroad. Sometimes, we manage to stop it. Other times, it just vanishes without a trace.'

'And you never had any idea?'

'We did have one clue, but nobody took it seriously. One of our officers said he saw something with long claws and a hunched back scuttling away along the dock once. But he drinks heavily, so no-one believed him.'

'Do you think Burt's involved with the smuggling?'

'He's been observed, put it like that. But in what capacity he's involved we don't know.'

'Yesterday Angelica and I had a look around Lettice's room. Someone tried to get in after us. When they couldn't, they gave the door a kick and left a muddy boot-print behind. We think that was Burt.'

'Really?'

'Uh-huh. And while we were there we found a note scrawled on a sheet of toilet paper. It also had a phone number on it. When I dialled it I got no reply. The writing looked very much like yours. The reason we went into the room was because of the cock-and-bull story you gave Angelica, and the fact you made sure she overheard the different story you gave Burt. Care to explain?'

Dingus rubbed at his oversized ears. 'Ah,' he said.

'That's it, "*Ah*"?'

'I told Angelica and Burt different things because I knew they'd both have reasons for wanting to check Lettice's room. I left the note and number to see who'd call first. I figured if it was Angelica it would be because she was involved in whatever Lettice was up to; if Burt called it would be to find out what was going on now Lettice was dead. But if *you* called, it meant that Angelica had asked you to look into Lettice's death, which she'd hinted at when I'd spoken to her previously. If that was the case, I knew I could tell you what was going on.'

'Only you weren't in when I telephoned. And if Burt hadn't whacked me on the head you wouldn't be here now.'

'You'd have called again until you got an answer.'

I sniffed. 'Bit elaborate, isn't it?'

'It worked, didn't it? Well, kind of. I mean, not in the way I'd planned, but it still worked.' As usual with Dingus, when you looked at things from his perspective they made sense.

'So she is involved?' Angelica said sadly.

'Before we moved her body we found a large quantity of money on her.'

'Along with a bunch of coconut hairs,' I put in.

'You knew about this?' Angelica said, facing me. 'And did you just say "coconuts hairs"?'

I nodded in answer to both questions.

'Oh, well. I can't say it's a complete surprise she was up to something.' She was quiet for a few seconds before saying,

'Am I the only one who's thirsty? Benji, you must be starving; I'll order some sandwiches too.'

As we waited for the tea and sandwiches to arrive, a weird, expectant atmosphere hung over the room which lasted until the tea things arrived. 'All right, Lieutenant,' Angelica said eventually, 'just what exactly *was* she involved in? Smuggling? It must be widespread, that's all I can say.'

'It all goes back to the shortages,' he told her, filling his teacup again. 'Since The Terror, lots of businesses have gone bust because the demand for certain products doesn't exist anymore, or there aren't animals interested in taking over certain manufacturing businesses, or don't have the skills. So once the Human supplies of certain items ran out, that was that.

'Then one day we pulled in this Mutt for being drunk and disorderly. His pockets were full of things we hadn't seen in months: cosmetics, certain brands of stationery, he even had these candy bars that none of us had ever heard of before. We got the Mutt sobered up and asked him where he'd got these things. Of course he wouldn't tell us; but someone in the station noticed that certain words on the packages were spelled differently.'

'British spellings?' Angelica asked.

'Right. But we had bigger Fish to fry. And as it didn't seem to be doing anyone any harm, we left it at that. But then we got to hear about these faulty lighters on sale at a downtown market. We had something like ten singed Cats and Dogs come through our doors one week. A couple of them had to be hospitalised.'

'But lighters aren't in short supply,' I said.

'That was the next part of it: goods started appearing that *weren't* in short supply, but were cheap. Legitimate businesses were being undercut and didn't like it. A few weeks later an old lush was found dead in the park, with a bottle in a paper bag clutched in his mitt. When the lab boys analysed the contents of the bottle they found the stuff inside was so strong it could have floored an Elephant.'

'Moonshine?'

He nodded. 'Rotgut. Within ten days we had another four dead winos and two that were permanently blinded. Reports kept coming in: quack medicines, blankets which were a fire-hazard, that kind of thing. Of course, those at the top were more concerned about their financial losses. We were told in no uncertain terms to sort it out.'

'But this is small fry. Where does Lettice come into it?'

It *was* small fry. But it's grown. That's why I'm involved. Some of the stuff that's coming in now...' turning to Angelica he said, 'Have you heard of a place called Brierley Hall?'

'Why, yes, it's about an hour from where we — *I* — live. In the Old days it used to be a stately home; even had its own zoo, apparently.'

'So you know what happened there at the start of the year?'

'There was a robbery. A lot of old paintings were taken and some irreplaceable jewellery. I believe that even some of the old animals were taken too. Lieutenant,' her voice took on a tone I'd never heard before, 'you're surely not suggesting that Lettice was involved in the robbery?'

'Not that I'm aware of. At least, that's not what your local police told us.'

'What *did* they tell you, Lieutenant?'

'Well, that's the problem. The occupants of Brierley Hall want their possessions back, but resent the fact that the case is in the public eye so they aren't being as cooperative as the local police over there would like. What we do know is that certain extremely valuable goods are suspected to either be on their way over or are in this district now, so we're keeping a look out for anything that seems unusual. So far, nothing's shown up.'

'And this is where Lettice comes in?' asked Angelica.

'Not long before the robbery she was apparently spotted "acting suspiciously" around Brierley Hall. When asked what she was doing, she said she was a writer doing research for a book. Later someone read in a local paper you were both coming over here on a book promotion tour, by which time the police had heard some of the stolen goods might be heading this way. So they asked us if we could make a few discreet inquiries. Unfortunately, there was a mix-up when you arrived and we ended up searching a completely different boat. And by the time we got to the right one, we found nothing.'

'She was at home with me that night,' Angelica said. 'The night of the robbery, I mean. It was in the paper the next day. She read it aloud to me, as I recall.' Angelica suddenly went quiet.

'So if she wasn't involved in the robbery, what was she involved in?' I asked.

'I'm working on the theory that she was fencing the goods, and what I found in her room backs it up. You say Lettice spent a lot of time away from home?'

'She used to tell me she was going off to sell some of *her* books. I just thought she enjoyed being out on her own without me cramping her style.'

'What did you find in her room, Dingus?'

'Well, there was a suitcase packed full of clothes, which struck me as suggestive,' Angelica and I exchanged glances, 'but the other thing I found I took any with me: a small wooden crate. And do you know what I found at the bottom of that crate? A hell of a lot of coconut hairs.'

'Didn't you say she kicked up a stink on the boat and demanded her own cabin? I asked Angelica.

'That's right, said she wanted her own space; and when she got here, she did the same thing again with the turret... *she wanted her own rooms so I wouldn't see what she was doing.*' The look on her face was an odd mixture of shock and begrudging admiration. She turned to Dingus. 'But coconut hairs? Why would she try and smuggle coconuts? And if she did, where are they now?'

'I don't think it's so much the coconuts as what you could smuggle *inside* a coconut,' he said. 'The inside's hollow. As long as you just pierce the eyes —'

'Eyes?'

'Eyes. Coconuts have eyes. That's how you get into them. You puncture the eyes and it makes it easier to crack them open. But supposing you didn't open the coconut up after puncturing the eyes? Once you'd drained the milk out, there'd be just enough room to hide something inside — like a piece of jewellery, for instance — then the holes could easily be sealed up again. And even if customs *had* found the crate, do you think they'd really want to smash apart a bunch of coconuts?'

'Good Lord, she's done it again,' Angelica said. 'Surprised me. Twice in five minutes. *The Haggling of Rosa Worth*?' we shook our heads in unison. 'It's just like the subplot from one of my novels. The main character comes into possession of a code which he needs to sneak off the island he's being held prisoner on.

'Anyway, one of the jobs of the prisoners is packing crates of bananas to be shipped to England. So our hero writes the code onto a small piece of card, and when the prison guards are changing over, unzips one of the bananas and removes a small piece. He then slides the card into the flesh of the banana and seals it up again using a small nail from the side of the crate. Finally, he puts the banana at the bottom of the crate, thus getting the code off the island. She... she used an idea from one of my novels to do all this but changed the fruit,' she said quietly. 'Maybe I misjudged her. Maybe she did have some talent after all.'

Before she could think about it anymore, I asked her if Lettice had been carrying extra baggage.

'I don't think so, but I got on board before her. I wanted to look around the boat, you see. Get the feel of it.'

'You didn't see much of her on board?'

'After she got her own cabin, the only time I clapped eyes on her was at mealtimes.'

'What about when you got off the boat?'

'I was one of the first ones off. She'd kicked up such a fuss on board I couldn't get off quick enough.'

'Which is how she wanted it. Damn, she's planned the whole thing down to the last detail.'

Beside us, the Mouse emitted a squeak.

'This room of hers; it's on the ground floor, right?'

'She could hardly walk around the hotel with a crate and not expect to be noticed,' I said.

'Exactly. But maybe after that she didn't *have to* remove it from the room...'

Dingus slapped his head as if he was an imbecile. 'I checked it pretty thoroughly. But if they did it properly this time —'

'— you wouldn't have noticed,' the Mouse said, smiling.

'I knew there was some reason I paid your wages,' I told the Mouse, who beamed at me.

‡ ‡ ‡

'Look at the way the carpet's curled up at the edges,' Dingus said as Lettice's door closed behind us. 'Any bets?'

Grabbing a pawful, he walked it backwards until he reached the bed. Several floorboards had recently been removed and put back in place minus their screws. Stepping over the folded carpet, Dingus began lifting them up. The earth beneath had been freshly turned and was packed solid.

'Burt must have got her this room, told the Moles where to dig and Lettice passed the coconuts down to them,' he said. 'In return I'll bet they gave her some of the money they took from the safe. That would explain why she had all that money on her.'

'So she must've done the deal the day of the book launch,' Angelica said.

'But it doesn't explain why her pockets were full of coconut hairs,' I said.

'What I don't understand is if she'd done everything that was required of her, why kill her at all? And who was responsible?'

'It can't have been the Moles,' I said. 'Not even they could be that clever.' I turned to Dingus. 'Could they?'

'If they did, they lost a lot of money in the process.'

'Burt, then. He's gone AWOL.'

'But why would he if they're in on it together?'

'Some kind of row between them?' Angelica wondered aloud. 'Lettice could be funny where money was concerned. Maybe that's why he wanted to get back in the room; perhaps he thought she'd have it stashed away somewhere.

'Well, I don't know about anybody else, but I'm getting rather dizzy with it all. I suggest that maybe we adjourn for a while. And afterwards I may take another look at those letters you brought me.'

A break sounded good to me as my head was still pounding, and Dingus looked in favour of one as well. The Mouse as usual looked as if he was still raring to go.

'See if you can find Burt,' I told him when Angelica had gone back to her room.

I asked Dingus if he knew any good walks that might help clear my head. Nodding, he made a sign for me to follow.

A few minutes later, we were on the beach. Walking to the water's edge, we stopped and turned round.

'It's hard to believe, isn't it,' Dingus said, looking at the slab of cliff the town was built on, the hotel perched on the left, 'that in that cliff there could be a whole army of Moles, burrowing away. And we didn't even think about them.

'Well, so long, Benji.' Clapping me on the back, he walked back up the beach.

Realising that I had the beach to myself, I suddenly felt lonely and depressed. With the sun in my eyes, I started thinking about the hotel's residents and what The Terror had done for them, turning a bunch of elderly domestic animals on four legs into elderly hybrids on two who were no better off than they were before. And for what? To sit in a chair all day waiting for it to end. Unless you liked dancing, that is. My headache suddenly worse, I reluctantly made my way back to the hotel.

Going up to my room I lay on the bed, only intending to shut my eyes for a few minutes. When I opened them again, the room was in darkness. Suddenly craving company, I headed for the Mouse's room and found his door unlocked. He was over at the window, looking out at the cliff.

'Anything to report?' I asked.

'No. No sign of him anywhere. Nothing suspicious going on. It's as quiet as the grave. I did see the Lieutenant though, a few minutes ago, wandering up and down.'

I made a decision. 'Listen, Linus, I'm going back to the city tomorrow. I don't feel too good and this place is starting to depress me. You think you can cope with the Lieutenant and Angelica?'

I'd expected a torrent of questions about why I was going but he never even turned round. His face was pressed up against the window. 'What is it?'

'Might be nothing,' he said, his voice steaming up the glass. 'But — look — it's doing it again.'

I was just about to ask what he was talking about when I saw it: a large 'gull, swooping in the air before diving towards the earth at breakneck speed. When it was only a matter of feet from the ground it stopped its descent, took a sharp left and glided maybe a foot above the ground.

'That's the third time,' the Mouse said. 'But watch what it does next.'

While he'd been talking, the 'gull had dropped onto the grass and waddled back to the point at which it had descended before bearing left. It appeared to be looking at something we couldn't see, and when its beak started opening and closing I thought I could just make out its cry. Then it leapt up into the air, hovering about five feet from the ground, with its head still angled down towards whatever it had been looking at. It hovered there for perhaps thirty seconds before flying off completely.

'Did it do that before?' I asked.

'No; the other times it did what you saw. Look,' moving away from the window slightly, he pointed over to the right, 'the Lieutenant's coming back.'

'And how,' I said.

He was striding purposefully; he only walked like that when he was onto something important. Stopping at roughly the same spot that the 'gull had been diving at, he bent slightly before crouching down and looking at the grass. Only for some reason I didn't think he was looking at the grass; I thought he was looking *beyond* it.

'What's that noise?' the Mouse said, opening the window as far as it would go. 'It sounds like a Dog barking; listen!'

'I can't hear anything,' I said.

The Mouse and I jerked backwards, mirroring the Lieutenant's movements on the ground. Then we watched him bend forward again.

'What's he doing now?' the Mouse asked.

'Wiping the spray of dirt that just shot up from his shoes. Come on,' I said, heading for the door.

As soon as I opened the door leading out onto the cliffs, I heard the Dog barking. A few of the residents were outside now, trying to find where the noise was coming from. Dingus spotted us and walked over.

'I was just coming to get you,' he said. 'It's up the back here. Linus, do you think you could keep these animals away for me?'

Following him up the cliffside through the lengthening grass, the barking of the unseen Dog became louder, occasionally changing to a snarl or a low growl. Thanks to the lights from some of the residents' windows, I saw the pile of earth flattening the long grass.

'Don't go too close, Benji,' Dingus said, reaching into his pocket and handing me a flashlight, 'he's pretty riled up. And be sure you don't fall in.'

Standing beside the pile of earth, I turned on Dingus's flashlight.

From above it was hard to judge how deep the hole was — but as the small, stocky dog inside was nowhere near close to freeing itself despite its frantic efforts, I judged about five feet. Across, it was much bigger than that, say eight feet: wide enough anyway for another, much larger Dog to be lying face down in it and not touching the sides. All the time as I shone the torch around, the smaller Dog continued its barking in front of the body. It was only when I nearly dropped the flashlight that he stopped.

As the light passed over the larger Dog, I saw something long, white and thin in the small of its back, right under its ribcage. It was sticking up at an odd angle and had thick, sticky blood congealed around it, turned pink by the beam of the flashlight.

'Burt,' Dingus said. I nodded.

'How are we going to get him out? I don't want to take my chances with the Dog like that.' The Dog barked even louder, as if it knew it was being talked about.

'Tricky,' I said. And then, something very nice and very rare happened to me.

Unlike the Lieutenant, it's not often that I'm troubled by inspiration. But on the few occasions when it does strike, I enjoy it.

Laying flat over the lip of the hole, I stuck my head over the edge, so the Dog's snapping jaws were only a foot or so away when it jumped. Then, very slowly, I stuck one of my paws down into the hole.

'Benji, what are you doing?' Dingus called out.

'Oh, he's not going to hurt me,' I shouted above the barking. 'Are you, Trix?'

Straight away the barking stopped. Below, Trix wagged his tail.

Leaning down beside me, Dingus watched as I patted at Trix, who, as well as jumping, was now trying to lick my outstretched paw.

'How —' he started.

'Oh, just a guess, you know,' I said, as modestly as I could.

Part Three: Of Moles and Magpies

‡ ‡ ‡

20. DISCUSSIONS

'WELL I JUST WISH you'd told me, that's all,' Angelica said. Next to her on the back seat Trix wriggled about, his tongue lolling with the motion of the car.

'I told you, there wasn't time,' I said. 'It all happened so quickly. Besides, it sounds like you were busy anyway.'

'That's not the point and you know it,' she replied, barely audible over Trix's panting.

The three of us — Dingus, the Mouse, and myself — had been up all night. By the time the local police showed, it was well after midnight, and we'd had a hell of a time trying to keep the old dears away from the crime scene. In the end, the Mouse had to rig up a makeshift tent around the hole using a bed-sheet he borrowed from the laundry. Thankfully, the police arrived not long after.

Once we'd explained the situation, it was left to me to remove Trix from the hole. When I'd got him clear of the drop, he leapt from my arms straight into the Mouse's. When we finally managed to tear him away, we got Trix checked over by a local vet we'd had to drag out of bed. He said apart from being a bit underweight and in serious need of a bath, Trix was fine.

When pictures had been taken, the body was looked over and the murder weapon removed from Burt's back. Dingus looked at it thoughtfully for a while before bagging it up. Finally, the body was removed from the hole.

Then Dingus surprised me by jumping in the pit. He looked up at me eagerly.

'I don't think Burt came in this way,' he said when I joined him. 'Digging a hole this size, he would've been spotted. A lot of the residents walk along here during the day.'

'It could've been dug recently. We know they work quickly.'

'Unh-unh,' he said, shaking his head. 'This wall's been freshly dug.' He rapped the earth to our left. 'And the body's facing outwards. He came through from below.'

'You think he knew his way around the Moles' tunnel system?'

'That, or he was taken against his will. Either way, I think he was killed somewhere else. Then they put him in here and filled in the hole after them.'

'So what the hell was Trix doing down here?' I said. 'Working on the assumption Betsy Oatland took him, that means she's either in with the Moles or Burt.'

'Or both,' Dingus added. 'If Trix has been in the Moles' burrows all the time, it would explain the lack of sightings.'

Back at the hotel, I, along with the Lieutenant and the Mouse, had passed various theories around between us, each one more far-fetched than the last, while Trix snored contentedly next to us. But in the end it all seemed to come back to the same thing: What part did Trix play in everything, and why was he in the hole in the first place?

After a while I noticed daylight streaming through the windows. Deciding that some shuteye was in order, Dingus left the hotel, while the Mouse and I headed for the elevator. Only we never got there.

'Where have you been?' Angelica called, coming down the staircase.

She looked as shocked to see us as we were to see her.

'Talking,' I told her. 'And now it's time for bed.'

'Time for bed? It's time to get up,' she said incredulously. 'Not that I've had much sleep, looking over everything you gave me. I thought we could discuss it over breakfast.'

'Breakfast?' I looked at my watch.

'You can't have been up all night talking. What's been going on?'

'You know, breakfast sounds like a good idea,' I said, walking towards the dining room, leaving Linus to explain the night's events.

After breakfast, I phoned Alannah Foxton to give her the good news. She emitted a shriek of joy down the line that nearly pierced my eardrum. Once she'd calmed down, I told her we'd bring Trix over right away.

'You can drop me off in the town after that,' Angelica said, standing next to me.

I decided not to argue. 'Sure. A bit of sightseeing?'

Not amused, she let out a heavy sigh. 'After reading all your case notes, I think I need to look at those stories of yours, so I've phoned Mr. Laidlaw to bring forward our interview. After which, I can go to your office and read the stories.'

'You have some ideas?'

'I might have,' she said sniffily. I got the feeling that she knew something but didn't want to share it.

As we pulled into Alannah Foxton's drive, I noticed the Mouse's eyes starting to droop. They snapped open when Trix leapt from Angelica's open window and shot off up the path. Within seconds the Dachshund was missing again, this time in a sea of bristling fur and wagging tails. At the centre of it all was Alannah Foxton, looking like she'd just won a million dollars. 'Go round to the summerhouse,' she called above the din, 'Liney knows the way.' When we got there, he plonked himself down into a wicker chair, he went out like a light.

'Oh, look, bless him.'

It was Alannah, standing in the doorway with a tray full of drinks, Trix by her side.

'We had a long night,' I explained. Angelica muttered something unintelligible.

'Let's go sit in the garden and leave him in peace,' Alannah said, moving away.

'So who took him, where did you find him?' she asked when we were settled.

'It looks like Betsy Oatland snatched him. We found him in a hole next to the body of an old Mutt called Burt who was the hotel detective at the Rockway Plaza. Does his name mean anything to you?' shocked, she shook her head.

'But why take him at all?'

'We're not entirely sure,' I yawned. 'You said that Trix was usually one of the first to come to you when he heard food being put out. Perhaps, if he was the first one out of the house, he was taken because he was the easiest to take.' Yawning again, I shut my eyes and stretched my paws in the air. 'We don't know yet.'

'This is a lovely garden,' Angelica put in. 'I'm sorry, Benji should have introduced us. Angelica de Groot.'

'That name rings a bell... no, don't tell me...'

'Mr. Spriteman?'

Opening my eyes, I saw a large, white eager face staring down into mine. 'Angelica says she has to go now,' the Mouse informed me.

I was about to say we'd only just arrived when it dawned on me. 'How long have I —'

'Long enough,' Angelica said, standing a few feet away with her purse slung over her arm. 'But it gave Alannah and I plenty of time to have a nice chat.' She smiled at me sweetly. Too sweetly I thought.

'Benji, I can't thank you enough.' Standing on tiptoe, Alannah Foxton gave me a huge sloppy kiss and a hug. Over her shoulder I saw the Mouse enjoying my discomfort. 'I'll um, send you the bill in a few days,' I said, awkwardly.

I told "Liney" to drop me off at the office and, after he'd taken Angelica to the Henderson Building, I told him to go home for a nap.

'I've just had one,' he pointed out.

'Well, have another. Or go and play with your brothers and sisters.'

'And what are you going to do, Benji?' Angelica asked.

'I'm going to have a nap too.'

'*You've* just had one!' she spluttered.

'I closed my eyes for a few minutes, that was all.'

'So you heard everything Miss Foxton and I were discussing?' she said, slyly.

'Sure I did,' I lied. 'Every word.'

Turning to look at her in the back seat, I wondered what the strange smile on her face was for.

21. BETSY / BURT / BUPKIS

M Y HOPES FOR A few hours' sleep got no further than plonking myself in my chair and unlacing one of my shoes when the phone rang.

'Spriteman.'

It was Dingus. 'How soon can you get to the police station?'

'Which one?'

'Ours.'

'Why?'

'Betsy Oatland just handed herself in.'

'I'm on my way.'

Dingus was waiting for me in his office. Finishing the nub of his cigar, he filled me in. 'She was holed up in Rockway and picked up the early edition of the *Herald*. Burt's murder is on the front page. Scared her out of her wits. Says she got the first bus here.'

'Good thing for us she was staying in Rockway,' I said. 'If we'd been waiting for her to read about it in *Fuller News* she'd have been none the wiser in August.'

In a room at the back of the station, Betsy Oatland twitched behind an untouched cup of coffee. Her eyes darted back and forth across the small room. When she saw the Lieutenant she started to rise from her seat. As he introduced us both I took a quick look at her.

She was a mousy little Border Terrier with short, wiry, mostly white fur who looked like nothing was too much trouble for a quiet life.

'Why did you come here, Betsy?' Dingus asked.

'I want police protection. Because of what they did to Li.'

'Li... You mean Mr. Burt?'

'Burt wasn't his real name. His real name was Bupkis. Lionel Bupkis. He had to... he changed his name to Burt later. It was the only way he could get work after... after what happened at his last job.'

'What happened at his last job?'

'He... he was in charge of security. A security officer.' She played with the ruff of fur at her neck.

'Where was that, Betsy?'

She looked at me for a second then back at Dingus. 'The bank in Rockway. The manager caught him trying to break the combination of the safe. He said he wouldn't press charges if Li left straight away.' When she took a gulp of her cold coffee Dingus and I exchanged glances quickly: *That's how the Moles knew!*

'You said you want police protection Betsy, because of what they did to Lionel. Who are "they"?'

'The Moles. They're the ones who killed him.' She looked at us both to see if we believed her. 'Stealing the safes, that was Li's idea. He was obsessed with them. When he was at the bank he said he thought he knew how to crack the combination. But he didn't, and then he got caught.' She took a gulp of coffee. 'Eventually he got the job at the hotel. He knew where the safe was, but the manager was careful. But when he heard about the Moles and the smuggling, Li got this idea that if he gave the Moles the exact locations of the bank and hotel safes they could tunnel and get them, open them underground and split the money. And he said if they didn't split the money he'd tell the police about the smuggling. He thought he was so clever.' She laughed bitterly.

'The Moles agreed to it?'

She nodded. 'It was easy, Li said: the hotel safe was on the ground, and it had a wooden floor. And the bank's safe was in a crypt below the main building which was about a hundred years old, so with their digging skills they'd have no trouble getting to it. So they took the bank's safe and nobody was any the wiser.'

'So what was the problem?'

'Li could be suspicious. He was still sure he could crack the combinations of the safes himself and said he'd meet them underground to do it. But they said they'd break them open themselves. Then the first time he met them to split the money he said they'd short-changed him. But Li had no way of knowing one way or the other, did he? Besides, he was doing other business with them.'

'What sort of business?'

'I don't know. Something big, he said. But it might have just been talk.'

'Do you know how much money he did get?'

'No. But he showed me some of it. It looked like a lot to me.' Falling silent, she ran her claws across the table, around the coffee cup.

'What about the Hotel safe?' Dingus asked.

'Same thing again,' she said. 'He told them where to find it and the best time to get at it. Li said the manager always emptied the safe on the same day of the week, so he arranged it for the Moles to get in the night before, so they'd be guaranteed a fair bundle. He said if he didn't get a decent amount this time he'd know they'd ripped him off. But after that robbery he said his share was even less. He was furious.'

'But it was only a hotel safe,' I put in.

'That's what I said, but he told me I knew nothing. He was just being greedy and selfish. Son of a bitch was always selfish. Never let me have my own ideas...' her claws scratched at the table.

'So what did he do?' Dingus asked.

'He went crazy! He knew he couldn't go to the cops because he was implicated in both robberies. He said he was going to sort those Moles out even if he had to blow up the whole cliff to do it. It was mostly talk again. Most things with Bupkis were, apart from getting the Dog. Then, I knew he'd really flipped. The Dog — it *was* Trix, wasn't it? He didn't come to any harm…?'

'He's fine, Betsy. Benji here was looking into his disappearance.'

She looked at me properly for the first time. 'You came because of Trix?'

'It ties into other things I'm working on,' I told her. 'Why did he want a dog in the first place?'

She took a deep breath. 'One day, I don't know why, he decided to pick me up from Miss Foxton's. While he was waiting, he saw the Dogs running about and said he wanted the Dachshund.'

'Not just any Dog? It had to be Trix?'

'There was this Old Dog book in his house with a page on Dachshunds; about how small and strong they were, and how they'd been used as Hunting Dogs in the past and sent down holes to dig out prey. He said he could train Trix to do that. I told him Trix was domesticated, but he wouldn't listen.'

'It wouldn't have done him much good anyway without knowing where the Moles were,' I said.

'Oh, he said he knew *exactly* where they were and how to get at them.'

'But he must've met them somewhere, to get his money after the robberies. Let's say he did know how to get at them: I can't see a small Dog like Trix being much use against a gang of Moles.'

'He didn't want Trix to fight them. He was going to take him down with him the next time he saw the Moles. And if he didn't get what he wanted from them, he was going to let the

Dog loose to dig more holes — he thought that way Trix might find some of their money. And if he didn't, the extra digging would de-stabilise the cliffside. Crazy.' Betsy raised her paws palms upward to the ceiling.

'And what about Trix?'

'He said he'd try and get him back out if he could, maybe offer to give him back for a ransom. But knowing Bupkis, he'd probably have left him in there.'

'But you still took him.'

Instead of flaring up at me, she looked at me sadly. 'That's the one thing I can't forgive him for. I really liked Miss Foxton — she was always so good to me — and I really liked the Dogs too. He *knew* that. He said if she had that many, she wouldn't miss one. He tried to sweeten the pill by saying if things went well I could quit my jobs. I didn't believe him, but I didn't have a choice. If I'd said no —' she swiped the air violently with her paws. 'That was one thing he *was* good at. I just had to hope Trix would get out after all.'

'So how did you take him?'

'I went there on a day Miss Foxton wasn't expecting me. She has a set routine, and always feeds the Dogs at the same times. After she's done that, she goes for a bath. If the weather's nice she leaves them to run around the garden. At the time she'd have been taking her bath I was stood at the fence loosening one of the panels. Because the Dogs knew who I was, they didn't make no noise. With the panel loose, it was just a matter of calling Trix over, getting him through the gap, then taking him to the car.'

'Weren't you worried about being seen?'

Betsy Oatland surprised me by smiling. 'Nope,' she said, folding her paws across her chest, 'I wasn't worried at all.'

'You wanted to be caught,' Dingus stated.

'I told Li the street was always empty all the time, but usually there was somebody walking about. If we had seen someone, I was going to make sure they remembered us. But the luck was all his that day.'

I decided to see if the Mouse was right about something. 'You wrote a story about the whole thing, didn't you?' I said.

Her mouth dropped open. 'How did you know that?'

'Rusty Laidlaw passed it onto me in connection with the poison-pen letters he's been receiving.'

She looked at me blankly, and then at Dingus. 'I don't know anything about that.'

'So why did you send him the story?'

It took her about four attempts to get the words out. 'After I took Trix — well, *before* I took him too — I felt awful. I phoned in sick the week before; I couldn't face Miss Foxton. I told Bupkis if we took Trix I couldn't go back there. I was amazed when he agreed. He even gave me some money; enough to move away so I couldn't be contacted by anyone. Then I took him at his word and quit all my cleaning jobs.'

'So what did you do instead?'

'Nothing. I brooded. I thought about how much I hated him. You know before we took Trix he even made me write out a plan so I wouldn't mess it up? One day I was feeling sorry for myself and I read the plan again. It was like this really sad story without an ending. So I wrote it out in more detail and added one. I thought it might make me feel better. Instead it made me feel worse. But at least it was *mine*.'

'It was a good story,' I told her. 'Well-written.'

She laughed. 'It is?'

'I'm not the only one who thinks so. The editor of *No Shit Sherlock* thinks so too. But why go to all the trouble of sending it there?'

'One of my cleaning jobs was in the Henderson Building. There was a fiction magazine on the floor above. After a sleepless night I went in early one morning to drop it in their mail. I was just about to do it when I heard someone. Then

I remembered there was *another* magazine on the next floor. So I ran up the stairs and dropped it there instead.'

'But you didn't sign it, or leave an address.'

'I didn't want it published; it was a confession. It was like putting a message in a bottle and throwing it in the ocean. The chances are nobody's ever going to see it.'

'But at the same time, folks should know what we'd done. We deserve to be punished. But what it said in the paper... not even *he* deserved that. They must be savages.'

'You're still convinced that he was killed by the Moles?' Dingus asked.

'He was found in a Mole-hole, wasn't he?'

'But if he went down there with Trix to sort things out, why kill him and not the Dog?' I asked.

'Because they're animal lovers? Who knows?'

'The money,' Dingus asked. 'What happened to it?'

'He hid it in his house, I imagine.'

'Where did he keep Trix?'

'In the house. He was a quiet Dog.'

'Where's the house?'

Dingus wrote down the address she told us.

'Ever see anyone else in the house?'

'Nobody. But I was only ever there once.'

'What happened?'

'I walked in and he was on the phone. He hung up and asked me what I was doing there.'

'You didn't hear any of the conversation?'

'I heard him say someone was being difficult. That was all.'

Dingus smiled. 'Thanks, Betsy. Last question: you still want police protection?'

'Nah, I'll manage,' she said with a smile. 'I'll just have to get an apartment on the top floor of somewhere.'

‡ ‡ ‡

'What are you going to do with her?' I asked in the corridor.

'No idea,' Dingus said, yawning. 'I can't think straight. Either I've had too much coffee or not enough.' He thought about it. 'Let's go get some more.'

In the Lieutenant's office we were on our second cups when the phone rang. Soon as we'd finished we were going to Bupkis's apartment, which meant a further visit to Rockway. I was thinking of setting up another office there.

'Yeah?' Dingus said, stifling a yawn as he held the phone.

From the other side of the desk I heard what sounded like a miked-up Chimpanzee leaving an obscene message. Apart from the odd 'uh-huh', Dingus said nothing.

'Clancy,' he told me, putting the phone down. 'He wants us over there straight away. It's about the weapon that killed Bupkis.'

'Does he know what it is?'

'Yeah, he knows what it is.' Dingus sighed.

'So what's the problem?'

'The problem,' he said, grabbing his trench coat, 'isn't *what* it is. The problem is he can't believe that it *is* what it is.'

'What the hell does that mean?' Dingus shook his head. He didn't stop shaking it until we were in his car.

22. SAWN-OFF

'W HAT'S ON YOUR MIND?' Dingus asked on the way there.

'I was thinking about what Betsy heard at Bupkis's place, about someone being difficult. It sounds like a pretty good description of Lettice to me.'

'Do you think Burt killed her?'

'Who knows? He was trying to get into her room for some reason. Working at the hotel, it would've been easy enough to drug her food if he'd known about the strychnine. But if he killed Lettice, who killed *him*? We're back with the Moles.'

'Betsy did say she thought he was dealing with them in other ways,' Dingus agreed. But he didn't seem any more convinced than I was.

At the coroner's office, we were told to go straight to the lab. Clancy was waiting for us with an expression on his face that I doubted I'd ever see again: one of almost complete bafflement. For the few seconds it lasted it was a joy to behold.

'So doc,' Dingus asked, 'what's the big mystery?'

'It's the murder weapon,' he said, waving his paws around. 'You're not going to believe me. *I* didn't believe me. So I decided to check it one last time under the microscope. And you know what I found? A tiny piece of lettuce.'

Dingus shook his head, stunned. '*You mean she was stabbed as well?*'

'What?' Clancy snapped.

'You never mentioned stab wounds before, doc,' I said.

'Not lettice; *lettuce*. That stuff I've seen Dingus picking out of his sandwiches. A minute particle up at the blunt end. I even had Teo check I wasn't seeing things. But that's what it was: a tiny piece of lettuce.'

'Why on earth would it have a piece of lettuce stuck on it?' Dingus said.

'Because, Lieutenant, your murder weapon, despite its unusual length, is actually nothing more than part of a very large, sawn-off —'

'*Tooth.*' A chill ran through me as I said it.

Clancy looked the way I must look when Dingus stole *my* thunder. 'How the hell could you know that? Look, I'll show you.' As he brought it over, Dingus looked at me for an explanation.

All cleaned up, it looked rather ordinary, despite its length. It certainly didn't look like the bloody object Dingus had yanked out of Bupkis's back.

'Okay, Spriteman,' Clancy said, his arms folded across his chest. 'How did you know it was a tooth?'

'Because I've seen it before,' I said quietly, still looking at it.

'At the Plaza; in the hole,' Dingus said.

'No, somewhere else. With its twin, in someone's mouth, usually covered in mushed-up vegetables. My God, he went through with it after all.'

'Who did?' Clancy asked.

'Harvey,' I said.

23. HARVEY

IN THE ELEVATOR I explained about Harvey: big harmless lovable Harvey, who nobody took seriously because of his oversized teeth; Harvey, who couldn't get a regular job and worked as my informer; Harvey, who must've lived a life of constant torment and frustration, but who was possessed of the kind of inner resolve which could let him take a chisel to his own teeth in order to shorten them.

'When did you last see him?' Dingus asked.

'A week, two weeks ago. I tried to contact him after that but he wasn't at home.'

'What does he look like?'

I gave him a description. 'But then he had those two enormous teeth covering half his face. If he doesn't have them any more he'll be able to eat properly, and his face will have filled out. He could look completely different.'

'We'll circulate a description anyway.'

'You do that. I'm going to find him.'

Dingus narrowed his eyes. 'You sure that's a good idea?'

'I know him as well as anybody; at least I thought I did. Drop me at my office and I'll get the Mouse to tag along.'

Then I remembered: The Mouse, cornered by a Rabbit roughly the same height at the book launch. I told Dingus.

'Stop at the next callbox, will you?' I said.

Phoning the Spayley residence, I was told Linus got bored and had gone back to the office.

Back in the Lieutenant's car I found myself tapping my teeth. 'I wondered what he did with the other one,' I said.

'Pardon me?'

'The tooth. I wonder what Harvey did with the other tooth.'

'Oh Jeez. And you want to go talk to him?'

'I told you, I'll have the Mouse with me. Any sign of trouble we'll be out of there straight away, believe me.'

When the elevator doors opened on the fourth floor, I immediately heard two things: the mutt at the end of the corridor who spoke so loudly on the phone the entire floor could hear his conversations, and from my office a sound I very rarely heard there: laughter.

Shoving my head round the door the laughter stopped. Taki and Angelica, sitting side-by-side at Taki's desk, stared up at me.

'So I don't need to do introductions,' I mumbled. To Angelica I said, 'How did the interview with Laidlaw go?'

'It was satisfactory,' she said. 'But my interview with Peaches on the other hand was much better.'

I'd heard the name before somewhere. 'Peaches?'

'Laidlaw's cleaner. Nice girl. Stroke of luck she was there, really. And what about you? A productive few hours?'

'Very. Burt's not Burt, he's Bupkis. And we now know what the murder weapon is. The Mouse here yet?' I asked Taki.

'In there.'

I started to walk away. There was a none-too-subtle cough behind me. I turned round.

'*Well?*' Angelica said. 'The murder weapon; what is it?'

'A tooth,' I told her, stepping into my office before she had a chance to respond.

The Mouse was sitting in the client's chair, looking bored. I picked up the phone and dialled Harvey's number. No answer. Getting my address book from the second drawer, I tore out the O's and told the Mouse to start the car. Then I grabbed the huge pile of stories on my desk and took them through to Angelica. She had the same stunned expression on her face I'd left her with.

'I don't know how long we'll be,' I said, dropping the stories onto the desk in front of her.

She ignored them. 'Did... Did you say a *tooth*?'

'That's right, a great big one. Good luck with the stories.' Slamming the door behind me, I hurried down to the car.

'Where to?' the Mouse asked.

'I've no idea,' I said. 'But this is the address.' I handed him the torn page and pointed.

'I've never heard of it.'

'I thought you knew everywhere. But you know the district?'

'Y-yes,' he said, his voice going up a notch. 'Who are we going to see?'

'Possibly the Rabbit who buttonholed you at Sidwells. Remember him?'

'I remember that he never stopped talking.'

'What about?'

'It was hard to tell. I was trying to listen to him and keep an eye on everything at the same time. He spoke very quickly, but most Rabbits do. And with the noise in there it was quite hard to understand what he was saying.'

'He'd have been hard to understand anyway if he'd only been able to speak properly for the past few days. What did he look like?'

'I didn't really pay him much attention. Why? Who was he?' I told him.

'Wow. And you think he killed Burt?'

'Well, "Bupkis", which it turns out is Burt's real name. And if he was at Sidwells maybe he had something to do with Lettice's death too.'

'But he's your informer,' the Mouse said simply.

'So I'm a bad judge of character,' I said as I looked out the window.

Twenty minutes later, we were driving through streets I hadn't known existed. All the colour seemed to have been leeched from the buildings, and the only greenery to be seen were the weeds sprouting up through the broken sidewalks. Few of the buildings we passed had any glass in them, and most of them were fire-damaged.

These haunted brick shells were soon replaced by wooden ones, row upon row of cock-eyed lean-tos, seemingly held together by grease and sheer good fortune. Down here, The Terror had changed nothing: poor Humans had kept poor animals and now they'd inherited the squalor, if they were still here at all.

Eventually passing the last of the lean-tos, the road split in two. I remembered Harvey saying his place was off the beaten track on the right, past the houses. After shuddering up a dirt road for a quarter of a mile, we saw two wooden shacks in the distance, leaning against each other for support.

They looked empty, but the Mouse and I stuck together anyway. Knocking on what I hoped was Harvey's door got me half a dozen splinters. While I picked them out, the Mouse was looking through a window.

'Anything?'

'Hard to tell through the grime,' he said, lowering himself on his haunches. 'What a dump. If he did kill someone maybe it was for the money. You can see why he'd want to get away from a dive like th —'

'Help you at all?' a voice said behind us. The Mouse squeaked. Slowly, I turned round.

A few feet away, a scruffy Rabbit dressed in plaid was watching us carefully, but not suspiciously, his paws holding the small roll of fat on his sides.

'I hope so. I'm looking for Harvey O'Keefe. I believe he lives here?'

'Well,' the Rabbit said with a grunt, shifting his paws to support his back, 'that's open to debate. He did say he'd see me later, but I wouldn't be surprised if I never set eyes on him again.'

My fur began to prickle ever so slightly. 'Really?'

'You know Harvey, I take it,' he said, watching me closely. 'I mean to *look* at?'

'I know he's got big teeth.'

'Well, he ain't got 'em any more. At least not growing out of his mouth.' My fur prickled a bit more.

'What happened to them?'

'Why, I sawed 'em off myself. Was like a different animal after I'd done it.'

A different animal. 'How different?'

'More alive, like he had a lot of catching up to do. Didn't have much of a life with them teeth in. When I started sawing he was shaking so much I had to get him a drink to steady him. But when I'd done he said he hadn't been scared at all, just excited. I think he was a little crazy with it all.' This time, the prickle went up my back.

'What happened to the teeth?'

'He took 'em with him.'

'Where to?'

'Rockway. Said he'd send me a postcard and bring me a little something back as a "thank you", but if I was him I'd leave this craphole behind. 'Specially now he's got a little money.'

My head felt like it was full of fluttering Birds. 'He's gone to Rockway? And he's got money?'

'Yup. Quite a bit, he said. Imagine you need money to go to a place like that.'

'Did he tell you where he was staying?'

'No. Just said he'd check into a hotel when he got there.'

The Mouse started to speak. 'The Pl —'

'We'd have seen him,' I interrupted. 'Surely we'd have seen him? And he took his teeth with him?'

'Tidied 'em up a bit and put them in his case.'

'Did he say why he took them?'

'Nope. If it was me I'd throw 'em in the sea.'

As the Mouse and I headed back to the car, the Rabbit followed us over.

'If he comes back, who shall I say's looking for him?'

'Hopefully you won't get the opportunity,' I told him as we drove away.

24. HARVEY EXPLAINS

IT WOULD'VE BEEN TOO much to hope that Harvey *was* staying at the Rockway Plaza, but we went there anyway. Unfortunately nobody could recall a Rabbit having stayed at the Plaza for months. While we were enquiring, Sanders came out of his office and invited us in.

'Any progress?' he asked, rubbing his paws together.

I made a few encouraging noises. 'Does the name Harvey O'Keefe mean anything to you?' he shook his head.

'We think he's staying at a hotel in the town. How many are there?'

He didn't have to think about it. 'Twenty-seven,' he said.

'We'll need their phone numbers.'

'There's a directory on the shelf. You can call from here.'

Sitting down, we waited for Sanders to go, but he played dumb, looking at the phone expectantly. 'Aren't you going to —?'

'The second you leave, Mr. Sanders,' I said, smiling up at him.

'You don't need me for anything?'

'You've been a great help. Thank you.'

Reluctantly, he left. When the door closed the Mouse got the directory and picked up the phone. I shook my head.

'Check he's not standing outside,' I whispered.

When he opened the door, Sanders was standing there, looking like he was waiting for a bus. 'You sure you don't need me for anything?' he asked.

'Absolutely,' I called back. As Sanders slinked off, I told the Mouse to keep watch and make sure I wasn't overheard.

'He thinks he'll find out which hotel our murderer is staying at,' I said quietly in answer to the Mouse's unasked question, 'bad publicity for them. Grubby world, the hotel business.' Picking up the phone, I rang the first number.

'Good afternoon to you. I'd like to speak to a guest of yours, if that's possible? I'm afraid I have to cancel our meeting for later today. His name's Harvey O'Keefe... nobody of that name? I must have written down the wrong number. Sorry to have bothered you.'

After reciting the same little speech a further twenty-one times, the words were beginning to feel like slush in my mouth. And what were the chances that Harvey would book into a hotel in his own name anyway? Was he *that* crazy?

'Hello, Sea Breezes Inn, can I help you?'

'Good afternoon, I'd like to speak to a guest of yours, Harvey O'Keefe. I'm afraid I can't make our meeting later and —'

'Just a moment please. I'll try to put you through.'

Evidently he *was* that crazy.

'Mr. O'Keefe isn't answering. Is there anything I can do to help?'

Yes, don't tell him I've called. 'No, it's okay. Thanks for your help.'

The Sea Breezes Inn wasn't in the same league as the Plaza, but it looked like a nice little place anyway, set well back from the road. In its understated lobby, the few animals sitting there looked decades younger than those at the Plaza.

I wondered if Harvey was back yet. If he was, it was a fair bet the receptionist had mentioned my call; the idea of Harvey waiting for us in his room with his newly-sharpened tooth at the ready wasn't a pleasant one.

'I think it's time for you to use some of that Mousy charm,' I told my operative.

He was in character before he reached the reception desk. 'Um, excuse me? I was wondering if you could show me the way to the *um...* nearest restaurant?'

'Why certainly,' the matronly Alsatian behind the desk said, already leading him towards the exit. 'Now. Stand beside me and you'll have a clear view. See? First of all, you have to turn left as soon as —'

I smiled. Apparently there wasn't a female on the planet who could resist his little-lost-Mouse routine.

I gave it a few of seconds before heading towards the desk, making sure that nobody looked up from their newspapers. Behind the counter, a big red leather book sat open next to a wall full of keys. I got lucky for once; it was the right book, and it was open at the right page: Harvey O'Keefe, Single Room, 381. Scanning the keys, I saw that Harvey's wasn't on its hook; he'd either taken it out with him or he was back in his room: we were either going to have to break in and wait, or knock quickly and stand well back.

'Thanks for all your help!' The Mouse yelled. As he did, I moved away from the desk.

'My pleasure,' the receptionist said over her shoulder as she walked back to the counter. 'You make sure you enjoy that meal!' Firmly under the spell of Linus Spayley, she let out a contented sigh as she passed by, blissfully unaware of my presence.

'Well?' he asked me outside.

'Third floor. Looks like he might be in.'

A few minutes passed before the next animal went to reception. When they did we crept back inside and got in the elevator.

When the doors next opened, the gleaming brass plate of room 381 was right in front of us. Behind the door I heard voices; hopefully just a radio. With the Mouse on the left side of the door, I knocked and moved right.

The voices coming from the room were switched off. I breathed a sigh of relief.

'Yeah, what is it?' a muffled voice said from behind the door.

'Room service,' I said, my paw covering my mouth.

'I didn't order room service,' the voice said. 'You must have the wrong number.'

'It says room 381 here.'

'Wait a second.' After a moment's pause I heard a catch being taken off its chain. The door slowly opened. 'I didn't order room service,' the voice said again, clearer now, 'there must be some —'

Taking a step to my left I moved in front of the door.

I don't know which of us was most shocked — Harvey seeing me or me seeing Harvey without his teeth. We stared at each other. Then Harvey gulped.

He didn't do it.

The words were shrill in my head, like a blast from a whistle. But I knew I was right. I blinked at him stupidly.

'You'd better come in,' he said, holding the door open.

‡ ‡ ‡

'I'd offer to get us drinks, but this place is turning out more expensive than I thought.' He was sitting on the edge of the bed and he looked miserable.

'You look… well,' I said. It wasn't strictly a lie — his face didn't look caved-in like before, and he had a bit of weight around his cheeks. But you could still have picked him out of a crowd. 'By the way, this is my colleague, Linus Spayley.'

'Hullo,' Harvey said glumly.

'Sound better, too.' He laughed without looking up, and I caught a glance of his teeth. They were still quite long, but now when he closed his mouth they vanished from view.

203

'No I don't,' he said eventually. 'I sound like someone whose mouth's been clamped shut for two years and doesn't know how to speak properly.'

'It'll come,' I said.

To my right, the Mouse was trying every trick he knew to get my attention, wanting to know what was going on. So I said: 'You didn't kill him, did you Harvey?'

When Harvey looked up his eyes were wide with shock. There was a wearying sadness there too.

'Kill who?' he said clumsily.

'Lionel Burt, AKA Lionel Bupkis. Hotel detective at the Rockway Plaza.'

'I've never heard of him.'

'Don't you read the papers?'

'Naw. They depress me. I don't need the papers for that at the moment.'

I started to speak but he interrupted me. 'Look, I know what you're going to say. Believe me, I'm sorry. But I'd just got rid of those god-damned teeth and I was on a high; I had to do something. I'm sorry. Really sorry.'

Confused, I said, 'What have you to be sorry for? I came here thinking you'd murdered someone. I'm the one who should be sorry.'

'Why would you think I killed somebody?'

'Because when we found Bupkis he had a large stab wound in his back. The murder weapon was a large white object with a sharpened end. It was a tooth, Harvey. *Your* tooth.'

Harvey's face sagged, the way it had the last time I'd seen him. The little colour he had drained from his face. 'Oh my God.'

'What did you do with the teeth, Harvey?'

He tried to speak, but nothing of any sense came out.

'Take your time,' I told him.

Composing himself, he looked up at me from the bed. 'It was something you said the last time I saw you. It all happened after that.'

'What did I say?'

'You said I should get a chisel.'

I squirmed. 'Jeez, I was only joking, Harvey.'

'I know. But I told Ray and he took it seriously. He said that a chisel would be no good though. But a saw might manage it.'

'Ray's your neighbour?'

Harvey nodded. 'Said he'd given it a bit of thought and any time I wanted rid of 'em, I'd only to ask. He had a saw in his shed and his paws were steady. There's only so much misery you can take...' He looked at me pitifully. 'So, out came the saw. The worst that happened was I got a few cuts around my mouth.'

Beside me, the Mouse made retching noises. Me, I just winced.

'Ray said you went a little crazy afterwards.'

'I did. It felt like being let out of prison or something. That's when I had the idea about the holiday. But as soon as I got here I didn't feel so good any more.'

'It sounds like you deserved a holiday after all that.'

'Maybe. But I didn't deserve to pay for it with other Animals' money.'

So that's what this was all about. 'You feel guilty for using all the money you'd put away for the operation.'

He let out a long, sorry sigh. 'You weren't the only one who gave me something. The prices the dentists were quoting were more than I could afford: I'd still have been saving six months from now, and I couldn't wait any longer. So I spent the money on a vacation.' He sighed again.

'So what happened to the teeth? Ray said you brought them with you.'

'Silly as it sounds, I still felt attached to them,' he chuckled. 'The day I got here I walked round with them in a bag. Then I had an idea how I could pay everyone back.'

'What about we go for a walk, get something to eat? My treat.' Realising that I wasn't kidding, he nodded.

Outside, Harvey pepped up a bit. He asked a lot of questions and used a lot of words to do so, as though each word was like candy in his mouth. Like Ray said, he was a different Animal.

As I was telling him about the case it occurred to me I'd lost a damn good information gatherer. 'What are you going to do now?' I asked.

'I haven't given it much thought,' he said. 'Something a bit more normal, I hope.' For old times' sake I asked if he'd heard anything lately that would interest me. When he said that he hadn't, he looked pleased.

After watching the heart-warming but comical spectacle of Harvey drinking coffee and eating donuts, he told us he had something he wanted to show us.

Leading us into a street full of shops peddling beach towels, postcards and seashells glued to boards, he stopped outside what appeared to be a junkshop. Every inch of its window was filled with trinkets — fishbowls, dusty commodes, sets of dominos, jewellery, you name it — all gloriously overpriced.

'There was a pair of glass eyes here last time,' he said, tapping the window. 'You wouldn't believe what they were selling for. Anyway, I went inside and got talking to the owner. When I told him what I had he damn near snatched my arm off. Said he specialised in unusual items; the more unusual, the better.'

'So you sold him your teeth.'

'Not straight away. I felt like I had to... make them a bit more presentable first. So I went back to my room and used every last drop of my toothpaste cleaning them. Then, I asked the janitor at the hotel if he had any spare sandpaper. Did both ends; sharpened one, smoothed out the other. After that I polished 'em up until they were as smooth as marble. They looked good. One had a bit of a cavity in it, but that was okay; like it was part of a design or something.'

'A piece of lettuce was found in that cavity.'

He looked surprised. 'Is that a fact? Anyway, I came back here and sold 'em. Got a fair price for 'em too.'

We went inside. Barely ten feet away on the other side of a jumble of stock, a small Tabby with light fur was sitting behind a crowded desk. Looking up from a figurine, his gaze went straight to Harvey.

'I thought it was you outside,' he said, standing up. 'Come in. How's the speech?'

'A little better, thanks. I've brought some... friends along. They wanted to know about the teeth.'

'Oh, that's a pity,' the Tabby said. 'I'm afraid they're long gone. Went as a set; right quickly, too. It's not every day something like that comes on the market.'

'Do you remember who you sold them to?'

The Tabby made a little huffing noise. 'I'm hardly likely to forget, the amount of trouble he had getting in here. And it's always the same. When I saw him looking in the window I thought, here we go again. He's so *big,* you see, and those wings of his... every time he comes in he manages to smash something. Luckily it was only a cracked china doll that time.'

'A *Bird* bought those teeth?'

'Exactly. A great big Crow, rude as hell he is. Said he wanted "to look at the white things in the window." And when I did manage to squeeze past and get them for him he gave them a sharp tap with his beak! Then he said he'd be back in a few minutes and walked out. When he came back in, he had a mouthful of money and dropped it all on the counter. Before I could ask if he wanted them gift-wrapped, he picked the teeth up in his beak and waddled out of the shop. The thing is I don't think he buys these things for himself. He always goes out and comes back later with the money. And when he has, I always hear some car driving away afterwards.'

'You ever see it?'

'No, it doesn't pass this way.'

'What about the Crow? Where does he go?'

'He doesn't leave in the car, that's for sure. A customer came in shortly afterwards and said she'd just had her hat blown off by a giant Crow flying towards the town.'

Outside, the Mouse said 'So someone got the Crow to buy the teeth for them. Why?'

'Because whoever wanted them didn't want to be seen themselves.'

'The Moles? Maybe one of them was driving the car.'

'Not if their eyesight's as bad as the Lieutenant says. Anyway, maybe whoever the Crow bought them for is straight. Or straight-ish. They could've then sold them on and the Moles ended up with them.'

Harvey looked crestfallen. 'And I accepted the first price he offered me,' he said.

'You should've tried the place next door to the Plaza, Harvey,' I said, patting him on the back. 'You should see what they charge for a pack of playing cards.'

Leaving Harvey to his well-earned vacation, the Mouse went back to the Plaza and I headed back to town.

25. AUTHORS

'COFFEE?' TAKI SAID WHEN I got back to the office.
'Certainly coffee. And lots of it.' I looked down at the mug in front of Angelica. 'Seems like I'm not the only one hooked on it.'

'I'm slowly getting used to it,' she said rather huffily, 'having drunk a gallon of it waiting for you to come back from wherever you've been.'

'Didn't the stories keep you busy?'

'I finished reading them over an hour ago. If it hadn't been for Taki's good company, I'd have gone back to Rockway.'

'You've finished all those stories?'

'Yes, and when I'd done that, I phoned the Lieutenant to see if *he* would tell me what on earth a tooth has to do with Burt's murder.'

'Bupkis. So Dingus is back then?'

'I've no idea. I couldn't get hold of him.'

Sitting on the edge of Taki's desk, I sipped at my coffee. 'So, the stories. Find anything interesting?'

Angelica gave me a look that said enough was enough. 'No, Benjamin. *You* first.'

She sat stony-faced as I told her about Betsy Oatland but suddenly she started to smile.

'Something amusing?' I asked.

'Well, some of this I already know from talking to Alannah Foxton. Surely you remember? You did say you only had a few minutes sleep in her garden... You know, at the time I wondered if perhaps Burt — sorry, *Bupkis* — had wanted Trix to dig his way into the Mole's system of tunnels, only things hadn't gone according to plan.'

'It's a possibility, I suppose,' I said grudgingly.

As she continued to smirk, I told her the rest of it, about Harvey and the tooth, and the Crow in the junk shop. 'Oh, and it was Betsy who wrote "Rex Got Lost",' I added finally, hoping to move her along. 'Now. *Your* turn.'

Wiping the last of the smile off her face, she became serious.

'Right, then. First things first. These letter writers — Daphne DuMoralize, Bumper Fodder, Giddyfits — I think it's all the same animal.'

'Who?'

'Mungo Bickeridge.'

'Bickeridge did the whole lot?'

'I think so, yes. You said yourself he's tried to drum up publicity this way before.'

'True, but the last time I looked he only had two paws. What about all the different styles of writing? I don't have him down as being that creative.'

'Oh, but he is; just not at writing stories. I think he used both paws, and a few of the letters were typed. Also, all the envelopes bearing postmarks came from different places.'

'So?'

'Didn't you say that the only time you got to speak to him was when he contacted you? Because he kept moving?'

'That's because he said someone was trying to kill him.'

'Exactly — that's what *he* said. But where are the witnesses to these attacks? According to Bickeridge, when someone tried to run him down the street was empty; we've only got his word that it happened at all. And he never reported it to the police, because I checked. And as for his smashed window —'

'He could have broken it himself,' I said, recalling what I'd said to Finnegan at our first meeting. 'But this still doesn't explain all the different styles of writing. Like I said, I really can't see him being that talented.'

'Maybe not talented, no,' Angelica said as she lit her pipe. 'But *devious,* yes. It came to me while I was waiting in Rusty Laidlaw's office — the majority of the letters didn't have postmarks at all; they had claw-marks and beak-marks.'

'Birds deliver letters these days. It's a well-known fact.'

'Ah! But who said that was all Birds could do?'

I let that sink in: Shove Off earning a crust as a fan, the Crow as the happy shopper. Her eyes widened.

'I see you understand. Have you heard of Percival Dipton?' I shook my head.

'Writer friend of mine; a great big Parrot, rather like the one at the book launch. Percival has perfect use of his beak. Well, I say perfect; he can only manage about thirty-five words a minute and suffers terribly with neck cramp, but he can write legibly. Of course, his secretary has to type up the manuscripts for him.'

'I don't buy it,' I told her, finishing my coffee. 'I mean he's crazy enough but... '

'I rather thought you might be sceptical. When I thought of it, I wasn't entirely convinced myself. Anyway, we'll leave that for the time being. When my interview had finished I was lucky enough to bump into Laidlaw's cleaner, Peaches.

'I asked her if she'd seen anyone suspicious over the past few weeks. She remembered this rather odd-looking character hanging around outside the building, who had piggy eyes and a large tuft of fur growing from the top of his head. She said he was "the ugliest thing she'd ever seen outside of a Fish-tank". It reminded me of your description of Mr. Bickeridge.

'And what about the letter that was sent after Lettice was killed: "You can't pin that murder on me it had nothing to do with me not my fault"?' she quoted from the sheet in front of her. 'Even with the shaky writing, it's clearly the work of whoever's responsible for the "cheking the mails" letter. I think by the time Lettice was killed, Bickeridge realised he'd created a monster that couldn't be stopped and was terrified he'd get blamed for her death.'

'So that's it?' I said. 'Bickeridge for the whole lot? We can discard everything else?'

'Ah. Now, I didn't say that. In fact, I think there's a lot more going on here than silly letters.'

'Such as?'

'The stories. I'd already come to the conclusion that Bickeridge was responsible for the letters, but I began to wonder if he could be responsible for the stories too. Having read them, along with some of Bickeridge's work, I'm pretty sure he isn't.'

'You've read Bickeridge's stories?'

'The few he's had published anyway. Laidlaw phoned Finnegan and asked if he could bring me some back issues.'

'What did you think?' I asked.

She gave a small shiver. 'Absolutely dreadful.'

'I did warn you about "Sick Relish".'

'I'm not talking about the content, I'm talking about the style; or rather, lack of it. It's quite obvious he can't write for toffee, but he's too caught up in himself to see it. As for Nelson, his stories don't appear to have anything to do with anything except a painful lack of self-awareness. But two of the stories — "Rex Got Lost" and "The Invisible Feud" — were both written by animals that *can* write. And thanks to her confession, we know now that Betsy Oatland wrote the former, so we're left with the author of latter: *Jake Lake*.

'Now, I'm not saying that the story isn't innocent by itself. If it'd been the only one I would probably have thought so. But then I came across this one as well.'

From the pile on the desk she produced a manuscript I recognised by colour alone: the one that looked like it'd been doing the rounds since the Ark was built.

'That one?' I laughed. 'It's as old as the hills.'

' "Deadly Ink" it's called,' she said, waving the pages in my face. 'And look. These pages have been stained with tea to make them look old. It's the oldest trick in the book.'

'And you spotted it because you know tea. But what has that to do w —'

'Ask yourself this: why would anyone want to disguise a manuscript in the first place? What possible purpose can it serve? Also, the phrasing and tone in this story and "The Invisible Feud" are quite similar. Small things really. I wouldn't have expected you to notice.'

'How very good of you to say so.'

'But what possible reason could Lake have for dousing a story in tea, writing another one that's quite similar and sending both to the same magazine?'

'That's the point. Why do it *at all*? That's why I think it should be checked out.'

'I'll speak to her again,' I mumbled. 'And you think Nelson has nothing to do with it either?' I said, changing the subject.

'Not unless you're completely wrong about his character, which I don't think you are.'

'What about the knock-down?'

'Probably an accident. But we can't entirely rule out foul play. Although why anyone would want to kill *him*...' she shrugged.

'What about Wiedlin? Anything?'

Her eyes sparkled. 'Ah, yes. *Quentin P. Wiedlin.* Very interesting.'

'In what way?'

'That I'm not sure about. I'm certain he had nothing to do with the letters. Or the stories, for that matter. But there's something about that rejection letter he sent Rusty Laidlaw.'

'Did you ask Laidlaw about it?'

'I did. I was curious to find out if Laidlaw replied. He said he hadn't. And Wiedlin hasn't been in touch since he sent the story back. I noticed that the story in question wasn't in the pile?'

'Because Laidlaw only sent me stories he felt might have something to do with the poison-pen letters.'

'Yet he sent you Wiedlin's letter.'

'It was so strange, I don't blame him.'

'Well anyway, I've asked him to dig it out for me. He said he'd drop it off here in the morning.'

That seemed to be it. 'So how was the big interview?' I asked.

'Oh, the usual thing, I'm afraid,' she said, laying her pipe down. 'He stopped just short of asking me where I get my ideas from, which I suppose is something. As an interviewer, he makes a very good editor, that's all I can say.'

'Think you could do better?' I said, grinning.

'I'm sure I could,' she sniffed.

'Care to put it to the test?'

'What do you mean?'

'You're intrigued by him, right?'

'Certainly.'

'Well, let's go see him. Now. You can even ask him for a copy of his story.'

'Aren't you going to telephone him first?' she said, following me out of the office.

'No. It'll be a nice surprise for him when he opens his door.' The idea of getting up Wiedlin's nose had perked me up.

'But he might not be in,' Angelica said.

'We'll cross that bridge when we come to it,' I told her.

26. DÉJÀ VU

'PERHAPS WE SHOULD GO for something to eat first,' she said, her paw raised in the air.

Between leaving the office and stepping onto the street, the heavens had opened, the drops bouncing back off the sidewalk with loud pats.

'And maybe miss the opportunity of catching Wiedlin?' I said. 'Anyway, we won't be out in this much longer. And I'm sure the hotel could rustle up a sandwich later if you asked them nicely.'

Despite the hour, the subway was still pretty busy, the wonderful aroma of sweaty fur coming at us on all sides.

'You ever been in a subway before?'

'I can't say that I have,' she shouted above the noise of an approaching train.'

'You'll love it — think of it as your own giant advertising space.'

Stepping onto the escalator, she saw the first of the advertising posters for her book covered in little balls of gum. 'Oh dear. We won't be down here very long, will we?' she asked in a lull between platform announcements.

I doubted that she'd find Derry Park Flats any less unpleasant, but I was wrong; once inside, she brightened up considerably.

'Hold that lift!' she called, hurrying over to the grizzled looking pooch in the elevator.

The three of us stood in silence for about five seconds. 'A bit grim here, isn't it?' she said cheerfully to our companion.

The Dog, who looked like he'd seen all there was to see in this world plus half of what was in the next, looked her up and down slowly. 'You should try living here,' he told her.

'Until two years ago, I'd never set foot outside this building. If only I'd known what was out there.'

'A better world?' Angelica said hopefully.

'A worse one,' the Dog replied. 'But I gotta eat.' He nodded down at his groceries. 'Still, could be worse. I could be on the twenty-fourth.' Abruptly, the cage stopped, the light momentarily blinking off.

'Why, what's on twenty-fourth?' Angelica asked.

'A great big leaky roof that nobody wants to fix. See you kids later,' the Dog called back as he made his way down the corridor.

Approaching Apartment 1926, I saw it was still missing its numbers. I had a feeling it was also missing its tenant. Crouching by the door, I examined the lock.

'What are you doing?' Angelica asked.

'Seeing how much noise this door'll make if I give it a kick.' As the words were coming out of my mouth, the door handle rattled, then inched inwards. I'd just managed to straighten up, when his face appeared in the frame.

'Yes?'

Wiedlin, perhaps sensing movement behind me, looked over my shoulder. His eyes widened.

'I see you've spotted my surprise,' I said, moving aside. 'Remember how you said you were such a *big* fan of the de Groot's? Well, I decided to bring along half of the partnership.'

'How very... good of you,' Wiedlin said, looking only slightly less stunned, his attempt at withering sarcasm not up to his usual standard. 'I'm thrilled. Truly I am. But I'm busy right now, so —'

'This won't take long, Mr. Wiedlin,' Angelica said, stepping forward. 'Earlier today, I was being interviewed by Rusty Laidlaw for *No Sh* — for his magazine, and I mentioned that a lot of our stories came about as the result of a title, at which point he mentioned a story of yours with the delightful title "The Mystery of the Fifteenth Corkscrew", and I haven't been able to get it out of my head since. I was wondering — I know it's a bit of a cheek, but it's one of those itches I just have to scratch, I'm afraid — would it be possible for me to borrow a copy?'

'It isn't here,' he told her, seeming to fill more of the doorway the longer he stood there. 'I keep all my stories at my office.'

'Oh, that is a shame.'

'Yes,' he said tonelessly. 'Shame.'

'Well. Another time, perhaps.'

Instead of answering her, he looked at me. 'Like I said. I'm busy.'

'Sure. We have to be getting back anyway.' I was still bustling Angelica away from the door when it slammed shut behind us.

'I should have let you go for your dinner after all,' I said as we waited for the elevator.

She looked at me, surprised. 'You think it was a wasted trip?'

'Don't you?'

'I'm not sure. Is it me or has he got one of those faces that remind you of others?'

'He just looks like another Schnauzer to me. He was at the book launch. Maybe you recognise him from there.'

'No, I don't recall seeing him. I'd have remembered. Strange, that he doesn't have any of his stories in his apartment.'

'Isn't it. I'll check up about his "office" in the morning.'

After seeing her onto the next bus to Rockway, I went home.

As I was standing in front of my door, fishing around for my key, I heard scratching behind me. Turning, I knew the noise was coming from Shove Off's apartment. A little voice at the back of my head whispered two words: *ask him*. Deciding to risk the Parrot's wrath, I knocked on his door.

'Give me a second!' a voice yelled.

As often happened, the first thing to emerge from his apartment were cats. After spending a few seconds rubbing themselves against me and trying to trip me up, they scattered along the corridor.

'Half an hour they've been pestering to get out,' Shove Off said from the doorway, 'I don't know why I don't just put their basket outside. What can I do for you, anyhow?'

'I want to ask you about Birds. What kind of jobs you do.'

He opened his beak to make some funny comment but instead changed his mind. 'Come in,' he said.

By my reckoning it was the third time I'd been in the Parrot's apartment, but this familiarity didn't prepare me for the experience; because no matter how many of my questions Shove Off could answer, I'd leave with dozens more unanswered.

'Take a seat,' he said. 'Drink?'

'Soda, if you've got one.'

'Coming up.' He waddled off into the kitchen.

From the living room I heard what sounded like the fridge door being opened and closed, a bottle being opened, a glass being taken from a cupboard and finally the sound of a drink being poured into the glass. None of it bothered me. I realised these things could be done with his beak alone, as could lots of other tasks — simple meals could be prepared, baths drawn, linen folded — he could do hundreds of things that twenty-four months ago wouldn't have been possible. But there were certain other things I could never fathom: how come, despite having razor-sharp talons and a beak he could open bottles with, nothing in his apartment appeared to be ripped or marked? When he finished bathing, how did he dry himself? And how the hell did he operate a can opener? Unless —

'Clear a space on that table, will you?'

I'd been so lost in my thoughts I hadn't heard him come in. He was only a few feet away, and my glass of soda was wedged so firmly between his body and wing it looked like nothing short of a pickaxe would shift it. Moving a large, glossy picture book of sailing ships from the table (its pages free of beak marks), I watched as Shove Off bent the top half of his body forward before letting the glass slide slowly down from inside his wing and onto the table without spilling a drop. 'Back in a minute,' he said, returning to the kitchen.

Taking a drink of the soda, I looked at the book I'd moved. *Classic Naval Campaigns.*

'I didn't have you down as a reader of this kind of stuff,' I called out.

He came back in with another glass, this one clamped in his beak. Sitting in a chair opposite me, he placed the soda down in one smooth movement.

'I wasn't called "Captain" for nothing,' he told me. Sticking his beak under his wing, he brought out a long straw which he plopped into the soda. Taking a long, noisy drink he finally let it go, leaving it to float in the glass.

'You a ship's mascot or something?'

'Nah. Owner ran a series of boats. He got me when he retired.'

'Sounds impressive,' I said.

'Not really. He was in charge of the boating lake downtown, screaming kids every day of his life. No wonder he was grouchy. What is it you wanted to ask me?'

'Is any of that true?' I asked when I stopped laughing.

'You're the detective; you find out. You said something in the hall about jobs.'

I told him about the trouble with the magazines and the letters. 'Thing is, I don't think the suspect I've got in mind is that savvy. Some of the letters had been shoved into window frames; and, with both magazines being on the sixth and seventh floors of the Henderson Building, it has to be a Bird or Birds delivering them. So what I've been wondering is this: is it possible that our suspect, in order to throw us off the scent even more, not only employed Birds to deliver the notes, but write them as well?'

Shove Off looked at me levelly. 'Sure,' he said.

'So Birds *can* write?'

'Of course Birds can write,' the Parrot snapped. 'How do you think we sign checks?'

Try as I might, I couldn't think of a suitable reply.

'Look, I'll show you.' Waving a wing in the air, he stood up and waddled over to a writing desk in a den at the back of the room. Taking a pencil from a pot on the desk with his beak, he scrawled something across a sheet of paper which I couldn't see until he moved his head away. IF YOU CAN READ THIS YOU'RE NOT AS DUMB AS I THOUGHT the message read, the words all straight on the lines.

'That's neater than mine,' I said, impressed.

'I know. I still remember the Christmas card you sent me.' Rustling his wings, they made a noise like sheets of brittle paper.

'So it is possible that Birds wrote the letters.'

'Birds can do lots of things these days, chum, if the money's right.'

'That reminds me. How's the fan business going?'

'Not so good since the weather cooled. But at least it's legal. Some of the stuff that goes on...' going back to his soda, he took an even noisier drink than last time.

'Such as?'

'Magpies,' he said, spitting the straw back into the glass.

'What about them?'

'Not the species. Well, maybe the species, but Crows mostly. I'm talking about the gang called Magpies.'

'I've never heard of them.'

'You're not supposed to have heard of them. They take on anything with feathers that's big enough, ugly enough and nasty enough. Break-ins, maimings, money with menaces; they'll do anything. There's even stories of them muscling-in on legit Birds' activities.'

'You ever had trouble with them?'

He shook his head. 'Nope. Maybe it's no bad thing the heat-wave's finished. The idea of having my wings broken doesn't appeal to me.'

The image of a great big Crow suddenly popped into my head. 'Smuggling,' I said to myself.

'Smuggling?'

'Smuggling. They'd be perfect for it.'

'I'll say. As long as it wasn't pianos they were shifting they could move just about anything. Hell, it'd be the quickest way from A-to-B as the Crow flies.' He chuckled at his little joke. 'No traffic, and the cops could do nothing to stop them. Who's going to take any notice of a Bird carrying something *these* days? And if they did, the Bird would just fly a bit higher so nobody could see them. Hah! I'm wasted as a fan, Spriteman. You need another body in that office of yours, you give me a shout.'

'I will,' I said distractedly, the possibilities filling my head as I left. 'Take care of yourself, Cap.'

'Don't you worry about me. Shove off.' The door slammed behind me.

Back home, more ideas swirled around my head. If the Magpies *had* bought the teeth for the Moles, or someone who was working with the Moles, were they in on other things with them as well, like the coconuts? If so, then the coconuts — or whatever was inside them — could be thousands of miles away by now. After tying myself in knots with possible theories, I dozed off for a few seconds and fell into a strange dream in which a giant Mole and a giant Crow, surrounded by oversized coconuts, were playing tug-of-war with a gigantic tooth. It was time to go to bed.

Before I did, I phoned both the numbers I had for Dingus. The Dog on the desk at the station house told me that the Lieutenant hadn't reported in, so I tried the number written on the sheet of toilet paper. But that just rang and rang until I slammed the receiver down.

27.
DISAPPEARANCES / REAPPEARANCES

MY FIRST THOUGHT WHEN I heard it ringing again was that it must be Dingus. Half asleep, I eventually managed to grab hold of the receiver at the fourth or fifth attempt.

'Yeah?'

'Mr. Spriteman?' A shaky voice asked. 'It's Rusty Laidlaw.'

'What can I do for you?'

'Can you come to the office? Now?'

As he spoke I noticed how dark it was in the room. 'What time is it?'

'Six fifteen. I couldn't sleep, so I decided to come in early and do a bit of work.'

Six fifteen? 'A bit early for me, Rusty. Had a busy couple of days. Look, I'll come round about nine and we can talk th— '

'The office has been ransacked,' he blurted out.

'I'll be there in half an hour.'

I managed to get to the Henderson building ten minutes early. Laidlaw was waiting for me in the corridor when I got out of the elevator. Patch Finnegan was standing next to him. I looked past both of them towards the door. It looked intact.

'They have a key or something?'

'They didn't come in through the door,' Laidlaw said. We went inside. As soon as we did, my fur began to rise in the cool morning air.

There was so much glass on the floor I was surprised to see a few pieces still hanging in the frames. Stuck between two shards, a large, black feather rippled in the breeze. As I walked over to it, it broke free and spun backwards out of the frame towards the ground.

Turning, I looked back at the damage. Every cabinet and drawer in the room had been turned out and their contents thrown to the ground. Paper littered the floor, most of it ripped and covered with claw-marks. For good measure the seat of Laidlaw's chair had been pecked to pieces; chunks of stuffing covered the floor behind his desk.

I asked if either of them had heard of the Magpies. Both shook their heads.

'What's been taken?'

'That's what I don't understand: nothing.'

'Nothing at all?'

'No. I checked while I was waiting for you to arrive.'

'You've no valuables here?'

'Just manuscripts. After all the trouble started I took anything of value home.'

Somehow I didn't think this was part of the same thing. 'What about your place?' I asked Finnegan.

'As I left it last night. Rusty, I'm gonna go. See you later.' With that, the Jack Russell left. I gave Laidlaw a look asking what Finnegan was doing here.

'I called him before I called you.'

'Things must be improving between the two of you.'

'It seems the best thing to do. Stick together.' He looked around at the mess. 'But *why*? If they weren't here to steal anything, why cause all this damage?'

'You've called the police?'

Laidlaw looked at me wide-eyed. 'I haven't. I called Patch and I called you and then Patch turned up...' He put his paw up to his mouth.

'I'll call them now,' I said. I asked to speak to Dingus, but he still hadn't put in an appearance. I gave the details to one of the officers.

'I'll be on the phone all morning,' Laidlaw complained, 'asking writers for new copies of their stories.' Sticking his long nose in his paws, he sighed.

That reminded me. 'Looks like Angelica's not going to get her story then after all.'

Laidlaw looked up. 'I'm sorry?'

' "The Mystery of the Fifteenth Corkscrew." You were going to send it over to my office this morning. Not that it's important now.'

Laidlaw blinked a few times before answering. 'It's not here.'

'What?'

'I checked last night, before I left. Sometimes I take manuscripts home and read them in bed. It's in a pile in my study.'

It took a few seconds for my mouth to catch up with my brain. 'How soon can you get us to your house?'

'In about thirty-five minutes,' he said. 'Why?'

'Because whoever trashed this place didn't find what they were looking for. I think it's on the pile in your study.'

Laidlaw's fur stiffened. 'They might have been waiting for me to leave home. So they could get it.' He said it like his house had already been ransacked. I nodded.

I wouldn't have believed it of Laidlaw, but despite the increasing traffic we were at his house in under twenty minutes. I hadn't realised that Whippets could be so reckless.

‡ ‡ ‡

By the time I reached the last page of "The Mystery of the Fifteenth Corkscrew" the ink was running down the page like mascara on a distressed Poodle. Running a paw over my fur, I flicked another fistful of water onto the floor of the subway train. On the seat opposite, an old doll with a pompadour sniffed her disgust. Politely pointing out that it was raining quite heavily outside, she moved into the next carriage.

The rain hadn't started until we were almost at Laidlaw's. I realised we might be there when the car skidded to a halt roughly six inches away from a garden wall. Jumping out, he ran for the house. I took my time.

There's a certain atmosphere around properties that have been broken into and this one didn't have it. Finding the front door locked, Laidlaw gave me a hopeful look before dashing round the back. Seconds later he joined me back at the front door.

'Nothing,' he panted. 'The locks are fine and none of the windows are broken.' Opening the door, he let us in.

Unsurprisingly, the living room was full of books, most of them housed in cabinets. A door at the back of the room led into a small and extremely-comfortable looking study, also filled with the printed word, only this stuff was all loose, piles of manuscripts covering the floor and desk.

' "The Mystery of the Fifteenth Corkscrew",' Laidlaw said, digging out a manuscript from one of the piles. Then, suddenly remembering that the police were due at his office, we raced back to his car. Despite his reluctance to stop, I got him to drop me at the subway.

It turned out the fifteenth corkscrew wasn't a corkscrew at all, it was a tuning-fork. Well, kind of. I could see why Laidlaw had bounced it. As a source of information relating to the case however, it was a real page-turner. After blowing on the wet ink in a lame attempt to dry it, I folded the manuscript as carefully as I could and slid it into my pocket.

By the time I reached Derry Park Flats it was raining even heavier; the pigeon-droppings presumably holding the brickwork together were melting down the honeycombed walls in black-and-white streamers. Going up to the nineteenth floor, the only sign of life I noticed was on the seventh, where something of indeterminate age with white fur slouched along, dripping water all over the floor. As it did, something that old Dog said last time I was here came back to me. When the door opened on the nineteenth floor, I stayed put, and pressed the button for the twenty-fourth floor.

Getting closer, I thought I could hear the trickle of water. Sure enough, when I got there, the top floor was swimming. Looking for a way to the roof, I spotted an anonymous-looking door tucked away at the far end of the corridor that opened onto a set of stairs; at the top of it, I could see a glass door panel running with raindrops.

Unless someone was hiding behind the chimneys, the roof was empty apart from a few wilted flowers in terracotta pots. The rain slanted down into my eyes, slicking my fur back against my face. Shielding my face with my paws, I moved slowly across the roof looking for holes, wondering if my theory was correct; seeing a huge black feather stuck to the floor, I started to think it was. A few feet from the edge of the roof I found what I was looking for: pairs of gouge-marks, six, maybe eight inches long. The more I looked the more of them I found. Satisfied, I went back down to the nineteenth floor.

The corridor was empty. I could've knocked, but this time I was sure Weidlin wasn't in. Doing what I'd wanted to do last time, I raised my shoe to the lock and kicked hard, twice, the door smashing back against the narrow wall. Before anyone had a chance to come out and see what the noise was, I went inside, closing the door the best I could.

Like last time, everything was thick with dust and the curtains were closed. I could've kicked myself for imagining that he'd ever lived here. I started with the obvious places, removed books from shelves, looked under the sofas, but drew a blank. The bedroom was completely empty; if Wiedlin ever did sleep here, it must be on one of the sofas. In the bathroom I found nothing except a small bar of soap and mildew on the taps.

Which left the kitchen. There was tea and sugar on the worktop and a carton of milk in the fridge, but that was all: the cupboards were bare. Crouching down, I opened the cupboards under the sink. They were almost bare — no rags, no cleaning utensils or other odd things you usually find under sinks. There wasn't even any dust down there.

Just lots and lots of small, thick, brown hairs.

After pocketing a few, I went back through the other rooms, removing any signs that I'd ever been there. Looking out into the corridor, it was still empty. Pulling the door back in place, I headed for the elevator. Inside I tried to reason everything through. By the time the door opened, I had more than a few ideas. But I needed to speak to Dingus and Angelica.

The pay phone in the lobby was out of order, which meant trying to find one in the subway. After finding three in use and one out of order, it was with some disbelief I finally found one free. I called POLICE HQ first, only to be told that the Lieutenant still hadn't called in. Then I dialled the Rockway number, but there was no reply; I had the sensation that something was wrong. Then, as I was about to try for the Plaza's number, I realised that I didn't have enough change. At the other booths, several animals turned to see who was doing all the cursing. When my train turned up a few seconds later, I gratefully jumped on. When I got to the office, I asked Taki if there'd been any calls.

'No,' she said, 'but —' Soaking wet, I marched past her, opening my door.

A sopping wet Pigeon sat on the windowsill outside, giving me the eye.

When I opened the window, I expected the Pidge to jump in. Instead, it kicked a piece of paper into the office and flew away.

Taki was standing beside me now. 'Didn't you invite him in?' I said, picking the note off the floor.

'I offered but he just stood there, staring. And when I went to open the window he started pecking at the glass. So I decided to leave him where he was.'

'How long ago was this?'

'Maybe ten minutes. Coffee?' as she left I read the note.

Have a touch of the sniffles today. Have decided to stay at hotel. Best wishes, A.

I read it again, then looked at the paper. My feeling that something was wrong intensified. The two previous messages I'd received from Angelica had been handwritten on the Plaza's own headed notepaper, not typed on cheap lined paper. Plus the message was too short: it usually took Angelica a sentence and a half to say "good morning" — perhaps I had learned something about an author's 'tone' after all — and the idea of her crying off because she had a cold...

Then, as Taki put the coffee down on the desk with a bump, an image flared in my mind. Turning, I looked towards the window, as if the Bird was still there, sitting on the ledge looking in. I only saw it for a second or two, but I was certain it wasn't the same Bird who'd delivered the other notes.

It was the wrong Pigeon.

I phoned the Rockway Plaza. 'Angelica de Groot, please.'

There was a click and the phone rang. And rang.

'She's not answering,' the receptionist said.

'Try for Linus Spayley.'

It was a relief when he answered. 'Yeah?'

'Have you heard from Angelica this morning?'

'No,' the Mouse said. 'She said she'd see me after breakfast, but so far —'

'Go up and check her room,' I told him. 'Then call me back.'

I spent a long ten minutes staring at the clock, sipping coffee and listening to the rain. When the phone rang, I jumped.

'She's not here,' the Mouse said breathlessly. 'I knocked but got no answer, so I asked reception to let me in, in case she'd been taken ill. The room's a mess: the carpet's all messed up and some of her stuff's on the floor.'

'Stay there and try to get hold of Dingus. I'll be there as quick as I can.'

A half-hour wait in the depot later, a bus finally pulled up. The driver, who'd picked me up a couple of times before, nodded at me as I made my way to the back. Being the only passenger, I had the perfect opportunity to think through what I thought was going on, most of it involving Wiedlin.

I figured that Wiedlin as well as Bupkis were the Moles' contacts above ground. For some reason — perhaps as a result of Bupkis' death — he'd got the coconuts from the Moles and taken them to Derry Parks Flats, a place nobody would think to look for them. Then he passes them on to the Magpies — who he's in pretty deep with — who get them away, and he gets them to bust up Laidlaw's office looking for his story. Did he get the Crow to buy the teeth too? Was Wiedlin the unseen driver of the car outside the antique shop in Rockway? If it was Wiedlin and he *did* buy the teeth, that implicated him in Bupkis's murder.

Then there was the story itself, and Wiedlin's reaction when he saw Angelica. Her instinct had been correct: she might not have been able to place where she'd seen him, but his response when he saw her was stunned silence. Plus he'd gone to all that trouble to get the manuscript back. Why? Because he knew if she ever saw it, she'd figure it all out —

Which is why he took her.

Ten minutes later I was in Angelica's room at the Plaza.

'It looks pretty obvious what's happened,' the Mouse said, pointing to the raised carpet. 'She's been dragged out of bed in the middle of the night and put up some resistance.' I nodded. I checked the stairs and corridor, had a look in the elevator, but there was no evidence of a struggle after that.

'How was she last night?' I asked the Mouse back in the room.

'She kept talking about Wiedlin. Said if she hadn't seen him before, she'd seen someone who reminded her of him, and that a good night's sleep would tell her.'

'So what do we do now, Mr. S?'

'I've no idea. I don't suppose you managed to get hold of the Lieutenant?' He shook his head. 'Where the hell is he? Perhaps we should report *both* of them missing.' I walked heavily over towards the phone. I was almost there when it started ringing.

I snatched at it. 'Angelica?'

'Um, someone down here to see you,' a confused voice said. Before I could ask, the line went dead.

After phoning the police to tell them about Angelica, we both went down to see who it was.

The lobby was crowded with the usual old codgers slumped in chairs drinking coffee, but that was all. The receptionist must have dialled the wrong number by mistake.

'Right. I'd better go look for her. Where, I don't know. You look into Wiedlin's private affairs. He claims to have an office somewhere in the city; see if you can find it. And keep an eye out for Dingus.'

'Er, Mr. S...' the Mouse was staring into the far corner of the lobby. 'Isn't that...?'

Following his paw, it took me a while to see it: something resembling a sack of garbage propped up in a chair against the wall. Together, we walked over to it.

It was hard to imagine the Lieutenant looking any more dishevelled than usual, but somehow he'd managed it. We were a few feet away when he spotted us. Trying to raise himself up in his chair, he slid back down again.

'Dingus,' I said. 'Are you okay? Where have you been?'

'Well, Benji,' he said, sliding a shaky paw into his trench coat, 'that's the problem. You see, I'm not exactly sure.'

The Mouse and I watched as he took a cigar from his pocket. It wasn't until he was removing the cellophane with his trembling paws that I saw the small clumps of earth stuck to his claws, and the fresh streaks of dirt on his already dirty trench coat.

Part Four: The Process
of Weeding Out

‡ ‡ ‡

28. UNDER THE HOUSE (1)

W E WATCHED THE LIEUTENANT struggling to light his cigar for a while before I reached over and took it from him. His concentration now fully focused on his lighter, he eventually managed to strike a flame which I stuck the end of the stinking cigar into. When it was finally lit, I handed it back to him the way you'd hand over something retrieved from an un-flushed toilet.

'Thanks,' he said, taking a jittery drag.

'If you're not sure where you've been,' I said, blowing apart the bluish cloud of smoke separating us, 'can you remember where you started from?'

'Sure I can,' Dingus said, resting the cigar in the ashtray. 'Same place as I ended up: in Bupkis' basement.'

'Why did you start there?' the Mouse asked.

'Because that's where I found the entrance to the tunnels,' the Lieutenant told him, picking the dirt from his claws.

'I didn't go there for that, of course. But I half expected to find some way in. It was what Betsy said about him knowing where to find them. Half the houses on that cliff could have tunnels beneath them. So I went to the basement. I found a small door in one of the walls. I just thought it'd lead to a closet. Instead...' as he shivered, dust tumbled from the creases of his coat.

I couldn't take my eyes off it. 'What the hell did you do down there, dig yourself another hole?' He laughed nervously.

'Any longer down there, I might have,' he said. 'Nope. What happened was my curiosity got the better of me. I forgot all the stuff I'd read about Moles and charged straight in there. Good thing I always carry a little flashlight. If I'd taken a minute to think about it, I'd have looked for a map too.'

'Maybe there isn't one —' I began to say. At that, he pulled a large piece of crumpled paper out of his pocket. 'Ah.'

'I found it when I came back out, stuck behind a crate next to the door. The writing's identical to the stuff I saw while I was nosing around. I think he must have made several trips down there.' He handed me the map. It was so complicated it made my eyes cross.

'So how long were you down there?'

'What time is it?' I told him it was just past one. 'Well in that case, since maybe four o'clock yesterday. Roughly twenty hours.' He started to shake even more. 'After I'd been down there awhile I started to get really panicky. I stopped walking through the tunnels and started running, which got me even more lost. I tripped over something in the dark and must've been out cold for a long while. When I came-to, I ached like hell. The flashlight had been on all that time and was running down. When I looked at my watch I saw I'd busted it in the fall. Not long after that the flashlight went out too.'

'What was it you tripped over; a pile of earth?'

As much as it was possible, the colour drained from the Lieutenant's face. 'Before the flashlight broke I saw a lot of strange things down there. The burrows are huge, and go all over the place. Some of the chambers were as big as caves, and there's loads of rooms and little nooks, and passages that go through some of the rooms and lead to other paths... a few of the rooms looked like they'd been occupied; there was *stuff* in them, and in corridors in the middle of nowhere. In one of the last rooms I went in before the light finally cut out, I saw a pile of bones. And my guess was they weren't the kind of bones Clancy is used to sawing into.'

236

'Moles?'

'Moles. And Benji, if the bones I saw are anything to go by, then they're quite a size.' He sucked what little was left of his cigar into his lungs.

'So what *did* you trip over?'

He surprised me by laughing.

'You wanna know what I tripped over? I'll tell you.' He looked at me, then the Mouse, then back at me. 'A radio set.'

'A radio —' I started.

'Nuts, huh? But I didn't see it because of the light.'

I frowned. '*Your* light?'

'What? No. There was a light coming from the end of the tunnel I was in. I thought I'd found a way out. So I ran for it. The radio was on the floor near the light and I tripped over it. When I came around I hobbled towards the light. It's a good thing I wasn't in a fit state to run that last bit.'

'Why?'

'It was at the edge of a hole in the side of the cliff, looking out towards Rockway. Below was perhaps eighty feet of nothing; then some rocks; then the sea.'

'Wow,' the Mouse said.

'It was then I looked at my watch and saw it was broken.' Taking it from another of his pockets, he held it up by the strap. 'You think it can be repaired?' he asked me. 'It belonged to the Lieutenant. The *original* Lieutenant.' I shook my head sadly, wondering how I'd feel if I'd smashed one of Jimmy's possessions.

'Anyway,' Dingus continued, 'not long after, the lights went out and I was walking around in the dark. I mean, our eyes are good, but not as good as when we were on all fours. I kept hearing things in the distance; screaming, shouting. My imagination started to get the better of me. What if those screams were other animals who'd got lost down there? A lot of animals go missing in the city, Benji —'

237

'I think you need a drink,' I interrupted. Spotting the old boy I'd seen the first time I was here, I beckoned him over.

'A scotch here for my friend.'

'Yes sir.'

'Oh, Benji, really —' Dingus butted in, 'I don't drink.'

'In that case, make it a double,' I told the waiter who shuffled off to the bar. Perhaps sensing that the drink was for medicinal purposes the waiter, as much as he was able, hurried back with it. Reluctantly taking a sip, Dingus pulled a face.

'So how *did* you get out?' I said.

'I just kept stumbling about in the dark, half convinced I was going in and out of the same two or three tunnels each time. Suddenly I smelled kerosene and remembered that there was a can in the basement. So I followed the smell.'

When he picked up his whisky glass again, I noticed that his paws had stopped shaking.

'You needed that,' I said as he drained the glass. I ordered him another.

'I need this more,' he said, gesturing with his cigar. 'I didn't dare light one down there. They might not be great with sight or smell, but I wasn't taking any chances with the smoke. Thank you,' he said when the whisky arrived. 'Will you run me back there to get my car? I wasn't up to driving, so I walked here; well, staggered here. Down there I thought I'd never breathe fresh air again. It's not far.'

'Only when you've drunk your medicine like a good Dog,' I said. Knocking back the scotch in one go, he coughed a few times.

'Okay?' I asked.

'Sure,' he said, unsteadily getting to his feet. 'I'll be okay.'

29. GRIM SURROUNDINGS

'RIGHT. I MEAN LEFT! Uh-huh. Definitely left. Definitely. You know, I'm usually much better with directions than this. *Much* better. This heat haze must be affecting my coordination.'

'That or the whisky,' I said over my shoulder.

'The whisky? Oh no, no. You think so? You think the whisky's doing it? No. It's definitely the heat haze. Definitely. Don't you think so?'

It certainly wasn't helping. You couldn't see the sidewalk for the pulsing waves of heat.

'Do you think these lights are *ever* gonna change?' Dingus wondered. 'Hey, I forgot to ask: what's been happening while I've been gone? Did you get Harvey?'

Even though it didn't paint me in the best of lights, I gave him a brief account of things.

'Gee, this Harvey sounds like quite a guy.'

'Tell him what happened to the teeth,' the Mouse said excitedly.

'What about the teeth?' the Lieutenant asked.

I asked him if he'd heard of the Magpies.

'Sure. Big black and white Birds. What do they need teeth for? Are their beaks no good anymore?'

'No, the group known as the "Magpies". It looks like they're involved in the smuggling too.'

'Yeah, they do ring a bell now you mention it,' Dingus said.

I explained to him what I thought was going on. 'But there must be someone on the ground organizing all this; a contact between the Moles and the Magpies.'

'So who is he then? Or who is *she*?'

'Tell him about what's happened to Angelica!' the Mouse said, squirming in his seat.

'I'll get to her in a minute,' I told him. I pointed out the window at the green light. 'Go.'

'Aw, the middle man can wait for a while,' Dingus said impatiently. 'Tell me what happened to Angelica instead. It could be important.'

It was like having two kids in the car. 'She's gone missing from the Plaza,' I said, giving him the details. 'Your boys are looking into it. Now can I tell you about the middle man?'

'Sure,' he said. 'You fire away.'

So I told him.

'Wiedlin?' he said, suddenly sounding sober. 'You don't say?'

'I *do* say; and if you promise not to interrupt, I'll tell you all about it.'

'You know, Benji, you should lighten up once in a while,' he said in all seriousness. 'I *promise* I won't interrupt. Shoot.'

I told him the lot: about Angelica thinking she recognised Weidlin, and the story, right through to the coconut hairs I found under the sink in his apartment and why I thought Angelica had been taken.

'Holy Cow,' he said. 'So where's he taken her?'

'He mentioned an office when we spoke to him last night. After we've dropped you off we'll go and look for it. But my guess is it doesn't exist.'

'Lieutenant Dingus,' the Mouse said in a hushed voice, 'is this it?'

Dingus leaned forward between us. 'That's it. Creepy, huh?'

The two-storey building on the cliff was tall, thin and mainly grey, apart from the ancient white paintwork flaking off the door and windows. Lethal-looking strands of ivy held the centre of the house in a stranglehold, and faintly luminous clumps of moss clung to the moist lower sections of the brickwork. Around it danced small wisps of smoke, presumably a by-product of the sunshine beating down on the wet path.

Presumably.

The Mouse and I followed the Lieutenant into the living room. I was reminded of Lettice's room at the Plaza: it contained little apart from a beat-up sofa and a few mangy chairs. It was the kind of place you went to when there was nowhere else to go.

As I was admiring the décor, Dingus picked up the phone. 'Might as well see if there's any news about Angelica,' he told us. Listening to his one-sided conversation helped take my mind off the chill in the air. 'No news whatsoever,' he said, hanging up. 'So, what are you going to do n —'

A shrill squawk filled the room, coming from the chimney. As it died out, it was followed by a small flutter of soot.

'Jeez,' Dingus shivered, 'this place gives me the creeps.'

'It's just a Bird on the roof,' I told him.

'I know. But it was noises like that I kept hearing in the tunnels. Shrill, like someone was being —' he shivered again.

The Mouse and I seemed to be thinking the same thing. 'You don't think that Angelica —?' he started, alarmed.

'No,' Dingus told him. 'I'd have heard her, I'm sure.'

'But if Wiedlin is in with the Moles, she *might* be down there,' the Mouse said, turning to me. 'And we haven't a clue about this office of his, or if it even exists. I think we should go down and take a look.'

The expression on Dingus's face suggested he wasn't ready for a return visit. 'I need to go through the house, properly this time,' he said. 'But if you go down there, go prepared. In the meantime I'll call for backup,' He said, picking up the phone once more.

As he did, the Mouse and I looked around for anything we thought might be useful.

'They're on their way,' Dingus told us when we'd finished. 'Sure you don't want to wait and go down with them?'

'How long will they be?'

'Coming from the other side of town, it could be an hour or longer.'

I looked across at the Mouse. To me, holding back sounded like a great idea, but Ma Spayley's boy looked like he couldn't wait. And if some of the noises Dingus had heard down there *had* come from Angelica...

'We'll go now. I mean, we've got the map and there are two of us. How hard can it be?'

'Well, it's your funeral,' the Lieutenant said.

With Dingus's cheery words echoing in our ears, the Mouse and I headed for the basement.

30. UNDER THE HOUSE (2)

'THE LIEUTENANT'S RIGHT — IT DOES smell of kerosene in here.'

The basement was no less gloomy than the rest of the house and about ten degrees colder. Before we left, I had a quick look around for any signs of merchandise Bupkis might have had lying around, but found nothing.

'Scared?' I asked the Mouse.

'A little,' he said, strapping on his back the bag he'd found. 'But we're well prepared: rope, flashlights, matches, a few weapons... The only thing we haven't got are suits of armour.'

'If we did, the Moles would probably have can openers,' I said. Opening what looked like a closet door in the basement wall, a large black rectangle appeared, along with a heavy smell of earth. Taking a deep breath, I crouched slightly and crossed the threshold, the Mouse following.

As soon as he closed the door, I clicked on my flashlight. The beam lit up a solid, black tunnel, perhaps three feet across and five feet high, stretching as far as the light did. We walked in single file, occasionally banging into the walls as the tunnels narrowed. From time to time my head brushed the ceiling and small pieces of dislodged earth landed on my fur. For some reason when this happened, I half expected a face to come lunging forward out of the darkness. To stop myself from going gaga, I paid closer attention to the walls of earth; mostly they were rough, but some were so smooth they looked

243

like they'd been finished with a trowel. Behind me the Mouse was breathing heavily. Eventually, the ceiling began to stretch away from us and the walls began to retreat; now we were walking through a space the size of a small broom cupboard. With the extra room, the smell of earth became less intense.

Suddenly the tunnel divided into two. Consulting the map, I figured Dingus must've taken the right hand tunnel, leading to the smaller of the two burrows, and had somehow ended up moving away from the Moles. Stepping over to that side, I saw a narrow path which climbed steadily. It was full of boot-prints that could only have come from one animal.

I joined the Mouse at the left-hand tunnel. 'You think we should go in?' he asked.

'No,' I told him, 'but we will anyway.'

The tunnel was wide enough for us to walk side-by-side. We hadn't been walking long when the ceiling rose to a height of maybe three feet above us. Shining my light at it, I could see what I thought were small white shoots hanging from the crumbly soil, when one of them dropped down and began wriggling on the ground.

'Mr. S,' the Mouse hissed. '*Look!*'

Thinking that I was about to walk off the edge of something, I stopped.

At the far end of a wide-open space of perhaps twenty feet, four tunnel mouths were visible in the huge wall of soil ahead. Two were at ground level with a couple of feet between them. Another was a few feet above. The fourth was maybe eight or nine feet above that and was more ragged-looking than the others. And wriggling its way out of this one was a huge, Pig-like snout, while at either side of it two lethal-looking razor-tipped claws slashed around in midair.

'Kill the lights,' I whispered to the Mouse.

By the time our eyes adjusted once more to the darkness, the Mole had almost worked itself free from the packed earth surrounding it but was still gouging the air, as if looking for the ground. Suddenly, it lost its grip and toppled forward, tumbling through the air amid a stream of dislodged earth before landing on the ground head first with a dull thud.

It lay there for several seconds, showing no signs of life, curled into a tight, black ball. As I raised my paw to my mouth to muffle the heavy sound of my breathing, the lump on the ground began to chatter.

It did this for what felt like several minutes, and I was strangely relieved that it was too far away for me to hear what it was saying. Then, without any break in the chatter, the dark ball of curled-up flesh began to spread lengthways and its hind legs appeared, stamping at the soil. The top half of its squat body reared upwards, its shovel-like paws stretching in the air like it was waking from a long sleep. Completing its move from four legs to two, the paws quit stretching and the snout began quivering in the air.

Upright it must have been four, maybe five feet tall, a great patch of velvet blackness darker than the earth surrounding it. Slowly, the snout turned in our direction, and the small, button-like eyes buried at the back of that snout stared straight at us.

For several seconds we all looked at each other, nobody speaking, nobody breathing. I could see a faint, green light in his eyes which didn't make sense. The Mouse was shaking at my side. Then I realised what the light was. I lowered my head slowly. Three long seconds later the Mole moved away. As it did, it started muttering again before wandering off to the right, into a tunnel or cave we hadn't noticed.

'Did — did you see his eyes?' the Mouse whispered. 'That green light? He seemed to be looking straight at us.'

'It was the reflection of my eyes in his,' I told him. 'As soon as I looked away, he lost interest. I think he was more concerned that he'd fallen out of the hole.'

We waited a while before moving again, checking first that our friend had definitely gone.

'So where now?' the Mouse asked.

Shining my light on the map, we both tried to figure out where we were, but it was useless. Wherever it was, we had to try and find a way to get closer to the rest of the Moles and hopefully Angelica. 'These tunnels look a bit narrow,' I said, pointing at the four holes ahead. "I think we should try and find some others.'

Over to the left, past the four smaller holes, we came across another large bank of earth, host to half-a-dozen further holes all thankfully at ground level. One led into a small anteroom, which looked like it hadn't been used for quite some time. Four of the other holes looked too narrow.

The one remaining hole, as Mole-holes go, didn't look too bad. The entrance looked roughly seven feet high and wide enough for us to turn and run in if the need should arise.

Barely a few feet in, the path began to dip and wind to the right, eventually levelling out, with the ceiling remaining a good foot above us. With nothing to smell and nothing to hear, the walk was long and boring. After a while, I began to wonder how far from the surface of the earth we were, when the Mouse stopped dead and I almost walked into the back of him.

'What?' I said. 'I can't see anything.'

'Not see,' the Mouse said, '*smell.*'

Sniffing the air, I caught a scent which, although faint, I should've spotted earlier. I wondered if my knock on the head at the hotel had affected my sense of smell. 'What the hell is it?' I asked.

'I'll go have a look,' the Mouse said.

Before I had a chance to stop him, he was off. Suddenly, he took a left through what looked like a wall of solid earth. Then I heard a little squeak from somewhere up ahead. In the blink of an eye he reappeared, holding his nose and coughing.

'What is it?' Between coughs, he said something I wasn't sure I'd heard right.

'*Freezer*?' Not trusting my ears, I went in to see for myself.

It occupied about half of the small chamber, its lid covered with muddy smears and deep, claw-like scratches. I only managed to lift it an inch of two before I had to shut it again.

'They dragged a freezer down here, Mr. S,' the Mouse said, stunned, as I emerged spluttering from the room, 'somehow, they've actually dragged someone's freezer down here with all the food in it.'

We were still talking about it some time later when our flashlights picked out a long, hotel-like corridor full of roughly-hewn doorways further down. Sniffing the air and finding nothing threatening, we began to explore.

In total, we must have looked in a dozen chambers. Each was self-contained, and all the rooms displayed signs of being used at some point, most of which were plain baffling. There was nothing on a par with the freezer, but the room containing a pair of tennis rackets, three cocktail shakers, and four bicycles stacked against a wall stands out in my mind. It was as I was emerging from this room that I noticed a new smell.

Signalling to the Mouse, we inched forward together until we got to the smallish entrance where the smell seemed to be coming from. It wasn't as strong as the contents of the freezer, but was still pretty unpleasant. Slowly, I popped my head round the entrance. Seeing what looked like a pile of rotting offal on the other side of the room, I popped it back out again as quickly as I was able.

'What?' the Mouse asked excitedly, sticking his head through the entrance. 'Oh,' he said, sounding disappointed. 'Is that all?'

' "*All*"?' I hissed. 'What the hell is that thing?'

'Just a pile of worms,' he said, as if it was obvious. 'The Moles eat them. At least, the Old ones do. The smell must come from their droppings.'

'I'll take your word for it. Look, I think we should go back, we're getting nowhere. Let the cops find Angelica.'

To my surprise, he agreed. 'Yeah, we know the way back: past the bicycles and up. Still, it's been fun. We can always follow the cops again when they come down.'

'Hmm,' I murmured, heading back the way we came.

Coming to the last room we'd passed, I shone my flashlight onto the wall where the bicycles were standing. As before, a sharp glint of light struck my eyes, only this time lower down, at ground level. Wondering how the bikes could have fallen without us hearing them, I saw nothing except dozens of empty bottles scattered over the earth floor. And then the penny dropped.

'Linus,' I said, trying to sound calm, 'somehow we seem to have got lost.'

'But we followed the same path back —' He waved his flashlight into the room. 'Oh no,' he said. 'What do we do now?'

'We either wait for the cavalry or we try to find our own way out. Do you want to wait?'

'Not really,' he said. 'But if we keep moving, we might get even more lost.'

'I don't see how. We might get lucky, too. Come on.'

If it hadn't been for the different varieties of junk we kept finding in the various rooms, I would've sworn we were going through the same few tunnels over and over again. The things we kept finding were unnerving; not because they were weirder than what we'd found before, but because they looked less tarnished, less *abandoned* than what we'd seen earlier; even the worms hanging from the ceiling looked livelier. Then there were the scents: the piles of droppings, the rotten meat... One room even stank of beer; at the back we found dozens of cans full of ragged puncture marks, the beer dribbling onto the earth.

Whichever way we turned, it was the wrong way. Then, as another vile, rotting smell filled my nostrils, I saw a half-smiling face at the end of a corridor and nearly screamed out loud.

I should have turned, run; but there was something about that face, a familiarity that made me walk towards it, even though the smell grew stronger the closer I got to it. Its unblinking eyes held mine, even as I shone the torch beam straight into them. And there was something about that smile that made me think of… and then I realised who it was.

'Isn't that a famous picture, Mr. S?' the Mouse said behind me.

Somehow I managed to jump into the air and laugh with relief at the same time as the Mouse's torch beam played over the portrait of the "Mona Lisa" wedged firmly into the wall of soil.

'It is,' I said as I got my breath back. 'And the original's priceless. But I doubt even *they* could have been so resourceful as to —' I turned to face the Mouse, but he wasn't there. 'Linus?'

'Over here.'

I followed his voice into a room on the left. He was kneeling down, the flashlight playing ahead of him. The floor glittered like the sea on a sunny day. The Mouse looked up at me and smiled, but I couldn't speak. Digging one of his paws into the warm light, he fished it back out with something dangling from the end. As it sparkled in the beam of my torchlight, my first thought was that it was a worm; but if it was, it was the most beautiful worm the world had ever seen.

'The whole room's full of this stuff,' the Mouse squeaked as I stared at the gold chain in his mitt. 'Chains, watches, earrings; maybe it's the stuff from the Brierley Hall robbery.'

'Maybe,' I said. 'We'll let the cops know about it if we ever get out. In the meantime, grab a few things and put them in your pockets as proof.'

In the few seconds it took for all this to happen, we'd forgotten about the smell, and I was only reminded of it as I stepped back into the corridor. It was stronger now, as if it was coming from the next room. It wasn't pleasant, but that didn't stop us from sticking our heads round the entrance to look. It was me who saw it first: another pair of eyes, staring straight at us. Only this time they weren't in a picture: they were in a Mole.

The small black eyes that stared into mine were as lifeless as dull lumps of marble in an ancient statue. Through the odours of blood and earth I caught a faint whiff of gunpowder, then saw the thick gout of blood running down its chest.

'Mr. S!' the Mouse hissed behind me.

He was standing at the entrance to another chamber, waving his flashlight about. Slap in the middle was a safe with its door busted open. Inside was a Mole squashed up in a foetal position, as if it had crawled inside to die, its congealed blood running out onto the earth floor.

Quickly, I stepped back out into the corridor. Hearing the Mouse squeak behind me, my heart stopped: two, three beats. Turning as slowly as I could, I fully expected to see him standing there with either a Mole pressing a gun in his back, or worse, lying on the floor with Wiedlin standing above him, Harvey's tooth sticking out of his chest. After gulping down the tennis ball that seemed to be lodged in my windpipe, and turning to look and finding nothing wrong, I decided that swearing was the best policy.

'Why are you shining your light at the ceiling?' I asked, among my many profanities.

'I'm not!'

'Well if it isn't your light, then wh —'

Lowering his light on the ground, I saw a small pile of soil at his feet. Looking again at the beam of light, I realised two things. One, that the light came from above us; and two, so had the pile of earth on the floor. The tiny beam of light became the most beautiful thing I'd ever seen, its appearance even managing to distract me momentarily from the noise I could suddenly hear in the distance.

'Come on,' I said to the Mouse, 'let's get out of this madhouse.'

The noise was getting louder. I couldn't decide if it was coming from above or behind us. As we stared at the light, wondering how to reach it, the noise became clearer, clear enough to realise that it wasn't coming from above.

'Okay,' I said. 'Here's what we do —'

But my words were drowned out by the noise in the tunnel behind us. Turning, we saw nothing; but we both knew what we'd heard.

Screams.

31. THREE ESCAPE

'CROUCH DOWN. I'LL CLIMB onto your back.'

'Why me?'

'Because if we do it the other way round you'll squash me into the floor. Now do it.'

Reluctantly, the Mouse crouched down. With the racket getting louder and closer, I took a run and jumped onto him. Apart from a slight wobble he held firm.

'Right; now raise yourself slowly. And pass me your flashlight.'

'Why?'

'Just pass me the thing. And shut your eyes.'

Holding onto his shoulders, I was maybe a foot from the light. Grabbing the flashlight, I also retrieved my own and let go of his shoulders. Closing my eyes, I punched the gap in the soil with both flashlights, showering us with dirt. When I opened my eyes again a few seconds later, the hole was still only about a foot wide. Instead of pummeling it again, I swept my paws around the hole to widen the gap. When I stopped, my claws were caked with earth. The hole was now a couple of feet wide, the outer edge of it close enough for me to grab.

'I'm going to leapfrog my way out,' I shouted down to the Mouse amid the din. 'If you get a bad back, you can sue me later. Okay?'

'I've already got a bad back!' he shouted.

'Okay. Here goes!'

Clinging onto the Mouse's shoulders, I took a breath and leapt up in a way the Old me would've been proud of. Shooting up towards the light for what felt like the longest split-second of my life, I eventually landed on the grass, rolling away from the hole as I did.

I was still on the ground when I heard the unmistakable sound of gunfire from below. The Mouse shouted for me to hurry up. Lying flat on what I hoped was a firm section of soil near the hole, I reached down for him. When he jumped he was so close to reaching my paw it was painful. I heard another shot and the Mouse squeaked again.

'I'll see if I can find anything up here,' I called out to him.

I was quite close to the edge of the cliff, which was fenced-in by wire and metal rods. Bupkis's house was about half a mile in the other direction, too far away to get help. I had an idea. 'Throw me your backpack,' I shouted down the hole.

'What?' the Mouse shouted back.

'Your backpack; throw it up to me.'

He managed to get it up to me on the second attempt. Groping around inside it, I pulled out the rope we'd found at the house.

'Grab hold of this,' I yelled, lowering it into the hole. He yelled something back, but I couldn't hear what it was.

'*What?*'

'I said there's a Dog down here; at the other end of the tunnel. He's got a gun.'

'Has he seen you?' I shouted.

'I don't think so.' A shot was fired below. 'Hurry up!' he yelled.

Hoping the rope was long enough, I ran over to the fence and tied the end around one of the fence posts. Returning to the hole, I shouted down: 'Tie the rope around your wrists. When you've done that, start jumping at the hole.'

Hoping he'd heard me, I ran back toward the fence, where I started to wind the slack of the rope around the post.

253

I seemed to have been winding the rope a long time before I felt any pull from it. By the time I did, I was running out of post to knot it around. Then the rope suddenly became taut, burning through my paws. Gritting my teeth, I grabbed at the foot or so I had left, holding onto the post for support at the same time. As I did, I felt the post moving, drawing itself up out of the ground. I was so near the edge of the cliff that I couldn't move backwards; all I could do was try to hold on. The Mouse's end of the rope tightened again. Instinct took over: instead of grabbing at the post, I let it break free of the soil, then fell on top of it before it slithered away from me, keeping it in place with my weight. But still it wriggled beneath me, and was just starting to pull away from me when I saw the muddy-white paws of the Mouse gripping the edge of the hole, followed by his hasty scrabbling over the edge, where he rolled away before the ground around him collapsed.

'You okay?' I asked, running over to him.

'Only just,' the Mouse gasped, untying the rope from his paws. 'Just as I was getting out, that Dog started grabbing at my feet.'

'What kind of Dog?'

'Help!' a ragged voice shouted up from the hole.

Going over to it, I looked at the Schnauzer below, a smile breaking out on my face.

'Hello, Quentin,' I said. His look of astonishment turned my smile into a grin.

'Quick, help me out of here!' he barked, 'they're going to kill me!'

'Really,' I said, looking at the rope burns on one of my paws, 'who's "they," Quentin?'

He looked at me like I was an imbecile. 'Who? *The Moles!*'

'Oh,' I said, looking at my other paw. 'Them. Where's Angelica?'

'I don't know! Just get me out of here.'

'Tell me where she is, Quentin.'

'Look,' he snarled, waving his gun up at me, 'get me out of here now or I'll shoot.'

'I don't doubt it, Quentin,' I told him. 'But I'll bet you're shaking so much you won't hit me. Here's what we'll do. You throw that gun up here and *then* we'll get you out.'

He looked up at me, his eyes blazing, the gun wobbling in his paw. A shout from below made him turn his head for a second.

'Gun,' I shouted. '*Now.*'

Gritting his teeth, he threw the gun up from the hole.

'How're your paws?' I asked the Mouse.

'Sore,' he told me. 'But we have to get him out.'

'Yeah,' I said. 'Shame.'

With the Mouse at my back, I lowered the now fraying rope down. With two of us pulling, Quentin emerged pretty quickly. Grabbing hold of him, I pulled him over the side of the hole, where he lay gasping like a caught fish. Rope burns were the least of his worries: his face and body were covered in scratches, and dried blood caked his clothes and fur.

'We'd better go before they follow us,' the Mouse said.

'They won't follow,' Wiedlin panted. 'Not during the day. Listen.'

We did. We heard nothing but silence.

'Right,' I said, jabbing the gun in Wiedlin's direction, 'let's go and see the Lieutenant, shall we? Did I mention he's organised a raid of the tunnels? After I've introduced you, you can tell the three of us everything you know.'

'I don't think so,' Wiedlin grunted. 'Now, back off and throw me the gun.'

I hadn't been watching him closely enough. With Cat-like grace, Wiedlin had moved towards the Mouse, and now had one of his arms around as much of him as he could cover, while the other jabbed something into his back.

'Quentin,' I said, moving forward, 'now you're just being silly.'

'Stay where you are or I'll plug him,' the Schnauzer growled. 'And stop calling me that.' He shuffled himself and the Mouse away awkwardly. The Mouse, realising what was being stuck into his back, remained calm.

'Quentin, Quentin, Quentin,' I said, still going towards him, 'you're not plugging anyone. You haven't got the nerve or the skill. Besides, Linus has a thick skin. No offence intended,' I said to the Mouse.

'Another step, Spriteman, and I'll do it,' Wiedlin warned.

'Fine, have it your way. Linus, do what you have to. But remember, we still want him to be able to talk.'

With one swift movement, the Mouse dug his elbow into Wiedlin's side, doubling him in half. While the air was still coming out of him, I made a grab for the weapon.

'Come on, Linus,' I said, pushing Wiedlin ahead of me, 'let's go see the Lieutenant.'

'Only if you stop calling me Linus.'

'I can't call him Quentin *and* I can't call you Linus? Hell, I can't do anything right.'

Seconds later, Wiedlin was upright and complaining. Remembering what I had in my other paw, I gave him a jab with it.

'Mr. S,' the Mouse said, 'do you think I could —'

'Sure,' I said, tossing the weapon over.

'I was pretty sure that's what it was,' the Mouse said, rolling it around in his paws. 'Wow. You weren't kidding about the size of those teeth were you, Mr. S?'

32. SOME THINGS FOUND

'**W**ELL, HERE WE ARE, Quentin,' I said outside Bupkis's house. 'Home sweet home.'

'You should be taking me to a hospital,' Wiedlin complained, 'after what those Moles did to me.'

'Is that why you killed two of them?' I said, pushing him through the door. 'Still, the Lieutenant's a fair chap. Maybe after you've confessed we can get you a bath-chair. Dingus?' I called out, 'We're home.'

Despite the three of us stinking like grave robbers, our aromas were soon enveloped by the odours of scotch and cigar smoke in the living room emanating from the Lieutenant, who was staring up at us from a mangy-looking armchair. Beside him on the floor was a nearly empty pint whisky bottle.

'Where is she?' he said. 'You find her?'

'Neither hide nor hair,' I said. 'But we did find this on our travels. Dingus, I'd like you to meet Quentin P. Wiedlin.'

'How do you do, Mr. Wiedlin,' Dingus said, as if talking to the bereaved.

'Me? I'm just *ducky*,' Wiedlin spat, as I pushed him into a chair. I asked the Lieutenant if he was drunk.

'No, but I'm not sober either. Linus; you'll have to drive us back. You know, Mr. Wiedlin,' he said, leaning forward, 'I had a *terrible* time down there —'

'We all did,' I interrupted. 'Let's go on with it. Mr. Wiedlin here has lots of things he wants to share with you.'

'Does he? Well, fire away.'

Wiedlin said nothing.

'Mr. Wiedlin? Quentin? Can I call you Quentin?'

Nothing.

'Besides emptying that bottle of scotch, what else have you been doing?' I asked Dingus.

'Oh, I've been really busy.' Leaning across the table, he picked up several sheets of paper. 'In the-' he looked across at the clock on the mantelpiece 'forty or so minutes since you left, I've found a suitcase packed with clothes and a fair sum of money. After that, I called my overseas colleagues, and — after telling them we were close to solving the case — they put me in touch with Brierley Hall. I told them I needed an *exact* inventory of the goods stolen at the Hall, and no holding back this time. And they said "yes!" ' I tried to imagine what an argumentative Dingus must've sounded like. 'What else? Yes, I phoned police HQ and told them where I'd been. They were *very* interested, I have to tell you. I also asked them to look into the possible whereabouts of Mr. Wiedlin's "office." But now you're here, perhaps you could tell us yourself, Quentin?' Wiedlin, turning his face from the Lieutenant, muttered in disgust.

'What's the matter with him?' Dingus asked.

'He doesn't like being called Quentin,' I told him.

'Doesn't he,' Dingus chuckled to himself as he lit a cigar.

'*Forty minutes*?' the Mouse said.

'Excuse me?'

'You said we'd only been gone forty minutes.'

'That's right; you left here around two thirty and it's now just after a quarter past three. I make that about forty minutes. Didn't you check your watches?'

I was stunned. I never even thought about it. 'We must've been in longer than —' I looked at my watch: three fifteen. 'Forty minutes,' I said quietly.

'Yup. That was all,' the Lieutenant said, reaching for his glass on the table close to the chair, 'forty minutes. Anyway, have a drink. Oh,' he pointed at his glass. 'S'empty.'

'I'll get you a refill,' I said, pouring him the dregs from his bottle.

As I poured, the police search party arrived. They looked like they'd come prepared for anything, loaded up with weaponry. There was talk about flushing them out with tear gas, until it was pointed out the problems some Officers would have fitting pre-Terror gasmasks onto their snouts. With more than a little swagger in his walk, Dingus took most of them down to the basement. We told the ones that were left about the hole we'd come through, and the Mouse left to show them where it was.

With the Mouse and the Lieutenant out of the way, I turned to Wiedlin.

'Okay, Quentin. Where is she?'

'Who...?' he asked, raising his eyebrows innocently.

'Don't get cute with me, Wiedlin. Angelica de Groot.'

'Oh. *Her*. I've no idea.'

'Why did you take her into the tunnels?'

'Did I? I don't remember saying so.'

'Okay, what were *you* doing down there? And don't tell me you fancied a change of air.'

'In that case,' he said, 'I won't tell you anything.'

The door behind us slamming, I turned and saw Dingus stagger across the room and flop into the nearest chair.

'If you won't tell us about Angelica, tell us about the coconuts,' he said. 'Where can we find them?'

'Coconuts?' Wiedlin immediately brightened. 'Now that I *can* help you with. Little brown hairy things, right? The best place to find *them* would be the midway. Or the tropics.'

'I found coconut hairs at Derry Park Flats,' I told him. 'In that place you don't use as an apartment.'

'Really? I don't remember inviting you in,' Wiedlin said, his eyes widening, 'and I'm sure I locked the door on the way out, so you must have... Oh dear... that really won't do at all.'

You really think you're invincible, don't you?'

'The luck's on my side, let's put it that way. I mean, I'm not stuck down there in that hell-hole, am I? *I got out.*'

'Alright then, if you won't talk about Angelica *or* the coconuts, perhaps you *will* tell us about *Lettice,*' Dingus said.

'Ah, the lovely Lettice... first Lettice, then Angelica. I daresay we'll never see their like again.' Crossing his legs, he let out a long mournful sigh. 'Of course, there is a *remote* possibility that Angelica is still alive. But I doubt it. It's like a war-zone down there.'

'I know. I saw the bodies. Why did you kill the Moles?'

'I never killed any Moles. They probably killed each other. I'd imagine being cooped up like that would drive anybody to murder.'

'That didn't stop you dealing with them,' Dingus put in. 'Or the Magpies.'

'That reminds me,' I said. 'Did you get what you were looking for at Rusty Laidlaw's office?'

For the briefest of moments Wiedlin's mask slipped. 'What are we talking about now?' he snapped, resuming his defiance.

' "The Mystery of the Fifteenth Corkscrew": a rather mediocre story of yours set in a wine cellar. When I brought Angelica along to your apartment last night you looked like someone had stuck a Bee up your shirt and I couldn't figure out why. When we left she said she thought you looked familiar. The thing was, I only brought her along to get the story. But you knew if she read it, she'd know who you were; if she didn't already. So you got the Magpies to break into Laidlaw's office to get it back before she read it, only they didn't find it. So you took her instead. How close am I, Quentin?' Apart from the odd twitch, Wiedlin didn't respond. 'Your big mistake was sending that rejection letter to *No Shit Sherlock*. If you hadn't, I'd never have come into contact with you —'

'If you must know, I lost her down there. On purpose. Let the Moles deal with her. They'd probably have dealt with me too, if you hadn't dragged me out of there.'

'The search party will find her,' I said, icily.

'Oh, I doubt that *very* much.'

'You know, I just can't get that story of yours out of my head,' I told him. 'Would you like me to remind you what it's about?'

'Not especially,' Wiedlin said without looking up.

'Maybe you're right,' I said, sitting back down. 'We'll wait until Angelica's here. She'd love to hear it.'

'No doubt,' Wiedlin said, scratching himself.

We tried to get him to talk after that, but with no luck. In the silence, Dingus fell asleep. I wondered how much longer the search party would be.

The sound of the front door opening startled me. 'Only me,' said the Mouse, barely audible over the Lieutenant's snoring. I gave him a nudge.

'What's happening?' I asked.

'I don't know. I heard shooting though, and a lot of shouting. What about —' he indicated Wiedlin.

'He's pretending he's taken a vow of silence. When the search party comes back, we'll take him downtown. And if he's really good, we may let a doctor look at his cuts and bruises.' Wiedlin sniffed.

'Hey, where's the bottle?' Dingus asked groggily.

'You finished it.'

'*The whole bottle?*'

'Yep. Don't you remember? Clearly alcohol doesn't agree with you.'

Hearing a noise below, the four of us turned towards the basement door. Seconds later it burst open, and several grubby-looking and shell-shocked officers came into the room.

'How did it go?' Dingus asked.

'Tough,' the officer in charge said. 'They fought like lunatics. We managed to get quite a few of them, and a lot of stolen property. And we found a few other exits, too. One of them comes out close to town so we're taking most of them out that way. The nearer ones we're going to bring out at the bottom of the cliff there.'

'What about Miss de Groot?' I asked. 'Did you find her?'

'We never even saw her,' the officer said. 'There were dozens of tunnels we never even went into; she could be in any of them. But I don't fancy her chances.'

'Oh dear,' Wiedlin said, smiling down at his claws.

33. WASHED UP

'THEY DON'T LOOK SO big out in the open, do they?' said the Mouse.

'I think that's down to the blankets,' I replied.

At the back of the house, we watched as another Mole came up the ladder and out of the hole with its head covered.

'How come they get blankets and I don't?' Wiedlin complained.

'They need them to protect their eyes from the sun,' Dingus told him.

'Diddums,' Wiedlin muttered.

'Heaven knows where they're going to put them,' Dingus said. 'They'll need to line the walls with steel or something. And the ceilings and floors. Are we ready to go?'

'Certainly are,' I said, rattling the cuff on my wrist. On the other end, Wiedlin made his disgust known by spitting on the ground.

'You'll be wanting to sit in on the interview?' Dingus asked as we walked towards his car.

'Sure. It might be a good idea if one of us is sober.'

'What do you mean? I'm perfectly fine.'

'Lieutenant, you could strip wallpaper with your breath. And I'd seriously suggest you don't light a cigar for a while. What is it?'

He'd pulled up a few feet from the house, his head bent to one side. 'The phone's ringing.'

As he rushed back inside, Wiedlin wriggled his paw around inside his cuff, jerking my arm up into the air.

'Will you stop that?' I snarled.

'You've fastened it too tight and it's digging into my skin,' Wiedlin complained.

'Quit moaning or I'll reacquaint you with the tooth; and I don't mean the blunt end.'

When Dingus came back out of the house he looked grim. 'Change of plan,' he said. 'Linus, I'm in no fit state to drive; can you take us back to Rockway in my car, then come back here for yours? But be careful; it's rare model,' he said, throwing him the keys. Before the Mouse could reply Dingus settled himself in the passenger seat.

'Why are we going back to Rockway?' I asked, once I'd got Wiedlin into the back.

'Because something interesting just washed up on the beach,' Dingus said, his back to me.

Beside me, Wiedlin was edgier than I'd ever seen him.

'Okay Dingus; spill it. This is about Angelica, right? At least tell me if she's alive or dead.'

'Oh, she's alive all right,' he said.

Inside the Plaza, the lobby seemed livelier than usual and there was a faint odour of seaweed. All eyes were turned on us.

'So why are we here?'

'Just over an hour ago the captain of the *Pleasance*, a pleasure boat doing tours around the cliffs, spotted a large Blue-Cream Longhair Cat in a floral print dress clinging to a rock in the water about thirty feet away from the cliff as he was coming back into the harbour.'

'Angelica? Is she hurt?'

'A bit worse for wear apparently, but she'll live. She ended up there after escaping Mr. Wiedlin's clutches in the tunnels in the early hours of this morning. By the sound of things, she did exactly what I did: ran blindly through the tunnels until she saw a light up ahead and headed straight for it. Only she didn't stop in time and landed in the drink — the cliff-side must be peppered with holes like that. Luckily for her, the incoming tide washed her up onto a small outcrop of rock where the boat found her.'

We both looked at Wiedlin, who was trying his best to keep calm. 'It's her word against mine,' he said quietly.

'So what's she doing here? Shouldn't she be at the hospital getting checked out?'

'Yeah, she should. But she refuses to go to the hospital until she's spoken with us. She says that she knows who the murderer is.'

Wiedlin suddenly looked ill. 'Looks like your luck finally ran out Quentin,' I told him.

Getting out of the elevator, the three of us shuffled along the sixth floor corridor: me manacled to Wiedlin, and Dingus tottering along beside us. At the steps leading to the turret, he went on ahead and knocked on the door, the stink of the sea and rotting Fish wafting down to us.

'Sounds like they're having a tea party up here,' Dingus said as the door opened.

Manoeuvring an increasingly difficult Wiedlin up the narrow steps and closing the door behind us, I saw he wasn't wrong: the small room was packed. On one side, it was wall-to-wall biddies. On the other, for no reason that I could think of, stood a Guinea Pig squashed into a rumpled brown suit, a Toucan with a discoloured red beak, an elderly Rabbit wearing nothing but a pair of Bermuda shorts that stopped just below his chin, and a nervy Chinchilla who looked like he could jump out the window at any second.

We found Angelica propped up in bed, looking dishevelled and a little crazed: her fur and whiskers were straggly and her eyelids drooped heavily.

'Nice to see you again, Angelica,' I said as cheerfully as I could. 'But I think at the hospital would have been better. I could have got you a basket of fruit on the way.'

'This is no time for levity, Mr. Spriteman' she said, raising herself from the mattress. 'If you could make your way over there — that's right, next to the others — we can begin.'

I was a little taken aback by her tone, but I seemed to be the only one.

'And what about Mr. Wiedlin here?' I asked.

'Yes, him as well. But I want you away from each other. Lieutenant, if you could take those cuffs off...' without a word, Dingus unfastened the bracelet from Wiedlin's wrist.

'What's going on, Lieutenant?' I asked as he removed the cuff from my wrist.

'Okay Angelica,' he said, ignoring me. 'Who's to go where?'

'Mr. Spriteman nearest the window, Mr. Wiedlin at the other end of the line. The others are fine where they are.'

Feeling like I was heading for a firing squad, I went and stood next to the Guinea Pig. Realising I was the centre of attention, I put up with them all staring at me for a few seconds more before reacting.

'Is this necessary, Angelica? We know Wiedlin's responsible.'

The look she gave me suggested that I wasn't to talk again. Talking was not helping us get this thing finished.

So I didn't.

34. ANGELICA EXPLAINS

A NY HOPES I HAD of an early resolution were dashed.
Just as Angelica looked like she was ready to start,
Dingus ushered her towards the bathroom. Standing
in the doorway with their paws in front of their faces, I could
make out nothing, until Dingus whispered something that
appeared to knock Angelica back on her heels.

'*That's it!*' she hissed. 'My God; that's *it!*' Then, with a
strange happy-sad look on her face, she gazed over at me with
an expression I found impossible to read.

'Right!' she said, moving towards us all again but still
holding my gaze, 'I think we're about ready to begin.

'First of all, you're probably wondering why I've got you
here,' she said, surveying the assorted faces. 'Well, you're here
to assist in the solving of a crime, or rather, a series of crimes
ranging from blackmail and kidnapping, through to robbery
and smuggling, and finally murder; the perpetrator of which is
now standing among us in this room.' At that, a gasp of shock
and horror passed through the room.

'I think most of you know who I am. For those that do not, my
name is Angelica de Groot and, together with my sister Lettice,
I wrote crime novels. But, as has been recently discovered, that
arrangement was not all it seemed.' Explaining the real truth
behind their "collaborations," her audience gasped.

'So,' she carried on, 'I am not entirely blameless in this
affair. Anyway; to the crimes themselves.

'Back at home, Lettice had promised our publishers a novel featuring a Private Eye. She'd read an article in a journal about the infamous "Carlin Case", which, if you recall, was solved largely thanks to Lieutenant Dingus here,' she waved a paw in his direction, 'and by the Private Investigator, Benji Spriteman. As our books were proving quite popular over here, it was decided that we would undertake a promotional book tour; and as our first port of call led us here, we could also pay a visit to Mr. Spriteman himself, to learn something of his business.

'We arranged to meet him at the launch for our new book. Tragically, within a few minutes of meeting Mr. Spriteman, Lettice collapsed following a brief altercation they'd had, and died. It was later determined that Lettice had been killed as a result of Strychnine poisoning.' Again, several old dears gasped in horror, casting appalled glances in my direction. I didn't like where this was going.

'I wanted the Lieutenant here to look into my sister's death. Unfortunately he was busy working on another job, more of which later. But, recalling Mr. Spriteman's sterling work on the Carlin case and ignoring his silly spat with my sister, I engaged him to look into the matter. In return, I agreed to look into the case he was working on concerning a series of hate-filled letters being sent to local fiction magazines.'

'Is this going to last all day?' Wiedlin asked. 'It's fascinating stuff, but there are other things I'd rather be doing.'

'Ah, yes; Mr. Wiedlin. Perhaps now would be a good time to explain your role in the proceedings; indeed your part in my now looking like a drowned Rat.'

'Interesting comparison,' Wiedlin said quietly.

'In the early hours of the morning in this very room, Mr. Wiedlin forced his way in armed with a gun, bustled me out of the hotel and led me into the vast underground system of tunnels used by the Moles under this very cliff.' She gave a brief account of our underground friends before continuing. 'Why did he do this? He did it in order to stop me reading a story he'd written which he thought would come into my possession.'

'That sounds a bit extreme,' an old Siamese with blue fur pointed out.

'Yes, but this was no ordinary story. Mr. Wiedlin had only written it as a joke, but it was in fact extremely incriminating. Anyway, where was I? Yes: the story. Or rather not, because at the time it was not the story that interested me, but Mr. Wiedlin himself. When I met him earlier, I'd had the nagging feeling that I'd seen him somewhere before. Then, shortly before Mr. Wiedlin broke into my room, I realised where I knew him from: an article I'd read in our local paper about a robbery at a stately home called Brierley Hall. Next to the article had been a rather blurry photograph of a Dog the police wanted to talk to; *the same Dog who is now standing over there.*'

'This is ludicrous,' Wiedlin said, shaking his head.

'Oh, you look a bit different, I grant you — your fur's shorter and a shade darker and I'll bet that accent you're using now isn't your natural one — but it's you all right.

'So why would he go to such lengths to retrieve a story? For one simple reason: *it would blow his cover, because Mr. Wiedlin here is the mastermind behind the smuggling operation which involved my half-sister.*'

'Can you stop doing that?' I snapped, as another sharp intake of breath came from the biddies. 'You're sucking all the air out of the room.'

After waiting for the fuss to die down, Angelica continued.

'Unbeknownst to me, hidden among her luggage was a small crate containing coconuts, the insides of which are hollow, and therefore perfect for hiding contraband, such as jewellery. In particular, I now believe, the famous Greodot diamonds, thought to have been lost for over a century, but which were in fact in the vaults at Brierley Hall. And, unless I'm very much mistaken,' she said angrily, '*Greodot* is an anagram of *de Groot*; the very name that Lettice insisted we publish our novels under.'

Following this revelation, the shocked intakes of breath were so strong it felt like they were pulling out my fur. 'For God's sake, somebody open a window,' I said, flattening myself back down.

'From this hotel,' she carried on, 'I believe Lettice passed the coconuts onto the Moles who, until recently, nobody suspected of existing, let alone being involved in organised crime.

'They've already taken the hotel's safe and the one from the bank in town by burrowing up through the floors. They were able to do this with the help of Mr. Burt, the hotel detective. Burt had arranged for Lettice to have a room on the ground floor, where she was able to leave the coconuts under the floorboards for the Moles. In exchange, they'd give her some of the money they'd stolen in the safe robberies. But knowing Lettice, I'll bet she wasn't satisfied with her share of the profits, and it was at this point that I think Burt persuaded Lettice to join forces with him. They might not be able to locate the Moles, but they could go after the creature behind the whole scam — Quentin P. Wiedlin — and blackmail him. Only of course Wiedlin couldn't allow this to happen.'

'And now they're both dead. So you're saying the same animal killed both Lettice and Burt?' Dingus asked.

'That's correct. As well as killing Grover S. Nelson.'

'*What?*' I said, not believing what I was hearing.

'Nelson was obviously in on it too.'

'Dingus,' I protested, 'she's not making sense. We know Nelson's death was an accident and it's obvious that Wiedlin killed Lettice and Burt. Angelica's obviously concussed after her ordeal and it's affecting her judgement.'

'No,' Angelica put in, now sitting on the bed, 'we might *suspect* that Mr. Wiedlin was involved, but we can't prove he killed anyone. In fact, I explained this to Mr. Wiedlin as he was leading me into the tunnels. I said that I thought somebody else had killed them. He'd told them to do it, certainly, but we couldn't prove that either.'

All of a sudden Wiedlin looked positively relaxed, like he was eagerly awaiting what was coming next.

'So if Wiedlin didn't commit the murders, who the hell did?'

'*You did Benji,*' Angelica said, raising herself from the bed as she pointed at me.

If there was a gasp that time, I didn't hear it; I was too busy laughing. Looking around, I saw I was the only one; even the Lieutenant's face was immobile.

'I know more about you than you think, Benji,' Angelica said. 'The Carlin case was your finest hour. But, as you also admitted, your worst. How long did it take for the fuss to die down, before you could do your job again properly? A long time, I'll bet; and money must have been tight.'

'Things picked up. I never did anything my mother wouldn't have been proud of.'

'That's not what Taki told me.'

'*What?*'

'She told me it was terrible, watching you struggle to pay the rent. She said she didn't like to think about what you had to do in order to make ends meet.'

Shaking my head I looked over at Dingus. 'Do you believe *any* of this?'

'These are very serious accusations you're making, Miss de Groot,' Dingus said, ignoring me. 'Why would he kill three animals like that?'

'Because he was desperate. At some point, maybe as part of another investigation, I think Benji and Mr. Wiedlin's paths crossed and Benji started to do a few little jobs for him. This arrangement was satisfactory until Lettice arrived. By then, Benji, you were so far in with Wiedlin that you couldn't go back. And when he wanted someone troublesome putting out of harm's way... I daresay the job was made slightly easier because the two of you were like oil and water.'

'How am I supposed to have killed her?' I asked sarcastically.

'With the strychnine, of course. As to how you managed it, I'm not sure. We know Mr. Wiedlin couldn't have done the deed because he left the book signing shortly after Lettice arrived. My guess is that you did it one of two ways: either by poisoning the cigarette she was smoking, or tampering with her food at some point.'

The whole thing was so ridiculous that I couldn't think of a thing to say against it. 'So how did I kill Burt?' I asked.

'Ah, now that's a bit more straight-forward, as you were seen shortly before the crime occurred, running out of the ballroom to chase after him. There are several witnesses to that.' A couple of the old dears murmured in agreement. 'Eventually you caught up with him; you struggled; during this struggle he hit you hard on the head, but you managed to stab him in the back with the tooth. Then you dumped him in the hole, implicating the Moles.'

'What about the tooth; where did I get that from? How did I manage to dig that hole, *and* get the Dog down there without being seen or heard? Plus, of all the places in the world I could have hidden, why did I choose a laundry basket?'

Angelica looked unruffled. 'You could quite easily have got the tooth from Mr. Wiedlin —'

'— which you can't *prove*,' Wiedlin added helpfully.

'— which we can't prove. As for the hole, the Moles could've helped you with that. What would it matter to them if they were implicated? Nobody knew how to get at them! And we know that Burt took Trix and then vanished from view; or so we thought. But I think you suspected that Burt had Trix hidden at the hotel. In which case, you took him while Burt was out of the way, and put him in the hole to muddy the waters even further. As for the laundry basket, we know that Burt hit you hard enough to concuss you. But who says that concussion started immediately? Its effects can sometimes be delayed — in this case just long enough for you to add a little

272

coda to your crime — and by hiding in the basket after you killed him and pulling a sheet over you, it looked as though Burt left you for dead when he escaped.'

'But he did!' I shouted. 'That's what happened!'

'I'm afraid not,' Angelica said. 'Miss Marsh, would you step forward, please?'

Miss Marsh, an ageing Terrier whose dress was the same colour as her fur, shuffled towards Angelica.

'Now, Miss Marsh, will you tell everybody here what you saw from your bedroom window?'

'Certainly,' Miss Marsh said, enjoying her moment in the spotlight. 'On the night in question I was getting ready for bed when I heard a commotion outside and that's when I saw him: a large Cat staggering about as if he were drunk.'

'Would you recognise that Cat if you saw him again, Miss Marsh?'

'Of course I would. It's the one on the end of the line there. The Tortoiseshell.' Between the gasps, I heard Wiedlin tutting contentedly to himself.

'Well, I never,' he said to Angelica, as it went quiet again. 'I thought you were kidding.' Confused, I wondered if I'd missed something.

'Okay, so that leaves Nelson,' I said. 'And we know how he died. Why did I kill him?'

'Mr. Wiedlin wouldn't tell me in what capacity Nelson was involved. But I think you pushed him into the path of an oncoming car. You were seen in the area around that time.'

'Yes: on the bus going back to town after talking to you! Ask the driver!'

Dingus gave a little cough. 'I did, Benji. I'm afraid the driver has no recollection of seeing anyone matching your description.'

I finally snapped. 'What? I've been on that damned bus virtually every day since this thing started! If he can't —'

Then I stopped. God, what a fool I was. Looking at Angelica, she looked away. When I looked at Dingus, he did the same. 'Oh, what's the use,' I said feebly. Angelica continued.

'You could as easily have changed buses when you were a sufficient distance from the hotel and then caught a later bus to town. I don't blame you for what you've been a part of, Benjamin; heaven knows the hardships you must've faced as a result of the Carlin case. But justice is justice, and you must face the full force of the law.'

'Come on, Benji,' Dingus said, coming towards me with the cuffs. As Dingus slapped the bracelets on I could hear Wiedlin sniggering in the corner.

'What about him?' I said, waving my manacled paws in his direction. 'You're not letting him go, are you?'

'We've no proof — you were at all three crime scenes; he wasn't at any of them. But if Mr. Wiedlin knows what's good for him he won't leave town. We'll certainly be keeping a close eye on him.'

'No worries on that score, Lieutenant,' Wiedlin said seriously. 'I'm not going anywhere. You can be assured of that.'

'Why you —' Before Dingus could stop me, I lunged at Wiedlin, but the cuffs robbed my blows of any power.

'Come on, let's go,' Dingus said amid more tuts and gasps from the assembled crowd.

Along with another officer at the bottom of the stairs, we walked to the elevator in single file. Dingus pressed the button for the ground. Nobody spoke. As the small metal box began its descent, I wondered what was going to happen next.

All told, it was pretty much as I expected.

When the elevator door opened it was to a lobby full of rubbernecking old codgers, all vying to get a good look at the prisoner. Sometimes, the speed of the Jungle Telegraph is truly astonishing. Standing among them was the Mouse.

'Hey! He didn't do anything!' he shouted when the handbags started flying.

Somehow Dingus pushed us through the throng, taking as many handbag shots as I did. The other officer squeezed us through a small gap in the door before he shut it after us.

Now it was just me and the Lieutenant. He walked me down the hill, past a few cabs waiting for fares, until we were about a hundred yards from the hotel.

'Get in,' Dingus said, stopping before a car with an open back door.

Careful not to bang my head, I ducked inside. Dingus removed the handcuffs.

'Look,' he said, pointing.

Wiedlin was coming out of the hotel. Going over to the nearest cab, he jumped in the back. When it slid out into the road a few seconds later, the cab behind it did the same.

'You on him?' Dingus said, talking into a radio from the front passenger seat.

'Yep. I don't think he's spotted us,' a crackly voice replied.

'Right. We'll be along soon.'

Before I had a chance to ask any questions, I spotted Angelica and the Mouse walking towards us. The Mouse had a peculiar expression on his face, like he'd just been told something very interesting; like I hoped I was going to be.

'Okay Dingus,' I said when they were nearly at the car. 'When?'

'When what?' he said.

'When,' I repeated as Angelica joined me on the back seat and the Mouse got in the front, 'did you cook all this up? I'm guessing it was that telephone call you took as we were leaving Bupkis' place.'

'We'll explain it on the way,' Dingus told me. Pointing out to the Mouse which car we were following, he said, 'Remember, you're just following *our* car. No heroics.'

'I knew you were innocent, Mr. S,' the Mouse said. 'Angelica just told me what happened back there.'

'I wish someone would tell me,' I said, feigning irritation.

'There was no time to tell you back there,' Angelica said. 'Besides, if we had you wouldn't have been so convincing.'

'So tell me now.'

'Well, quite a bit of it was true. When I realised where I'd seen Wiedlin, it all started to fall into place. I'd just decided to get hold of you — by telephone this time, rather than Pigeon — when I heard the noise outside my door.'

I laughed. 'The thing is, I ended up with one anyway.' I explained about my visitor earlier on.

'Anyway, I knew it'd be him. I had to think quickly. He had a gun, but I knew he wouldn't use it; the noise would have been too great for a start, so I gave him the runaround for a while.'

'You certainly messed up the carpet in your room,' I said.

'I thought you'd notice that,' she smiled. 'But in the end I let him take me outside.

'I knew he wouldn't shoot because he'd want to know how much I knew or suspected first, and the best place to find out would be in the Moles' tunnels where he wouldn't be disturbed. And once he'd learned what he wanted to, he could leave me down there to fend for myself. Or I suppose he could have shot me...' Her voice trailed off for a moment.

'Anyway, I found I kept going back to that story of his, though, thinking it must have some significance. Did Laidlaw pass it on?'

'In the end,' I said, telling her about the break-in.

'And is it significant?'

'It is.'

'Well, pray tell.'

'It'll be more fun to confront Wiedlin with it first. Like it was more fun to keep me in the dark back at the hotel.'

I smiled to myself. Angelica didn't reply.

The traffic stopped suddenly. 'What's going on?' Dingus said into the radio.

'Some kind of hold-up,' the crackly voice replied, 'I can't see what.' Car horns blared.

'Look!' the Mouse said, pointing out the window.

Dodging between the cars, Wiedlin cut across both lanes of traffic towards a cab pulled in at the kerb on the next sidewalk along. Jumping into the back seat, the cab raced off.

'Does he know we're following him?' the Mouse asked.

'I don't think so,' I told him. 'He'd never have let himself be seen like that.'

'Either he's just being cautious, or he's in a hell of hurry to get somewhere,' Dingus added. Suddenly the traffic was moving again.

'We'll catch him up at the next junction,' Dingus told the radio.

'You were telling us about the tunnels,' I said, bringing Angelica back to her story'

'Yes; he took me to an overgrown spot on the cliffs. The hole was well covered up; I'd be surprised if anyone else knows it's there. And on the way there I remembered something I'd realised earlier: the only animal we knew for certain was either at or around all of the crimes scenes, Nelson's included, was you.' She smiled at me. 'Of course it was only a coincidence, but Wiedlin didn't need to know that. All *he* needed to do was believe that *I* believed it.

'We wandered around down there for a long time, but he still didn't speak. He started to get agitated. I assumed he knew his way around down there, but somewhere I think he took the wrong turning. I saw my chance and told him that I didn't like being closed in and because I was so desperate to get out I started to tell him everything I knew; how I'd recognised his picture in the paper, in the Brierley Hall robbery article. I gave a pretty convincing performance. In fact, for a moment I thought it was too good.

'He stopped me in the middle of a tunnel and stuck his gun in my face. He was smiling, but was clearly on edge. I think he was pretty sure that I wasn't going to get out of there, and, being the egotist he is, he started to tell me about the Moles and the Birds he used to transport things. In return I told him what I suspected about Lettice. Then he told me about the plan she and Bupkis hatched to get what they thought they deserved.'

'And what was that?' I asked.

'A bigger cut on what Lettice smuggled in: the *Greodot* diamonds,' Dingus said, leaning back. 'Each one is connected to a section of gold chain. There are twelve in all. Fasten the sections of chain together and apparently they make one hell of a beautiful necklace, and the centrepiece diamond is twice the size of the others and about four times as valuable. Without it, the necklace is still pretty special; but with it —'

'So when they traded the coconuts, they kept the one with the big diamond in it back?'

'Either that or they swapped it for a replica when they made the original trade; then they exchanged it again — presumably at the book launch — hence the money and coconut hairs on Lettice's body.'

'And if Wiedlin knew they were plotting against him, he'd have to kill them,' I said.

'I think Wiedlin was expecting me to say just that,' Angelica said. 'But then I wrong-footed him by saying that I thought *you'd* killed them.

'He didn't believe me at first; said that I just wanted to escape with my life. So I began to get hysterical again, which I don't think he was expecting, waving the gun at me as he was. And he certainly wasn't expecting the sharp kick I gave him in the bread basket.'

'Right,' I said, taken aback.

'By the time he got his breath back, I was busy getting myself lost in the labyrinth of tunnels down there. And, after God only knows how long, I escaped.'

'But why did Wiedlin kill the Moles?'

'A row over what was happening? He was pretty highly strung when I got away from him.'

'Okay,' I said, 'so if I didn't kill anyone, how did Wiedlin?'

Angelica smiled. 'What was it you said a little while ago, about being more fun to confront Wiedlin with it? I think the same thing applies here.'

'Fair enough,' I said.

'I think this is where we get out,' Dingus said.

We'd pulled up in what looked like a huge parking lot. I caught a waft of cotton candy and suddenly felt hungry. To our left, the taxi we'd been following shot past us with just the driver inside. I could feel the smile dissolving on my face.

'He's pretty cocky,' Dingus remarked, getting out of the car, 'you've got to give him that.'

'Yeah,' I said, remembering what the Schnauzer had said to me before.

Little brown hairy things, right? The best place to find them *would be the midway.*

Locking the doors, we followed the detective from the unmarked police car as he walked towards the midway.

35. WIEDLIN'S OFFICE

L EAVING BEHIND THE RELATIVE quiet of the parking
lot, my insides dig a little jig; the last time I'd been
anywhere near this place was during the Carlin case.

Among the rides, we kept a discreet distance from the
plainclothes. The place was choked solid. The Mouse walked
on in front; as well as being the tallest he was the only one who
seemed to know their way around.

'Where are they heading?' I asked above the blare of
an organ.

'Looks like the coconut shy,' Dingus said. 'I told you it was
about this time last year they were here before.' Again I thought
about Wiedlin and his arrogance. Would he hide them here,
under everyone's noses? I decided he probably would.

'He's level with it now,' the Mouse called back. 'Oh —'
Suddenly, he stopped.

'What's wrong?' Dingus asked.

'Look.'

We looked: through a gap in the crowds we saw Wiedlin
walking past the coconut shy and vanishing into the crowds.
The speed he was walking suggested he wasn't here for
the attractions.

Drawing level with the coconut shy, I made a decision.
'Right; Linus, stay here.'

The Mouse looked less than happy. 'Why me?'

'To see if anything suspicious happens. Or in case we lose him and he doubles back.'

'But he won't,' Linus said sulkily.

'He might if there's something hidden in one of those coconuts,' I told him, pointing to the 'shy. 'How much money have you got?'

'Not much,' he said, taking a few coins from his pockets.

'Here,' I said, giving him all the change I had. 'Try and win as many as you can.'

'But what if somebody else wins one?'

'Buy it off them. Promise them anything; within reason.'

By the time I caught up with Dingus and Angelica, all that remained of the midway was a hot-dog stand at the edge of the park. We had a clear view of the plainclothes guy, and Wiedlin was just ahead of him. If he turned 'round, he'd spot us.

The Midway behind us, we were on a path heading out of the park. A low wall and a few trees bordered the grounds. Over to the right Wiedlin was approaching the gate; I guessed he'd head right, taking him back towards town. Instead, he vaulted the low wall and turned left.

'What's up there?' I asked Dingus.

'Just houses. Nothing much happens around here as far as I know.'

I could believe it; beyond the gate, on the far side of the road, a long row of dull, faded red-brick houses crouched on a hill overlooking the park.

When he reached the gate the plainclothes was waiting for us. Together we watched Wiedlin cross the road, march down the drive of the nearest house, unlock its front door, and go inside.

'Wiedlin's "office"?' Dingus said. I nodded.

We waited a few minutes for some sign of activity, but saw nothing.

281

'Either he's in a back room or he has a basement,' Dingus said. 'Let's go look.' With the plainclothes waiting at the front of the house, we headed for the back.

The drive consisted of busted paving slabs and foot-high weeds. The door at the side of the house looked like it hadn't been opened since The Terror. I thought about his other "home" at Derry Park Flats. Somehow, I'd imagined a creature like Wiedlin living in decadent luxury.

Below the back window, a set of wooden steps led down to what looked like a fruit cellar, with a couple of planks fastened across its doors. Pencil-thin strips of yellow light shone through gaps in the wood.

Heading down the steps, we grabbed a plank each and started to slide them away. We'd just about finished when we heard a grunt on the other side of the door, followed by what sounded like something being dragged across the floor.

'*Now!*' I shouted.

Moving the planks away completely, we threw open the wooden doors and went inside, Angelica right behind us.

We found Wiedlin kneeling before a hole in the floor, surrounded by the kind of treasure trove the Mouse and I had seen in the Moles' tunnels: jewellery, antiques, and thick wads of crisp, green notes.

And sitting amongst it all next to a large suitcase: a dozen coconuts.

'Hi Quentin,' I said cheerily. 'Social call. Looks like a couple of minutes later and we'd have missed you.'

Wiedlin, not a creature to be stuck for words, didn't disappoint us. It's only my impeccable upbringing which prevents me from repeating what he said.

36. (NOT) COCONUT SHY

'COME ON, QUENTIN,' THE Lieutenant was saying, 'you may as well come clean now, just like you did when you were alone with Angelica in the burrows.'

'When she beat you up,' I added.

Evidently having exhausted his supply of expletives, Wiedlin remained silent.

'Perhaps I can fill in the gaps,' Angelica said. 'Once the coconuts were ashore, and Bupkis informed Lettice you'd short-changed him, they decided to do the same thing to you. So Lettice, *who'd packed the coconuts,* kept back the one designated to contain the most expensive diamond, and when you went to the Moles with only got *eleven* coconuts instead of twelve, and then realised that Lettice and Bupkis were holding you to ransom... You could have left it at that; even without the largest diamond, the necklace is extremely valuable. But you're greedy, and the idea of being cheated like that... No, getting the coconut back wouldn't be enough. *Nothing would be enough until the two who had wronged you were dead.* Then you found you could kill two Birds with one stone at the book launch.'

'But if you remember,' Wiedlin said, making a noise that sounded like he was about to be sick, 'I left the bookstore early that day, because I couldn't stand watching you acting like you owned the place.'

'Not so,' Angelica shook her head. 'You only made it *look* as if you left early. But in reality, I doubt you actually left at all. Instead I think you waited for Lettice in the washroom, where you'd arranged to meet her.'

Wiedlin snorted. 'And what am I supposed to have done? Put on some eyeliner and a pair of heels?'

'I didn't say you went into the female washroom, Mr. Wiedlin. And I don't think Lettice did either. She was never what you'd call feminine — she carried on wearing those terrible baggy suits of hers even after she'd been mistaken for a male half a dozen times — so she could have easily slipped into the male washroom unnoticed. If anybody saw her, all she had to do was say she'd made a mistake and try again when the coast was clear.'

'And the suit had great big pockets,' I said, 'big enough to hide a coconut or a stack of cash in them.'

'So you made the deal at Sidwells, safe in the knowledge you'd get your jewel back. But on top of that, you somehow managed to get into the kitchen at the Plaza earlier that morning to poison her kippers. You knew from the Moles that there was plenty of strychnine about the place, so nobody was likely to suspect foul play, at least for a while. You may have lost some of your money paying off Lettice, but you'd more than make up for that with the contents of that one coconut.

'This left you with Bupkis to deal with. When the fuss died down, I don't imagine for one minute he'd think Lettice had died of natural causes; he was sure to suspect you of being involved somewhere. Only now the price for his continued silence would have gone up.

'So you arranged to meet him on the night of the dance, when he wouldn't be missed. Only, luckily for you, before you got the chance to meet him, Benji did.'

'And I've got the lumps to prove it,' I put in.

'After their little scuffle, Bupkis met you as arranged, in the one place nobody would find either of you: the Moles' burrows.

Only he wasn't alone. I'll bet it was a bit of a surprise, seeing him with that Dachshund? What on earth had he brought a dog along for? Because Burt had plans of his own, and I'll bet you wanted to know why he looked so dishevelled too. And when he told you about giving that private detective a good thumping, you saw you could use it to your advantage. So you stabbed him in the back with the tooth and, with the Moles' help, you left him in an open grave near the hotel with the dog beside the body just to confuse matters further. A very clever plan, Mr. Wiedlin.'

'Clever, yes,' I put in, 'but a bit predictable.'

'What do you mean?' Angelica asked when Wiedlin didn't respond.

'I was just thinking that all Quentin's ideas seem to revolve around putting things in confined spaces; for example "The Mystery of the Fifteenth Corkscrew".'

'Ah yes,' Angelica said. 'I was wondering about that. Is now the right time to tell us?'

'Now's as good a time as any. Okay, are we all comfortable? Then I'll begin.

'It all starts after The Terror, when a vain, old Dog called Bracken inherits a large country estate in England called Lowry Hall. Tourists used to flock there in the Old days to see the exotic animals which were part of the estates' private zoo. But now, it was a rather sad place; the only thing left of any value was the former lady of the house's extremely valuable necklace. But Bracken was reluctant to part with it, even to get himself out of a financial scrape.

'One day, he sees a way out as he's taking a walk around the grounds and spots one of the few Old animals he has left: an Emu, moving awkwardly around on a small island surrounded by a large pond. Bracken knows why: it's about to lay an egg. So, he stops to watch.

'The egg pops out, but a strange thing happens: the egg has been laid on a slope at the top of the island. It rolls down the hill and, before anything can be done to stop it, it rolls into the pond and sinks to the bottom, so Bracken loses yet another exotic animal, even before it's hatched. But it gives him a hell of an idea: what if he could find a hiding place for the necklace and convince the police it's been stolen? Then he could cash in on the insurance policy. The problem was, where could he hide it?

'The answer came to him at lunch. He goes to pour himself a glass of wine, but finds the bottle empty. Following his usual pointless habit, he gets the cork and puts it back in the bottle. After staring at it for a while, he races down to the wine cellar, uncorks a bottle of cheap wine with one of his prized corkscrews, pours the contents down the drain and takes the bottle back up to the kitchen. There, he wraps the necklace in some cloth, slides it inside a glass vial, and bungs it up with a small piece of cork. *Then*, he pushes the vial into the bottle and, because the bottle already has dark glass, he fills it with water from the tap before securing the original cork and putting it back in his wine cellar.

'The police are baffled; there's no sign of a break-in. They suspect Bracken from the start, but he has a cast-iron alibi. With heavy hearts, the officers head for the cellar, with no real hope of finding anything.

'But down among the dusty bottles one of the officers sees something that catches his eye: hanging by hooks on the wall, are what appear to be a row of corkscrews. The officer is about to ask why when Bracken explains: his hobby is collecting unusual corkscrews — he has fifteen in total.

'The officers begin their search of the cellar. But one of them keeps looking back at the corkscrews, particularly one at the end of the row which had two prongs and looks more like a tuning fork, although one its prongs is considerably longer than the other. Smelling a rat, the officer asks if they could see this particular corkscrew in action. Bracken panics, he says that would be wasteful; he only opens a bottle on special occasions. But the officer, who knows his wine, says he's sure there must be a cheap bottle around somewhere.

'Going along the rows, he finds a bottle that isn't as dusty as the others. He also notes that the cork isn't level with the lip of the bottle; and when he picks it up, the weight feels all wrong too, and it makes an odd clonking sound when he moves it from side to side. He takes the fifteenth corkscrew from the hook on the wall, inserts the shorter of the two prongs into the cork and pulls it out; then he inserts the longer of the two prongs into the bottle, where it spears a small piece of cork floating around inside. He draws *that* out and finds it's attached to another, smaller bottle, inside which he finds the missing necklace, wrapped up in cloth.'

'That's really quite ingenious, in its way,' Angelica said. 'I mean it's not perfect, but —'

'I think it sums Quentin up pretty well,' I replied 'You're good, but not good enough. Not content with the planning and stealing of the Greodot diamonds, you can't resist showing how clever you think you are. So you write a story explaining how you're going to smuggle the diamonds into the country and send it to a magazine. But even then that isn't enough; the story gets bounced and you can't believe it. So you mail the editor a pompous letter demanding that the story be published! As for that crack you made about the coconuts at the midway —'

I never learned. Just like at the Mole-holes, I was blabbing so much that Wiedlin caught me off guard. In the blink of an eye he bent down, picked one of the coconuts off the floor, and hurled it at me so it bounced off my head. Sprawled on the deck, I watched him as he pushed past Dingus and Angelica, shot up the steps of the fruit cellar and out into the garden.

'Are you alright, dear?' Angelica said, offering me her paw.

'Fine, apart from the bells chiming in my head,' I said, rubbing the new bump above my ear.

By the time we got to the garden, all was quiet. A mown-down fence panel at the back told us where Wiedlin had gone. I was just about to follow him when I heard groaning over to my left.

Sitting in the grass was the plainclothes officer who'd been at the front door, holding his head as if something was about to burst out of it, a thin trickle of blood slicking down his fur.

'What happened?' I asked.

'The Lieutenant went chasing after him, so I followed. But Wiedlin doubled back on him and he clocked me as I came through the gap in the fence.'

'Stay here and look after him,' I told Angelica, 'and call for backup.'

'Why? Where are you going?' she asked.

'The midway!'

'But what about the Lieutenant?'

'Tell him where I've gone when he comes back,' I shouted above the ringing in my ears.

'But you're injured.' Angelica said.

'Not as badly as him,' I pointed at the officer. 'Get him an ambulance. Hell, call another for when I get back.'

I wasn't a great fan of the midway, but I was grateful that its noise blocked out the ringing sounds in my head. Making my way along, it felt like someone kept tilting the path from side-to-side. When a wave of queasiness washed over me, I slowed to a walk.

Seeing the harassed-looking Schnauzer ahead of me dodging his way through the crowds, I walked as quickly as I dared as the path zigzagged around me, trying to send me off in different directions.

I managed to gain a bit of ground as the crowds thickened around him. I lost sight of him for a second or two, then the crowd spat him back out of their midst like a piece of spoiled meat. I was close enough now to see he was getting frustrated. Here was my chance; forgetting that I'd decided not to run, I ran after him before he escaped.

I'd barely started when he turned and saw me. As I ran the ground lurched, sending me left; Wiedlin, a confused expression on his face, moved to my right. By the time I'd righted myself he seemed to be twice as far away from me as he had been seconds earlier; I was just about to pull up, disgusted with myself for losing him, when I saw what he was heading towards and laughed. I trotted gently after him as he headed towards the coconut shy.

The Mouse was standing next to a huge pile of coconuts, looking slightly embarrassed. The music all around us was deafening but I shouted as loud as I could and waved my paws in the air, which did nothing for my balance. It wasn't until Wiedlin was maybe twenty feet away from him that the Mouse turned.

'*Run after him!*' I yelled, pointing at Wiedlin. '*Head him off!*'

Thankfully he couldn't hear me; instead, he picked up a coconut from the pile, hefted it in his paw and hurled it. An instant later it smacked into the side of Wiedlin's head and split in two, both halves landing on the ground about the same time as he did.

As quickly as I could, I made my way over to the Mouse, half-laughing, half-panting, the ground still rippling beneath my feet. Misjudging the distance between us, I crashed into the side of him, Wiedlin lying face down in the mud a few feet away, the coconut halves of beside him.

'That's one way to get them open,' I said to the Mouse as he propped me up.

37. NUTCRACKING

A S MUCH AS I would've liked opening all the coconuts that way, it wasn't to be; soon after, the Lieutenant turned up, quickly followed by an ambulance.

'How did you catch him?' he asked as Wiedlin was loaded into the ambulance.

'The Mouse mistook him for the coconut shy,' I said, pointing at the halves on the grass. 'That's one way to get them open,' Dingus remarked, picking up the segments.

'That's exactly what Mr S said,' the Mouse noted.

'Mr S should've gone in the ambulance with Wiedlin,' Dingus said as we walked away, me with my arm around the Mouse.

'I'll be fine,' I told him.

'I hope Wiedlin will be okay,' the Mouse said, dragging along the sack full of coconuts he'd won as well as propping up yours truly.

'He'll be okay. He's got a thick skull.'

Angelica was waiting for us in Wiedlin's front garden. 'Good heavens,' she said, 'what happened? Did you get him?'

'The Mouse scored a direct hit,' I told her. 'And as well as clocking the bad guy, he managed to win lots of coconuts.' The Mouse gave an embarrassed smile.

'Do you think there's anything in them?' Angelica asked.

'If this was one of your novels, I'd say without a doubt. But probably not.'

'Yes...' she said uncertainly. 'Still, we have to make sure. Lieutenant, I believe you're the expert at opening them?'

'Just lead me to a screwdriver and a hammer,' he said, grinning.

‡ ‡ ‡

'You know, we should really be doing this with a corkscrew.' Dingus said.

The first time he hit the coconut nothing happened. Nor the second. But the third blow split the 'nut in two. A clear, almost odourless liquid spilled onto the ground. Inside, it was slightly bigger than the size of an egg, and held nothing except smooth white coconut meat.

'How many left?' the Lieutenant asked.

'Sixteen,' the Mouse said proudly.

The three of us watched the Lieutenant take another of the Mouse's coconuts and place it on the floor. After checking it for any tell-tale signs of tampering, he pierced the small 'eyes' of the fruit with the screwdriver before securing it between his knees. Whacking it with the hammer, the coconut split open. It was also empty.

'Where did you learn to do this, Dingus?' I asked.

'The stallholder told me how when I won one for my nephew last year. Anybody else want to try?' he asked, splitting a third one open.

'Me!' the Mouse said, grabbing the screwdriver.

'Oh, while I remember,' Angelica said after half a dozen more had been opened, 'I had a look 'round while you were gone.'

'And?'

'It's very unusual. The rest of the house is in much the same state as this place, except for a bedroom upstairs which is done up like a palace, full of unusual *objets d'art* and trinkets which he's presumably picked up on his travels. It seems he's a bit of a Magpie himself.

'There was a hefty sum of money too. And talk about being self-obsessed; he's kept the notes and plans of all the robberies he's been involved in, including articles in local newspapers and pasted them into a scrapbook. Can I have a bash?' she asked the Mouse, grabbing a coconut.

With the kind of whacks you wouldn't want to be on the end of, Angelica made quick work of the last of the Mouse's winnings; every one of them was empty. 'Well,' she said, getting to her feet, 'that just leaves the ones Lettice brought over in the crate. Lieutenant?'

Taking one of them in his paw, he held it up to the bare bulb hanging in the middle of the room and began turning it slowly. 'Hmm,' he said. 'Pass me the screwdriver.'

The Mouse passed it over, and Dingus scratched at one of the eyes with its point. Small brown flakes began falling to the ground.

'The holes have been sealed with some kind of gum,' he said. 'And look; the eye's bigger.'

He was right: the eyes of the first batch of coconuts were roughly the same width as the screwdriver head. These were at least twice as wide.

'Can you see anything inside?'

'There's something in there,' Dingus said, clearing the rest of the hole, 'but it's not going to come out.'

'So what do we do?'

'Only one thing we can do. Smash each of them open as carefully as possible.'

'You want to try, Benji?' Dingus asked when all the eyes in the 'nuts had been removed.

'Why not,' I said, 'I'll imagine it's Wiedlin's head.'

I put a coconut between my knees.

'What you said earlier wasn't true,' Angelica informed me as I picked up the hammer. 'In one of *my* novels, all the coconuts would be empty.'

'Wouldn't *that* be funny,' I said, raising the hammer.

It took me seven goes to split the 'nut open. This time, instead of a thin trickle of juice, there was a small cloth packet inside. My paw trembled slightly as I worked it open.

Inside that was smaller packet, also made of cloth. Inside that was one of the most beautiful objects I'd ever seen in my life, even under the harsh light of the naked bulb. A flash of gold seemed to sparkle in one of my eyes, while a blood red gleam lit the other.

I handed the section of necklace to Angelica.

'This... this must be the really expensive one, surely,' she said. 'It's so...' at a loss for words, she shook her head.

'Let's find out,' I started on the next coconut. The segment inside was equally stunning.

'Let me!' Angelica said, grabbing the hammer.

And so it went on, the four of us taking it in turns. As we did it, we fastened the sections of necklace together.

'And then there were two,' I said, looking at the remaining coconuts. 'I don't think we've opened the big one yet.'

'We haven't,' Dingus said, picking up the coconuts. There was a look in his eye that I'd seen many times before.

'Perhaps you could pass me one, Lieutenant?' I said, smiling.

He handed me the one in his left paw.

'Any particular reason for keeping that other one back, Lieutenant?' Dingus just smiled.

Opening it, I found another beautiful section inside. But that was all it was: a section. After it was added it to the necklace, we all turned to Dingus.

'How did you know it was that one?' I asked, looking at the 'nut.

'The hole's considerably wider,' he said. 'And there's a small cross scratched into it. I doubt it was there when it fell from its tree.'

'The Designated Coconut,' Angelica said quietly. 'Well, as you think you've found it, Lieutenant, I think you should be the one to open it.'

So, kneeling on the floor for the final time, the Lieutenant jammed the coconut between his knees and raised the hammer. The fourteen very careful blows it took to open the coconut all seemed to be an hour apart. Finally, there was a small cracking sound, and the two halves of the fruit split open. While they were still wobbling around on the floor like dropped crockery, the Lieutenant picked up the small cloth bag which had been inside. His paws shaking, he fumbled it open and took out its contents.

'Son of a gun,' he said quietly, holding it up for us to see.

'Indeed,' Angelica said eventually.

'Wow,' offered the Mouse.

'Indeed,' I said, mirroring Angelica.

Epilogue: Three Months Later

‡ ‡ ‡

'N O REALLY,' THE MOUSE said after getting out and righting the trashcan, 'that was much better.'

'Linus, if you're lying to me, I'll —'

'No, no. Honestly. Try it again.'

After a heavy sigh and with some reluctance, I tried again and somehow managed it perfectly. Turning to look at the Mouse, he looked pleased for me; genuinely pleased.

Smiling, I shook my head, marvelling once more at his patience and optimism. Try as I might, I couldn't think of another individual who after an hour of my constant cursing and snarling would not only still be here, but also be in good spirits.

'So you really think that one was okay?'

'Perfect,' he told me. 'Carry on like this, you'll be driving yourself to Rockway or anywhere else in no time.'

At the mention of Rockway the smile fell from my lips.

I still wasn't sure what it was about driving that made me so nervous, but I'd decided that it was better than relying on the Mouse all the time, or riding the subway. I might even save a bit on shoe leather.

'Okay,' I said, getting out of the driver's seat. 'That's enough for today.'

As we swapped seats, the wind rose again, blowing stray leaves down the empty street and onto the windshield. The sky was a dingy grey. I was glad to see the back of summer; we'd had a couple more mini-heat-waves, none of which seemed to please anybody, the vogue for shaved bodies at last going out of style. For me, the worst problem was trying to sleep, a situation only marginally improved once the bell-ringers in my head finally moved on after Wiedlin cracked me with that coconut. But I got my own back in the end, so I shouldn't complain.

‡ ‡ ‡

In all, I saw Wiedlin three times after the events at the midway. The first time was at the hospital, an hour or so after we'd been left stunned by what we'd found inside the last coconut.

After being given the once-over and told I was basically fine, I hurried to the ward. Wiedlin was delirious, or at least pretending to be. Whichever it was, it certainly seemed to have affected his voice.

'You tricked me,' he said in a pathetic, snooty little English accent, 'into going towards that Mouse. He nearly split my skull open.'

'He's short-sighted,' I said. 'Thought your head was a coconut.'

'Yes, that's right,' he said, attempting to sit up in bed, 'coconut. I remember now... And a necklace. With diamonds on...'

Dingus, Angelica and I looked at each other. None of us said a word.

‡ ‡ ‡

'Oh, I forgot to tell you,' the Mouse said, once we'd started back for the office, 'I got another postcard from Angelica this morning.' Digging it out of his pocket as he drove, it was a relief when both his paws went back on the steering wheel.

'Couldn't she have written it any smaller?' I said, squinting at the writing.

Dear Linus,

In answer to your letter, I know you don't like being called Linus but in all conscience I can't keep referring to you as 'The Mouse.' Anyway, I hope you are well.

Work on The Malignant Meerschaum of Murry Munster *is progressing well, thank you for asking. A 'Meerschaum' is a kind of pipe, incidentally. Perhaps it is a bit obscure — maybe I should change it to 'Briar'... Anyway, it's about a poisoned pipe — such a simple idea! I think it was seeing all those coconut hairs which started me off on it — the similarity between them and strands of tobacco is quite striking.*

Well, I'd better be getting back to it now. But while I remember, I forgot to mention in my last note to Benji how pleased I was to hear he'd welcomed Harvey back into the fold. Sounds like quite a transformation!

Best wishes,
Angelica Hartley

P.S.: It's not only a certain soon-to-be-launched magazine that'll be appearing with a change of title. My story 'Poisoned Pen, Poisoned Letter' will appear in its pages under my 'proper' name. It feels like the right thing to do, now that the dust has settled.

'Settled as well as it can, anyway,' I said, handing the postcard back to the Mouse when we pulled up outside the office.

‡ ‡ ‡

The second time I saw Wiedlin was a couple of days later, after we'd put Angelica onto the bus for the next leg of her — now extremely-well publicised — book tour. The last thing she said to me was this: ' "There is also such a thing as making nothing out of a molehill, in consequence of your head being too high to see it". Take care, Benji.'

It made me smile. 'Something you wrote?' I asked.

'Something I read,' she replied.

'I just got word from the hospital that Wiedlin's stopped pretending he's insane,' Dingus told me as we waved her off. 'Want to pay him a visit?'

When we got there his mood was no better, even if his memory apparently was. Dingus read out the charges: four counts of murder — which included the two as yet unnamed Moles — along with various other offences, such as theft and kidnapping.

'All on the flimsiest of evidence,' Wiedlin sniffed.

'Well, it *was* flimsy,' Dingus said. 'We're now pretty certain you killed Lettice by spiking her kippers with strychnine. And although we can't put you at the Plaza on the morning of the book launch, we do have several members of staff, along with the manager, who distinctly remember seeing you at the hotel on previous occasions, so it's not too much of a stretch to imagine you were there to see Bupkis. Knowing the area, you'd have been aware of the problem with Moles, plus on top of that, you were in possession of one of the teeth known to have killed Bupkis.'

'And there's the Moles you shot at in the tunnel, the ones you didn't successfully kill,' I added. 'They seem quite willing to testify that you murdered two of their brethren. Oh, and there's the smuggling of course.'

Wiedlin looked daggers at me.

'Tell me what happened to the diamonds,' he said, breathing heavily through his nose.

'I think we'll save that for next time,' Dingus said on our way out.

Over the next week or so, a few other things fell into place.

'I heard about you cracking the case,' a voice soft as silk purred at the other end of my phone-line a few days after I'd visited Wiedlin. 'I was wondering if you felt like celebrating.' Jake Lake.

'Not especially,' I told her, my ears still ringing.

'Well, it's your loss. Be seeing you around.' She hung up.

The next time the phone rang, it was Dingus. 'I thought you should know: we just found Mungo Bickeridge.'

'Really? What's he saying?'

'He's not saying anything; he's dead. A demolition crew found him inside a building that was about to be pulled down. Looks like he stuck a gun in his mouth and pulled the trigger. There was a note beside the body.'

When Dingus read it aloud to me it was Bickeridge's voice I heard.

' "To the police; I can't live like this any longer. Despite not being there when she died, I'm the one who's responsible for the death of Lettice de Groot because it was me who wrote the poison-pen letters to *Dismemberment Monthly* and *No Shit Sherlock*, and who later broke into both magazine's offices. By the time I realised that my letters had acted as a trigger to some deranged animal, it was already too late.

' "As soon as it happened, I feared for my life. I knew you'd hold me responsible. Since that moment I've moved from place to place so you wouldn't find me, and sent letters to both magazines protesting my innocence. Then I heard that another writer, Grover S. Nelson, was killed by a car, the killer clearly using my 'Bumper Fodder' letters in which I claimed I'd been the victim of an attempted knock-down as cover. From that point onwards, I've been afraid to look at the newspapers which I now use for blankets in case I read about another death I've caused. I have tried to live with what I've done, but find it is impossible. My only hope is that my death, along with this confession, will spare other writers from meeting the same fates as Lettice de Groot and Grover S. Nelson and that the maniac responsible for their deaths is soon brought to justice.

' "Mungo Bickeridge." '

When I didn't speak, Dingus said, 'Benji? You still there?'

'Yeah, I was just thinking; if it hadn't been for Bickeridge's letters, we wouldn't have come across Wiedlin the way we did.'

Later, I called Lake's number. 'I've changed my mind,' I told her. 'Let's meet up.'

The next day I sat in the park, waiting. I even bought an ice cream for her.

'So,' she said, 'what made you change your mind?'

'Tea,' I said, passing her the ice cream.

She smiled a confused smile. 'I'm sorry?'

'Tea; that stuff they drink across the pond until it's coming out of their ears.'

'What about tea, Benji? I'm not following.'

'You used it to stain a manuscript to make it look older than it was. It was among the stories I read during the poison-pen letters investigation.'

Lake looked at me blankly; sweetly, but blankly.

'I got Angelica de Groot to take a look at all those stories. She said she was certain whoever wrote "The Invisible Feud" also wrote "Deadly Ink," about a deranged individual sending threatening letters to his neighbours for the hell of it, and that they'd made the manuscript look old by staining it with tea. Why did you do it?'

I got that same blank look for a few seconds before she dropped it. Then, in a voice equal parts glee and irritation she said, ' "Why?" *Why not*? It was fun. The letters were too good an opportunity to miss. I couldn't pass up on an idea like that.'

'Fair enough. Here's another one for you. Those letters were sent by a deluded mutt called Mungo Bickeridge. He wrote them in a desperate bid to draw attention to his work; he even went as far as to make up death-threats. The thing is, Bickeridge was *so* deluded that when Lettice de Groot was killed, he convinced himself that he'd as good as done it himself. He was found earlier today in a condemned building where he'd been hiding out with a bullet in the back of his skull. Anything to say?'

Lake shrugged. 'They were only stories,' she said.

'Some stories. Why did you really want to meet up?'

'Because I liked you. At least, I thought I did.' She glared at me.

I glared back long enough for the foolishness I felt to pass. 'So it's nothing to do with getting a bit of inside information on the murders? With a view to writing further stories, say?'

Her stumbling reply told me all I needed to know. Throwing my ice cream in the nearest trashcan, I walked away.

‡ ‡ ‡

'The Mouse here got a postcard from Angelica,' I said as we walked into the office.

'Big deal,' Taki said with a smile. 'I got a letter.'

'It was something like the fourth she'd had since Angelica had returned home. 'Must be nice to be so popular.'

'There's no need to feel left out,' she assured me. 'Angelica says to tell you you've got one coming your way soon.'

Her most recent postcard was still on my desk. *Remember and tell me what you think about the story in the new magazine* was the gist of it. I picked up the phone.

To everyone's surprise, the business with the poison-pen letters seemed to have resulted in a thaw in Finnegan's and Laidlaw's relationship; when I met them now they reminded me of a pair of squabbling brothers. The resulting publicity seemed to have dampened both editors' enthusiasm for their respective periodicals, and it was soon announced that *No Shit Sherlock* and *Dismemberment Monthly* were to fold and be replaced by a new magazine featuring the best aspects of both: half crime, half spooky stuff. Hell, they even merged the name.

'Hello, *No Shit Monthly*,' Patch Finnegan said.

'I just wondered how things were going.'

'Hello, Benji. Well, things would be going a lot better if my co-editor wasn't being such a pain. We've just been sent this *wonderful* story —'

'Wonderful nothing,' I heard Laidlaw shout out.

'— but he doesn't like it. Says it'll lower the tone of the magazine, can you believe that? From *him*? Hey, maybe you could read it for us?'

'Uhn-uh. Those days are over,' I said. 'I hear Angelica's got a story in the first issue.'

'Yeah, we've bought a couple off her. And now the quality of the work is consistently good, if you know what I mean.'

I smiled. 'What about Betsy Oatland? Did she sell you "Trix Got Lost"?'

'No dice. We even offered her "triple-scale" for it but she wouldn't budge. Said it was a part of her life she didn't want to be reminded of. Apparently Alannah Foxton even offered Betsy her old cleaning job back but she wouldn't take it.'

'So I heard. But she managed to get her other ones back and Alannah didn't press charges. Tell me: did you take either of those Jake Lake stories?'

'Hell no,' Patch Finnegan laughed. 'After Angelica's poison-pen story sees print I doubt we'll be publishing anything like that again for a while.'

‡ ‡ ‡

The final time I saw Wiedlin was in the police station. On the way, I asked Dingus if there'd been any progress.

'Some. A few of the Moles have agreed to talk but they're not very reliable. We reinforced the fifth floor and put them up there; steel walls, floors, the lot. You can still taste the metal in your mouth an hour after you've left. But it keeps them secure.'

'Anyone gone back down the holes?'

'The search team have been down and found a few things, but the Moles themselves just scattered. And they probably took all the really good stuff with them. It wouldn't surprise me if they were tunnelling under the sea.' I laughed. 'But we're keeping an eye on the new entrances we've found. Hopefully the smuggling will drop off soon, too.'

'Arrested any Magpies?' at that we both laughed.

'Come on. Let's go see Wiedlin.'

We were hardly in the door when he started. 'Okay, enough's enough. I need to know: what happened to the diamonds?'

'Why so interested?' I asked. 'It doesn't concern you anymore, does it?'

'Personally I don't think it's the diamonds he's interested in,' Dingus said. 'I think he wants to know how much of his plan worked out.'

'Maybe you should tell him,' I said. We looked at each other. Then at Wiedlin.

'Look,' Wiedlin said. 'Tell me and I'll cooperate. I promise.'

'Try the other way round, Quentin. *You* tell us what we want to know and *then* we'll tell you.' After a slight pause he nodded.

'You seem to know most of it anyway,' he said grouchily. Sighing, he went on. 'Burt... Bupkis... whatever... He arranged for Lettice to have a room on the ground floor so the Moles could get the coconuts, and they passed them on to the Magpies. I met the Magpies on the roof of Derry Park Flats and hid the coconuts in my apartment. I should've checked they were all there, but I didn't. I put them in a suitcase, ordered a cab to take me home and was about to hide them under the floor of the fruit cellar when I realised one was missing. A meeting was arranged. You know what happened at that meeting. When Lettice and I did the trade I checked the coconut first, but didn't open it. It was sealed the same as the others, so I knew it was okay. Then I put it with the rest.'

'Why didn't you leave straight away?'

'I had a few other business matters to attend to first,' he said, sighing. 'But, after that pantomime at the Plaza when you said you'd be keeping an eye on me, I knew I couldn't hang around any longer. So I went back to the fruit cellar to crack open the coconuts and leave with the diamonds when you lot showed up.'

'Those business matters presumably being the counterfeit money operation you're involved in. We checked the notes you gave Lettice. But we'll leave that for another time. What happened with you, Angelica, and the Moles?' Dingus asked.

'You want to know about that as *well*?' Wiedlin snapped. 'I took Angelica down there and got lost. She gave me the slip. Eventually I came across the Moles. By then I wasn't in the best frame of mind and got into an argument with them. One of them took a swipe at me with his claws, so I ran. Then I remembered: I had the gun. When any Moles got in my way, I shot at them. Now, for the love of God, will you *please* tell me what happened to the diamonds?'

I looked at the Lieutenant and grinned. 'Let me,' I begged. 'Please.' With a shrug in Wiedlin's direction, the Lieutenant stepped back.

'Well, Quentin,' I said, moving towards him, 'it was like I said before; you're good but not good enough. Your plan worked out almost perfectly. But for one small detail...'

Once I'd told him, the Lieutenant and I managed to get to the door before he really lost it. Later, it was said he was so loud that the Moles could hear him yelling on the fifth floor.

‡ ‡ ‡

Things quietened down over the next few months: Wiedlin remained in custody along with several Moles, and the recovered items stolen from Brierley Hall were returned. I didn't miss my little trips to Rockway, or reading substandard manuscripts penned by half-crazed lunatics. In fact, I got out of the habit of reading altogether for a while. During that whole period, there was only one thing I did miss.

Then, last week, we had a visitor.

'Look, it's no good,' I heard Taki saying next door, 'I can't understand a word you're — *my God, that's disgusting!*'

Even with the door closed I heard that soft plopping sound.

'I'll just go straight through,' another voice said.

A Rabbit-shaped silhouette covered the glass in my door. 'Benji?'

'Come on in, Harvey,' I told him. 'How's the donut business going?' I asked as he entered, with what looked like two enormous candles gripped in his fist.

'It isn't,' he said, his speech now no different from anyone else's. 'I packed it in; nothing but animals with no manners all day long, and not an ounce of excitement.'

'I see you got your teeth back,' I said, nodding at his paw.

'Yep.' He dropped them on my desk where they made an oddly attractive clonking sound. 'I did think of selling them, knowing how much they'd fetch, but...'

'You couldn't let them go.' He shook his head.

'You want your job back, don't you?' Harvey nodded. 'But without the teeth —' I started.

'I've been wearing them for the past few days,' he said. 'Ask your secretary. She couldn't understand a word I said 'til I took 'em out again.'

'You mean you've been wearing them, knowing where at least one of them has been?'

'I washed 'em first,' he said, defensively. 'I used this really powerful cleaning stuff my dentist recommended. They were clean as bone after a few hours' soaking.'

'But what about all the animals who've seen you without them the past few months?'

'I doubt they'll recognise me when I suck in my cheeks. And as for the ones who knew me before, I don't think I look that different.'

'But word must have spread, Harvey. About what you did.'

'The only animals who know what happened are Ray, the folks in your office, that writer and the Lieutenant. I keep myself to myself most of the time. And if anyone does say anything, I'll tell 'em the whole thing was a joke someone put around. I mean, can *you* imagine anyone being crazy enough to let someone take a saw to their teeth?'

'I try not to,' I said, wincing.

'Right.' With that, Harvey raised his oversized teeth towards his face. And somehow — I looked away before he did it — managed to fasten them into his mouth. Sucking his cheeks in, I had to hand it to him: he really *didn't* look much different than he had before.

'Tho,' he said, his mouth barely moving behind the enormous teeth, 'Tha a haa na na noh nack?'

'Sure,' I managed to say when I'd stopped laughing, 'you can have your old job back.'

‡ ‡ ‡

Yesterday, the first issue of *No Shit Monthly* arrived in the mail, and I read it from cover-to-cover in my lunch break. Angelica's story was by far the best thing in it, but the rest of it was pretty good too.

Today, the mail brought me the letter she'd promised:

Dear Benji,

I trust you are well.

By the time you receive this, hopefully you will have read "Poisoned Pen, Poisoned Letter", and I welcome any comments you may have, although I think (if I may be so bold) that you will find little, if anything, in it to criticise. Since reverting to my "proper" name, I seem to be going through a bit of a purple patch — so much so in fact that I was able to fit in another short story a few days ago, called "All That Glitters is Not Gold". I've taken the liberty of including a copy for your perusal, but I have a specific reason for doing so, as you will find out.

The story centres around the theme of coincidences; and unsolved mysteries; and the way a simple, seemingly insignificant occurrence can alter the

308

entire complexion of a series of events. Most of these things often don't matter, even if they do remain a mystery. For example, how did all those writers know that Patch Finnegan was the author of "Giddyfits" if he never told anyone? Or why was Lettice so insistent to speak with you that day at the book launch? Was she just keeping up the illusion of working on her book, or was there some other reason? And what about the fact that both she and Burt had their bags packed? A coincidence, or were they planning to elope with their ill-gotten gains? And who killed Grover S. Nelson? Chances are we'll never find out any of these things.

Anyway. Let me know what you think of the story. If nothing else, I'm sure you'll be able to recognise some of the events chronicled therein.

With best wishes,
Angelica

Taking the story out of the envelope I read it through. Then, as soon as I'd finished, I drafted her a letter.

Angelica,

Good to hear from you. I read "All That Glitters..." with interest. Although not an editor, I feel that I can make a few salient points.

One: when the jewel thief Letitia collapses on the ground next to the tree, and the passing Jackdaw sees the jewel glinting in the top of her pocket, the likelihood that it would turn out to be a trained Bird seems a bit too convenient. I think it's more likely to have been just a passing Bird who, having spotted something shiny, decides to swoop down and make off with it (Jackdaws of course being notorious thieves).

Two: Later on, when Tarquin, the original thief, opens the cloth package he's exchanged with Letitia and, instead of finding the missing jewel inside, only finds a note, I'd say that that note would be far more abusive than it currently is. Letitia, after all, is a pretty unpleasant character. I'd also say that Tarquin's response to this note would be much more violent than you have written it.

Three: I don't think the jewel, despite being much sought after by its original owners, would be recovered. I'd say it's more likely that the Jackdaw used it to line its nest or something similar and that's where it would probably remain.

Otherwise I enjoyed the story.

With best wishes,
— Benji

After putting the letter into an envelope, I stood at my window and looked out over the city. Autumn sunshine glinted on the windows of the buildings opposite. To their left, far off in the distance, something also glinted in the top of a tree on the other side of the river for a second before winking out.

I seem to see a lot of things that glint lately. If I was different kind of animal, I could drive myself mad with it. Sure, the chances are that I'm seeing nothing more exotic than a drop of dew on a leaf or a discarded piece of tinfoil, but it doesn't stop me wondering.

Moving away from the window, I sat back down. I reckoned Angelica had it about right in her letter: the world was full of coincidences and unsolved mysteries. And to be honest, I think I prefer it that way.

At least some of the time.

The End

Acknowledgements

THANKS TO MUM, SHARON and Peter McAuley for reading the book in manuscript form, Ian Alexander Martin (AKA 'The Butcher') for thankfully noticing things I should have spotted myself, and Sunila Sen-Gupta for the great cover.

The quote in the Epilogue is from *The Moonstone* by Wilkie Collins.

RIP PF

— JOHN TRAVIS, WAKEFIELD, UK; MAY, 2012

About the Author

JOHN TRAVIS HAS HAD over 70 stories published in places such as *British Invasion*, *At Ease with the Dead* and both *Humdrumming Books of Horror Stories*. Recent appearances have been in the anthologies *Where the Heart Is*, *The Monster Book for Girls*, and *Darker Minds*. Besides *The Designated Coconut*, he has two other books in print: a short story collection, *Mostly Monochrome Stories* (Exaggerated Press) and a novel, *The Terror and the Tortoiseshell* (Atomic Fez).

One day he hopes to make a living out of writing. He also hopes to be about six inches taller, a stone lighter and wake up to find he doesn't have a broad Yorkshire accent any more. Wish him luck.

ATOMIC FEZ PUBLISHING
Eclectic, Genre-Busting Fiction
www.AtomicFez.com

Earlier he wrote...

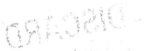

THE TERROR AND THE TORTOISESHELL
A novel by JOHN TRAVIS

John Travis's first novel, *The Terror and the Tortoiseshell*, is a
noir–styled murder mystery with deft touches of both the Comedy
and Science Fiction genres, but primary in it is the honouring
of the classic hard-boiled detective novels of the 1940s.

Benji Spriteman takes over the "Spriteman Detective Agency"
after the world is changed overnight by 'The Terror', resulting
in the animal kingdom moving from four legs to two and
banishing the now crazy human population from existence
to become the dominant species. Oh, and Benji Spriteman
is a sentient, six-foot tall, suit-wearing, Tortoiseshell cat.
Yeah, that's a bit of a jolt, especially to Benji.

In this strange environment, which sees animals taking on
some of the characteristics of the humans they were closest to,
human beings have become a bit like flying saucers – despite
occasional sightings, there is never any definite proof that they
still exist. But when humans do start to appear it's always in the
most bizarre situations – always dead, and 'displayed' as if they
were animals. And it's just as Benji's life is starting to become
a bit more 'normal' that he gets drawn into the investigation
into these murders, and soon finds himself involved in ways
he could never have imagined...

Animal Farm *meets* The Big Sleep... *compelling hard-boiled
mystery... superior work... fully realized imaginary world.*
— *Publishers Weekly* **(starred review)**

*John Travis is a madcap cross between Monty Python and
Clive Barker. His stories percolate like a popcorn machine full
of jungle beetles!*
— **Mark Mclaughlin**

Jacket-less Hardback: $34⁹⁹/£19⁹⁹ ‡ ISBN: 978-0-9811597-3-7
E-Book: $4⁹⁹/£2⁹⁹ ‡ ISBN: 978-0-9811597-4-4

6/13

CPSIA information can be obtained at www.ICGtesting.com
Printed in the USA
LVOW011452160513

334167LV00021B/780/P

9 781927 609002